Yvonne, and family.
Thanks for calling & starting our reconnection.

Hope you enjoy this. Let me know what you think.

Joe G.

Stolen Votes

Joseph Guion

Alltap Publishing
Williamsburg, Virginia

This book is a work of fiction. The characters are fictional except for a few public figures who are named. Conversations with them are part fact and part fiction.

Copyright © 2008 by Joseph Guion. All rights reserved.

Printed in the United States of America.
No part of this book may be used, reproduced or scanned, or distributed in any printed or electronic form whatsoever without written permission, except in the case of brief quotations embodied in articles or reviews.

For information, address Alltap Publishing
2202 Westgate Circle, Williamsburg, VA, 23185.

Design by Wolko Design Group, Inc.

Photo by Ramone

First edition

ISBN: 978-0-9820513-1-3

10 9 8 7 6 5 4 3 2 1

Alltap Publishing
2202 Westgate Circle
Williamsburg, VA 23185
www.alltap.net

DEDICATION

To all special forces people, especially the U.S. Navy SEALs, who are seldom undone, except by fumbling planners and outsiders who do not know or appreciate the expertise and dedication of these great military people. And to all military persons, past present and future who carry a legacy of sacrifice and willingness to go beyond the usual to accomplish the mission.

Finally, to the families of these men and women in service to their country. Their service and sacrifice is not acknowledged enough.

Thank you for serving.

                Joseph Guion CDR U.S. Navy (Retired)

Stolen Votes

CHAPTER ONE

The D.C. boss of Operation GRASS ROOTS had demanded witnesses for the third murder. Two of the victim's friends would see the horror that evening. The disgraced former Navy SEAL Dan, The Cat, Haggerty ushered his girl friend from the 1986 Oktoberfest dance in Virginia Beach earlier than expected.

Beth Olson's laughter reminded him of a kid's stream of bubbles. She gestured and did a reprise of their last dance. "I enjoyed myself tremendously. It's unfortunate that we had to leave early. What was Tony's hurry?"

The Cat padded along, inhaled wood smoke and the biting scent of burned leaves that pressed down in layers. Leading her to his car, he could not prevent his eyes from darting from one group of revelers to another. Was he on a recon op again? Where?

She interrupted. "Why did we have to leave now?"

Could he tell Beth how frightened Tony had sounded? Dan walked with his head lowered and his hands working into fists. Could he tell her what Tony had said? What he had shouted? Something about two previous killings?

Tony Garbossa was a expert programmer at the Truth Television Network where Beth was the Satellite Division Manager. Should he tell her? Should he bring her along? Was there danger for her in meeting Tony. A white lie to protect her was okay. He blinked away honesty and said, "Nothing to worry about."

She shrugged and touched his cheek. "The music was super, 'oldies' and some recent ones. You enjoyed those Stan Kenton arrangements, drumming on the table. Did you play?"

His grin appeared as a slight upward curl at the ends of his mouth. "Before I joined the Navy, I played drums in a fourteen piece band and we did a lot of his music."

She touched his stiff shoulder. "That's wonderful and you have good rhythm dancing. You surprised me, another thing I didn't know about you. What other secrets have you been hiding from me?"

He closed his eyes for a moment hoping to cut that off.

After a silence she said, "I was having such a wonderful time. I hated to leave."

"Me too. Sorry about that. Guess I'll have to take you dancing again. Not too often though."

"I beg your pardon? Is it impossible for you to ask me for more dates?" An impish grin accompanied her remark. She frowned. "You haven't explained why Tony needed to see you immediately. Why?"

"Uh, Tony said he was in a hurry, had to see me right away."

He was still confused about her; sometimes she seemed sophisticated, with her big job and everything. Tonight the Minnesota farm girl wore a black, conservative length dress, accented by a single strand of pearls. A light blue shawl matched her eyes. She pressed. "What's going on?"

"Tell you after we see him." He had hung up the phone at St. John's gym with Tony's words echoing in his head. *"Dan! Dan! Help! Help me! I'm running for my life. Meet me at the church parking lot. Fifteen, maybe twenty minutes. Don't let me down. I'm in deep shit. Two of my ex-*

programmer buddies from the Agency were killed. I'm next."

The blonde woman frowned and her eyes crinkled at the corners, as if she could actually see into his mind. "You look different, on the edge. Please tell me what is happening."

Yellow sodium vapor lights on celery stalk poles cast an eerie glow on couples moving toward their cars. Images of ghostly North Vietnamese troops slipping down a trail near the Bassac River filled his brain. He halted, caught by a memory switch. Damn the recall! His thoughts staggered backward into a forbidden zone, burning hootches in the South Vietnam Delta, the nauseating stink of mud, burning bodies. And here? Swirls of dead leaves surrounded a few dozen cars, parked in a random manner, like tombstones in an old graveyard, gap-toothed, asymmetrical.

His eyes became like slits in a mask, absorbing the surroundings. He wondered if he were more pissed because he couldn't stop gathering intel, or because this was a half-assed attempt. His eyes probed the lot, and then focused on the back corner on a man in a dark sedan. Was that a walkie-talkie in his hand? Why? Was it connected to Tony? He blinked and let it go, not wanting to revive his past skills. When he realized that he was far from the warrior's edge he had in 'Nam, his shoulders sagged. That damned shotgun screwed up my life! Never want to see one again. He turned away from her and stared at nothing.

She asked again, "What is wrong? Please tell me." She slipped her arm in his. "I'm here to help you, honestly. Won't you explain?"

He shook his head. "Wanna sit in the car and wait?"

"Not really."

He glanced around the lot again, too late to keep her away from their good friend. He pointed. "Hey, there he is."

Tony's Trans Am announced its arrival, tires screeching, scattering several couples. Two men followed in a dark green Ford. One looked like he held a walkie-talkie too. What the hell? A light blue pickup, its wheels and fenders splashed with red clay, pulled in and stopped.

Dan waved and shouted, "Hey, Tony! Tony, over here! We're here." He took Beth's arm and walked toward their friend.

The pickup rolled up next to Tony's car, driver's side to driver's side. The man leaned out of the window and Dan heard a shout. "Take that you fucking queer!"

"Blam!" A shotgun blast lighted up the inside of the car. Another "Blam!"

Haggerty shoved Beth to the pavement and covered her with his body. The pickup screeched tires. Lurching ahead, it sped out of the parking lot dripping red clay.

Screams and shouts darted about like fireflies. A cloak of silence dropped over the murder scene with each person frozen into a statue for a moment, before breaking into waves of movement. To Dan they seemed like roaches surprised in an infested kitchen. He rolled off Beth and crouched in a wrestler's stance. "You okay? Stay there!"

"Lord Jesus! You almost crushed me. What happened?"

"Stay there!"

He leaped towards the Trans Am, running with silent cat-like strides. He leaned into the driver's window. Tony's head was nearly blown away, his brains and face splattered around the car. The body twitched once, twice.

Dan sagged against the car. He saw images of a shotgun, his, blowing away his best buddy's face. It had happened again! Damn it all to hell! He covered his eyes with his hands and slumped to the ground.

Beth struggled to her feet and glanced into the Trans Am. A gory mess oozed from the top of a sprawled, grotesque body. She screamed. Leaning against the death car, she could hardly breathe. Her words came out in staccato phrases. "Oh, my God! Lord Jesus! No! No! Oh, Dan! Dan, are you hurt?" She bent over and strained to sit him up. "Dan, what's wrong? What happened to you?"

CHAPTER TWO

Two miles away five armed men waited for a report from the murder scene. The rented office suite in Norfolk wore frost blue walls. Desktops displayed no personal effects. The men were so intent on their efforts that they seldom spoke. Two of them used communications equipment linked to a satellite.

Charles R. Best sat on a desk corner, lifted his gray trouser cuff, and rubbed a painful toe. The husky leader was agitated because of the delay in reporting from the murder location. In the past five minutes his contact had called him three times on a secure phone, accusing him of incompetence.

A lean nerd-type with chrome-rimmed glasses picked up a buzzing walkie-talkie and reported. "Ford guy says Mack got away clean. Backup is trailin' the hitter to Carolina. Spotter in the dark blue car is long gone with the rest of 'em to Richmond. You got lotsa witnesses like you wanted. I'll relay the info on the secure phone."

Best's voice rasped from too many cigarettes. "State that the action was completed exactly as required. Nothing more."

"Okay."

He lit another cigarette and sighed. Two additional steps

before I have this group sanitize the office and depart with the equipment. Now perhaps the son of a bitch will get off my ass! Until another job surfaced, he would hide his identity in his cover career.

A walkie-talkie spit static. The first communications man answered and handed it to Best.

"Speak."

"Courier here. Got the package, be there in ten."

"Bullshit! Hurry your ass."

He returned the handset to the communications man and stuffed out his smoke. He nearly smiled. The stud on the radio had stolen the dead man's mail, the last opportunity that the "vic" could have passed on what he had found at the Truth Network. Now Best could tell the bastard above him that all loose ends were covered. Or were they? What about the large fellow and his girlfriend at the victim's car? The report said they seemed to know the dead homosexual. He lighted another Camel.

Now that the hit had been completed successfully, he wouldn't have to use The Mechanic. That pleased him for the spook had been difficult to control. The leader watched as the snake-eyed killer continued to sharpen his knife and smoke a joint. He never seemed to blink.

Five minutes later the courier arrived and handed over the murder victim's stolen mail. The muscular control man received the package, passed the courier an envelope, and jerked his thumb toward the door. "Get lost. Don't call me."

Best limped into his office and locked the door. The manila envelope had a scrawled "T.G." in the upper left corner, addressed to Dan Haggerty. When he slit open the package with his pearl-handled letter opener, a stack of computer printouts and five floppy disks fell on the desk. He read the victim's note on the stack and dropped his cigarette. "Dynamite!"

The note revealed that the stiff had hacked into "a secret program" at the local Truth Network. He read aloud and frowned at the next sentence. "I worked on the program when

I was at The Agency seven years ago—." His eyes and mouth opened wide when he read about "a national scheme."

He felt perspiration break out and placed his Armani suit coat on the back of his chair. The "vic" had left a printout on Haggerty's boat, showing how to hack into the program that was connected to satellites. Son of a Bitch! Computers. Satellites. National. What the hell is this? He stood and cursed as gout pain took another bite.

He skimmed through suggestions on how the program could be penetrated along with a warning. "It's dangerous to know this. Two of my former Agency teammates are dead."

Best rubbed his toe. His contact had told him, "This is easy, run a quick kill job and disappear." Bullshit! This had become a large and complex effort, more than he had anticipated.

The note continued. "Ask Beth if some odd things are going on in her Satellite Division, but don't tell her about this. The less she knows the better. The program is a bugger, got five levels of security. Be damned careful. You gotta know and trust the one you ask for help. Dan, you've been a good friend. I couldn't have hung in without you. Tony."

Best threw the note across the desk. "Son of a Bitch!"

He smoked quietly. I'm the only one aware of a weird kind of a deep and mysterious plan. Like the faggot said, this crap is dangerous. Okay, "C," self-protection comes first. My contact knows about the stolen mail. He can decide what to do with this package in the morning. I'll take out an insurance policy, keep the note, and sneak those printouts off the boat. No, I'd better not. He'll know about the disks so I'm not about to take any chances. I've got to place Haggerty and his sweetheart under surveillance immediately. I'll report it tomorrow.

Being curious didn't pay in his field of work, but he wondered about his contact. Where does a freaking ex-CIA guy fit into this thing? And to whom did he report? Bullshit! Don't pry; you're better off not knowing more than the essentials. The bastard running this can of worms has maximum clout and substantial amounts of money. He certainly owned a large pair of *cojones*. Obviously he didn't have qualms about killing his hirelings, for the "hitter" was on his way to be eliminated. Best, you'd better cover your ass and keep questions to yourself.

CHAPTER THREE

In an expensive mansion in Chevy Chase, Maryland, a man with the bulk and sneer of an NFL defensive tackle sat in his custom easy chair oblivious of the threatening weather outside. He glanced at the large television screen and grunted.

"Looks like they're going to investigate that contra aid plane crash. Too freaking bad. Screw you, Fox."

Nelson Wallace The Third turned from the scene that had generated that emotional response. He poured several fingers of Jack Daniels into an iced glass. After a gulp that matched his man-size appetites, he allowed a long "Aaaaah," to escape before continuing his orders on a secure phone.

On October fifth, a C-143K carrying clandestine arms for the contras had been shot down over that country. Since then, national press coverage and outcries from Congress had caused sleepless nights in the White House and elsewhere. The "cargo kicker's" public statements brought considerable concern to the people involved with illegally supporting the Nicaraguan rebels. They wondered if their clandestine efforts were going to be exposed. Wallace had more pressing action to consider.

"I'll say it again." Wallace used the affected "ah-gain" handed down from FDR to former President Johnson. "Look, Shadow, you get that freaking report to me in the next hour. I don't give a damn if you have to wake five admirals."

The ex-CIA man on the receiving end answered. "Sir, the ex-frogman isn't going anywhere soon. I have he and is girl under surveillance already. My contact's contact ordered it and the initial group is already in place. It might not be the appropriate moment to get people out of bed or to rush a request for service records that are already filed away. And gaining access to a court-martial record is not very easy to accomplish. You don't want any eyebrows raised."

Wallace sipped before he answered. "I accept that. Make sure that my orders are clear and carried out to the nth degree. Surveillance only. No one. I repeat, no one, tries to challenge that frogman in any way unless I give you specific orders. No freaking free-lancing."

"Yes sir. I understand. I'll have the report on his service record and the court-martial tomorrow."

Wallace frowned. "And that won't raise eyebrows?"

"No sir. A couple of people in the Bureau of Naval Personnel owe me many times over."

"I'll be tied up with the Speaker of the House tomorrow morning anyway. Got to fight that freaking Fox. I know he's going to try to stop the investigation on the contras. That bastard! He tried to bankrupt me two years ago. One of these days, I'll forge ahead of his projects and crush him. He'll become an ex-billionaire. That's secret information; so don't repeat it to anyone. Don't think of letting any of that slip out, or you'll join that shooter."

"No sir, never crossed my mind. I know what can happen and I want to retire again."

Wallace hung up. His threat might have been overkill, but he wanted to remind Shadow every so often that he was as expendable as the entire crew he had hired.

He downed the bourbon and refilled the tumbler. He had covered all possible glitches and leaks in GRASS ROOTS.

Stolen Votes

But you never knew when something unexpected could arise. The third team of killers was traveling to Virginia's Hampton Roads Area. Nelson had prepared the plan with built-in redundancy, and the separate groups had no communications or connections to one another. In addition, he had layers of "cut-out" people who only knew the next person in line, giving him denial opportunity, which was the second commandment in the nation's capital.

And tomorrow, he'd grab that son of a bitch Magee by the *cojones*. The stupid shit didn't realize that their occasional joint ventures were only meant to ingratiate him with The Fox. The last one had cost the a-hole the loss of a Nigerian lobby contract. He thought about rumors that Magee was getting tired of his mistress, Whitney Carlton. Too freaking bad. I want that bitch myself and I'll get her one way or the other. He laughed and shook his fist. "Up yours, Fox."

He poured more Jack and headed for tonight's cutie in the bedroom. If she didn't like rough stuff it was too damned bad. He was paying a big price for her body.

Dark clouds lurked over buildings in the nation's capital, like ancient gods brooding over obstinate mortals. In Washington, DC, there was one true god, worshipped by man and woman, in government and out. The god of Power. Coveted, seldom owned, power was often achieved through access to its cathedral, The White House. The magnificent white castle basked in floodlights that night with a select few invited to a small reception.

A silver-gray stretch limousine stopped at the White House gate and earned immediate recognition and a salute from the guards. Their superior spoke. "Evening, Mister Magee. Going to the reception, sir?"

The rear seat occupant on the left side waved, "That's correct, Ben. How's the family?"

"Fine, sir, thank you. The reception is ready to begin."

Francis Xavier Magee owned the "Foxmobile" limo, and

more than a few members of Congress. The super lobbyist known by the sobriquet, "The Fox," escorted his wife up the entrance stairs. He was impeccably dressed and no one knew whether his black hair or the temples of gray were natural. His dark eyes were agate marbles and his frown contradicted his pleasure in receiving tonight's invitation.

He had been waiting for a call about the secret plan JUST CAUSE, an adjunct to the Iran Contra effort conducted from a National Security Council group in the White House. The Fox handled several deals at the same time without flinching, but he hated delays and incompetence. He had said in private that the people running the hostage release hopes and the contra efforts couldn't run a Seven Eleven store.

Tonight's event was publicized as a tribute to the President for refusing to give in to Gorbachev on the Strategic Defense Initiative at the Iceland summit. Its true purpose was to respond to congressional demands for an investigation of aid to the contras.

"Mister and Mrs. Francis X. Magee." The announcement sounded like royalty had arrived. Why not? *Forbes* had called the multi-millionaire "a prince of capitalism." FX headed a large credit bureau, a public relations firm and an alleged non-profit enterprise. He was one of the centers of influence in the DC power game, confidant of the mighty, the powerful, and the moneyed.

"Good evening, Mister President. It was wonderful that you invited us."

The rangy, aged head of state grinned. "You know you've always got a friend here, Frank. Estelle, you look wonderful. Doesn't she, Nancy?"

He leaned toward Magee and whispered, "Frank, I want to thank you again for your sizable contributions to the cause of the Freedom Fighters in Central America. You've been tireless in your support. Thanks to your suggestion, I'm doing an all-out effort aimed at the people who are calling for an investigation. I don't know why Congress is so up in arms."

"Perhaps they're incensed because they won't believe

your statement that the people involved in helping the contras were volunteers." He didn't mention his negative evaluation of the group running the secret operation. Someone should have shut the "kicker's" mouth.

"Well, yes. It's unfortunate that the man talked so much." The free world leader grasped Magee's hand to move him toward the party. "I can always count on you."

FX believed that JUST CAUSE could be in trouble. Failure was not in Magee's lexicon. He had plans to strike back quickly, before the convoluted operation unraveled. He had warned his National Security Council contact that the "shoot-down" could be another step in exposing the scheme.

The Fox ushered Estelle to a group of "A List" women and joined a small group of generals, admirals and an assistant to the Deputy Director of Operations for the CIA.

The crew cut three-star Army General Norman nodded at him. "Evening Fox. Come join the conversation. As I was saying, most 'Demos' and a few Republicans are convinced that the cargo plane shot down in Nicaragua was an illegal CIA operation. Crash evidence and the survivor's statements inferred connections to The Agency."

The CIA rep shook his head. "Not true. Congress cut off aid in eighty-four. But your private groups have been sending military material to that embattled country for years."

The general said, "Even though Congress released a hundred million aid packages as part of the '87 spending bill last week, the furor still hasn't died down."

The Agency man smiled. "I hear on the grapevine that the FBI and Customs went to Miami to investigate Southern Air Transport. One of your outfits, Fox?"

"Of course not." Magee grasped the general's elbow. "Can we talk?" He ushered the "three star" to a corner. "I didn't want to disclose this with the others present. I'm not certain on how much you know about what has happened, so here's the scoop. After the Sandinistas shot down our cargo plane The RIG—"

"What the hell is that?"

"You didn't know? That's the Restricted Inter-Agency Group or the Core Group. They've got some high powered people in there running the contra re-supply. They have State, The Pentagon, ex-CIA people. One of them is Ollie North's leader. From what I hear, their main job was to cut red tape so they could carry out their mission of helping the contras."

"Re the FBI investigation of Southern Air Transport by the FBI and Customs, our cowboy in the Security Council started pressure, then Admiral Poindexter called Attorney General Meese to ask about delaying the investigation of Southern Air. Meese called Webster, head of FBI, and he agreed to delay the investigation for 10 days. Discussions held with the Assistant Commissioner of Customs, William Rosenblatt, resulted in their investigation to focus only on the C-123K that had been shot down instead of Southern Air in its entirety."

"That helps."

"So, supposedly the RIG started to plan how to develop a cover story that would be plausible and cover up that the U.S. Government was not involved at all. As you know deniability is not a dirty word in this town. Guess we'd better get back. I'll get in touch and fill you in on some other events that came from that crash. Not good. I'm damned mad about the columnists who exposed Colonel North, and I intend to counter-attack in my own way. Regarding the congressional investigation, I'm contacting Tip O'Neill tomorrow."

"Thank you, sir."

"Some of the dolts I'm working with don't seem to realize that exposure of the missiles sales and the connection to Nicaragua seems to becoming more likely. In early June the Miami Herald had a front-page piece on North and inferred or accused the White House of trying to side step the Boland Amendment. When he appeared before the House Intelligence Committee on August 6th, he had the good sense to obfuscate the truth about raising money for the contras."

The general agreed. "Like we used to say, sometimes you have to lie, cheat and steal to accomplish the mission. I understand that North is still staying on top of trying to keep everything secret. I heard that he tried to intervene with a Honduran General for fear that he would disclose the contra support. Wasn't there another threat of exposure back in September?"

FX nodded. "Oscar Arias, the new president of Costa Rica, was going to talk about the secret airstrip for the southern front at Santa Elena. Colonel North brought in Elliott Abrams and the Ambassador to help but it didn't work except to delay the inevitable."

He didn't want to spend a minute more in the White House than necessary. He'd schmooze with people he needed to contact later in the week, and then depart. He wanted to see how his JUST CAUSE Plan was doing. It was a support and back-up plan to release hostages in the Middle East with his hired paramilitary force. More urgent was his need to contact the Speaker of the House tomorrow to get a congressional investigation squashed.

CHAPTER FOUR

At the murder scene the shrieking voice of an ambulance growled to a snort. Circling red lights splashed urgency around the parking lot. Many drivers had departed in a hurry after their initial shock. Those who had remained were either curious or eager to make a statement to the police. Two persons pointed to Tony's car parked there. A dispatcher's voice rattled through spits of static. Two uniformed medical personnel disembarked with equipment.

The howl of sirens coming from both directions on Virginia Beach Boulevard shuffled people back and forth. Shock and anger created uncertainty. Rumors rolled and broke over the crowd, splashing stories, true and false.

A uniformed paramedic looked at Tony. "This one is gone." He checked Dan sitting against the car. "What's your name, sir? You okay? Any wounds?"

Dan shook his head, fighting dry heaves.

A female ambulance driver asked Beth, "Are you hurt? What's your name?"

Beth moaned. "My Lord Jesus, they killed him. They killed him!"

She sat Beth down nearby and placed a blanket over her shoulders.

Haggerty's eyes were glassy, out of focus. He remained in a sitting Buddha position, rocking, mumbling. "Bobby, Bobby. My fault. Sorry, man. Oh, God, what did I do?"

The medic managed to get Dan to give out his name.

A police officer muscled through the crowd to question him. He caught jumbled answers. "Tony? Bobby? What the hell?" He turned to the medical rep. "What gives?"

"The guy in the car is dead. Shotgun to the head. Guess his name is Tony. This guy has some kind of 'Nam flashback about a buddy being killed. Really screwed up."

Dan sat against the death car, dulled with shock. In The Teams, he had lived by the belief that when a SEAL was killed or wounded, somebody had screwed up. Bobby Douglass died in a shotgun blast because Dan had screwed up. The official investigation agreed, ending his usefulness in the SEALs.

He shook his head and tried to eliminate the dazzling lights that pulsed in his eyes and circled the cop leaning over him. He felt as if he were sliding into a VC pungi pit. He gritted his teeth and clenched his fists, struggling to see, to speak, trying to gulp in oxygen. Don't give in! Don't give in!

The officer continued to press questions and Haggerty attempted to answer, mumbling and fumbling with words. The policeman pried enough details out of Haggerty that he could radio in the information.

"Pickup, uh Tony's car. Driver blasted him Tony, twice."

"Take it easy, sir. Ya said the color of the pickup was blue. And the shooter had a cowboy hat."

When the policeman returned he asked, "You feel good enough to talk?"

"No! Too much like 'Nam. Like Bobby's death. God. Hey, is Beth okay?"

"Yeah. Anything else?"

When Dan told him what the shooter had shouted, the policeman's intent expression changed to disinterest. "This guy was queer?"

"Hell, I don't know. He was a friend. Never knew it." The Cat shook his head. "What the hell does it matter? Shit. He didn't deserve being blown away like that."

The policeman nodded. "You sure the driver said that?"

"Yeah. Pickup came alongside. Saw flash of the shotgun. Bastard shot him twice, close range." The Cat struggled to stand. He touched the death car. It was cold, clammy, like a gravestone in a Pittsburgh winter.

Beth approached and held his hand. "Dan, are you okay? You fell. Are you hurt?"

The Cat's answer was more like a groan.

Two detectives arrived, spoke with the uniformed officers and separated the couple. The older one wore a faded plaid sport jacket and dark slacks. He looked like he had five hundred thousand miles on him. He asked about Tony.

In a halting jumble of words Haggerty managed to say that Tony was a computer programmer at the local Truth TV Network. "Tony was a, a friend of mine. He, uh, taught me computers. Um, I taught him diving. Scuba diving."

"Tell me. Off the record. Are you gay too?"

Dan's anger energized him enough to stand without support. He wanted to punch out the detective, but his arms felt like they were chained.

"You, you some bitch! None of your freaking business." He staggered toward Beth and put his arm around her. The detectives separated them again. Dan's questioner lectured him about following orders and pressed for more details.

Dan's head and shoulders leaned to one side. He was slipping. Suddenly he couldn't wait to get drunk. Tony's shattered head was more gruesome than Bobby's. And just like those terrible events, he felt responsible. He had to get away. He pulled his arm from the detective's grasp. "Can't take this shit. For God's sake take her home. I'm shoving off."

After the detectives released them, The Cat paced near his car with his fists clamped. Damned 'Nam again. Tony's death. His fault. Bobby's death. His fault. He wanted to help

Stolen Votes

Beth, but he couldn't think straight. He needed booze.

Beth touched his face. "Honey, this really hit you hard. Another Vietnam problem? Let me drive you to your boat."

"No! I'll drive you home. Then I get blasted."

"Oh, please. Don't do that again. You've got to get away from that terrible drinking. You just started with AA. Why?"

"Dammit! This was like 'Nam. Bobby killed. That was my fault. Tony. Another buddy killed. My fault again. I called out Tony's name and pointed to him."

"But you didn't call him to meet us here. He called us. It wasn't your fault! Please, I want to help you. Don't get drunk again. I hate alcohol and everything associated with it. Drinks do not help."

"There you go again. Helps me to relax." If only he could. He swayed and grabbed her arm.

She covered his hand and spoke about his drinking without scolding. "You had too much to drink, and now you need me to walk you to the car."

"Come on, babe. It's not that. Tony's death."

"Dan. I'm speaking to you. You're not looking at me again. I'm present. Here. Not somewhere in a distance."

"Uh. Sorry, kid. I—."

"You don't like me to bring up your drinking."

He tightened his jaw. He couldn't tell her about of the shadows that enveloped him. Maybe someday. No, not now.

She placed her hand on his diver's chest.

"My dear, you're changing the subject. I wish you could tell me what's bothering you, why you have to drink. I want to help. Please go back to AA. At least call your sponsor."

He sighed. "Hey, it's not a big deal. You got a choice. Hit a bar with me and get blasted. Or find your way home."

"Lord, Jesus. You know I'd never go to a bar. Please."

He shook her away. "Let me alone. Don't call me. I'll be hung over."

Anger burned on her face and she stood, fists planted into her waist with her legs wide apart.

"Precisely like you when something terrible happens!

You attempt to hide in a bottle. Gosh darn it! You make me so angry. You and that terrible liquor." She touched his face again and her eyes had tears. "Oh, honey, let me help you."

He wasn't hiding. He was hoping to separate reality from dreams, 'Nam dreams, where you blew your best buddy into pieces. "Bullshit! You and your frigging Reverend Jethro. He hates homos. Somebody from the network could have done it. They hate queers like I do."

"How dare you! How dare you say that, Dan Haggerty. Lord Jesus, you've sinned by judging others. Accusing our beloved leader or his people makes it more serious. Better ask the Lord Jesus for forgiveness."

"Get out of my way! I'm getting drunk! You comin'?"

Beth's anger found her target. She shouted, "You, you, big lunk-head you. You think that you're so macho. Look at you. Sick! Folding up. What happened to your strength, your gumption?"

"Thanks a helluva lot. You don't know." Images of Tony and Bobby merged. He covered his face with his hands. "Get the hell out of here. I don't wanna see you again!"

"That's perfectly acceptable to me. I never want to see you either."

Haggerty cursed and staggered toward his car. "Booze is the only answer!"

At home later that evening The Fox retired to his private den. He washed his hands and pulled out the Top Secret NSA KL-43 encryption device furnished by his White House contact. He had placed a new cassette containing a new code into the machine that morning so he could communicate securely to other members of the cabal. He typed out two messages concerning a pending arms drop in Central America. An incoming message on the device indicated that his White House contact might be departing CONUS shortly. He also reported that if the trip were successful, some "packages" might be delivered. They'd better get our hostages out.

Stolen Votes

The Fox knew that the secret National Security Agency had given Lieutenant Colonel North around fifteen top-secret KL-43 encryption devices. The equipment enabled the alleged "Project Democracy" players to communicate through coded messages. He had heard that North gave units to a retired General who was into financial arrangements. Others that Magee could communicate with were a liaison in Central America, a U.S. military advisor in El Salvador and the station chief in a Central American country. The Fox found out that a another machine went to a rep from Southern Transport, the aircraft company that had worked for the CIA. He shook his head and smiled. It was amazing how rules could be bent if people thought that it was all for a mission signed off by the president. That was questionable too. Where did the other devices go? He never asked.

An incoming indicated that his JUST CAUSE people on the ground in Lebanon still could not locate the hostages. His reply was an angry "Find Them! No matter the cost."

FX shut down the machine and returned it to its locked container. Yes, they were still pursuing Iran assistance for recovering hostages. The arms shipments were part of the deal. Well, at least I'm doing something worthwhile. The anti-tank missiles should be delivered next week to Israel, to replace the ones they had sent to Iran.

He sat at his desk and sipped one hundred-year-old Grand Marnier. He glanced over to the framed M-1 Garand rifle equipped with a sniper scope. He had knocked off a couple dozen ChiComs with that piece in Korea. By God, I can still squeeze off rounds with it. Too bad I can't do that to some of the anti-contra ass-holes. He poured more Grand Marnier, sniffed it and enjoyed his peace, his last for a while. He raised the glass, "To JUST CAUSE!"

CHAPTER FIVE

Near the western gate of the Naval Amphibious Base on the Norfolk side, The Anchor Inn's noise level was normal at that time of the night. The sailor's hangout required the voice of an old time Bos'n's Mate to order a drink. Shit-kicking music held sway now, with the latest female vocalist from Grand Old Opry expressing her misery for losing her man again.

A fight was stirring between men from different ships, triggered by the claims that one LST, Tank Landing Ship, captain was a better shiphandler than his counterpart. Norfolk-based Shore Patrol Headquarters would have been better served if it had a permanent organization in the area and a small brig outside the premises.

"Cat" Haggerty's head was the centerpiece of a small table with a full beer on each side. Another had spilled on his face drained on the dirty floor. The over-endowed waitress on the far side of forty-five shook her head. She swiped another five-dollar bill from the crumpled mess inches from his outstretched hand and slipped it into her stuffed bra.

Two hard-faced men entered, glanced around and sat at a table near Haggerty. The older one in a shaggy sweater ordered. "Two double Glenlivets on the rocks, please." He grabbed her hand and squeezed. "And no freaking bar scotch, Honey. We're first class guys."

The fight beyond them erupted with curses, shouts and errant punches from two combatants, their efficiency reduced by their consumption of alcohol. Companions supported them with shouts of, "Hit him harder." Or, "Grab his jumper and blast his face." The melee spread with another two boxing experts until the floor was jammed with struggling fighters.

Shaggy sweater spoke. "Jeff, move our buddy, so he don't get hurt or put in the brig."

His crew cut companion disagreed. "Shit let him get his. We ain't gonna get blamed. I wanna see what kind of balls he got. He sure lost his moxie with that hit."

The older man leaned toward the other and stared him down. "What I say goes, got it? You're a last minute pick-up on this job and you don't show your muscle to me or anyone else."

They slid Haggerty and his table farther away from the center of the room and sat with him. Crew cut snared the roll of bills and slipped them into his jacket.

"Geez thought you gave up robbery. Don't start any suspicion here or else."

"Mike, this bastard is out. You wanna nursemaid him. Be my guest."

He answered by grabbing his companion's wrist in a painful grip. "You may want to play games, but not me. I know the Best guy. He acts smooth and kinda sophisticated, but he ain't one of your forgiving contact men. You know what happened to the shooter, don't you?"

Jeff pulled his wrist away and sat back to allow the waitress to deliver the drinks. After she left, he mumbled, "No I don't know. Don't need to know."

Mike sniffed at the drink and sipped, satisfied that they hadn't been slipped bar scotch. "You need to know damned little, your only job's to keep surveillance and not allow anyone to put him in the hospital. The shooter is dead. D-E-A-D! I ain't gonna let you get me that way by fucking up. You follow orders or you'll be out over the ocean for a one-way plane ride. These people are top-notch highly dangerous bastards, but they got clout and money up to their ass. I'm willing to bet they got one or two other groups down here or on their way. They do not take chances on somebody or something screwing up their plans."

He took a long drink and hit the table with the glass. "Good scotch. I worked with Best before and he only takes big jobs. And this is probably over your head, kid. So keep your mouth shut. Don't think. Follow orders to the letter."

Jeff shrugged. "Okay, I got the warning."

"One more thing. There's a guy they call The Mechanic. He's Best's boy. Kind of looney tunes. But he can kill any way they want. Never stops sharpening his freaking knife. When he's out on a job, he carries five weapons including a sawed off shotgun, always loaded. Hangs it from a loop on his belt. They say nobody ever saw him blink. He's after you? No chance. So don't cross Best. You do something wrong while I'm with you, I'll beat The Mechanic to you, cause I know what's coming."

The younger man raised his glass and his companion saw a slight shake in the guy's hand. Apparently, he had the message.

"So, now we nursemaid the ex-SEAL back to his boat when I get a phone call. The other team will have the damned thing bugged. Until then, enjoy your scotch. And shut up!"

Five Shore Patrol members ran into the bar and began separating the bloody but barely maimed combatants. After unsuccessful questioning of everyone nearby, they hustled the damaged ones off to the brig for first aid. They would deliver them to their ships with a nasty Shore Patrol Report pending for the captains. Mike shook his head. Some things never change.

CHAPTER SIX

In bed the next morning Beth felt as if an axe had split open her head. The pain was deepened by thoughts of the horrible killing and the argument with Dan. She drifted off for a moment and saw the grotesque scene again. Poor Tony. She struggled to free herself from the sheet and blanket wrapped around her like a shroud.

She prayed for Tony, for Dan, and herself. Gritty eyes scanned the flowered bedroom. Her dress had been tossed on the beige upholstered chair, her panty hose and underwear were scattered about on the gold carpet. Her shoes were pointed in different directions in the middle of the floor. She scolded herself for a moment.

Poor Tony. Oh God, have mercy on him. I cannot believe that he was a homosexual. She called Dan's boat and let it ring ten times. Gosh darn it; he's either drunk, or hung over. I ought to wake him for that reason. No. No vindictiveness. In the shower with hot water coursing down her body, she prayed for the strength to deal with Tony's death. Dan's failure to handle the situation spun through her mind. She placed her palm on the shower wall to regain her balance. Hot water helped to wash away some of the pain. She swiped at the steamed mirror with a towel. *Uf Dah!*

The old country remark that meant nothing or something flushed out memories. Bad ones of her father beating her Mom when the farm had been lost. She still struggled to forgive him and herself for running away. Stop the guilt!

She dressed in a gray tailored suit with a royal blue blouse and bow. Her earrings and lapel pin were conservative. She marched out. Minnesota farm girls were tough.

On the way to the Truth Network complex near the Norfolk airport, she was unaware that her apartment and phone had been bugged and that two men were tailing her.

Tony's death had stunned her. Was he killed because he a homosexual? Some people were capable of terrible acts like that. Could it have been mistaken identity? She thought of Tony's questions last week about tying a secret computer program to her satellite system. She shook off that possibility.

The Reverend Jethro Creed believed that God's people should go first class, that the laborers in the vineyard were worthy of their pay. Apparently he had overlooked Matthew's passage when Jesus sent his disciples forth with nothing extra. The boardroom reflected his philosophy with plush, mauve carpeting, trimmed in Williamsburg Blue. Expensive drapes with bishop's sleeves prevented outside light from penetrating the inner sanctum. The centerpiece, a twenty-foot oak table, was buffed to a mirror finish and shimmered from overhead lights. The boardroom had audio-visual aids and briefing equipment that would have made the Pentagon jealous. A mural of the Last Supper covered the sidewall.

He nodded at the higher-level network staff like a king acknowledging his court. A large, heavyset man, his bulk was hidden by carefully cut, expensive suits. His dark hair was touched at the temples with distinguished light grey patches. His smile seemed pasted on, as if he were a poster of himself.

He intoned his blessing on the meeting in cathedral-like tones. "Oh, Lawd, help us stay in your grace. Let us hear your word, almighty Gawd, forever and ever."

"Ahmen!" The assembled answered in a thunderclap.

He read from the Third Chapter of Paul's Letter to the Colossians, "stripping off the old man, putting on the new man." He gave a stirring, ten-minute sermon urging them (including the three women present) to become, "new men."

He flopped into his plush swivel chair. The temperature was set at 68 but he was perspiring. "Brother John, please report the contributions."

"Yes, sir. We have, uh," The treasurer cleared his throat and consulted the figures for the twentieth time. "We received four hundred thousand this week from donations for the election telethon, two hundred and fifty thousand for the missionary crusade in the Far East, two hundred thousand for the missionary crusade in the Middle East, and uncommitted donations of two hundred thousand."

The numbers cascaded over them like a waterfall, not washing them all in pleasure because of worry. Donations were down thirty percent from last year. The anxious face of the treasurer was not reflected in the beaming appearance of the great leader. The preacher nodded with each subtotal.

Beth wondered. Were the smaller donations caused by the television evangelist's sex scandal in California? It was terrible that the man had fallen. It would be worse if his behavior damaged the good work that other televangelists were performing. She hoped that Reverend Creed's call for a "Religious Summit" next week in Williamsburg would offset the negative publicity. The morning headlines had reported the murder of a homosexual employed at the network. She wondered how that would affect their local financial support.

She turned to her beloved leader and blushed. He was smiling in a strange way and his eyes were focused on her breasts. She closed her suit jacket.

When his eyes flicked to hers his smile had vanished. "Ahem!" His voice caused an immediate response. They sat straight, shoulders back, alert.

The treasurer stopped. "Yes sir?"

"Nothing wrong. Ahem. Jes cleared my throat, y'all please continue." He sipped water from a cut glass tumbler.

Beth was embarrassed for him and for herself. He was only human. She knew how his ministry had helped millions of people. She acknowledged his call from God, his service to help those in need and offered a silent prayer for him.

The treasurer's figures were of little interest except that she wanted more funds in the budget for automatic tracking equipment. She frowned and scribbled "five million dollars" received this week on her pad. She was too loyal to question The Reverend's motives. He needed considerable operating funds to continue his work all over the world.

Tony's remarks about him pierced her thoughts. He claimed that the poor lambs were sending their savings to a hungry shepherd. And that Creed rhymed with Greed. Poor Tony. She thought of her friend's statement about her shop. "We're setting up data transmission output for your satellite system. A special program. Pretty secret."

"Data transmission?"

"Yeah. The Computer Center is being set up to provide a direct data output on the uplink to your satellite during the election telethon."

"And I haven't been told about this?"

"Ah, Miz Lizabeth?"

Creed's voice called her back and she felt her face burn. "I'm sorry, Reverend. I, uh, I'm afraid I was thinking satellites."

"Well, that's all right as long as you come back to earth right quick."

The assemblage fulfilled its duty by echoing his laugh.

"Well, now it seems like we are in fine shape for the coming Far East campaign. Any questions about the telethon for November fourth? We go on the air, when, Ned?"

Creed's executive assistant, Ned Henshaw, cleared his throat. Thin and balding, he had a voice that grated, like scraping sandpaper. "We go on the air at six a.m. and we'll be on; as you know, for twenty-four hours straight. The theme is back to Christ and back to the founders of our country who entrusted us with the precious vote."

"Ahmen." from The Reverend.

"Praise The Lord." The automatic response came from two yes men.

Ned wiped his head with a white handkerchief. His smile reminded Beth of an iguana. "Well, what is more appropriate than to have a Truth telethon on Election Day?"

She felt that it was ill advised. The network would report the results of voting around the state and the U.S. before the polls were closed. The Truth Network would provide up-to-date information. Was that the secret data transmission?

Ned finished his summary of the telethon plan and appeared to be relieved. He asked, "Are there any questions?"

Beth sighed. "Well, not exactly a question. But I want to remind you that my crews will be on double shifts to carry out the telethon. I will have a problem getting them all off during the day so that they can vote. I was wondering."

The preacher answered. "Well, thank you my dear. Of course, they must have the right to exercise their franchise. Please do anything that's necessary to permit them to vote. The computerized systems in Nawfuk and Virginia Beach should help."

Beth saw nodding heads. "Yes, Reverend. However, they could be delayed. A question, please. Aren't we doing what the major networks promised not to do? We're giving out voting information before the polls are closed. Last year the three major networks had an agreement with the House Task Force on Elections. They promised not to project the probable winners of a presidential election in any state until the polls closed." She flashed a frown at Henshaw who seemed ready to interrupt.

"I know that this is a not a presidential election but... Another question. Do we have data transmission hooked up to my satellite? Is that part of the telethon?"

Ned seemed to become vicious. "Who told you that? We're using people on telephone lines. There will be summaries from time to time. It's a continuing effort to get Christians to go out and vote. To tell them what the vote IS. We're not telling them how to vote. You shouldn't make any accusations without—."

"I wasn't making any accusations. I was—."

Creed's sunny smile preceded his gentle chiding. "Now. Now. My brother and my sister are all fired up. Heh. Heh. No need for that. We don't need details right quick." His chuckle brought smiles around the table. "Miz Elizabeth, why don't you and Mister Ned get together after the meeting and discuss it. We need to move on."

"I'm sorry. Reverend, forgive me. Ned, I'm sorry."

When the meeting ended, Beth was angry. No one had acknowledged Tony's death. Her mentor hadn't prayed for him. Any network person who was sick, or in some kind of difficulty was listed in their prayers before the meeting. Had Ned forgotten? Was silence the network's way of dealing with a homosexual in their midst? She had thought about bringing up Tony's death. Now she was sorry that she had kept quiet.

The great man smiled and touched her arm. "Ah thank you, Miz Elizabeth for your concern. Please tell your people how much ah appreciate their dedication."

She smiled, awed by the man. She owed Jethro Creed so much, a second chance at life and more. Beth realized that he was holding her arm for quite a while and the grip was stronger than normal. She frowned.

"You take care, heah?" He released her and swept out of the room followed in train by Ned and his entourage.

She was puzzled about the data transmission issue, the election information, and the sudden anger from Ned. The Reverend's touch had helped to ease her mind, but that brought up questions too. His hand had always been soft and reassuring. Why had he gripped her so tightly? She shrugged it off. Maybe she could find out something from Ned if he cooled down. She'd never seen him so irritable.

She tried to call Dan four times without success. Was he okay? She gave her secretary his number and asked her to call before she returned. After that, she marched to Ned's office and stood in front of his desk with her arms folded. "Why didn't we pray for one of our own, one who was just killed? Tony Garbossa. The least we could do was to pray for him."

"Are you serious? You knew he was a homo. You were there last night. I saw your name in the paper. What did you have to do with him? If we had known he was a public sinner we would have fired him. You know the rules."

She leaned forward with her fists into her waist. "You, you hypocrite! You knew about that little sweetie in Accounting who was servicing the night shift."

"That's not true. I fired her as soon as I found out. I can't believe you. You, a Christian woman, meeting with a known homosexual. You'd better read your Bible."

"I read it all the time. You fired that woman. Did you fire any of the men on the night shift? Do we have a double standard of Christianity here?"

"How dare you talk to me like that? Why, I'll, I'll. "

"You'll what, report me to our leader? I'll report to him myself this afternoon."

He was silent, but anger seemed to flood his face. His hands gripped the desk; the knuckles were white, fingers vibrating. What in the Lord's name was wrong? He was always anxious and nervous, but this was quite different. Perspiration oozed from his forehead. She felt the kind of fear that had been constant when she had been hooking on the street, before Reverend Creed and Jesus had saved her. She dashed out the door, not bothering to close it.

CHAPTER SEVEN

That morning damp streets in the nation's capital reflected sunlight in disturbing patterns. Too many cars dashed in and out of crowded traffic lanes generating rising tempers. Government workers and the larger supporting cast rushed to offices before the boss arrived. Early lobbyists were lying in wait for congressional staffers and aides at "Gucci Gulch," outside of the Ways And Means Committee office, hoping to peddle their wares.

Francis X. Magee's driver brought his boss toward Georgetown in a circuitous, rapid route to the office on K Street. The Fox reviewed his appointments for the morning. He had to talk to The Speaker of The House ASAP because of the damned contra investigation already proposed. He ran an arrow downward from the original entry, "Wes- TV, Creed." After a sly smile he thought, yes, I'll get that Creed television business on the road this week.

He disembarked from the "Foxmobile" at front door of the office. Red blotches marred his Miami tan. His stride was jerky and erratic and his eyes were diamond drill-points.

The doorman braced and saluted. "Good. Good Morning,

Mister Magee, sir."

After the dark gray power suit whisked by, the doorman alerted the office staff by phone. When they heard that the boss was in a terrible mood they scurried for cover.

Magee's profile was not publicized as much as lobbyists Richard Deaver and Robert Gray. He was one of about eight thousand and some eight hundred registered lobbyists. A curious and connected person would probably find out that there were nearly twenty-thousand of them. The Fox had more influence on legislation, taxes, foreign affairs and government action than the Minority Whip. In a town where access, influence and advice were the coin of the realm, he held thousand dollar bills. He was part of the "secret government" of lawyers, lobbyists, members of Congress and top level bureaucrats who never seemed to leave the nation's capital. Their agenda was often at odds with the citizens they were supposed to serve.

Magee's offices covered the third floor. A security man and the receptionist stood when he stepped from the elevator. The security officer saluted. "Good Morning, Mister Magee."

The lobbyist didn't respond. He walked past "Suite Able," named after older Navy, Marine Corps parlance. His conglomerate offices of finance, insurance, a major credit bureau, and an international service firm were housed there. Suite "Baker" was his control center and lobbyist's lair. A leading designer from the Baltimore-Washington corridor had decorated it in splashes of lavender, black and mauve against an off-white ceiling. The executive staff stood at attention in the outer office.

He bellowed. "Marcy, get The Speaker on the phone damned quick! Don't let his little ass-kissers keep me from talking to him. Got that?"

Magee's Executive Secretary looked like she had wet her panty hose.

"Get Wes at 'Charlie' after my ten o'clock with the General."

"Yes. Uh. Yes, sir! I'm punching The Speaker's private

line, sir."

Magee was a phone call from the official and unofficial leadership in Congress.

He was home free in The Senate, but enemies controlled The House. With The Speaker's nod, he was able to persuade enough members to consider his views. Their dealings were carried on with mutual respect and trade-offs. Tip's son was a fellow lobbyist, and the lobbying lists included the daughters of two Senators plus a son of the House Appropriations Committee Chair.

"Tip, my dear friend. How did you survive Casey's party?"

"You just have to remain in control, Frank. I missed you and Estelle. You're not getting old are you? By the way, the wife thanks you for those roses, and so do I."

"My pleasure." Magee cut off the social and meaningless chitchat, the grease that kept the capital's machinery in operation. "Tip, I'm reluctant to request a change in your busy schedule, but I cannot meet you and Nelson Wallace today because of changes brought about at the last moment. I hope that this will not cause difficulty in your own busy schedule."

"Not a problem for a good friend. I know that you can't stand Wallace. Consider it done."

"I owe you, thanks. Now the subject this morning is the Freedom Fighters in Nicaragua."

"My gracious. So, 'The Fox' is really pissed this morning. Are you hiring lawyers for The Hasenfus Defense Fund? Too bad your survivor of the Nicaraguan plane crash talked as much as he did. Your people in the Senate are raising hell about being given the mushroom treatment on the contra supplies. Some members of the Judiciary Committee are asking Attorney General Meese for an independent probe. Again, I'm not involved."

The Fox grimaced. "You told me that you weren't going to have the contras investigated. What's with the rumors? The President signed the bill last Thursday. The Freedom Fighters are in desperate need."

"Cut the blarney, Fox. They're a creation of the CIA and the administration. Ron's people are blowing a smoke screen. Your friends can't even produce a complete bill to aid the so-called Freedom Fighters for the President to sign. There were pages missing. So Ron will still have to sign a complete one. Remember, we have Public Law 99-569 ready too. If he signs that one the CIA is banned from using its dandy multi-million contingency fund to arm your friends. Then what?"

"What will I do? I'm not involved with the CIA."

"Fox, this is Tip you're talking to."

"You people keep changing the rules in the Boland Amendment. You're making it more difficult to help the freedom fighters. By the way, I see that your party needs fund raising. I can probably swing some cash their way. No publicity of course."

"Why thank you, Frank. I appreciate that. You know that I'm retiring this year anyway. As Dickie Nixon said you won't have me to kick around."

"You're not really going to retire are you? I thought that you were pressuring some of the laggards with that statement. You know, to get them in line on the drug bill with the death penalty. You can't retire. No one can take your place, Tip."

"Hogwash. The truth is, I'm very unhappy about the impact of money in politics. It's getting worse. I need a rest too. Need to get back to Barry's Corner in North Cambridge. Some of my colleagues enjoyed your dinner at the reopened Willard Hotel. Were you trying to cultivate new influence centers? My replacements?"

"Who, me? Not hardly. Now back to the contras."

"Sure and Ron is breakin' me heart, sayin' American boys will die."

"It could happen."

"What? Fox, you're a helluva lot smarter than that. My compatriots and the press are all over my neck, saying you lobbyists are crucifying the democratic process. However, I won't forget that you helped me on the president's tax reform bill."

"Ah, you remembered!"

"Absolutely. The Lobbyists' Full Employment Act? You know an Irishman never forgets a slight or a helping hand. I'll call a few folks about the investigation. Will that help?"

"You know it will. Thanks again for that and the things you've done for me. I won't forget either. I have one last favor to ask before you do leave this God-forsaken rat race. It's very important to me and I don't want my involvement known."

"Name it, and it shall be."

"I think it's about time that we did something positive for the young girls who have no safe place safe to go. Uh, something like the Boys Club. I mean, look at all the teen pregnancies and kid prostitution. I—."

"Sure, I know what you mean. What can I do?"

"It would be great if Congress could change the charter of the Boys Club to include girls too. Uh, something to think about, okay?"

"You really mean this, don't you?"

"I certainly do, Tip. It would be a great favor and I—."

"It may not happen right away, but consider it done. On the agenda for the next Congress, and I'll keep my eye on it back home. I still have many favors to collect here."

"Thanks, my friend. And thank you for not asking questions."

They rang off and Magee sighed. God, that was a tough request. He blinked and thought of his wayward sister for a micro-second. He blinked her away and rearranged his perfectly aligned marble desk set presented by The President. Back to work. Damn! I'll use every hole card I have to block an investigation. And that bastard Wallace better not get in my way.

Best's thoughts were interrupted by a light blinking on his secure phone. He verified that it was on the scrambler mode and answered. It was his contact somewhere, nicknamed "Shadow" for his obvious CIA connections.

"Best, you're sure you got the two lovebirds under surveillance?"

"Dammit! I told you they were covered."

"Listen up. The guy could be trouble. Right now he's back in 'Nam reliving the murder of his swim buddy from the SEALs."

His phone contact sounded like he was reading a report. "Daniel Haggerty nicknamed 'The Cat.' Thirty-eight years old. Former SEAL. Court-martial found him guilty of killing his 'swim buddy' Bobby Douglass in action at Dung Island, Bassac River, Vietnam. Discharged on less than honorable conditions. Rated dishonorable discharge but previous combat actions mitigated the sentence."

"Wait a freaking minute. How did you happen to receive court-martial information?" As soon as Best asked, he knew he had made a mistake, possibly a fatal one.

"Shut up! None of your damned business! More on Haggerty, recurring visits to Veterans Hospital in Hampton, Virginia. Wife divorced him. Alcoholic. Numerous arrests for bar fights. Can't hold a job, except current one, night watchman in a marina next to U.S. Naval Amphibious Base. Lives on an old boat."

Best interrupted. "I know most of that from the bugs. He talks to himself aloud. I do not consider him to be a first class threat."

"Keep your damned mouth shut or someone will do it for you. Priest friend, Father Carl Steward, counseled him. Now running and exercising with him. That enough?"

"That fills in the details, but I believe that he is a lesser threat than you do."

"None of that bullshit. He could get back to being a warrior and, like I said, trouble."

Best thought of the Mechanic parked in the outer office. "Remember, I have an asset here who could eat him for breakfast, no matter how tough he is. He's—."

"He's shit and so are you. I'm warning you. Just for insurance, I got a team going down today. They report to you and me. Since the 'vic' lives on a boat, got two divers with them. And, remember, no freaking action on either of them, unless I give you direct orders. Understand?"

"Yes, I have it. Ease up will you? I carried out my job perfectly. You wanted witnesses; you had more than you needed. You wanted him labeled as a queer, many people on the scene heard the shouts and the newspapers identified him as a homo. I am neither dumb nor anxious to get wasted."

He heard a soft laugh and, "Don't you worry. You're on a list too, and so am I. You continue to do the job perfectly and follow orders to the 't' and you'll retire someplace. Better not let anybody know where. You get me?"

"Yeah. I'll give you a daily report."

"And I'll be calling to check on you."

Best sat back and perspiration ran down his face. He was dealing with badass people who had clout galore. They had connections that enabled "friends" to open up court-martial proceedings regardless of security classifications. He lighted another cigarette. After his part of the project was completed, could these bastards find him in his hideout? Better start a new self-protection plan, one with two more options. He reached for the secure phone.

Magee's long-desired goal of creating and controlling a right wing media empire had been set aside temporarily. Now was the time. He hated the liberal media for trashing the President and his many supporters. He called his security chief. "Wes, Fox here. Sorry to call without advance notice, but I need to see you tomorrow for several projects. Remember LIGHT HOUSE?"

"Yes, sir. No problem calling me any time, sir. When?"

"I may have to sandwich you in between several meetings. You may be waiting a lot."

"Sir, we did a lot of waiting in The Corps. No sweat,

sir."

"When you come in, Marcy can give you The Reverend Jethro Creed's private number."

"The Truth Network owner in the Tidewater area of Virginia? Yes, sir. I believe that you have some material on that project in your special safe, sir. About the media info. I'll have it ready for you shortly after I arrive, sir.

"Thank you."

After he rang off, The Fox rubbed his hands before he washed them again. A smile crept on his face as he thought of Creed's Truth Network. Yes, now that would be a fine fish to catch.

CHAPTER EIGHT

The Anchor Inn hangout was as dark as the innermost passages of a cave. The smoke in the sailors' watering hole was like a cobweb requiring one to sweep it aside with a hand. Many of the chrome and Naugahyde bar stools wore the same cuts and bruises that some patrons sported.

Dan Haggerty continued his two-day drunk, now beyond the slurred words stage. Although he had a port list, the inside seat of a booth kept him somewhat vertical. Mumbling aloud, he tried to rid his mind of Tony's gruesome appearance.

"Tony. Tony. Dam-dammit! Why'd you die?" He saluted with a glass and downed the cutting bar scotch. "Shit! S'like, like Bull Piss. Tony. Homo! Can't be. Never showed signs. Poor bastud killed. My fault. Again. Dammit. You fugguh, mother. Kill frrruh, uh, friends. Cat, better off no friends."

He had two old SEAL friends. Maybe Beth? Other friendships were with booze and the gutter. It had been a long fall, barhopping, jail. He was almost conscious that he was sinking that way again.

"Hey, Cat! Come alongside. Where you been?"

Haggerty weaved over to a small table. He peered at a late thirties, chunky civilian, with rumpled brown hair and a mustache. "Hey, Charlie. That you? What you been doing? Jus what I need. A 'slick' driver." He called out like he was trying to overcome battle noise. "Come on down. Clear LZ. Bring that chopper down. Get me the hell outta here."

Charlie laughed. "You got a real snoot full, man. Want me to retract you? Sorry 'bout that. I left my MedEvac back at the hospital. You need one to get outta here."

"Med. Whah? Hos? Spit? Whacha mean?"

The support helicopter pilot from Vietnam grinned. "Hey. Got a good job. Flying Nightingale bird for Norfolk General. Keeps me off the streets. Just come off duty. You better shove off soon, man. Want me to load you?"

"Shit, no. C'mon. Have a, a one for the road." He waved a floppy arm. "Hey, honey, dub, double scotch, rocks."

The painted waitress with the skirt up to her buns sidled up to him. Her eyes were tired inside deep crow's feet. "You had enough fella. Better shove off. We don't serve drunks."

Dan tried to focus. "You're bootiful, baby. Jus' what I need. Hey, how 'bout one for my pal here and me. Go back a long way. Us."

She snatched the twenty-dollar bill and stuffed it into her bra. Her ample endowments had received new life with a push-up model. "Sure, Baby, I'll get you a drink. Just one. I been in enough trouble with the fuzz."

She returned with watered down bar scotch. Haggerty downed it in one gulp and shuddered. He called out, "Crap! Aberdeen Bull Piss. Freakin' rotgut? Hit us again."

Charlie had been near Dan's platoon on the Mekong Delta and in many support and rescue missions. They talked about the nutty stunts they had pulled when they were together.

"Cat. Remember? Saigon with Doc Warner and a couple a SEALs in Sixty Eight?"

Haggerty shook his head trying to remember. "You mean at the Victory, uh—."

"Victoria Hotel. You know, when the MPs grabbed us." Haggerty seemed so fog bound that Charlie poked his arm. "Remember? Old Doc had to do fast talkin' to get us away from the MPs. I almost shit when he told them the cats we used for target practice under the hotel were VC booby traps."

Dan seemed puzzled. "Oh, yeah."

"MPs said prove it. We hit the street, and you had a Whiz-Bang grenade in your pocket. When you pulled the pin before you handed it over, they ran their asses off."

Dan bent over laughing and ended up coughing. Charlie slapped him on the back until he stopped. "You okay, Cat?"

"No sweat."

They laughed about a stunt they had pulled when Westmoreland came around on an inspection tour. "Hey, I hear they busted you in your second tour. What the hell happened?"

Dan shook his head and Charlie continued. "Sorry about that. Gotta date, have to shove off. Cat, you want a ride back?"

"No. Got the duty here. Some a-hole got to see the dogs die. That's me. See you."

"Likewise. Be careful here. Got some shit heads with quick tempers."

Haggerty shrugged and dropped his head into his arms on the table.

An hour later a husky sailor in dress blues peered into the bar and strode in. For a man barely under six feet, Doc Warner had wide shoulders and a barrel chest. The SEAL had a small curved scar on his left cheek. Beneath his "Budweiser" SEAL insignia, he had more combat decorations than the average general. When he stepped up to the bar, nearby sailors opened a space.

He questioned the bartender and the man answered, "Yes, sir. Had a short bar fight." He pointed to the back door.

Doc halted at the door and placed his left shoulder against it. He shoved it open and stepped out quickly, fists at the ready. Nothing there except a civilian's body lying face down. "Cat, you son of a bitch! Good thing Charlie called me."

He turned Dan over and examined his body carefully. The First Class Navy Corpsman had seen a helluva lot worse. "Guess he don't need any stitches in his face. No broken bones. "Hey, Cat, come on here. What the hell went down?"

Doc sighed and lifted Haggerty in a fireman's carry. He struggled with the weight and managed to get him sitting against the building. He gently cuffed Dan on a bloody cheek.

"Hey, bud. I'm gonna call for help and get you on the boat. Sit there."

He returned in five minutes and told a comatose Cat that he called his priest friend. He squatted alongside Haggerty and smoked a cigarette. "Seems like old times, Cat. I've seen you worse than this. What the hell kicked you off this time?"

When Father Steward arrived Haggerty was still out. Doc rose and nodded at the young priest. The clergyman had an eager face and curly black hair. "You Father Steward?"

"Yes. You must be Doc Warner. Pleased to meet you, except under these circumstances."

He shook the priest's hand. "The old Cat got beat up again. Think you can give me a hand and haul him to my car?"

The priest grinned. "I'm in shape, Doc. Let's go."

In a short time they laid the unconscious body in Dan's bunk on his boat. The doc cleaned up the damage and bandaged his friend. On the way up from the small bedroom he grabbed a bottle of Glenfiddich from the saloon. They sat back in the transom of the aged Bertram cabin cruiser sipping on Dan's scotch and discussing his condition.

"I don't know who beat him up, Father. Just found him on the deck. They rolled him too. Least he's got his wallet and keys. Somethin' must have sent him off again."

"Perhaps because he was at a murder last night at Saint

John's Church."

" Murder? No shit! He wasn't—?"

"Accused? No. He was there with his friend Beth Olson. Well, she called me to get a ride home. Apparently she and Dan had a terrible argument after the murder."

The doc shook his head. "Dint hear about it. Anyways, last I knew he was doin' good. At least I ain't heard about anything lately."

"Beth said something about a flashback from Viet Nam. Maybe that's what started this."

Doc sipped his drink and glanced at the water. "Well, he had a bad time his second tour. Trouble was, well, he blamed himself for an incident."

"Could you tell me about it?"

Doc sipped. Like most combat veterans he seldom spoke of his experiences. "Maybe it might help. Ain't much to tell. Seems like we was near the end of our second tour in 'Nam in '69. We kidnapped a VC tax collector and ran our asses off back to the canal to get extracted. We all knew what our positions were supposed to be even when bugging out. Cat was point man on the way in and rear guard on the way out. His Buddy Bobby got lost or went in the wrong direction into a free fire zone. Cat hears movement or saw something, so he fired the Ithaca couple times. Uh, that's a shotgun, and Bobby bought the big one. Blew poor Bobby's face off. After that Cat was nearly a basket case. Couldn't touch that freakin' weapon. He kinda lost his warrior psyche. See what I'm saying?

"Oh, my God."

"Yeah. I worked on Cat. He sez all he could see was a white-hot haze. His sight cleared, but not his head. The Navy blamed him. Nobody blamed him more'n he did. He was a freakin' mess. If it hadn't been for his record, they might have given him a General Court. Instead, a Special Court trashed his career. The Navy discharged him as a Second Class Quartermaster."

"Trouble was that around that time they reorganized. We

had a SEAL team leader but they put us under some little twit rear echelon Lieutenant Commander. Our Lieutenant would have handled it so Cat probably wouldn't even got a court-martial. He tried but the bastard, sorry Father, in the chain of command wanted to make a name for himself and pushed a court to higher authority. The little desk jockey never even saw a drop of blood on his tour of duty. Our leader testified but they disregarded most of his testimony.

The doc hit the scotch again. "I tole Cat to get a JAG lawyer to help with the trial. Guess he felt too guilty. The only good thing about it was that they pulled us out from under that jerk so we could do our job right. Didn't help. Anyways, he couldn't even handle explosives, not much use to SEALs." He had another sip of scotch. "How come you know him?"

The clergyman nodded when Doc filled his glass. "I met him at the Veterans Hospital. We did a lot of sharing and I invited him to stay with me at the retreat house in Hampton. He stayed for a year. He never told me about what happened in Vietnam. Apparently, just before he returned home he received a letter from Ruthie, his wife of 5 years, and it affected him terribly."

"Yeah, a 'Dear John.' I mean she dumped him. Heard they poured him out of the aircraft at NAS Norfolk. She didn't meet him at the plane. 'Cause she was sittin' in the street with a bunch of 'Nam war protesters at the Main Gate." He fixed the clergyman with a hard look. "Some bearded, scroungy-looking priest with her was leading chants against the "Baby Killers."

Stew frowned. "Really. That's unfortunate."

"Helluva lot worse than that. He was ready to kill the sneaky bastard with his bare hands. When he found out that they were shacking up together, it blew his mind."

Father Stew shook his head. He explained how he had started their friend on running, then racquetball. "His physical condition was improving and he was coming around to a better frame of mind. Then this, again."

"Yeah." The doc sighed. "Guess I better be getting on. Thanks for helping. Me and the Cat were pretty tight, guess we still are. I helped to get him this crummy job here as a night watchman. Ain't much of a job for a first class warrior like him. That's the way it is. You think of anythin' I can do, call me at SEAL TEAM TWO, huh? Take it light." Doc went below to check on him. Before he shoved off he noticed a large Hatteras sports fisherman model across the narrow slip from Dan's boat. He frowned for a second. Three occupants out on deck and two on the bridge seemed to be interested in watching Cat's boat. Intel? Or curiosity? He shoved off.

Father Steward put the glasses and scotch away then made a last minute check on Dan. He said a short prayer and blessed him before he departed for his car.

Sometime later Haggerty awakened with a screaming headache and pain in many places. "What the hell?" He wondered why his face was bandaged, why he hurt so much. He was caught between 'Nam and the present. He thought of Tony, then Bobby's death. He leaned against the bulkhead. "Where's Beth? Shit, that Beth. Her and her freaking 'Praise the Lord' crap. That network sure has rubbed off on her. She thinks the Reverend Jethro is Jesus himself."

He staggered up to the saloon and hunted for the bottle. He wondered where the physical pain came from. He felt other pain, from his fight with Beth, from Tony's death. He fell against the corner of the table and felt the sharp, familiar pain in his hip. "Shit." He slid back toward the transom bench and sipped at a scotch. His wounds and SEAL TEAM TWO memories in 'Nam roused him for a moment. He thought of his best friend Bobby Douglass and had a crying jag.

Drinking rapidly, he lost consciousness in stages. The computer monitor in the cabin levitated and floated around. Then it spun away. He followed it with his eyes and the inside of the boat began moving, around and around. He shook his head. "Whoops. Hold it there. Slow down. Jump on the merry-go-round." He stood, lost his balance and staggered against the table.

"Hey! Stand by for heavy rolls. Man. Got heavy weather here. Whoops! Batten down the hatches men." His words ended in crazy laughter. It felt good. He finished his second glass, missed the bench and flopped on the deck. The cabin disconnected itself. It rose up and down, spinning clockwise.

He was lying on deck, barely conscious. There was a sound on the boat like somebody was coming aboard. He opened one eye and mumbled, "The last thing to go is hearing. Hey! Anybody there? Sound off, dammit." After a long silence he heard footsteps. A board on the boat creaked. "Who goes there, foe or fugging foe?" He giggled for a moment and drifted off into oblivion.

Joseph Guion

CHAPTER NINE

Thunder echoed around the inside of the Lincoln Memorial. Wallace wore a raglan-sleeved beige raincoat, which made him look stouter than he was. A casual observer would guess that he was a jolly fat man. If he were to play Santa Claus, parents would be better off taking their children to a wino on the street. Wallace was stronger and tougher now than when he played tackle on the Tennessee football team. There was steel in his eyes and in his bear's paw hands. He inhaled with a slight noise from damaged cartilage.

The gold Cartier watch that had cost him five big ones indicated that Cliff was late. Damn him. Need to get to The Hill. He watched a group of schoolchildren scamper from the rain under the portico like squirrels from shotguns.

He searched for something unusual, perhaps a vehicle parked nearby containing a listening device. There were no signs of other surveillance tricks, like street repairs, workmen in the park, utility vans. He nodded. Come on, Cliff. I don't have all freaking day.

He thought of The Fox. That bastard is trying to steal my business, and he skipped our meeting this morning, afraid that I'd show him up. I'll keep dropping more hints about how he's deeply involved with the freaking missile deliveries to Iran. He almost grinned. Yeah and the president says they'll never negotiate with terrorists. Bullshit!

He wagged his head and his jowls vibrated. "Project Democracy" run by the NSC was as hidden as a walkin' horse's ass. Maybe I could get a contact to make Hasenfus talk more about a CIA or White House connection. That would frost FX for sure.

A cab swooped to the curb like a bird of prey. New passengers jostled the well-dressed businessman stepping out wearing dark aviator glasses If they knew the former CIA operative's reputation, they would have backed away. Cliff popped open a large black umbrella, paid the driver and strolled to the far side of the memorial. He slipped around children and visitors, slowly coming closer. He stood behind Wallace and spoke quietly. "Sorry about the delay. People are scurrying around about the contra crap."

"Never mind that shit! What the hell happened with GRASS ROOTS?"

"Yes, sir. There was a minor glitch and—."

"Minor glitch? That was a glitch? Some assholes free-lancing and beating up my target? That was a loss of control and I won't have it!" He turned and his eyes pinned the ex-CIA man. The words hit like machine gun bullets. "Y'all don't get it! I'm fucking serious about the project. That means no glitches, no means of discovery. The operation will be a complete and unqualified success. Do I make mahself clear?"

"Yes, sir! I'm taking care of it. Those two won't see the light of day. The Mechanic will take them out."

"He ought to take you out, shit head. You want me to jump in and take over?" Wallace was pleased when he saw Cliff back off half a step. "What about the system?"

"It's in place and almost ready. A complicated system like that has to be tested and debugged. We're on schedule. The computer-satellite hookup is ready to operate. All they have to do is keep it under wraps."

"Seems to me the wraps are openin' up, one seam after another. After that hit down at that beach, the Redneck A-hole should have stripped the weapon and dumped it in the ocean. He's history. One more screw up and somebody else will go. The system's got to be one hundred percent by two November. Without fail!"

"Yes, sir. What if I have to leave the country on short notice?"

"What? You leave and your ass is mine. I have a special unit down there already. Tell me about those two pigeons in Norfolk?"

"The frogman and the woman are under surveillance. The team knows their orders cold. No fatal action without permission. Anyway, most of the stuff on the tapes is a bunch of shit. The SEAL is half drunk all the time. The Mechanic can't wait to get him."

"He'd better wait or your ass is grass! You get something interesting from those two birds, call. I want a big push on them, understand?"

"Yes, sir. Is that it?"

Wallace nodded. He watched Cliff slip away and spotted a young woman walking briskly toward the memorial. He thought of Magee's mistress and wagged his jowls. Some day I'm gonna have her, the hard way. That would be the biggest coup I could pull on that Fox bastard.

Better call my other contact in Norfolk. Maybe it's time to ease Cliff out of the loop and send reinforcements down there. He knows too freakin' much. Might be better to send The Mechanic after him. There were too many loose ends.

The Fox ordered Marcy to send his chief security man into Suite Baker. His entry into the world of television and other media would begin with a deal with Reverend Jethro Creed. He knew that his request would be distasteful, disgraceful to some, but like many deals The Fox had made, the means were irrelevant. This security man, a former Marine, would follow any of his orders, albeit this awkward one. Wes was the only man on earth that he trusted with his life. He'd proven that in Korea.

The former "Gunny" Sergeant slipped into the suite through a private door wearing his five-o'clock shadow face, black hair and no smile. Average in height and weight, he was dedicated to serving his boss. The coal-hued eyes were alert and probing, like those of a point man on a night recon patrol.

"Wes, I've got a special favor to ask of you."

The answer was snapped out with precision. "Never a problem, sir."

"Excellent. Well, I need to involve two people in order to accomplish two important tasks. The first person is the television evangelist, Reverend Creed. Your efforts to mine his foibles and financial status have been exemplary."

"Thank you, sir."

"It becomes complicated because I need to compromise some of my values for the better gain. Nevertheless, I have decided that I will sacrifice these ethical concepts to insure that Creed ends up in my pocket. To do this, I need your excellent services and—." He paused to display a practiced sad face.

"I have promised Miss Whitney Carlton a red Mercedes for six months now to whet her large appetite. This is the time to dangle that prize in front of her greedy eyes. It's also the time for me to dispose of her. She's been getting too demanding for a mistress and frankly, I'm getting tired of her."

Wes frowned. "You want me to take her out?"

"No, no! No such violence. You are to pass on this offer and the keys to said Mercedes to Miss Whitney, when she completes the assignment I have for her." He handed the security man an open envelope. "Take a seat and your time reading this. Ask any questions you need and we'll discuss the exact steps I want taken."

While Wes read the instructions, FX poured some green

mint tea shipped from Hong Kong by an associate. His face was calm, but his mind raced around the reactions he was going to get from Creed and from dear Whitney. The shadow of a smile flickered on his mouth. Marcy reported that there was an urgent call from the White House.

"I'll take it."

The person on the phone identified himself properly and said, "It's about the Relative."

The Fox frowned. The Core Group had been unhappy with the failures concerning their contacts in Iran. General Secord's business partner, Albert Hakim, had started a second channel with Iran and a new contact. He was a member of the Revolutionary Guard and a nephew of the Parliament Speaker Rafsanjani. That was why the Americans called him the Relative.

Magee wasn't happy. "Listen, after a year's dealing with Iran to get two hostages out, in four days two more were kidnapped."

"We think that the Relative is sincere and worth working with. After all, in late September he wired seven mil to 'the enterprise' Swiss bank account as a deposit toward the next arms purchase. It was a 'good faith' effort and that's why we considered his request for another meeting with our people in Frankfurt on October Sixth."

"I don't know. I think we're still buying a pig in a poke. You guys think that they'll do exactly what you want, but they always drag their feet. Next thing you know, they have the funds and we're empty handed with no people delivered to us. I've told you several times that those people are experts at bargaining and we're not."

"We're trying. It's a great cause."

"I know. Just make sure that our people do some hard bargaining. No pussy cats." After hanging up, he turned to his security man. "Forget what I said on the phone. Questions?"

"No, sir. Seems clear-cut. I'm sure that Miss Carlton will be extremely upset."

"Good point. There are others who have been interested

in her for quite a while." He grinned. "Indeed, my worst enemy, Nelson Wallace, has had the 'hots for her' ever since he saw us in Hong Kong last year. Knowing him, he'll punish her as well as screw her."

Wes raised an eyebrow, possibly at the blunt expression.

"Any questions?"

"No sir. I'll contact her right away."

Magee smiled and nodded. "I know that this type of an assignment is not something you like to do, and I appreciate your willingness to perform such a distasteful act. However, I need to have it done quickly."

"ASAP, sir!"

He handed Wes a stuffed brown envelope. "Just a little bonus. You always do such a complete and professional job in everything I ask."

"Thank you, sir. It's really unnecessary."

"Yes, it is. You're a trooper like I was. Call this an early Christmas bonus."

The security man braced at attention. "Sir!" He spun around and walked out of the office.

FX rubbed his hands. Time to wash them again. In the private bathroom he spoke to the mirror. "Well, Fox. You did it. The wheels are turning even though you'll piss off Whitney so badly, she'll take off as soon as she can. Maybe not. I'll crush the little whore yet. Wes will be very uncomfortable with this. But the bonus will make it more palatable."

Later that day Father Steward called Beth from the retreat center in Hampton. He asked how she was doing and her answers seemed guarded but reasonable in light of the trauma she had experienced with the murder of her friend. She had told him about the argument at the murder scene. He wanted to cool the atmosphere, so he asked how The Reverend was dealing with the headlines of Tony's death.

She assured him that her mentor was dealing with the

event calmly. Her voice betrayed concern when he said that he had news about Dan.

"Is he all right, Father? Did something happen to him? Can I see him?"

"Now, don't get too excited about it. He's okay, had a few scratches and cuts in a bar fight."

"Oh, Lord Jesus. Is he all right?"

"Certainly. One of his SEAL friends and I brought him to the boat. It will be better, I think if you wait until tomorrow to see him."

"You're telling me that it would be better if I didn't see the results." Her voice sounded commanding, "Father, I want to know precisely what his injuries are."

The priest sighed. "Okay, Beth. He has a black eye, a fat lip and some scratches on his neck. Probably has a bruise or two on his chest. Remember, his SEAL friend is a medic and he knows very well how to handle those kinds of injuries. He'll be okay to go to Tony's memorial service tomorrow night. I hope that you'll bring him. I'm helping to officiate the non-denominational service."

"Oh, dear God. Yes, I've forgotten all about poor Tony. Couldn't think much beyond work to keep me busy and worrying about Dan. Are you sure that he's not in trouble?"

"Sure. I think he might take some convincing to go to the service. He has quite a homophobic outlook. I think that if you appeal to the friendship you three had it might win him over. This has been a terrible experience for you. As you know from his reaction, Dan had a post-traumatic experience with Tony's murder. He needs some comfort and TLC."

After a long silence, she responded. "Yes, Father, you are correct. I've never seen him so helpless. His first action was to protect me, but then he ran, I guess to help Tony. Dear Jesus, it was so horrible. Are you sure that I shouldn't go there right now?"

"Whatever you think, but there isn't much you can do except sit by his side. Doc sedated him and he'll be out for some hours. Try to be gentle and forgiving with him. He's had a difficult life."

"I know. I know. I love him, Father. I only want what's best for him. If only he could break the hold that alcohol has on him."

"Yes. Between us we'll bring him around. But it wont be easy. Let's try to get him back to AA without pushing. In the meantime I'll continue to get him into a physical regimen. That will provide some help. With your care, I know that he'll respond. I'll see you tomorrow evening. Take care, Beth. And God bless you."

"Thank you, Father. You're a great help and friend. I know that you are in great favor with our Lord, Jesus."

"Thanks."

The priest placed the phone on the cradle carefully. Poor Dan would be a mess tomorrow evening, but he needed to get out and away from that boat and his solitary routine. Maybe he ought to suggest that Doc and his buddies visit him. He'd refuse to see them though. Father Stew wasn't sure why.

CHAPTER TEN

Later that day The Fox strolled through the private hall to Suite Charlie, home of his tax-free foundations. He reviewed the latest reports on large political contributions and smiled. Last October he had escorted several millionaires to the White House. Their contributions to the National Endowment for the Preservation of Liberty had done much to influence the government in his direction. He had worked PACs to insure that the "right" Congressmen and Senators would be elected or reelected. His direct mail organization collected checks from all stops on the political spectrum, making money on people he opposed for political reasons.

His ten o'clock appointment entered, a former three-star General Officer of the United States Air Force. The Fox stood at attention. He knew how to appear to be subservient while remaining in control. You stroked the man's fur in the right direction and became the ideal subordinate. He assumed a flag officer's aide mode; sharp, anxious to please, vibrating to jump in the direction the officer ordered. He waited for the crew cut, red-faced visitor to offer a handshake.

"Welcome back from Central America, General. How

was the trip?"

"Glad to see yah, Frank." The general's voice rasped from too many bourbons and cigars. "Had the three-dollar tour around the Southern Command with 'Squeaky' Moore. Damned good man. I'd like to see him kick ass and jump on those Sandyneestas. I spent a day with a-hole congressmen on their 'fact-finding' tour. Shit! They wouldn't know a fact if they fell over it."

The general sat and lighted off an Upmann, next to a "THANK YOU FOR NOT SMOKING" sign. "That damned House! Investigating contra support. Dumb wimps! They'd vote against aid to Texas if the Mexican Army were invading. We gonna win that one?"

"Well, I'm quite positive. The President turned his cabinet people loose. I heard rumors that he signed a finding to authorize intelligence aid for the contras. There was a major publicity campaign supported by our people and others. We might be better off to forget Congress and supply them the way we're doing now. How about deliveries?"

The general puffed. "Not good. You know the bastards closed the airfield in Costa Rica the end of September. As for airdrops, we had near a hundred since August, about five hundred tons. We needed to get the drops in before the dry season in the winter."

"Yes. I learned that the Costa Rican government was going to have a press conference early last month. They were going to identify the secret airstrip that we used for direct supply up to February. Too bad it's only available for an abort base for damaged aircraft. Fortunately, the influence supplied from some of my sources worked and they backed down."

"Good. Glad you were involved. I'm pissed about the FBI investigating Secord's Southern Air Transport. They could expose some of our flights."

"As a matter of fact, there's been influence applied there too." Magee explained Attorney General Meese had helped to delay and narrow the investigations by the FBI and Customs.

"Anything new on finances? We're about running out of cash. I think it's an idiotic method of running the funds around a couple of circles."

"Not certain if you aware of it. An Assistant Secretary of State reported to the Senate Foreign Relations Committee on the tenth of this month that we have not received funds from a foreign government. Which was, of course, not factual, but the way he had said it there was an element of truth in it."

"I did see him on that Cable News Network around that time, where he denied any U.S. government involvement. He sure knows to wiggle around facts. Guess he was talking about the official story, not what was really going on."

The Fox grinned. "That's one of the first principles you learn in DC Course 101. Learn how to state things and answer questions without exposing the actual situation. He and a couple of CIA spooks testified before the House Permanent Select Committee on Intelligence on the fourteenth. That title is a misnomer at least, intelligence, indeed. They did the DC thing in that closed hearing too."

The general wagged his head and blew smoke at the "...NOT SMOKING" sign. The dolt. Magee pursed his lips but didn't comment. He reflected on his personal growth in the DC process. He had taken the lack of truth as his own, even though he abhorred the lack of accountability in the nation's capital. It was a helluva lot different in The Corps.

"I'm counting on the President signing the revised bill soon. That's a hundred mil for the contras. Some banks are using part of that bill to float loans. If the CIA runs arms deliveries, we may be partially out of business."

"Yeah, could be. Those ass-holes in Nicaragua ought to quit infighting, get off their asses and hit the *Federales* hard. We need a honcho there with a frigging whip. You ought to be down there. We need an ex-grunt Marine in charge on the scene."

"My best contribution is to pry money out of people, the like-minded ones and the fence-sitters. Frankly there's so much stirring here since the C-123 was shot down that some people are getting uneasy. Too many have covered their asses already." He did not mention that one of his contacts in the White House had started to shred documents for fear of discovery.

"No shit! Meantime, those contras need some heat seekers to fire up the ass of those Russian Mi-21 choppers. Anything new on getting Stingers?"

Magee updated the General on the missiles and other arms supplies.

"Frank, that plane crash on the fifth was UNSAT! The press claims that Corporate Air Services was connected to that flight. I heard something about Swiss bank accounts. What the hell was that? Somebody skimming bucks?"

"Not that I know of." The Fox would not allow that can of worms to be opened up. Better that this retired officer didn't know. "Sir, have you read about that Russian nuke sub that sank off the Bahamas? Shows that they aren't that good."

"Yeah. But the bastards are still nosing around in our backyard. Too bad a few more of them aren't sunk." The General stood. "Frank, keep it up. Until Congress gets some backbone, you guys are the only hope we have of turning the thing around in Central America."

"Yes sir! I'll give it everything I can to make sure that we control the efforts."

After the general departed, Magee thought of his beloved USA. He hated the direction it was taking. Drug abuse, sexual excess and a loss of moral fiber convinced him that the country was heading for destruction from within. Dedicated and principled people had fallen to his persona, to his pressure and to his financial acumen. His credit bureau in Suite Able provided access to important people with financial problems. He leaned on people in key positions to accomplish his objectives. He had no qualms about making deals with enemies to gain his ends.

When his security chief entered, The Fox grinned. "Good afternoon, Wes. What's the latest on the TV acquisition?"

"Yes sir. Here's an update on the those evangelists. Had their annual meeting here at the Sheraton in the spring. The report has the details. As you suspected, The Reverend Creed's network in Norfolk is in financial trouble. Donations are down and there's trouble with the IRS. Possibly about non-taxable funds. Some question of his own finances. I'll provide more when I contact the right person at the IRS."

Wes cleared his throat and hesitated. "For personal preferences, the preacher likes young, athletic women. But he's very discreet. Some financial and sex scandals are about ready to blow the TV evangelists apart. Creed's not involved, but the preacher from California is one of them. There's the couple in Carolina too. It's all in the report, sir."

"Thank you, Wes. I know that you aren't comfortable in such areas. You've done a great job, as usual."

"Yes sir."

Wes paused at the door. "Good luck with the contras, sir. They need your help."

"Thank you."

The Fox wore a wicked smile when he washed his hands in the lavatory. He needed access to media power for many of his plans. He glanced through the TV report. "Bunch of weak people who are great on TV. I'll get in there without fail." Thinking about his moves to get into television brought on the same facial expression he wore after killing an enemy soldier. He raised his chin and nodded. The Reverend Jethro Creed is not an enemy, unless he refuses my plan. Then? He slapped an open hand on the desk as if he were killing a fly.

Stolen Votes

CHAPTER ELEVEN

Haggerty didn't know what time it was. He was pretty sure he was still at the Anchor Inn. Loudmouth drunks tossed out challenges that their ship was better than anyone else's. With no takers, they tried to empty the bar of liquid.

Dan tried to down a drink but he ended up coughing and spitting. Damn, Cat. You lost your diving lungs. Yeah, me and Doc were hot shits in SEAL TEAM TWO. He thought of a few tricks that they had played with new guys just coming into BUDS. Although his eyes were half closed there was a glimmer of a spark that surfaced and winked out.

The SEALs had made him special, a warrior. Now he was nothing. Tony. Tony. Dammit! Why'd you have to die? Poor Tony. A homo! Hard to believe. Never showed signs.

He grabbed another glass. Geez, I hope the hell he dint give me AIDS. Shit. He used my glasses and cups lots of times. Killed. God! My fault. Again. Dammit. You kill your friends, Cat.

His eyes locked on Go-Go Deena's current performance. Bumping and gyrating, her beautiful young body glistened with perspiration. Big, bouncing breasts kept time with the music. He wondered if he was too far-gone to function if he could get her on his boat. When he was lying at the bottom of a cliff, he would need a woman. Beth had rejected him at the crime scene. She was so freaking straight anyway. She was the woman he really wanted. Why did they fight so much?

He tipped his glass at the young woman as her routine ended. Eyes flashing with excitement and exertion, Deena picked up crumbled currency lying on the stage and stuffed the bills into her G-string. She waved at Dan and smiled. He pointed at the chair next to him. She called out, "One more dance before a break."

He nodded. Later, in the sack with that gorgeous body. The Cat purred.

When she sat at his table he asked her to come to his boat and stay. "Look, Dan, I, well, I have to get home for the baby sitter."

Geez, she's got a kid. "Can't delay goin' home?"

She shook her head. "Besides, my hubby is calling from Naples. His ship's getting underway."

Shit! Another freakin' Med Widow, wife of a deployed sailor. The Cat knew he shouldn't screw around with her, for the guy's sake. Bullshit. He was beyond caring anyway. Damn sailor's wives, you couldn't trust them. Like his ex.

He thought of Tony's death. Was Bobby's worse? They had been swim buddies in BUDS, the Basic Underwater Demolition and SEALs training. They went through jump school and final training together. They had deployed in the same detachment, Det Bravo in Foxtrot Platoon in the late 60s. They had a helluva lot of hit and run ops in the Mekong Delta. Bobby had caught the big one in '69 during their second tour in country. Dammit to hell!

Later Deena drove him to his boat and shoved off. Dan's intel capability had deserted him. He never noticed the large Hatteras sports fisherman across the narrow slip of water between the piers. He didn't realize that a new crop of killers had been installed there, monitoring the bugs on his boat and ready to kill when ordered. He roused himself enough to hit the scotch again. Tipping the bottle up, he downed several gulps straight. Coughing and cursing, he snatched a glass and filled it with ice. Filling it to the brim he flopped on the bench in the tiny kitchen.

Three men had watched Deena help Dan to his boat. The Mechanic's flat, humorless grin widened a quarter of an inch. "Let's follow them on the boat. I want that bastard. Then I can cut up the blonde's nice tits." He slipped the knife out of his sleeve and snapped it open.

Ace Murphy said, "No. We got orders to wait. Say, he's a big bastard, ain't he."

"I'll cut him down." The knife snapped open and closed, open and closed.

They watched the sexy blonde take off. The frogman staggered and sprawled on the deck of his boat. They heard him snoring. Ace brought The Mechanic and the tall guy over to Dan's boat.

When they arrived The Mechanic whispered, "He's gone. Let's take him now."

"No. We got our orders. No killing now. We check for more computer shit."

They checked the open stern and inside the cabin without speaking. The tall man stepped over Haggerty in a careful manner. He located printouts in a drawer and took them.

The Mechanic stood over Haggerty, knife poised and said, "This is too easy."

The tall man shook his head. "Hey, cut it out. We got orders. I wanna get paid."

They walked silently down the small pier to their boat. There they checked out the tape recorder. Ace said, "Call our man and tell him we've got the printouts. Might as well get some sleep. The bastard will be out for hours."

The other one nodded and strolled down to a pay phone.

They had a phone, radios and other equipment on the boat but he was insistent on how to communicate with him. Their contact had given them specific instructions on how they would carry out their surveillance and neutralization. On the boat Ace thought, Tommy don't like being told all the details. But, hell, with this kind of dough they can tell me when to shit. He grinned. This thing's a piece of cake. That ass-hole's a hopeless stew bum.

Mikanos Landros, aka The Mechanic, existed and worked in the excrement of society as well as in the gilded and lofty levels of privilege. In politics and other power games, these extremes were often braided together into a hangman's noose. He had flopped on the queen-size bed in the Hatteras owner's cabin. Lying there he watched a late movie, smoking a joint, playing with his switchblade. He could slip aboard and knife that big bastard easy.

Ace called out, "Hey, Mechanic, you got a phone call. Your boy friend?"

The Mechanic stuck the knife blade under Murphy's chin. "Want your balls cut off? Gimme the freakin' phone." After he hung up, he picked up his traveling bag and started to leave.

Ace asked, "Hey, where you goin'?"

"Kiss my ass! None of your business." The killer walked down the pier.

"Geez, he ain't gonna kill the frog now, is he?" Ace ran after The Mechanic and grabbed his arm. "Where you goin? On the drunk's boat?"

Unblinking eyes drifted to Ace and riveted him.

Murphy swallowed. This guy's the worst killer I've seen. "Dammit! We follow orders. They just told me again. No killin' yet! You'll get your chance damned soon."

Before Ace realized what had happened, he was bent backwards and the knife was an inch from his crotch. "Jesus, don't. We gotta follow orders. Or else."

"Else what? I got my own orders. Fuck off!" He released Murphy and walked toward the pier where Haggerty's boat laid, the knife still in his hand.

Murphy raced back to the Hatteras. Gotta get help before the Mechanic takes the drunken bastard out. If something happened to the drunk without orders from Best, he and his crew would be up Shit Creek.

CHAPTER TWELVE

Wallace and Cliff, his top control man in GRASS ROOTS, strolled along with a noisy tour group in the Smithsonian. They stayed near the rear of the group, just close enough to seem part of it. They spoke softly so that no one else could hear.

Wallace grumbled. "It seems that there are too many holes for exposure in this plan. I'm paying high prices for competent, silent people. They don't seem to be first class."

The former CIA man shook his head. "They came high, but the game isn't over. I'd prefer to keep them in place. I figure it's too soon to knock off the two lovebirds at the same time. Ace and his people are ready. The Mechanic can take care of an army."

"What's your opinion about the woman? Is she a real threat?"

Cliff half-turned to check for anyone close. "She's under tight surveillance. Ace can move in anytime. I'd like to find out what she knows before we put her away."

"That makes sense." He poked Cliff. "Listen heah, I don't want any suspicions. No accidents, contrived or otherwise. This removal has to be so smooth that it will seem completely natural. Any, quote, accident, unquote, and the police might be too curious. I have additional resources there but—."

"Understood. We'll find out what she knows. She's very loyal to The Reverend."

Wallace responded. "She ought to be loyal. He redeemed her, sent her to college and hired her. She may have an inkling that something is going on, but she can't put her finger on it. Put the squeeze on Ned to get everything out of her. He's a damned nervous Nellie"

Cliff agreed. "Weak. Yeah. He could be dangerous. You have him covered?"

"Absolutely. In many ways. He's afraid to take a crap without lookin' down first."

"Boss, I have a good tail on the woman, a tap, and listening at her apartment. She has no friends, no people she goes around with, except the dude with the boat."

"Find anything more about him?"

He told Wallace what he knew about Haggerty and added, "Got 'Nam flashbacks, mind wanders. Very unreliable. We might have to watch out for him, if he got his balls back."

Wallace squinted. "What do you mean? Think he's on to something?"

"No. But he could put up a fight if he were in shape. Not to worry, boss. The Mechanic can handle him whenever you choose."

"Is the frog a computer whiz?"

Cliff shook his head. "Not really. Not even a low level hacker."

"Better be sure about that."

"I'll deliver a clean job by getting both. So far it's just the woman and the washed out frogman. Nobody they know has the computer smarts to hack into it. When the system is completely checked out and proofed, there's no way to stop it."

Wallace jostled him. "I'll tell you this. I've made my way

to the top by not talkin' that way. There's always a chance that some A-hole can blow a complicated plan. That's why you have to stay on top of it to the bitter end. I don't like this remote control position for me. But I don't want to step in and take charge."

"You don't need to boss, I'm trying to ease your mind a bit. If the woman doesn't go to New York like she's supposed to, I'll have her snatched."

The big man nodded. "Fine. So the man is an Ex-SEAL and has psych problems? Think I might add to them. Make him believe that he's had one too many Viet Nam flashbacks. Maybe he butts his head into a wall and knocks himself off." He laughed and laid out an idea that had his companion grinning.

"Just for an added insurance policy, contact Best. Tell him to hire two first class hitters. He knows a few to say the least. Lay out the whole idea so he knows what I'm after, a quick kill, professional, and no loose ends. And they don't move unless I order it personally. Keep them down in the Tidewater area, ready to go after that frog with a snap of my finger."

When Cliff nodded, he continued. "Now remember, get all you can out of her. First, the approaches I told you. If they do not work, get it out of her no matter what you have to do. And no publicity." He poked his contact in the chest. "Got That?"

On his way home, Nelson thought of when this had started. A spook Rear Admiral had told him of a secret computer program. The officer had given him names of the five "dirty tricks" unit programmers. Last night The Mechanic had dusted the fourth in another "accident." With the queer hit in Virginia Beach there was one left, their man working for GRASS ROOTS at the network. The Mechanic was now free to take on the frogman and his girlfriend any time. And the nut would enjoy it. He gives me an ace in the hole. Wallace drove off with a wicked smile creasing his face.

CHAPTER THIRTEEN

Before noon Magee finished the newspapers and leaned back at his desk in Charlie, the tax-free suite. Creed was coming in to discuss their hopes for the election. *The great TV reverend will resist my proposition, but later on I won't give him a choice.* His quiet laugh sounded more like Fagan sending his boys out on a thieving mission. *I'd better get ready for that knuckle-headed director of JUST CAUSE.*

He glanced at the wall behind his desk. *Shit! That damned frame with our statement of purpose is out of line again.* While he straightened the offending frame his eyes scanned the words. "The purpose of JUST CAUSE is to keep America free from interference with the democratic process."

In many ways the organization subverted its purpose. It was the conservative's answer to the ACLU and Common Cause. The Board of Directors contained a Who's Who of columnists, publishers and TV network executives. The Fox was not on The Board. He had no official position, only a controlling role in the tax-free organization. Others included retired flag officers, high-priced lawyers, current and former government executives, and some of the "secret government."

When Retired Army Major General Beretulli arrived at Magee's office, The Fox stood at attention. The grizzled soldier had a straight back and a crew cut. His voice sounded like a tank rumbling down a dirt road.

"Greetings, Frank. I don't have much time, so let's just stand. I don't like the pre-election news. Are we going to get the 'right' people into The House and Senate."

"Yes. We already have a thin majority in The Senate."

"Yeah. But are we going to keep it? This election is crucial."

The Fox placed a reassuring hand on the general's shoulder. "I know, Marty. But this isn't the time to worry. You can't always believe the polls!"

"I don't know, Frank. We've got a fight on our hands."

"We do. The Senate has narrowed down to some key states. Alabama will probably be ours. Things look even in Colorado, Nevada, North Dakota and Washington. We've added funds in those states and the commercial 'spots' are pretty effective."

"Yes, I know. But I've got problems. I've spent years building up my organization to give support to the contras. The news media claims that the supply aircraft was a CIA operation. I've been calling Bill Casey for days. He won't see me. Do you know if there's something called 'the enterprise?' A covert op of some kind?"

FX shook his head, not wanting to go there. "Well, Bill has a lot of things on his plate besides running the CIA. I'll get after him and he'll give you a call. I admit that things have been popping in Nicaragua. The hearings will die down soon. Look at the bright side. If it weren't for the Star Wars chip, the Iceland Summit would have been a setback. The Russians are worried about their missiles becoming extinct."

"Frank, have you read about all the terrorism? They say that Syria is a connection. Dammit, we ought to go over there and shake some 'nukes' in their face."

"Yes, the President has spoken against terrorists many

times. Remember what we did to Libya earlier this year."

The General passed a gnarled hand through his gray crew cut. "Frank, I get pissed when we listen to the ninnies and play around with disarmament. The Russians have hundreds of thousands of tanks and artillery over us. Without our 'nukes,' they could sweep through the Fulga Gap in Germany into Italy, France, and Belgium no sweat."

Magee agreed. "That's why we need our Senate, more people in the House and state houses. And we need changes in congressional districts. Eighty-eight is the year, Marty. If we don't get a right-thinker in the White House, it's all she wrote. We need more PAC money in those close races. Getting out the vote is critical. Take care, give my regards to your wife."

The Fox had uncomplimentary thoughts about the well-meaning, but inadequate General. The real work done in this group was through a Casey connection, a retired Navy Rear Admiral.

Well, Fox, Creed's coming in. Now it's time for some fun. He washed his hands and resumed his seat behind the desk. He'd send the preacher back to Norfolk happy and worried. Sometimes he thought that Jethro was a lightweight. His corn-pone manner covered a sharp and inventive mind. He knew how the televangelist would react to the suggestion concerning his TV network.

The Reverend strode into the office, his face flushed and a frown indenting lines over his bushy eyebrows. He flashed his television smile and pumped Magee's hand. "Great to see you, Frank. Lawd almighty, good thing y'all are heah for us. Think we stand a possum's chance with the election? Those ABC, TIME, New York Times polls claim it's closer than we thought."

After reviewing close races and those leaning for or against their candidates, The Fox reminded him. "Remember, Jethro, four is the 'magic number' in The Senate. All we need is fifty seats, ties are ours. That's why we've targeted all but the hopeless ones. We need the power in the Senate to consent to the proper federal judges."

"Judges? Look how the liberals kept tryin' to keep that Judge Rehnquist from being Chief Justice. The courts wander around like sheep, all over the place. Six months ago, a judge fined a Catholic bishop. Yes, your faith. Thank the gracious Lawd the Supreme Court agreed to allow states to outlaw homosexual sodomy. We evangelicals went to court to get the right books in school."

Magee tried to calm him down so he could bring up his proposal. "I know that things have been rough this year. That's why we're counting on your telethon to get out the vote. You're set up to provide commercial breaks for our people aren't you? The broadcast should provide an edge. Probably enough to win."

"Ah have a gut feeling that things won't work out like we had planned."

The Fox spread his hands. "Jethro, everything is in place. The money has been targeted. The direct mail has flooded key precincts and the doorknockers are ready to get the vote out. Haven't you preached, 'Ye with little faith'? Trust me."

"Ah'd feel better if ya'll would come on the telethon. I mean, why can't you? My folks have been hearin' about JUST CAUSE for a long time. They'd love to see and hear you. Ah have an open speaking spot for y'all up at the Religious Broadcasters Convention too."

The Fox could feel that this was the time to spring his proposal. "Well, I'll do it on one condition." He saw Creed's nod and continued. "I'd like you to consider a consortium to share in your TV network. There's considerable financial support."

The churchman jumped. "What? Share? Share? What do you mean? Y'all want part of my network? My network? You must be joking. Ah built that up from nothin'."

"I'm well aware of that. And your financial situation too. With all the negative publicity the past few years, you television evangelists have been taking a financial beating. You've tapped me for considerable sums of money. Has it

72

been used properly?"

"Frank. I'm shamed here. Are y'all accusing me of some hanky panky? I can't believe that you would even think of such a thing. Maybe I better get along."

"Now, now. Sit down my friend. You've asked me to search out ways for you to get around the IRS investigation. You've told me how desperate you are for funds. You said that you might have to lay off some of your people. Here's a chance to recoup. Believe me, I have a solid commitment from people. I have to stay in the background but I have a person who can work with you. A man with an impeccable record. He could easily be accepted by the FCC and any watchdog group. I'd be the silent, but flush partner in it."

Creed wrung his hands. "Frank, you don't know how much blood, sweat and tears I have poured into my ministry, my network. And you want me to give it up, to share it?"

"Give it up? Of course not. Your ministry is the key to this idea. You're well established, have a large audience and support. Let's face it. Costs and expenses are rising. You've got to have backing to expand your network. Isn't that what you want?"

Creed paced. "Expand, yes. Ah need a larger share of the market to attract more advertisin.' Ah didn't want to get into any commercial spot hunting, but it may be my only choice. That would really put the IRS on me."

Magee patted the preacher's shoulder. "I'll take care of the IRS. You need funds; this idea will supply a tremendous amount without becoming a commercial venue. You retain the control over programming, content, and whatever else you wish. Wouldn't you like to develop your own family-based TV programs? You could offset the sex and violence that permeates the networks. I only want to have an outlet for our message without dealing with those damned commercial networks. Come on, friend, what say?"

They argued, discussed and argued again with Magee slowly winning. He played his trump. "I have a large donation right here in my desk to tide you over for a while as you consider this. It's a no-strings offer. There's no obligation."

"You sure you're not shittin' me?"

The Fox smiled. Creed's use of the vulgarity was the sign of a concession. He removed a thick envelope from the desk drawer and handed it over. "There's half a mil there, friend. Cash. No way to trace it. And it is, as I said, a donation with no obligation."

The preacher snatched the envelope like a bass sweeping in a lure. "Ah don't know. Let me think about it, eh?"

"Not a problem. How about if we set up another meeting next week? Just to talk about it. I realize that this was quite sudden. I'm not trying to stampede you."

With Creed's agreement, they parted at the door. Magee laughed aloud. After this evening he'd have that hole card against The Reverend.

CHAPTER FOURTEEN

The lounge in the Washington National Airport was busy with people knocking off booze, steeling themselves for delays and bumpy rides. Wes wasn't waiting for a flight. He sat at a booth in a far corner waiting for Magee's mistress.

Whitney Carlton had wanted to meet him at the Willard Hotel, the recently reopened dowager queen of DC hotels. There she would snatch the eyes of every male and most females in the vicinity, but he was too well known as Magee's security chief. Press eyes could trace her origins, perhaps more. At the airport she could be mistaken for a movie or TV star, perhaps a flight attendant based in any city.

He was uncomfortable with public exposure, more used to being and working in the background. He checked his chronometer watch, a gift from his boss. You're late Miss Whitney. That will cost you. And suddenly there she was. Every male head turned to view Miss Carlton's entrance. The statuesque young woman wore a full-length mink, opened to display part of her physical attributes.

Wes thought of an ancient Greek city, alluring, aloof, anticipating a conquest of her or the opposite, her charms seducing a powerful, rich king. He could imagine painting her in his hidden studio, capturing a regal pose, festooned with jewels from exotic places. He shook his head. Back to the business at hand.

Today she wore a haute couture dress of warm pumpkin with a cream sash, and a belt matched by suede boots. She was quite a sophisticated and beautiful package, a gorgeous young woman who knew her way around this town. Mister Magee was about to drop her out of sheer boredom, if nothing else. Then she would be available. He wasn't in the running, for he knew his place. The paintings help him to soar above his state in life into a more lofty position.

His tone was gruff. "You're late, Miss Whitney." He paused for the waiter to take her order and leave. "How is the arrangement going?"

The young woman raised her head and smiled. Her voice was well modulated, her diction perfect. "Things are quite satisfactory, Wesley. However, I'm waiting for the promised large gift. It is so difficult for a woman to travel around this town without a good car. The metro is gross, taxis are expensive and terribly difficult to find at the right moment."

He needled her about using a taxi to make a three-block trip from The Watergate to The Kennedy Center. His reward was the usual Whitney pout. Sensuous lips extended, trimmed eyebrows arched and her classic cheekbones elevated. Her patrician nose was her only flaw, slightly off the vertical. The result was a more approachable look than she had displayed before the surgery.

"Mister Magee made you a promise. Today you receive your just reward." He withdrew a set of car keys from his coat pocket. A miniature Mercedes hood ornament glinted in the light. Her green eyes locked on the dangling keys. There was a slight movement of her mouth, like a cat licking its lips. He closed a fist over the keys and her eyes darkened.

"The only trouble is that Mister Magee has a problem. And there's only one person who can bail him out." He went on with a sales pitch about the momentous deal that his boss had been developing. He opened his fist occasionally to let her glimpse her gift.

She lifted her chin, bringing a flush that tinted her professional makeup. "I have accomplished everything Frank desired. I have given up my other means of income. I'm completely dependent on him. When I am called, I fly to California, Europe, Hong Kong to meet him. I have given up my freedom, including my competitive target shooting. And that was quite important to me."

He allowed a rare grin to surface. "First place in the match before Quantico. Too bad the Corps can't use your talents."

She nodded and frowned. "If there is something else, why can't he ask me?"

A twitch on his face accompanied his reply. "Well, you know that he's quite bashful sometimes. That's why he has me around to help out. I'm like his John Alden, you know?"

Her stare was crisp and cold. "More like his muscle, aren't you?"

"Who me? You know I'm just a small pussy cat." He reminded her how much she wanted the car and how long she had asked for it. He pointed out that his boss had to fly to cities and countries to keep high-priced people happy. "And he has to be discreet about you."

"Yes, the hidden consort. I would love to accompany him at the Kennedy Center."

"That's out of the question. Look, he's taken care of your every wish. He didn't ask you to cut out Wednesdays with the crippled kids."

She pointed a slim finger. "Dammit! They are not crippled, nor are they handicapped. They are special children. I refuse to give them up!"

He waved his hand, "Course not. How about giving him a break. You know it's impossible to do something about his wife. If she got suspicious, there could be trouble, publicity." He pointed at her. "Too much publicity for you too."

She downed her scotch, held the glass near his face and

shook it, clinking the ice cubes.

He waved to a waitress and ordered. "This is one of those difficult maneuvers. The deal is almost complete. Down to the last half-inch but the guy won't budge. There's so much riding on the thing." He glanced at empty booths nearby. "He's tried every angle. You know him. He can find a solution to anything. If he can't, there just isn't any."

"What does this have to do with me? And with my, uh, the car?"

Wes had enough discussion. "I know you'd do anything for Mister Magee." He leaned toward her and captured her eyes with his, knowing that he could intimidate her. "After all, he brought you out of the high-priced whore class to be a retainer-paid mistress. I imagine you aren't too unhappy with the first class travel and five-star accommodations. And those expensive trinkets he gives you, like that heavy diamond and the emerald necklace."

He displayed the keys on the table like a manager at Cartier's on his side of the table. "This is really hush-hush. I mean, you tell no one, not even your shrink."

She glared. "Now look, I need counseling—. It, it has been a long term problem."

"Sure, sure. Only kidding. Mister Magee regrets this deeply, I mean, he'd do anything not to have this happen." He heard her inhale. "Like I said, he has to be so careful, that's why you can't be seen with him around here. So he's got this personal problem, as well as this business one. Looks like the only way to solve them both is with you."

She pressed her lips together and spilled her drink. "He, he's going to drop me?"

"Aw, nothing like that. Listen, he's got to be careful right now. People are watching everyone associated with a PAC. Lobbyists are under fire with accusations in The Post about influencing the election. And he's on a sweet deal worth half a bill. I mean billion a year. But this other man, he just won't move. FX needs an edge. You know? The gent has people supplying him with everything you could imagine, including." He leaned closer. "Some of Miss Barbara's best ladies. You know some of them."

She lifted her chin. "I do not choose to discuss that."

He slid the keys a few inches closer to her. Long lashes drooped as she looked at the prize. Whitney's tongue slipped along her lips. She swallowed. Raising her head, she looked him in the eye. Her voice was quite low. "What does he want me to do?"

"Take it easy. It's not that bad. He just wants you to meet this guy tomorrow evening. Show him a real night. That's all."

Color flooded her face. She stood and held out her fists. "What! What? He wants me to screw some man so he can get a business deal. What the hell does he think I am?"

He took her hands in a stinging grip, squeezed and pulled her back into her seat. "Keep your voice down. We already know what you are, a high-priced whore. One who wants a Mercedes so badly she'll do anything for it. And she has a guy who meets her every whim."

Her anger was obvious. "What if I refuse? I mean, dammit, the son of a bitch won't come around and ask me to my face. God! I deserve some dignity. Why he's, he's nothing but a fucking pimp. And so are you, you, bastard!"

"I said lower your voice. We wouldn't want anyone to hear this would we?" He patted the back of her hand, still holding it in a vise-grip with the other. "Mister Magee will give you the shirt off his back, but he does need help." He squeezed her hand hard enough to hear her gasp.

"You know, you're nothing but a product, a commodity, a deal. You were meant to be what you are, a world-class whore. Hell, even your name was manufactured, Whitney Carlton. If this were my problem, I'd give you a Corvette and call it a Mercedes."

"You're attacking me because you can't have me."

His grin was a slit on his face. "Already planned. When you get dumped, he's promised you to his former associate."

Tears ran small rivers down through her makeup. "He

wouldn't do that. He wouldn't."

Wes picked her apart then, reciting her past. She tried to pull her hand away but he gripped her so hard that she whimpered. He attacked her, jabbing with cruel words, reminding her again and again that she was nothing but a whore.

"A damned expensive one, I grant you that working in Miss Barbara's, the top madam of DC. We know your story about your mother dying and you had to go to Miss Barbara's stable of girls to save her life is all bullshit. And she died anyway."

He stuffed a white handkerchief in her mouth to smother the sound of her crying. He saw something different in her face, like hate burning in her eyes. He squeezed again.

She pulled out the handkerchief and threw it at him. "You're the one making the bargain. Frank will not soil his lily-white hands. He washes the damned things fifty times a day. Since he might need muscle, you were chosen. You know what you are, Wes? You are a fucking whore yourself."

He swept the keys off the table and dangled them in front of her. "You get these when you come across with your assignment for Frank. Not before!" He whispered the hotel and room number. "Be there by six. Remember, all night. Give him everything he wants and then some. Say, the car's a real beauty, a 450 SEL, fire engine red, like you wanted. It'll be parked in your space next day. Don't bother to say thanks."

"What if I do not show up?"

His answer was a malevolent grin. "A Mercedes can get smashed and burned just like any other car." He leaned forward, putting his face close to hers. "So can a beautiful woman's face." He marched out, mission accomplished.

Whitney cried on her way to the powder room and thought about that bastard Frank. Pimping her again like he did in Hong Kong last year. And she had the poor nose job to prove his anger when she had first refused. Was it her fault, getting into the profession? Her mother had been a divorcee in the social set in DC with a married young Air Force General as her lover. She had been attracted to him too. But the son of a bitch had raped her. She wiped away tears, cursed him and restored her makeup.

She had found healing through hard work in college and modeling. The General had given her a woman's business card and explained that if she ever needed a friend, or was broke, to call her. To help her Mom she had called Miss Barbara.

Dammit! I won't let that bastard do this to me again. She marched out of the restroom with her shoulders back and her appealing chest out until second thoughts crept in.

CHAPTER FIFTEEN

That evening Dan and Beth argued on the way to the funeral home. They were unaware that two men in a surveillance car trailed them. Dan found a space in the crowded parking lot. The trailing vehicle ended in a dark corner at the far end. A van jammed with electronics was parked on the opposite side, listening to their conversation.

They sat in Dan's Chevy. "Dan, you promised to attend, not just to sit out here."

"Go inside? No way, Jose! Me go to a queer wake, forget it."

Beth pleaded with him, reminding him that Tony had been a close friend. "How many times did we go diving together? He was always so helpful and kind to both of us, and he provided considerable assistance with your computer."

"Yeah, I know that. Geez, you want me to run into a bunch of queers?"

"We don't have to, to fraternize with others. I'm quite sure that he didn't have family here. We'll just go to the wake and go back to my apartment." She kissed him. "Please, darling?"

The Cat folded his arms. "Dammit, Beth, I wouldn't be caught dead with queers. I thought your bible said being a homo was a sin."

"Precisely. This is quite difficult for me. Jesus said that we should not judge others, that God is the only judge. And Our Lord Jesus said we should love one another."

"Look, I'm tryin' to come back. Cleaned up. I'm sober. But queers? They'll be all over the place like roaches in a diner. Any come near me, I give 'em this!!" He showed a fist. "They're all alike, always trying to draw you into their trap. I got propositioned in movie houses, bars, heads. Damn, even on a ship. You want me to go in there and meet 'em? Bull!"

"Please come with me. I'm putting my job in jeopardy by going in there. If the network discovered that I attended his funeral, the powers that be wouldn't like it." She touched his face, near a bandage. "Please, dear, for me?"

He sighed. "Well, okay. Just the wake. No socializing, nothin' like that. I don't want no homo shaking hands and givin' me AIDS." He got out of the car and opened her door. "I'll go in. But I'm keeping my right hand free all night."

They walked down a long hallway in the funeral home. Each step caused a shot of adrenaline that tightened his muscles. "How the hell did I get talked into this?" He was in a Cat fighting mood, on the balls of his feet, balanced, wary. "Just let one of those bastards touch me."

A white-haired man in a conservative gray suit greeted them at the door to the viewing room. The guy, or gay, wore a maroon tie and a gray textured shirt, and he seemed sure of himself, in charge. Haggerty lifted his chin. Still, Dan wondered if the guy lisped.

The greeter had a deep baritone and his manner was correct, almost formal. He smiled and greeted Beth with a half bow. "Thank you, thank you for coming. I'm Peter Dunn." He offered his hand to Dan and held it out as Haggerty delayed. Dan gave in and shook hands. The Cat felt a strong grip, so he gripped harder. He glared and met a satisfied look in return.

Dunn invited them to enter with a friendly gesture. "Please. You may see someone you know. Most of us haven't come out of the closet as yet. Gays or lesbians aren't just artists and hairdressers. We're mechanics, police officers, bulldozer operators, and business people."

Dan was on the balls of his feet, ready to punch out someone. "Let's go." I'll let the bastards know I'm straight. He took Beth's arm and marched toward the closed casket.

Banks of flowers permeated the room with a sweet, nauseating scent. Dan knew that people were watching. Kiss, my ass. He put his arm around Beth and stood at the casket. Trying to pray he wondered, would God forgive Tony for what he did? For what he was? He shook his head. Would God forgive me for what I did in 'Nam? For what I am? A damned drunk. He stepped back from the casket, confused and unhappy.

He spotted a gorgeous young woman with blonde hair draped to her shoulders. The light blue dress showed off a well-rounded body. She must have been in her mid, late twenties, maybe even low thirties. Geez, he thought. Don't tell me she's queer too.

His interest must have been obvious, because Pete invited him to join her group. "Let me introduce you to some people. This is Bob Weatherby."

Haggerty set his jaw and shook another strong hand. The guy was almost his size. His suit didn't fit and his tie was about half-mast. He seemed to be a weak-kneed slob, not like Pete.

Weatherby nodded. "I see that you've noticed Rita."

"What? Uh, oh yeah, the blonde? Is she uh, a—."

Weatherby's grin revealed even, white teeth. "Contrary to what you expect, she's a lesbian. Don't let that bother you. We're quite open-minded here tonight. You might not know it, but there is often much antagonism between gay men and lesbians."

Beth seemed to be biting her lip. She slipped her arm around Dan's.

Pete smiled and asked, "Well, do we look much different from you and Beth?"

Haggerty was puzzled and didn't answer. He saw two men kiss each other on the mouth and felt his gut convulse. Son of a bitch! He made a show of holding Beth closely.

Pete moved away to greet Father Steward. The slim priest shook hands with Dunn and hugged Beth. "How are you doing, Beth? Have you had some counseling after Tony's death?"

"Yes, Father. The Reverend is such a wonderful person. He's helped me."

"Good. You know, I'm spending some time at your network. My religious order sent me to get computer and television smarts. Some day we may be broadcasting."

"That's wonderful. Please call me and we can have lunch together."

Stew nodded. "Hi, Dan, you're looking better. Are you okay now?"

"Yeah." Not true. The queers had him on edge.

The priest grinned and brought out a prayer book. After a short non-denominational service Stew spoke briefly about the value of life. And the need not to judge others. He blessed the casket with holy water and rejoined Beth, Dan and Pete.

Dunn invited them to a reception at the Ramada nearby. "We're joining together in a more relaxed setting to celebrate Tony's life. We have catered food and quite a broad range of drinks. Please join us. I understand that you and Beth were good friends of Tony's."

Dan shook his head. "We better take a rain check on the invite. Me and Beth had plans."

Pete shrugged. "We'd love to have you come."

The priest spoke. "It would be nice if you would, Dan. It helps if we try to accept people as our brothers and sisters regardless of who or what they are. That's the only reason why I'm suggesting it. I'm sure that the alcohol will be very tempting. You must be the one to choose."

Beth tugged at Dan's arm. "I'm sorry. I won't be around

liquor. Please take me home. Father, please don't encourage him to drink. He's had too much lately. Look at his face."

"I know, Beth. But Dan can only rid himself of his problem if he begins to see it."

Haggerty decided that free booze was worth a short-term compromise and accepted.

Beth shook her head and touched him. "Please, Dan. Please don't drink. For me?"

"I'll be okay. I promise." That was easy.

She looked angry and accepted the priest's invitation to take her home.

The service ended and Beth walked off with Father Steward without saying goodnight to Dan. Here we go again. She's pissed no end. What the hell, I'll get some free queer booze.

The surveillance car followed the priest's car and the van trailed Dan.

Pete waited for him at the Ramada entrance. They walked silently to a plush room set with a bar and straight back chairs matching the green carpet. "Thank you for joining us, Dan. Would you like a bit of refreshments before we start moving around to meet people? Tell the waiter or bartender. Would you prefer scotch, bourbon, gin, rum, or vodka?"

Dan thought of Beth, shrugged off her influence, and grinned. "I'll take all of them."

Pete laughed. "A man after my own heart."

Dan didn't look around until he had downed a three-fingered belt of expensive scotch. He stood with his back to most of the people, shoulders hunched up and muscles taut. Weatherby joined him, weaving, tie askew.

Rita waved, strolled over and introduced several women. During the introductions, Dan had an urge to blurt out that he was straight. He stood apart as they engaged in conversation. Rita turned and asked, "How long have you known Tony?"

He was embarrassed to answer. "Um, I guess a couple of

years. I taught him Scuba and he taught me a lot about computers. I got one on my boat."

Rita smiled. "That's interesting. How do you manage to have steady power?"

"I'm afraid I don't get her underway much." He wondered how she'd take the female pronoun. He felt anxious about words that had a sexual connotation. He frowned, wondering why he didn't want to offend them. He sure as hell didn't want them to think he was queer. "I got a special power line in port and a peak filter. It's for—."

"I know. It should keep power surges from crashing your computer."

A crew-cut woman with her arm hooked into Rita's spoke. "She ought to know. She runs the Operations Center for the Virginia State Bank."

Dan's surprise became a question. "The whole thing?"

Rita's laugh was light and musical. "You're not a male chauvinist, are you? I have the Ops Center. We run the computer operations for this area. Honestly, it's a zoo around the end of the month. But we do have some slack moments. You ought to come down and see my place."

"Gee, I'd like to do that some time." He thought of Tony's programming skill and how he had zipped through problems. "You got good security there? Can a 'hacker' get in?"

Rita tilted her head. Dark eyebrows curved over gorgeous blues eyes. "We have considerable automatic security with all operations audited in real time. And we have people doing random checks on the system. Why? Are you a 'hacker'?"

The group seemed to close in on him, so he slugged down scotch. "Me? Hey, I can turn on my 'Trash 80' and that's about it. I know Tony was a 'hacker.' He told me about some stuff but it's way over my head. Somethin' about main frames and security."

Weatherby moved in. "Could you tell me specifics about what he said? I'm a systems man at the Naval Supply Center.

Maybe I can help you find out what he was talking about."

Dan shrugged and sipped. All he wanted was more free booze.

Rita pressed him about Tony's remarks. "Do you know what he was working on? They have one of the latest mainframes at the Truth Network. Was he talking about security there? Maybe somewhere else?" She sipped at her drink. "I wonder what kind of security they need in such a strong Christian organization."

Her butch said, "They must be hiding lists of sinners like us. I wonder how he could have stayed at that network. They're so uptight about people like us."

Haggerty gave the Amphibious Force salute, palms out and up, shoulders high. "I don't know what the heck he was talking about."

Rita looked thoughtful for a moment, and then smiled. "Well, you'll just have to come down and see my mainframe. I've got an upgraded IBM 360 with *mucho* tape drives. I can access our other mainframes in Richmond and Alexandria.

When Weatherby handed Dan a business card, the queer's hands trembled. He said, "Here's my card. I have some large number crunchers at the Supply Center too. You might want to stop in and see me. We can talk about Tony's thoughts about security or whatever."

Haggerty took it. It would be a long freaking day before he called any of these weirdos.

Rita handed him her card too. "Now promise you'll give me a call. I mean that, Dan."

She touched his arm and his muscles tingled. Geez, she acted like a one hundred percent female. He shook his head and downed the scotch. Was she really a lesbian? Damn, she touched me. Hope the card ain't contaminated. He needed another drink damned quick.

The conversation moved to the AIDS epidemic. When Dan eased away, Rita smiled. "Too much for you? You can't catch AIDS from shaking hands or touching an infected person."

Stolen Votes

Rita's friend added in a baritone voice, "Can't get it from a toilet seat either. Relax Dan. We're not going to make you ill. You need to find out more about the disease before you get uptight about it. There's some small hope with a new drug, AZT."

Haggerty was damned uncomfortable and getting thirsty. "Never heard of it."

Rita explained that the new drug had bad side effects and that AIDS hot lines were swamped with calls. "Dan, you seem uncomfortable. Let's talk about computers again."

He was damned glad to get off the AIDS shit and shoved off shortly after that.

On the way back to the boat he never noticed the surveillance van. He was too busy replaying the evening at the Ramada. Some great booze, but. Those people are so damned hard to figure out. That Rita is a doll. And she likes girls? He thought of Tony and it helped to sober him up. How the hell could I have missed that he was a homo? And I let him stay on the boat with me. It's a damned good thing he didn't try anything.

What the hell is an IBM 360? Never mind that. Rita sure has a helluva main frame herself. Why was she so interested in what Tony was doing? And that Weatherby guy too. He shrugged. What the hell, they're computer nuts. And that was four-oh scotch. Geez, I feel like I need a shower. Yeah, alone too!"

Joseph Guion

CHAPTER SIXTEEN

A ringing telephone woke Charles R. Best from a half-sleep facing the TV picture. It was almost ten pm. Who the hell? He stretched to grab the phone with a muffled, "Yeah."

"Get on the secure phone."

He sighed. "Shit!" He struggled to shake off sleep and crossed the room to the phone, punched two buttons and said, "Yeah."

"You on scramble?"

"No, I'm in a phone booth, ass-hole. What's so damned important at this time of the night?"

"Shut up! The frog and his squeeze were talking about computers with a couple of experts at the fag's wake. The lovebirds are gonna take a boat ride in the morning. I'm gonna try to get an explosive guy there with some gear before they take off. It's a made-to-order chance to get them both with a good cover, a boat fire."

Best shook his head and blinked twice. "How the hell am I going to get that accomplished before morning? Ask them to stay off the boat while I set up an explosion? Why didn't you call me while they were still at the funeral home?"

Stolen Votes

"Had to get permission. Remember the orders, no fatal work till my contact tells me. Well, he just told me."

"This is not smart. We should have had an emergency line with an automatic cut in, so we could respond ASAP! Can't guarantee the job. You can tell your contact."

"Bullshit! You do something now."

"I'll get the wheels turning and divers ready, but unless we can board the boat and put the frogman to sleep, we'd better wait for a better opportunity. That's my opinion."

"No! I'm gonna have a pissed off contact."

"Too freakin' bad. Your boss has to loosen the reins a bit so I can do my job. I have an expert explosive guy who could put some shit on the underside of the boat. If I get it done, I'll let you know. Any idea of where they're going to take the boat?"

"They're going diving someplace. Haven't found out yet where, or even when."

Best shook his head. "That makes it doubly difficult. If I get it done, I'll call." After hanging up, he rubbed his foot. Son of a bitch. You would think this outfit could plan ahead. He could have had an army of explosive experts ready to jump in a second. He limped to his carry-on bag and pulled out a book. He dialed a local number and identified himself as "C."

"Henry, got a fast job. You got enough C-4 to blow a thirty-foot boat tonight?" After a short pause, he said. "It's tonight. Now! And it must be rigged underneath the boat without waking the owner if he's on board."

"You crazy, C? I got the goods, but you're talking about leaving no trace, right?"

"Right."

"Wrong. Is it a diesel or gas?"

"What difference does it make?"

"Gas boats are easy to have accidental fires and explosions, not diesels. Anyhow, my diving gear is screwed up. You got a diver? Explosive qualified?"

"Yeah. Can you do it, Henry?"

"Where the hell is it?"

"Marina next to Amphib Base. I have a boat there with divers aboard."

"What the hell? You want it blown there?"

"No. Can you rig it so it will blow later when the people are on a trip to go diving?"

"C, how the fuck can I do that if I have no idea when they're getting underway or where they're going? Jesus, friend. You better get more info for me or I can't do it."

"Shit! Seems like an easy job, set the stuff to blow with some kind of signal, and—."

"You got somebody near with a transmitter that will work underwater? How far away will the trigger man be?"

"I don't know, Henry. I thought you were an expert?"

"Fuck you!"

Best heard the phone click and then a dial tone. He slammed the phone on the cradle. Now what? He dialed another expert. The man was more receptive to the job and said that he'd do it on one condition. Best had to use his own divers.

"How come?"

"Sounds like a Chinese Fire Drill. I'll be damned if I'll get under a boat, rig it, check it and set a timer or a radio receiver. And who the hell is the owner? Is he a light sleeper? Suspicious?"

"He's a freaking drunk and he couldn't hear a cannon going off."

After a long silence, Best heard, "Okay. I'll do it. Meet me at Shore Drive and Pleasure House Road in an hour. Bring cash."

"Great. Ten bills okay?"

"Fifteen or I stay home."

"You got it." Best hung up and poured a large scotch before he called his contact to verify the job. He had another before he dressed for the meeting. He called Ace Murphy on the Hatteras and told him the plan. The divers were already aboard. They could take on the frog if this didn't work.

Murphy told him that they were both experts with years of SEAL training, more recent than their target. If it came to an underwater battle, they had the newest diving equipment that was incredibly quiet if they had to sneak up on Haggerty.

Best didn't want to think about using them. He was too focused on blowing up the lovebirds. He rubbed his hands and went to his traveling safe in the car trunk for the money. Goodbye, you two. We'll waste both at the same time. The Mechanic will be pissed. He wanted that woman before he knocked her off. Now he won't even have that pleasure. I'll give him a list of others that we need to eliminate. That will make him feel better.

CHAPTER SEVENTEEN

In the Hampton Roads area Saturday, early fall had returned with the temperature in the seventies. Pleasure boats streamed out of yacht clubs, marinas and boat ramps, like bees leaving the hive for nectar-laden flowers. Dan's thirty-two foot Bertram labored to one of their favorite spots, between the York River Channel and Plumtree Point, close to Langley Air Force Base in Hampton.

When they were planning this day of diving, Dan was happy to accommodate Beth's desire to relax and mosey around on the bottom. Now, he felt cold for some reason. He needed a quick morning shooter of scotch. If Beth saw it, she would have insisted on staying home. Was he afraid of diving again? In the SEALs, diving was their ticket to fun besides the thrill of HALO jumping, High Altitude Low Opening of chutes. He shook off those distant thoughts.

Beth hooked her arm in his. "What a gorgeous day. The breeze seems to blow troubles away. What do you think?"

He shrugged and glanced back at the Hatteras Sports Fisherman that was trailing half a mile behind them. Were they following? Or just out for a great day too? He felt uneasy, as if something was wrong, but he couldn't uncover a clue. He anchored, helped Beth suit up and donned his.

At the stern she asked, "Do you want to check the patch by the bow? After Tony ran us aground and you patched it up, you said you'd make sure that it was still holding."

He grimaced. "Naw. Let's get in the water."

She tilted her head. "Dan, that's not like you lately. You had been finishing things that you started. Except, of course your promise to get back to AA."

"You would say that."

"Only take a minute." She gave him a sly glance. "I want to see precisely how you patch things up."

"Double meaning there, huh? Okay, let's get going, I'm sweating."

They discussed the issue for a moment. Dan turned and saw the Hatteras moving closer.

She continued, "Come on down. I'll check the hull."

"Geez, kid. Okay, I'm following."

She slipped along the underside of the boat. The bay bottom hadn't been disturbed much so she could see quite well. Looking upward she saw an object that she had never seen before, a small cube-like box that was attached to the hull. She touched it and saw a black box next to it with a wire sticking out. She turned and waved to Dan waiting at the stern. He spread his hands in a manner that seemed to mean he was puzzled and didn't know what she wanted.

Her hand waves became more agitated, so he took his time easing along the boat. She pointed at the gray object and gestured as if she wanted to know what it was.

When Dan came close enough to see it, a stab of fear hit his gut. "Jesus." He grabbed Beth and shoved her toward the stern. A quick glance and he was sure it looked like a block of C-4. The black box was probably a transmitter or receiver. When he touched the object he felt like an electric shock had hit him. He felt around the backside and found a metal, cylindrical stub, like a golf pencil. His hand shook as he pulled the detonator from the wire attached to the receiver.

He stuffed it into his pouch and swam rapidly to Beth's side. He jerked his thumb upward, indicating that she should surface and get back into the boat. He followed her aboard, coughing and spitting water.

"What's wrong? What was that?"

For the first time since he had left 'Nam his mind had accelerated and he was partially The Cat again. Don't frighten her. "Just those damned SEALs. Wait till I get them."

"What do you mean? Who?"

"Oh, my old buddies from our team. They rigged a fake explosive setup. Doc was over the other night kidding me about going fishing. They probably attached the damned thing then."

"Is it dangerous? Could it have gone off?"

He kept his hands slightly behind him so she wouldn't see them trembling. "Not really. That gray part was supposed to look like a block of C-4, a pretty strong explosive. But you have to have a detonator stuck into it to make it work." He fingered it in his pocket. "Let's get some diving in, huh?"

"What was that black box with a wire?"

"Oh, you saw something like that? Probably a miniature radio receiver. Just another trick we used to pull on non-SEALs when we wanted to get rid of them in a hurry. Let's go." He noticed the Hatteras underway and turning away from them.

They slipped into the water together. He allowed her to lead, because he was still all shook up. They spent the rest of the morning enjoying the dives and Dan forgot about the incident until he touched the detonator still in his pouch. After they surfaced, he slipped the piece into a drawer before they had lunch. He had difficulty overcoming his frown and anxiety. Would those idiots try to scare him like that? Or was there someone or something else? Beth took him out of that mood with a long kiss and hug.

Late that afternoon Dan's boat chugged toward the marina at Little Creek. He threaded the boat through pleasure craft into Hampton Roads. He smiled, watching Beth braid her long blonde hair. She was a fine picture of strength and beauty. Although she carried more than 160 pounds, they were well distributed on her five ten frame. Her weight was more than current women's magazines promoted, but Dan liked women who had some meat on their bones. Their relationship was becoming serious. Did he want that? Did she? Sometimes, she seemed distant, holding him off.

Technically Hampton Roads identified the water passage at the confluence of the Elizabeth and James Rivers before they met the majestic Chesapeake Bay. The water barrier seemed deeper than the Grand Canyon between the peninsula cities of Hampton and Newport News and their south side sisters. Indeed, attempts had been made to unify the Tidewater area, but the jealousy and independence of these cities prevented a cohesive and more powerful economic base. The Hampton Tunnel and the James River Bridge, five miles northwest of it, were the only means of driving across Hampton Roads.

He picked his way through seagoing traffic off Fort Monroe and headed east. He searched Chesapeake Bay to port. "Okay, Beth. Wanna take over? See that buoy there?" She nodded. "Head for it. When you get close, keep it to starboard. That's the right side."

Haggerty's laugh floated by as she took the wheel. In the saloon he pulled a moisture-coated beer from the refrigerator. The drink would frost her, but he needed something after the nervous discovery earlier. And the last dive had disturbed him.

He had stepped into mud that felt like quicksand. The grasping feeling of being caught by an unknown force tripped the trigger. Wisps of jungle rivers and firefights hit. Damned 'Nam. Trying to sneak silently into a VC camp at night. Racing from an ambush and trying to pull out of that freaking mud that created a sucking sound that seemed louder than a

Swift Boat running at full throttle.

The pain of Bobby's loss and his discharge remained. He had been getting better until Tony's murder flipped him. He was back there, face in that damned mud, waiting, ants and bugs crawling up his nose, in and out of his ears. He didn't dare move. The smell of the jungle, explosives, and fire. Burning hootches and bodies. Should he quit diving?

A warm hand on his arm snapped him around to see smiling eyes. Round eyes. He held her. "Honey, I like your big diver's chest. You can hold your breath for a long time."

"That's not why you like my chest." She pointed at the beer. "You'd be a lot stronger and more stable if you'd get away from that awful liquor. How can you keep going back to it?"

"Yes, dear. I'll try to remember. After this great day with you I just wanted to relax."

Beth shook her head.

The Cat checked astern and the channel approach. A tug towing its barge of railroad cars was two miles north, coming across from Cape Charles. No problem. He noticed a big Hatteras Sports Fisherman. It seemed like the one that had nosed nearby when they were diving. The boat accelerated, passing by a couple of hundred yards.

His shoulders tightened when a sailboat worked its way out of the Little Creek Channel. The two-masted ketch must have had a rank amateur at the helm. It was all over the channel. "Come on, dummy! Use your rudder." He saluted Beth with the beer.

"Drinking again! That's _your_ fault. When will you learn? When you have too much to drink, you end up getting in trouble."

"Aw, come on. I've been good lately. It's just that I'm gettin' feisty again. Last time I had a fight because two sailors were picking on a kid with a young wife. He was scared. He needed help. Me, the knight in shining armor."

Beth smiled. "Maybe like dented armor?"

He knew that Beth was kidding. She didn't know how

close he was to something bad. It was like being on the edge of a bottomless pit. Sometimes you were dizzy and leaning over the edge, and there was nothing to grab for safety.

"Dammit, move over, you freakin' jerk!" The Cat spun the wheel, swinging near the western side of the narrow channel and then back again. He put the beer in the holder and shook his fist at the passing sailboat, now flapping its sails and wandering.

He turned right into Fisherman's Cove, edging close to his past. Amphibious ships in haze gray lined up alongside the piers, large landing ships and small craft. Damn! There it is again. Every time he saw an LCM it claimed memories. How many insertions and retractions did they make in an armed Landing Craft Medium in country? Weapons ready, each one pointing away from the boat and team members. Taking his Stoner off safety. The feeling of power it gave him. Son of a bitch, Cat. Get off it! He eased alongside his berth nearest to the parking lot.

Beth took the bow line ashore and secured it. He connected the shore power lead and shut off the generator.

"Okay, babe, I've got power for my computer. You know, Tony used to play around with my Trash Eighty at night, doing some mysterious stuff. Hope he wasn't breaking into a bank system or something like that."

She frowned. "I was thinking about the last time we were on the boat with him. Before he died? He said something to me about working quite late at the network. Something about a secret program. I asked Reverend Creed about it and he assured me that it was a special program that we needed."

"Oh sure, he told the truth."

"Please don't start a large argument about The Reverend. You don't know how many people he's helped. Honestly, if you could read some of the thousands of letters he gets, thanking him for his ministry. After all, so many people have no connection to any church and he provides the Bible message and helps them to get closer to Jesus. He's a great man."

"Okay, okay. Only kidding. Tony was an ace hacker. If he had the time, he could get into any program even with plenty of security. I came back to the boat one night after he had shoved off and there was still a message on the monitor. Said something like, um I don't know, maybe some levels of security. And a Trap Door? A Trojan Horse?"

Beth nodded. "Those are some tricks that hackers use to penetrate and manipulate computers. But I can hardly see what he could have been looking for at our place."

After a short goodbye kiss at her apartment door, Dan returned to his boat, feeling hot to trot from the day of being with Beth and diving. Bad memories had succeeded in bringing back some training and skills. He grinned. Yeah, and what about the "det?" He pulled the slim cylinder from the drawer and examined it carefully. When he looked up, someone on the Hatteras' bridge seemed to be watching. He wagged his head. "Get off it, Cat. Shit. Next thing, you'll be looking around for VC. Boat needs a fresh water wash-down."

He liked the old boat because of the large amount of wood in its construction. He'd shine it with linseed oil and buff the shellac to a fine gloss. He worked hard for hours and sweated, even with the light evening breeze. He stopped periodically and glanced at the Hatteras with someone always watching. What for? Don't get paranoid. Maybe they want to buy this old tub. He finally laughed.

CHAPTER EIGHTEEN

Charles R. Best sent his men into another office. He pushed the scrambler button on the phone. "Okay, boss, I'm alone and I'm on scrambler. Here's the dope. They came back from diving."

The contact sounded pissed. "Wait a freakin' minute. You mean they're alive?"

"Yeah. My guy attached the explosives and checked it out. Our boat got close so the signal would be strong enough to work. They triggered it and it didn't blow. They tried a couple times, even juiced up the transmitter. The two were underwater before the shot. Maybe he found it and disarmed it."

"Son of a bitch!"

"Hey, there were planes and helicopters flying all over the place. We'll set up the boat when it's dark. Trouble is, when he does the night watchman trick we don't know where he'll show up. He's got no routine, just wanders around the whole marina. Stops at odd times, doubles back, all sorts of shit. If we get a chance tonight, we'll do it. Otherwise we'll try tomorrow night."

"Okay. You sent me the tape?"

"Yeah, by courier. They were discussing some computer material, including the freakin' network system. That ring a bell?"

"None of your business."

"Okay. You said Cliff was out of the loop. You want me to call him anyway?"

After a long silence Wallace spoke. "Don't bother. He's gone on a long trip."

"The Mechanic?"

"Yeah. The Mechanic will be back after another job. I'll send him to you for orders. Keep after those two and keep me informed, no matter what. New subject. Get two pro hitters ready. Keep them down there in contact with you constantly. But! No action unless I call, or you get it from a guy called Mister Big."

"Mister Big? You shitting me?"

"Shut up! Make sure they're pros. No evidence, no witnesses. Just a clean kill. Make sure that you have people ready to take the body out to sea. Probably a good idea if you used his boat for that. The hitters can be heard on your surveillance, so you'll know when to get the Mate or Captain from the Hatteras to take his boat out to dump him, he can return on our boat."

Best agreed, hung up and thought about the job. First, two pro hitters. I'll use Denny and Fred. Either one has the skills to do it himself. Important thing is, no action without orders. I don't know why, but what the hell they're paying big bucks. Mister Big. Geez that's original. He almost laughed until he thought about it.

Best rubbed his aching toe. Cliff wasted too? Jesus, these guys don't take prisoners. If I get a sniff of trouble for me, I'm gone. Could I make it to the island before they sniffed out any trouble? The woman would take care of me whenever I showed up. I need to keep ahead of their thinking in case I'm the next guy in the barrel. Sometimes the job ended up being more dangerous than expected, and this was in spades.

After one of the early retreat sessions ended, Father Steward remained with a group of his people at the retreat center in Hampton. He received a call from Beth Olson. She sounded frantic, her voice breaking at times, and her words tumbling over each other.

"Father, Father, I've called Dan's boat, uh, his boat, five times this morning and there's no answer. I, I haven't been able to contact him since, since I left the boat Saturday afternoon. Please tell me. Do you know where he is?"

"Gosh, I'm sorry, Beth. Say, try to take it easy. I'm sure he's around somewhere. Tell you what; I'm heading over in that direction and I'll stop by at the marina. I'll call you. I promise."

"Thank you. Thank you, Father."

When the priest drove to the marina, he realized that Dan's boat was missing. He wandered around searching for it, then he went to the office and asked the owner about Dan.

The chubby man pulled a cigar from his mouth. "Well, sir, uh, Father. I ain't seen him since last night when we tried to get all the people back aboard their boats without them fallin' to the water. Seems like they had quite a party. Anyways, when I come in this mornin' his boat was gone. I was gonna ask the people on the big Hatteras across from him when he shoved off, but they was gone too. Lots of boats out today, good weather."

CHAPTER NINETEEN

Beth arrived at her office wearing a cobalt dress of clinging velour because she hoped to see Dan later in the day. The dress would show how soft and alluring she could be. At work, she wanted to disguise her determination to find out what Tony was seeking at the Computer Center.

Walking back and forth, she fidgeted around her desk and twisted a handkerchief around her fingers. She called Dan's boat again. What could have kept Father Steward from calling her? She couldn't concentrate on dealing with her new assistant. When the priest called she was first relieved then puzzled. Was Dan really fishing or was he drinking somewhere? Was the priest covering up for Dan? Why was she so suspicious?

Her hands clenched into fists. Her anxiety added to her irritation with Jules, the new assistant. Her intuition warned her to be careful. He was long and angular, like some space satellite antenna. He sat in her office appearing to be half-asleep. She had requested an assistant for months without results. Why had he been hired now without her approval?

"Well, where were we, Jules?"

"Oh, we were talking about the uplink for the telethon. Guess we need two people on the control console, because the telethon would be goin' on twenty-four hours. You got somebody in mind? I don't know these people."

Beth clamped her jaw. She had brought that subject up to test him, and he had failed miserably. He should have remembered her main point, that one person was able to operate the entire board. He was unable to meet her eyes. What was this man here for? To observe her? Was Tony correct about a secret program at the network?

She knocked and marched into Ned's office. He jumped at his desk and papers flew onto the floor. His hands were shaking and his face was more pale and drawn than usual. He picked up the papers and jammed them into a drawer. He placed his hands on the desk and his fingers drummed on its top. His tie was pulled sideways and his eyes were swollen.

She announced, "Ned, I'm going over to the Computer Center."

He jumped. "What? What? What for? You don't need to do that. Call Dawson. He knows everything that's going on over there. After all, you told me you had too much work to do to go to New York or Williamsburg. And you were off the other day to go to that queer's funeral." He wiped his face with a handkerchief and his hands trembled.

How did he know that? "Listen here, Ned. That was the first day I've taken off in six months. I'm going over to the center precisely because I'm involved with their work. How do you expect me to handle the data transmission with the telethon, if I don't have any idea of what it is? You never told me that I was going to have to transmit data."

He seemed to get control of himself. "We talked about it enough last week."

"I need to go over there. I want to find out precisely how they'll work with us on the telethon." She had to get to the computer center to satisfy herself. Idle curiosity? Or was she searching for something strange? "Darn it, Ned. I have to go over there. I didn't want to tell you. Please don't tell anyone.

It's about Tony. He. Well, I want to collect his things." She blinked rapidly as if she were going to cry. "You wouldn't understand."

"Oh, yes, my dear. I understand. You and Tony. Hmmm, some kind of perversion? Never mind that. Certainly. Please go over there right now." He pushed a buzzer on his desk. "I'll call Dawson and I'll send The Reverend's new chauffer, Ace Murphy, to help you."

"A new chauffer? I don't need anyone to drive."

"He can help you carry Tony's possessions. Besides, it's good to have someone else along. It's very sad when we have to gather someone's things after their death. I remember how Momma felt when she had to pick up Daddy's clothes and personal belongings."

Beth realized that a relationship with Tony could be a good cover. Actually, she felt better with someone going along. The new chauffeur's name was Ace? What a strange name? "Thank you. I'm sorry about what I said. I've been lost since he was killed."

Beth tapped her purse waiting for the guard at the Computer Center's security desk to identify and sign in Murphy. And Dawson's assistant seemed to be taking too long to find the security logs.

"Look here, Davis. I want to see those logs right now! You've been delaying me here by telling me that they aren't complete. Your job is to make sure that the logs are up to date. Don't you have an automatic tie-in with the computer?"

"Yes we do, Miz Olson. But, well, we've been so busy and there's been a lot of night work here because of the Middle East campaign and the telethon."

"Yes, I know that. I'd rather look at the logs as they come off the printer anyway. Let's go in there." She pushed him toward the entrance.

Entering the Computer Operations Center was like entering Orwell's 1984, with TV monitors at strategic places on stark gray walls. The clean, controlled environment was often too cool for people. The motor generator sets purred constantly, supporting the relentless needs of the computer. A portrait of Reverend Creed overlooked a column of computer tape drives that stood guard near the central console. The other walls had the simple word "TRUTH" placed in gold frames.

Eight technicians in white coats checked tapes, removed, or installed them in the drives. The people working in the console area seemed to move like programmed automatons. When they spoke their voices were subdued, as if they were in the presence of a god. She wondered which one was Doug, the new tech. Tony had mentioned him several times.

Davis had a Systems Operator punch commands at a keyboard. The printer zipped out data with continuous feed paper snaking up the printer frame. The green and white sheets dropped off the back to flip-flop into a pasteboard box on the floor. Beth walked behind the console and picked up the printout. She scanned the columns and data, listing the daily routine logging in and out. There was a separate category for off-hours work. Summaries were listed by day, by work project and by employee. The printer stopped.

Beth tore the paper from the machine. The projects were difficult to identify because they were listed in eight letter and digit codes. She crosschecked, tying operators with projects. Sam, Doug, and Tony's records had working patterns that extended into after hours and also showed up at odd times. She frowned and tapped her pen against the printouts. Tony had done a lot of night work lately. She wrote the project codes on her memo pad and marked them on the printout. "Could you tell me what these three projects are with all the night work?"

Davis looked at the printout and frowned. "I really don't know. I'd have to look them up. Besides, I don't know if you have the need to know."

"What do you mean? I'm a Division Head. I have a right to know most everything that goes on here. And some or all of these may be associated with the Satellite Division." Three names were connected to three unidentified projects. Tony's name was not logged on any of them. "You people are supposed to be providing me with data for the telethon, and I'll be darned if I'll wait until Election Day to find out what it is."

"Providing data for the telethon? 'Fraid you're mistaken Miz Olson. We aren't doing that. It would take a special feed from 'him.' We aren't set up for that."

Beth knew that many of the geeks used the masculine pronouns "he" or "him" instead of saying "the computer." Personifying the machine or worshipping it? "All right. Maybe you don't. But if I needed to transmit data directly from the computer, how long would it take to provide me with a feed?"

He shrugged. "Heck I don't know. Maybe a couple hours. But we'd have to check it out, measure the signal at your end to see that it was coming in properly."

"Yes, and I'd have to check it on the transmission side. If there any problems surfaced I'd let you know. I'd have to monitor the bird too. We don't want another Captain Video to capture the signal. You know, the guy who pirated the video signal?"

Davis grinned. "Yeah, I remember. We had a semi-panic in May to make sure the guy didn't penetrate here."

"Let me ask a foolish question. Let's say I want to play some games. Couldn't I disguise it by using a regular project 'id'?"

"Sure you could. But, we know pretty darned well how much time it takes to do our projects. If there's a lot of extra hours on a project we start to ask questions."

He explained how the constant audit trail combined with the clock in the main frame to provide automatic verification of the tasks. He laughed. "Seems like there's been a rash of computer crime, and Dawson is scared stiff that somebody might try something here. But we don't have to worry. We check at random times and review the overtime work pretty closely."

There was little else she would get. Try feminine wiles. She moved closer and placed a hand on his. "I really didn't want to say anything about this. Please keep it confidential. It's about Tony. I need to check on his night work."

"Oh? You and Tony? Well, gosh, I didn't know. Say I'm real sorry about what happened to him. The papers were pretty bad. I mean, accusing him of being a homosexual. Bet The Reverend didn't like that. Tony was a real good worker, a good guy."

"Thank you so much. Could I take part of this printout?"

"Gee. The policy is not to let any printouts go out."

"Well, could you do this for me? The police asked what nights I was with Tony. If I could have a list of the times he was here at night it would help me remember."

"Sure, I can have the operator do that. You want to wait in the office?"

"I'll wait here." She shuddered for a moment. Was it the lower temperature here or a touch of fear? She had to find out about the three unnamed projects. Did Tony leave anything in his apartment? If he did, the police would have it anyway. Why was she thinking this way? She wondered if Tony had hidden anything at Dan's boat. As soon as she left the center she'd try to call him again. Perhaps he was back at the marina. She smiled. The poor dear. God protect him.

She felt uncomfortable in the center for many reasons. Covering up her real reason for being there was a break in trust. That was alien to her love for Jesus. Beth, why are you searching for something strange here? You know how truthful The Reverend is. She shook her head.

CHAPTER TWENTY

Best met Denny and Fred in a secluded parking area of Virginia Beach near the Chesapeake Bay. Denny was a tall muscular man with light features and a strong jaw. He worked out daily and could bench press more than most NFL linemen. He carried a garroting wire, a stiletto and a *lupara*, a sawed off shotgun with a beautifully carved stock with silver inlays. The Italian word meant "wolf shot" because of its lethality and its use in Mafia killings.

    Fred could have been mistaken for an atypical Italian mobster, heavy with jowls. His bulk seemed to be a handicap, but his large hands were powerful enough to break necks, arms and legs without much effort. He was an expert in the use of silenced handguns. His favorite act was the double tap, shooting the victim twice in rapid succession.

    Best went through his instructions and emphasized three times that they were not to carry out the kill unless he called and identified himself with a code word. "Take a look at the wino's boat when he's off and make sure you aren't seen together. He hangs out at the Anchor Inn" He showed them the location on a map. "Any questions?"

Fred spoke as if he had a frog firmly located in his throat. "Where we staying?"

"Got a rooming house for you that's safe and clean." He showed them a map. "Anybody asks, you're cousins looking for a long lost uncle by the name of Carmine Stiglioni. The house is empty. Enjoy the scenery and some good seafood."

They nodded and parted. Denny drove a Chevy sedan rental in someone's name that he couldn't decipher.

Wallace was on his way to The Hill when he received a call from Best in his car. After hanging up without a word, he drove to a secluded place and called back from a phone booth. "What the hell do you mean you couldn't take him? What's this bullshit about two hard-ass guys being with him? How many men do you need?"

"The son of a bitch went fishin' with two SEAL buddies. You want to take them on?"

"They couldn't be armed."

"We didn't know that. What were we going to do? Board the damned boat? There were fishing boats all over the fucking place. I figured we could jump on him after they came back in and the SEALs left. The bastards never did. They stayed all night, drinkin,' tellin' war stories. Listen to the tapes I sent you. If they're tellin' anywhere near the truth, they probably knocked off a couple hundred VCs."

"Son of a bitch!"

"Yes! I certainly agree."

"You meet your guys?"

"Yes. They have your complete instructions including the wait for orders. No slip-ups. They'll deliver. They worked for me three or four times before. I've always been satisfied."

"They'd better be first class. Or you'll be meeting the Mechanic in a different way than you're used to. He'll be there tomorrow."

CHAPTER TWENTY ONE

An overcast crept over the nation's capital bringing a chill outside and inside. The Fox reflected the opposite of the changing weather. Today he would put enormous pressure on Creed. An offer he couldn't refuse? He rubbed his hands at his desk and called Marcy to bring in his security chief.

Magee patted his label tie so that it lay perfectly. He brushed a tiny piece of forbidden lint from his gray power suit. "Wes, thank you for waiting. About my dear friend, the Reverend Creed?"

"Caught in the act, sir. This envelope has the pictures, negatives and the video of his, uh, his athletic ability with the young woman." He seemed embarrassed for his boss; the man's own mistress had been caught with someone else.

"Is she recognizable?"

"Yes, sir. I could have blocked that out easily. I didn't know. Should I have the material changed?"

"Don't do anything. You've done a fine job again, and I want to give you a bonus. Will twenty-five be enough?"

"Twenty five? Sir, I, I don't know what to say. I think that's overly generous."

"Nonsense. You've earned it. You will continue to earn it with your work and silence."

The security man nodded at the door. "You never have to worry about that, sir."

Magee weighed good and bad news concerning JUST CAUSE. Through his efforts, the chances of investigating the contras were slipping away as rapidly as congressman near a recess.

Bad news came from The Speaker complaining on the phone about the tactics being used to stifle an investigation. "It gets my Irish up, Frank. They'd better not push me."

"Tip, The President is ready to sign the revised contra aid bill tomorrow. Why not let it go away? I told you that the administration would come through. Don't be so angry with Ron's Chief of Staff. I know he tried to pull a fast one and have the President come before the House."

After a long line of profanity that many constituents wouldn't have believed, The Speaker replied. "Frank, I'm going public on that. You know that there are Shanty Irish and Lace Curtain Irish. That Chief's somewhere under the outhouse lid." His tone changed to a bargaining mode. "Are you going to oppose me on the South African sanctions? I understand that there are some of your important clients who won't like the idea."

"As long as you don't go too far, at the present time I'm playing it close. You should have accepted the President's offer to make the sanctions part of an Executive Order. You can't have the whole pie. Besides, the President will probably veto it anyway."

"You think?"

"Hmmmm, I'm not at liberty to say, but he's moving in that direction." They made a luncheon date and rang off.

Later that morning, Marcy ushered the preacher into Magee's office. "Well, well, Reverend Creed, thanks for returning. You know, I was thinking of your spring trip to Central

America when you reviewed those troops. That was a fine thing for you to do. I understand from official sources that they greatly appreciated it."

The TV personality's tan matched that of his host. His gray suit had a slightly different shade from the one worn by Magee. Head bobbing and smiling, he was the epitome of a political hand-shaker. His face was creased with a toothy smile, and his voice carried to the corners of the large office. "Frank, ah'm glad to see you. How are the JUST CAUSE efforts comin'?"

"They're doing extremely well. The feedback this week tells me that we may have bought TV time at the perfect moment. By the way, I have something important for you."

The Fox handed over a bulging envelope containing a quarter of a million dollars out of sequence. Whether it was a payoff or donation to the network, no one would know. Creed slipped the envelope into his coat pocket. They discussed the latest polls for next week's elections.

"Ah am just afraid that there will be too many liberals comin' back to Washington. Are y'all sure that the PACs will be able to deliver the votes to hang on to the Senate? The President is bound to appoint one or two Supreme Court Justices. With the Senate's help, we'll be able to reverse that awful, murderous pro-abortion case. My Gawd, when I think of all those little babies bein' killed. I tell you."

"I agree. By the way, I have another envelope for you to see. My security man has been watching some people for another reason, and he came across these interesting photos." He opened a large manila envelope and silently handed over the incriminating pictures. He watched with great pleasure, as a shocked expression swept a white wave over the florid face.

"Maybe, you'd better sit down, Jethro. Apparently this video was filmed at the same time." He inserted the cartridge into a VHS. The large television set showed a young woman in a sexy black negligee lying on a couch. She watched a man come in, glance around, and walk toward her. The camera swung and focused in on the face of Reverend Creed.

The young woman undressed the grinning evangelist. He grabbed her negligee and almost tore it off. He fondled and kissed her, bending her over backwards. They were soon in bed and involved in heavy intercourse. The camera moved in for close-ups, then panned outward to cover the entire room. The effect of the scene was one of lusty sex.

"Uh, Jethro, would you like a bourbon?"

The television evangelist found his voice. He spoke so rapidly that The Fox had difficulty understanding every word. There was no doubt about the content.

"Yes! Yes! Quickly. My Lawd. This is terrible. Who could have—?"

"Some enemy of yours, I suppose. That's not the point. What would it be worth to make sure that these pictures never see the light of day?"

"Worth? Worth? How can you talk like that? Ah am ruined. Ruined!" He was on his feet, pacing and wringing his hands. He gulped down the large bourbon.

Magee explained that the source of the pictures had held the negatives. "And there's another copy of the video that is being held."

"Held? Held by who? Where did y'all get this?"

"I'm not at liberty to say, because it involves people who cannot be exposed. I'm certain that I can receive the negatives and the other video, but it will take extreme pressure and considerable funds. I've already offered half a million."

"Half a million? My Gawd."

"Surely, your reputation is worth much more than that, my friend. This group is attempting to take over a failing television network. Run by a television evangelist, like you. There is resistance, not only by the current owners, but also by some of your more powerful brothers in the business. Now, I'm quite sure that I can convince this group to join me in aiding your network. I know that we can come to some satisfactory arrangement."

"You mean y'all talked to the bastards holdin' these

pictures?"

"I'm afraid so. I have tried considerable pressure and even more funds. They are determined to get into evangelical television. It seems to me that we can kill two birds with one stone, so to speak. All I have to do is convince them to change the direction to join your interests." The Fox poured a generous three fingers into the preacher's empty glass.

The Reverend drained the refill. "This, this is blackmail. How can—."

"Blackmail? It's nothing like that at all, merely one of the many ways that business deals are made around here. I thought you knew that. One party has something the other wants and finds a way to persuade a reluctant buyer or seller to accept. And, from what I understand, this group could be persuaded to give up all the evidence."

"How? Why? Why wouldn't they hold out?"

The Fox smiled as only a fox can smile. "My security people have already collected enough information, so that I can easily neutralize anything they might consider. They are willing to trade pictures for involvement plus funds to expand your market."

Magee spotted a different light in the man's eyes. Greed and ambition were propelling the evangelist toward accepting the idea. His intelligence collection on the man was accurate. Creed had tried many times to expand his Truth Network with little success. The lure of new horizons for his ministry could provide the right amount of forward thrust to the transaction.

"What do you think? I don't see how you can lose."

"Ah must think about it. My Lawd, this is serious. I'd lose everything."

"I doubt it. Tell you what. I'll arrange for a meeting with the head of this group. Between us we'll be able to persuade the man. Perhaps dinner at my home?"

Creed wiped perspiration from his brow with two white handkerchiefs. "Anything, Frank. Anything."

"I hate to bring this up, my friend. But you know there

will be a sex scandal breaking very soon that will implicate several of your confreres. The man from California, one in Texas and the couple in Carolina."

Creed's eyes opened roundly to match his mouth. "How? How did you know?"

Magee patted the man on the shoulder and eased him toward the door. "It's my business to know many things, to protect my friends as well as to deal with my enemies. Here, don't forget to take the video. By the way, athletic wasn't she?"

Creed left silently.

The Fox closed the door, made an obscene gesture, and exclaimed, "Gotcha!"

Joseph Guion

CHAPTER TWENTY TWO

Ned did more than pace in his office; he seemed to lope around near the walls. If he could have climbed them he would have tried. He reached for a forbidden cigarette and stuffed it into his pocket. Beth had left for the computer center and he was frantic. What was she searching for? Did she know anything about the secret program? Oh, my God. Oh, my God. What can I do? What should I do?

    He reached for the phone three times, then withdrew a shaking hand. He was only supposed to call his contact in an emergency. This situation was more compelling than that. He remembered that he couldn't use a network phone anyway. He could be discovered.

Ned drove his compact to the nearest shopping center and called a local number. Leaving a message that he needed an urgent call, he took a wandering drive around Virginia Beach. He chain-smoked, looked for a tail, drove up the on-ramp to the expressway at First Colonial and down at the same exit. He took a side street and looped around to the expressway.

Satisfied that he wasn't being followed he headed east.

"Lord Jesus help me. Yes. It's for you I'm doing this. I have to finish it." He was working for a new, moral America. The forces of evil had penetrated government at every level and throughout society. He was a part of the process of reversing that trend, battling atheistic humanists, Satanists and immoral leadership. The Bible led the way. At the A & P parking lot on Rosemont Road he answered the ringing pay phone in a whisper. "'H' here."

" 'J' here. Talk louder friend."

Ned glanced around. No one was within a hundred feet of the booth, but he was certain that he could be heard a block away. "I've got a terrible problem. I need to see someone today! Right away! Things are coming apart."

"Impossible to see anyone. What kind of trouble?"

Ned was angry at the refusal. He explained in an obtuse way. "Curious person on the job. I'm trying to cover, but it doesn't seem to help. That person is suspicious."

"True suspicion or just curiosity?"

Ned's answer had a ring of desperation. "I'm talking real, real suspicion!"

"That could make a difference. Give me some details. What questions were asked?"

Ned gave the contact a detailed narrative of Beth and her actions, statements and questions without mentioning her name. The information was passed without identifying his position, the network, or the type of activity. After he finished there was silence. He was hyperventilating, perspiring and trembling. "Did you hear what I said?"

"Easy, easy. Some of the questions were legitimate and relevant. Others weren't."

"I'm exposed here. Perhaps you ought to get someone else down here."

"Already there, chump. We're watching you too."

Ned's hands shook so much that he couldn't use a match to light a cigarette. "I had to call. She knows!"

"What do you mean? She knows what? Spell it out."

"She went to the computer center. She knows about data transmission."

"Where is she now?"

He almost dropped the phone. "At the computer center."

"Listen. Ace is with her, right? He'll keep an eye on her."

"You mean he's one of, uh, of ours? Lord Jesus. What would he do?"

"None of your freaking business. Contact Ace. Tell him she has to be kept in sight all the time. Don't let her drive from work."

"How will I do that?"

"Get her keys, stupid. I'll call your office at eleven forty-five. Be there!"

"Yes, sir, yes, sir!"

"Check this out immediately. Find out if she talked to her boyfriend."

Ned started to protest, then he heard a dial tone. A car entered the parking lot headed toward him. He slammed the phone down and bolted. Back on the expressway heading west, he realized that he had acted suspicious when he had left the phone booth. He felt his shirt sticking to his back from perspiration. He turned on the air conditioning.

"How can I find out about Beth's boyfriend? How did they find out? Lord, Jesus. They probably have someone watching me. Oh, God. How did I get into this?"

He realized that he was the one most vulnerable to exposure. Before Tony's death, he had refused to admit that they might use deadly force. What could he do? He raced to his office and felt his heart throbbing. What will they do to Beth? Oh, God, I don't want to know. He had to save his wife Cherry and himself, the kids. How could he do that?

Charles R. Best cursed when he eased the gray BMW into a MacDonald's parking lot. It was crowded with an early crew of construction workers with four-wheel drives, pickups and battered muscle cars. A man with cut off shirtsleeves and bulging biceps had long, unkempt hair straggling down from his hard hat. He made a nasty remark at C's car, not knowing how close he was to a desperate, armed man.

Best was to meet Ned at this fast food location. He'd gotten there in record time. Stepping on the parking brake was a chore though, with gout pain piercing his foot. He was sweating out the hit list. Now that Cliff had been eliminated, he was more vulnerable than ever. The rest of the contract had to be completed without another problem or he'd be dog meat somewhere. It would be ironic if they had The Mechanic do it to him. This meeting with Nervous Nellie Ned was the key to his survival.

He motioned for Creed's assistant to approach his car. He waited and whispered, "In here, dammit! Your car might be bugged."

"Oh, my Lord Jesus. I—."

"Shut up!" Best questioned him for thirty minutes and focused on anything that concerned a relationship between Tony and Beth. "Dammit! Now you tell me that she's uptight about Jules being here. You were supposed to smooth that over."

He whined. "I tried to. Oh, God, that awful murder. I had no idea that you people would go that far. I haven't been able to sleep."

"You won't sleep at all if you screw this up. Now listen. Who did she talk to at the computer center? Dawson? Sam?"

"I don't know! Dawson told me that she had asked about hiding time and work in the computer system. She asked about penetrating a secure system. I don't know what to do."

Best frowned. "Not good. I want her pumped with questions. Ask what she was doing with the faggot. Ask about her friend, Haggerty. If she wants to know why, you saw it in the paper. Tell her you can't have any homos in the Network. You want them there?"

Ned shook his head. "No! No, of course not."

"Ask her if Tony talked about anything weird at the computer center. Tell her that The Reverend wants to find out if there was something from Tony's past."

"Besides his being a, a, a faggot?"

"Yes, stupid. Now listen here. It's up to you to find out everything she knows and find it out today! You're on the hot seat. If this thing ever comes to light you're the first asshole who gets it at the network. Don't play coy or dumb. If you screw up, I'm on the griddle and I won't be there by myself. Find out what she knows."

Best shoved his fist under Ned's chin, against his Adam's apple. "Make sure Ace keeps her in sight. Or somebody in your family may get sick. I may have to move today!"

Ned grabbed the man's jacket. "Oh my God! Please. Please. Don't let them do anything to my wife and family. I'll do anything, anything."

"Make the woman stay at work!" He poked Ned in the ribs with a steel rod-like finger. "Get back to me before two. If you don't find out what she knows about the plan your ass is grass. By the way, how is your wife Cherry's health? I hear that she's on diabetes medication. I hope that nothing else happens to her."

Ned's hands covered his face as if he could hide from the truth. "Oh, God, please. Leave my wife alone. I'll do anything. Anything!"

Best slapped Ned on the back hard enough to hear him whimper. "I know you will, my friend. I know you will. Call at one fifty-five. Here's the number. Memorize it. Now get the hell out of the car! Don't call me again, ever. Don't remember what I look like or your wife will disappear."

Best watched Ned walk to his car. The shithead dropped his keys twice. I have to keep the pressure on that bastard. If he goes, so do I. I'll put my own man on him.

CHAPTER TWENTY THREE

After Ace Murphy had reported that he held Beth's keys, Ned paced around his office. His hands twitched when he tried to wipe perspiration from his face. He wondered what he could do to satisfy the contact. What does Beth know? Can I get any information from her? If he failed what would they do to him, his family?

He dropped to his knees by his desk. "Dear, God, forgive me a sinner, for tying myself to the Devil." All the secret work was done for the good of the country, a land so blessed by the Lord Himself. There were many Bible passages where God's people smote the enemy in God's name.

Later he slouched into Beth's office with a worried look on his face. He chewed on his lip and blinked several times. "I need to talk to you."

"Look who's here. I was going to ask to see you. I have an appointment with The Reverend at two and I want to tell you what I'm going to say."

"What did you find out at the Computer Center? Davis tells me that you—."

"What? I needed to find out what programs are using my

overtime funds."

"Now look, Miss Olson, who do you think you are? You act like everyone owes you an explanation, when you're the one who owes us."

"I beg your pardon?"

"You know what I mean. You and that queer Tony."

She watched Ned shift back and forth, blinking his eyes. Should she ask about Tony's suspicions? Could Ned be the one involved in a scheme? "I have something important to discuss. I want to know the truth, straight, no equivocation or sidestepping. Do we or don't we have a secret project going on here in the network?"

"If there is a secret project going on and you don't need to know about it, will it be enough for me to say that there is?"

"Not quite. If our pastor tells me that, I'll accept it. I'm sorry. Frankly, right now, I don't trust you. That's the way it is."

"Thanks. Trust is a two-way street. You haven't told me about you and Tony"

"That was a personal matter."

"No. Not with all the negative publicity since his death. That's not personal."

Her eyes drilled daggers. "That's what I would expect of you. You don't give a damn about Tony. All you care about is the reputation and the growth of the network."

"Somebody has to. You don't. Associating with a drunk and a homosexual."

She stood. "And who is the drunk, pray tell?"

Ned looked away and fidgeted with his hands. "Well, you've been calling that Haggerty fellow all day. You were with him when Tony was killed."

Her words jabbed at him like the measured blasts of her grandpa's shotgun when he was shooting quail. "How. Do. You. Know. That. He. Drinks?" He didn't answer. "Tell me, Ned. You seem to know so much about my private life."

"It's my business to know how our people live their

lives. We are ministers of the Lord Jesus. Our people have to be like the driven snow."

Beth was back in the street, trying to survive. "Bullshit! What you're saying is that you can spy on people. Did you have Tony followed before he was murdered?" She repeated the question. "Who was following him? The police would love to hear this."

Ned stood and held out his hands. "Don't, don't tell them anything." He licked his lips. "I mean, Beth we are under a terrible strain here. Don't you realize how the network is under scrutiny because of the murder? I'm trying to protect all of us."

"Protect us from whom? Secret agents? Homos? Queers? The Public?"

He sat down and covered his eyes. He reminded her how the sexual scandals in California had damaged all television ministers. "If the drop in contributions continues we'll be in trouble."

He sighed. "We do have a secret project. It has to do with national security. That's all I can say." He jumped from the chair and grabbed her wrists. "You must not tell anyone. Not even your friend, Mister Haggerty." He dashed out.

Beth was stunned. "National Security?" There had been rumors that churches had been asked by the government for assistance. Church efforts overseas often coincided with military and foreign aid support. The CIA had used religious organizations for questionable actions, and The Reverend had extremely close ties with the White House.

After Ned had left, she tried to call Dan again without success. "Oh, dear God. Please help him. Beth felt that she was a whisper from disaster. Her intuitive sense had been heightened by Tony's death and the possibility of secrets. The Reverend could help her.

A mural of Jesus preaching to a crowd dominated Creed's spacious sitting room. A caption in bold letters proclaimed, "I am the Way, the Truth, and the Life." Beth paused. The painting always had an impact on her. The Reverend sat with his face in his hands, elbows propped on the desk. Was he meditating?

She felt better, until she saw Ned there holding several files. "I asked for a meeting with The Reverend, Ned. Not with you too."

Creed raised his head and rewarded her with a toothy smile. "Now, my dear Lizbeth. Please come over here, and let's just see if we can make some peace. Please, sit down. Right here, child." He patted the textured beige sofa. She didn't move, so he came around his desk and took her hand. "How are you, my dear? Ned, has told me that y'all are feeling peaked. Would you like some tea?"

He led her to the sofa. She fought her feelings about the great man. Her mind paraded images of him helping her out of her past life, giving her assistance, consoling her. "Yes, I'd like some tea. Thank you. I'm sorry, Ned."

The man nodded and poured tea into Wedgwood cups.

"Theah now." Her mentor held her hand and stroked it. The millions who thought that he was God's gift to television ministry didn't know how good he was one on one. "Let us bow our heads and ask the Lawd Jesus to come to us." They prayed together, heads bowed, intent on the words. "... and we trust in the Lawd Jee-sus, Amen!"

Beth echoed the "Amen," and felt better. It was as if she were coming back home, returning from a bad dream, and the Lord was there in person to help her. She felt embarrassed that she had bothered her mentor over something that she should have resolved with Ned. She thought, "Lord, forgive me for my lack of Faith."

"Now mah dear. Ned tells me you have a troubled mind. What can I do for you?"

Ned's face was stiff, but his eyes never stopped moving. She gazed at her counselor, her pastor. She had never lied to him, even when he was delving into her past. He knew everything about her, her worst secrets. "I hate to bother you." He waved at her to continue. "I've had a difficult time in the past few days. Tony's death was—."

He patted her hand again. "Go on, mah dear."

"Well, my relationship with Tony was, uh very close. " She glanced up at the mural. There was truth in that statement, not the follow up. "I wanted to review the times that Tony and I." A tear wandered slowly then slid rapidly down her cheek. "Well, we were together sometimes and we, uh, talked a lot about things, personal things." She sat straight. "Our relationship isn't anyone's business. It wasn't, uh, carnal."

"Praise the Lord. I'm sure it wasn't, my dear"

Could she lie again to the wonderful minister who had saved her? "The police asked me to tell them when Tony was working at night, so that I could remember the dates that we were together. I found that out at the computer center."

"Hmmm. You went there and looked them up. Ah see nothing wrong."

So Ned had told him about her visit. "I found out the dates, and something else. He and another technician were working on some special projects. A secret project of some kind?" It was a question and Creed seemed puzzled. He didn't know about it?

Ned broke in. "She's asking about the special project we were requested to carry out by the Federal Communications Commission. You remember? Project Zero-Zero-Five?

Creed's face regained its sunny brightness. "Yes, Ned. Ah remember. They asked that we set up some computer systems to check on, let me see. " He shook his head. "That government name-calling is right good; never know what the thing is. The one where we send out data and check it back again. Why shucks, that's no secret from you."

"It isn't? I'm sorry, but I don't know a thing about it."

Ned handed her a file folder. "I beg to differ with you, Beth. Here take a look at this.

It was one of her own files identified properly as SatCom001124. She didn't remember. She read Ned's cover memo and glanced at some pages.

"Your initials are on the cover sheet. I'm sure you'll remember it when you read it again. It's no problem anyway. It's almost finished. The report will go through you."

Could she have missed this? She was proud of her memory for projects, so she examined the initials. They looked like her flowing scrawl. She had a private tickler file in a locked drawer in her desk. She'd double-check that later. This was puzzling. She felt warm, dizzy.

"I'm sorry. I don't remember this. I'm sure that I would have gone over to the center periodically to talk with the technicians first hand." The memo date was October 2, 1986.

"Isn't there a project plan? I should have seen that plan and agreed to it."

Ned showed her a Project File. "Take a look. It has your name on it."

She saw her name and signature approving the project. "No. No! This couldn't be. I'm not losing my mind here. I did not sign this plan. I did not!"

"Now, now, don't worry your pretty head about it right now. We're not as concerned about this project as much as we're worried bout our Lizbeth. You've been through a large strain these past few days. The Lawd God knows that."

"I'm going back to my office and check this. I am not losing my grip here. Something is wrong. I've heard about things."

"Things? What things, my poor dear?" His voice seemed too smooth, unctuous.

He reached for her hand and Beth removed it from his grasp. "Things going on in the computer center; some kind of data transmission from my satellites during the election. And you brought in a new assistant who doesn't know beans. And, and, you're against me because I knew a homosexual. Is that what is going on here? "

"Why that's not it at all. Now you know we're goin' to send out information during the telethon. Shucks y'all have known that for weeks."

She stood. "Information yes. Data no! What type of data? Where is it going? They're supposed to get the information by voice and picture. Why do they get data?" Her voice rose and her face became red.

Ned finally spoke. "Wait. Don't get so worked up."

The Reverend placed his arm around her shoulder. "You heard Ned, there, relax, child. Just settle down a tad. No sense getting' all riled up. Take some time off."

His hand felt like a vise. She struggled to free herself.

"Please, Lizbeth. Why don't you take the rest of the day off? Please. Maybe couple days. Just go home and get some rest."

"I don't want rest. I want to find out what's going on."

He stroked her arm. She relaxed, somewhat reassured. This man was a man of God. How could she not trust him? If he knew about the secret program, it had to be okay. She was confused, tired. She needed to get away, now. She needed Dan. She wandered to her office.

Her car keys were missing from her desk. "Louise, where are my keys?"

"The Reverend's chauffer has them. He's waiting to take you to Mister Haggerty's. Here is a note from his last call."

She read the first sentences. "Need to see you right away. Please come to the boat. Dan." She could tell Dan everything and they would decide what to do. Wanting to be with him urged her forward. Gosh-darn-it! You're falling for a married man with a terrible hang-up, an awful drinker at that. She thought about leaving everything and taking off with Dan. With him, she could actually do that. Run away? Leave your wonderful job? My mentor, my pastor? How could you? She finally admitted it. With Dan she could walk away. From God? No, no. Lord Jesus, help us.

Murphy held the car door and she smiled at his grin. It was difficult to see his eyes behind the sunglasses. When her car entered the marina parking lot, she frowned. "I don't see his car."

"Maybe he's off for a minute or so. We can wait on the boat. Here he comes now."

Ace took her arm. His fingers were like the talons of a hawk. "Come on."

She relaxed and let him lead. She called out. "Hey, Dan. Wait up."

Obviously he hadn't heard her. A bit annoyed but feeling safe, she walked forward, smiling and happy. The driver waited until she came up by the rear fender, then he swung the door in front of her and jumped out. Ace pinned her arms behind her back.

"Oh, God. It's not Dan." She felt a surgical mask cover her face.

She inhaled sweet oil, then felt nothing.

CHAPTER TWENTY FOUR

That evening one surveillance team watched the Anchor Inn from inside, the other waited outside. They were ordered to eliminate Haggerty that night. The men inside never let him out of their sight. One man spelled the other, following him into the men's room twice. They watched Haggerty and his flying buddy down drinks, laughing and joking.

"Hey, Cat, remember the time I had to extract you from that world of shit off Dung Island?"

"That time? Geez, you hauled our asses out of there a helluva lot of times."

"Yeah. But you had the shits and I could smell you over the jungle rot."

"You bastard. You said you weren't going let me in the chopper and the VC were spraying bullets all over hell."

"Good thing Doc grabbed your arm and hauled you in. Otherwise you would have had a windy ride on the skids. It took me half a day to clean the bastard after you shoved off."

"Shoulda told me. I'd a brought a momasan. It was some old rations."

"Like hell, you jungle boys were eating snakes, eels and

all sorts of shit."

At the marina, the wind howled through boat rigging and tossed paper about.

The other thugs were holding Beth on Haggerty's boat, waiting for him to arrive. Ace was on the phone. "Yeah, the action guys are here. Okay, we'll wait till they finish him. Then it's a one-way ride huh? No sweat." Ace hung up and stopped The Mechanic from torturing Beth.

The killer complained. "Shit! She's singing like a bird. One more jab at her."

"It don't matter. The Big Mahoff wants us off the boat now. The Anchor Inn guys on the frogman say he's gettin' ready to leave. Take her to the other boat. The others will take the big bastard when he gets here. Then they swim with the fish."

"Bullshit. She's a ton. Damned if I'll carry her over there."

"Stick the knife in her back and she'll walk like a trouper. Won't you, baby?"

Beth's eyes answered. He put the gag back in her mouth. The Mechanic showed her the blood-stained knife. She shivered and covered her nakedness with the torn dress. Ace told the other man to follow after he cleaned up the boat. "Make sure you double-check."

Beth had never been so frightened. The snake-eyed man with the knife was the most cold-blooded person she had ever seen.

"No screwing around bitch!" He pushed her to the side of the boat. "Don't try any shit or this will be up your back."

She bit her lip and staggered. She thought of jumping over the side, screaming, anything to get away from this monster. It was hopeless. She knew that they were going to kill Dan as soon as he arrived. How could she warn him? She had tried. Would it work? She prayed.

Stolen Votes

Denny and Fred waited on Haggerty's boat with their primary weapons, silenced guns, a garroting wire and surprise. They had agreed that Denny would begin the festivities with the wire, backed up by Fred's silenced double tap. Denny had brought his *lupara* slung around his neck on a lanyard in the event that things got out of hand. He had polished the wood with care and before he had finished, he kissed the stock for luck. It had never failed him.

They spoke in muffled tones and rehearsed as if they were practicing for a *pas de deux*. They tried different positions in the small cabin to ascertain that one would not interfere with the other. More importantly, they went through the steps through the killing until they knew exactly where the other person was located at all times. They agreed that Fred should use a knife instead of the silenced pistol to avoid a friendly fire casualty in close quarters.

After fifteen dry runs Fred nodded and said, "Got it, pal. We're ready."

Denny agreed. From that moment on they were silent and placed themselves so that Haggerty would be unable to avoid their expert efforts. Waiting was a part of a professional hit. So the two men chose positions in the dark where they could relax and stay alert at the same time. They had done this many times together and similar actions individually.

Smoking was not allowed because the pro never knew if the "vic" had a sensitive nose. Fred chewed gum while Denny sucked on lemon drops, a substitute for the snuff bulge in his cheek he normally wore when not on the job. A half hour passed without any noise or movement that could have been detected by the sensitive bugs rigged on the boat.

They heard a car approach and both became tense, ready. They were like two hair triggers on a revolver; only a slight movement would explode them into action.

Haggerty stepped out of the helicopter pilot's car. "See, you,

Slick. Thanks for the ride. Damn sight right. We coulda beat those gooks if they let us. Watch out for SAMs!"

He waved and weaved toward the boat. His mind was jumbled with crazy thoughts of Tony's horrible death and Beth's absence. Where the heck was she? He had tried calling her several times during the day but couldn't get through to her at work. He had tried her apartment before he went out earlier and she wasn't there.

He glanced around the marina for a moment. Nothing out of the ordinary. It was dark outside the arc of overhead lights in strategic places and in the parking lot. Each pier had small lights at regular intervals for sure footing. He hadn't carried out a good check on the boats, so he strolled around the marina, walking down each pier with a flashlight in his left hand. He had a slight buzz on. He and Charlie had a great time. His fishing trip with Doc and Bennie had started him out of his slump. Yeah. I can keep it going too. All I have to do is listen to Beth some more.

He finished his marina tour after picking up paper and trash that had bounced off expensive boats. He made sure that his car was locked, looked at the sky and nodded at the overcast. Maybe rain soon. He walked on the pier toward his boat. I'll call Beth right away. He ached and his sloped shoulders reflected fatigue. He shoved the light into his side pocket and stepped aboard; grinning, relaxed, unaware.

Stolen Votes

CHAPTER TWENTY FIVE

While the killers waited for Haggerty to step aboard, a small, but elegant dinner party was underway at Freeland, Magee's estate in suburban, upscale Maryland. Estelle was beaming, assured that everyone was having a wonderful time. At first, she had expressed annoyance at using a substitute hostess. However, the beautiful young woman had excellent taste and knew the Washington scene. She wondered where Frank had located her. If she had known that the young woman was her husband's mistress she would have imploded.

The guests included two couples from the A-1 list and two DC party matrons to pair off with the two television executives, Reverend Jethro Creed and Mortimer Zoljak. The latter was Magee's collaborator aimed at taking over the Truth Network.

On their way to the dining room, the target grabbed The Fox and whispered. "Frank! Frank, I can't go in there."

"Is everything all right, Jethro? You look a bit peaked. Can I get you something?"

"Mah Gaw-wed. Frank. Didn't you recognize her?"

"Recognize who? You mean, the publisher's wife, Denise? She's on television all the time."

"No, no! Not that. The, the hostess, the young woman in black. She, she——."

The Fox stifled laughter. "The hostess? Is there something wrong with her service? She's a temp, and I don't want her to give a bad impression."

Creed grabbed Magee's lapels, holding on, as if he would slide to the floor. "Frank, don't you recognize her? She's the, the, you know, the woman in those pitchers of me. The whore. The blackmail. It's her I swear."

"She couldn't be. Let me check. Good Lord, you'd better go back and wash off with cold water. You're absolutely white. Go ahead, take your time. I'll delay the meal."

The nine-course Chinese dinner was elegant, superb. The conversation never lagged and the wine was exquisite. Everyone enjoyed the evening, except for Reverend Creed. He was, literally, in a sweat. When Whitney came near him, his shoulders curled in and he bent over his food as if he were trying to hide. The host coughed a few times trying to suppress laughter.

When she tried to catch his eye, The Fox focused past her as if she were part of the Louis XIV sideboard near her. She had become just that, a piece of furniture, used twice. His mistress was probably pissed. Too damned bad! Tonight, he was collecting on her monthly retainer.

The television madam spoke. "Frank, I'm sorry to report that I have an urgent meeting after dinner. It seems that we have a new poll that reinforces the shift toward a more liberal House and Senate. I've told my staff that I may be delayed, but I must make the eleven o'clock news. I have no desire to leave. This is an exceptional evening."

"Not a problem, Denise. I know how important this news is, and I'll not restrain you for a moment. Please know that after desserts I do have a small token of my appreciation for all of you, for making this such a special evening."

The Fox watched the preacher's obvious discomfort and had to call on his immense control to keep from exploding with laughter. He was amazed that the man had stayed. After all, he could have feigned illness. Obviously, the temptation for more funds and the promise of a wider audience had overcome his embarrassment. Once again, Magee's studious knowledge of his victim would come to fruition with a deal.

During coffee and sumptuous desserts, Frank stood. "Ladies and gentlemen, Estelle and I thank you for attending and making this a special evening." He grinned. "Now, don't get the impression that I am shooing you out. Denise must leave when she feels she needs to, but the rest of you can stay as long as you wish. Unfortunately, Reverend Creed and Mister Zoljak and I have a meeting too. Estelle and our hostess will ensure that you will continue to have the refreshments you desire. If you'll excuse me, I need to get that small gift for each of you."

The Fox's departure implied that there was no hurry for anyone to depart. It was also a calculated move to heighten Creed's anxiety over Whitney's presence. It would place the mark more under his control.

He slipped into his study and erupted with laughter. He said, "Oh, Fox. You are terrible. This is rich. It worked better than I had expected. And later, the *coup de gras*." He thought of Creed, desperately trying to hide his emotions, in order to see the network deal through. The Truth Network was in trouble and he needed the financial support that they had discussed. The Fox thought of a murder story. While everyone was having a merry time at the dinner table, the murderer and the victim knew a dark secret that dominated their evening.

At a suitable hour, the extras departed with exuberant thanks to the Magees. Estelle excused herself and Creed, The Fox and Mort Zoljack sat in the study. After Whitney departed the clergyman finally smiled and engaged in the discussion for the network situation and possibilities. They reviewed Truth Network's financial situation and Zoljak's proposal too. The network would receive an immediate infusion of fifty million with an agreement to pay fifty percent of operating expenses.

The two public partners would jointly petition the FCC to expand, buying out stations in the southeast and on the West Coast.

Creed would handle the programming and fund raising in the United States and eventually worldwide. Zoljak would handle support activities. He ended his pitch with a promise that another satellite, dedicated to their use, would be in orbit by 1988.

The public figure rubbed his hands, possibly thinking of the funds rolling in. "Ah have to go back to my financial people to review the figures y'all have given me. Ahm also concerned about how all of this will look to the agencies of the federal government. Justice? IRS? FCC?"

Magee answered. "Jethro, my friend. Those avenues have been explored. Here, take a look at the correspondence I have from those organizations. And there are notes here of support from Senators and Congressmen." He presented copies to both men. "I'm sure that these will help to alleviate your concerns. I do have excellent access here in DC."

After reading the material they agreed that the possibility of approval and support had become a high probability. Creed seemed to return to his jovial, expansive self, grinning and joshing. Magee was sure that they had an agreement. The Fox had the blackmail material ready whenever he needed it. He stood, signaling that the meeting was over.

The two erstwhile partners shook hands and Creed spoke. "Tell you what, Mort. Could you come to the television summit meeting that ah called for this weekend in Williamsburg? I know that it's very short notice, but I'd love to have you as my guest. We can get together and also provide good news for the media. Press conferences are on Saturday and Sunday."

They agreed to meet in Williamsburg that Friday. They would finalize their acceptance and announce success there. The Reverend was more anxious than his companions for the news. He would leave the religious broadcaster's conference in triumph, in a stronger position than before. Expanding to new markets with the promise of a dedicated satellite would put him into the elite of television ministry. The possibilities were enormous. With Magee's assurances of cash, Reverend Jethro departed in a great mood, his mind freed from the young whore.

The Fox toasted himself with Drambuie when the alert light on the secure phone and its ring alerted him. Another job accomplished? He agreed and hung up. Opening the small safe, he pulled out the KL-43 encryption machine. The contra thing was exposed to a point, but they could still get in some weapons deliveries if they hurried.

If the White House people could resolve that damned landing glitch in Portugal they'd be set. He contributed to the decision that they'd offer an additional thousand missiles. One or two hostages would probably be released at that time. He closed the machine and smiled. "God, I wish I could tell someone about Creed and Whitney."

Filled with success, he thought of some loose ends, like inviting his archenemy, Nelson Wallace to join him in Williamsburg. The big bastard would be livid with envy when he learned of his newly acquired nation-wide, and later, a worldwide television presence. He'd probably have diarrhea in those large trousers.

I'll make it easier for him by pawning off the African lobby deal. Those idiots were getting more difficult to handle and their plans for the future were doomed to failure. Why not screw Wallace twice? He laid his forehead on the desk and laughed until he cried.

Joseph Guion

CHAPTER TWENTY SIX

Dan walked on the pier, unaware that he was cruising toward his killers. When he stepped aboard, the sweet scent of perfume raised the hair on the back of his neck. Something wrong! He crouched and his hands swung upward as if jerked by a puppeteer, a second too late.

Denny brought the wire over The Cat's head, tightened it and choked him. Too late to grab it, the victim fought instinct and went hard for the man's groin with a clenched fist. There was a satisfactory grunt and the wire slackened. Dan was on him, chopping twice at his neck. Silence. A noise behind. He jumped to the side and caught the glint of a knife. He slammed down on the knife hand, but the big man didn't drop it. He slashed twice and Dan heard the clatter of a weapon hitting the deck. In the glow of pier lights, he saw a shotgun swing toward him. Watch out for the first guy. Seconds left. The water! The SEALs escape route. He was trained to fight there.

He drove against the knifer and tumbled over the side with him. As they hit the water the Cat felt a sharp pain in his left side. He dragged the man down to the bottom and stuffed his head into the silt. The killer was strong enough to swing the knife in the water, but self-preservation won. Fred tried to push off from the slimy bottom with both hands. Dan's lungs screamed for attention, but he locked the killer's neck in a death grip. His opponent gurgled. The body convulsed and jerked in its death throes. He felt the man become limp.

Watch coming up! Dan blew out air carefully as he surfaced, hands reaching for the boat's bottom. He surfaced under the flare of the bow where the other killer wouldn't see him. His chest was heaving from exertion and excitement. He gulped air with little sound and heard a thud aft on the boat. It would be tough climbing on board without making noise. He slipped under the pier and paddled quietly toward the stern.

He spotted Denny on the outboard side trying to see what had happened, a shotgun at the ready. The Cat slipped silently up on the diving shelf at the transom and was on the man's back in seconds. He tried to grab the gun barrel but it slipped from his muddy hand. The killer was muscular and tough. They sparred in the open deck area, wrestling for a hold, trying to beat the other against something solid. He saw flashes of lights and felt a hard blow to the side of the head. The guy had an arm lock. Too powerful to wrestle. Dan jammed his heel down on the killer's instep and felt the grip loosen. He slipped out of it.

The killer swung the shotgun and Dan kicked at it. Too slow. His opponent slammed his shin with it and Haggerty grunted. He hobbled to the after end of the boat. Get him in the water? After a kick in the groin, the killer doubled over and dropped the weapon. Stepping behind Denny he grabbed the man's arm and bent it backward. He felt the bone give. A scream echoed around the marina. He drove the guy into a stanchion head first and the man dropped to the deck.

Haggerty was on him slugging with the dropped gun. "Take that, you bastard." He stood over the unconscious form. Panting. Out of shape. You're one lucky dude, tie him up.

The Cat heard diesel engines start up across the slip. He

touched blood from his wound and spoke aloud as if his voice could marshal his thoughts. "Better call the cops! What the hell is going on? A garroting wire indicated that they were professional killers. Why were they here? Where is Beth?"

He went through the boat rapidly, checking lockers and every space to make sure that no one was hiding. He heard the sound of powerful boat engines receding and light traffic on Shore Drive. He realized that he held the shotgun in his hand. "Dammit!" He threw it on the deck.

He went below to check the wound. A puncture job, oozing blood. The bunk was messed and he smelled perfume. There was blood on the slipcover. He spotted a shiny object in the folds of the covers. "Beth's ring! Oh my God!" Somebody had Beth aboard. They hurt her. Dammit to hell! What was going on?"

The Cat felt as if he were perched on top of a barbed wire fence. On one side was the past, 'Nam with its terror and recurring dreams. The other side was now, reality. Was it real? He shook his head, uncertain. He shouted, "What the hell?"

Physically and mentally exhausted, he felt unwilling or unable to do anything. He knew he would be easy prey to a quick follow up by other killers. Part of him didn't give a shit. But Beth was in danger. He cursed at himself for feeling immobilized. What should he do with two dead bodies? The big man on deck had no pulse, no life signs.

You stupid bastard. Those aren't the first you killed in combat. 'Nam thoughts howled through his mind. Was he back there? What was real and what wasn't? He tossed down a glass of neat scotch. Hands trembling. He grunted at the pain. Get hold of it! Think. Dammit, think!

He eased back on the stiff sofa. The knife wound was throbbing, oozing, even though he had taped it down tightly. If it was really bad, he'd find out later. If he went to a doctor or emergency room with a stab wound, the cops would be called. Too many questions. His SEAL buddy Doc Warner could fix him up. Don't get him involved. Where was Beth?

Who had attacked her? Where did they take her? Why?

He thought about calling the police again. No, not till I figure out what's going down. How badly was Beth injured? The blood on the bunk wasn't much, but it was enough to make him mad. Shit, if I call the police, they'll be here for hours. How the hell am I gonna explain two bodies? I can't search for Beth with them around.

The cut, the bruises, and welts on his head and arms would be proof of self-defense. But the body in the water wouldn't show much, except for drowning and superficial injuries. Better try to find the body. Keep a lid on this.

Satisfied with his first good decision, he gathered his shallow water breathing gear. He stood on the boat's fantail in his wet suit and felt better. Back in harness again? You got the guts to get on this thing? Come on, Cat, let's do it.

He set his watch timer for thirty minutes and slipped into the water. He tested his facemask and tank operation and went under. He probed the murky water with a high intensity light and searched the immediate area.

Best was livid when Ace Murphy reported on the phone that the frogman had probably killed the two hit men. "There wasn't supposed to be any fight."

"Yeah, but he talks to himself, and he said he's gonna call the police. I didn't want to take a chance on it. That's why we got the boat ready to beat it."

Best answered. "Damn you! Take the woman out and dump her. We'll take care of him. Take off!"

Two cars approached the marina. Four men looked around and moved silently to Haggerty's boat. The leader stepped aboard and motioned the others to follow. They searched the boat rapidly. The first man to board said, "Je-sus. He aced Denny. Fred missing. Frog ain't here either, Gus. Now what?"

"Shit. Wait a minute. Look, some diving gear broken

out. Maybe he went in the water again looking for Fred."

"Yeah, we can pop him when he comes back."

"If he comes back."

Jeff Stone positioned one man in the shadows ashore near the boat. He stationed a second on the bridge with a shotgun. The third man was in the open stern with an Uzi. He stayed in the cabin, covering the exposed man outside. "Don't forget, soon as he breaks out of the water, blow the shit out of him. And stay freaking alert. He already wasted two guys."

The boat's telephone rang. Jeff answered it. "Hello? Who? Yeah. We're waiting for him. No sweat. He's probably in the water, got his diving gear out. Hey we're not going in after him. I got a surprise party for him. Okay. Gotcha. I told my boys, hit him on sight." He shifted his position so he could observe the man ashore and the one in the open stern. They'd waste the bastard and pack him up for a sea trip.

The man in the open stern asked, "How long we gonna wait for the asshole? What if he went somewhere else?"

"It's not your worry, Nip. Just stay freaking alert, huh? The man on the phone told me he got bout a half hour of air. Ought a be coming back soon. You up there, Gus?"

"Yeah. Don't see shit. Saw a light out past some of the boats. I ain't seen it again."

Stone grunted. Hits were always like this. Waiting and waiting for the mark, stewing if something went wrong, then it would go down in a rush, spotting and aiming at the target. Blasting away, making sure the guy was really dead.

Haggerty remembered that the tide was going out. He started from underneath the boat out toward the channel, working silently. His life started to return in pieces. The underwater sounds, the air system, being on an op. It felt good. He had to be careful that he didn't cut his suit with all the junk on the bottom. The body could be caught somewhere or long gone. His side and head ached. Was searching the thing to do? Working in the water helped to clear his mind.

Stolen Votes

He was tired and found nothing along the bottom but silt, boots, tires, pieces of seagoing gear, and even a commode. No body. Ten minutes remained on his watch. He felt a trickle of cold water around his ankle and was ready to pack it in and get coffee. He could cover more with his skiff anyway. He searched toward the channel, close to the shallow areas. The Cat was so intent that his watch alarm jerked him. Geez! Scared the hell out of me. Man, you're too nervous.

When he surfaced, his boat was behind a line of others about a hundred yards away. Sure didn't get very far. He pulled off his mask and disconnected the breathing apparatus. He poked around in the weeds working his way back to the boat. He kept looking back at the marina periodically. This is a helluva way to make your night rounds. He made a wide swing to the other side of the channel, approaching with some semblance of surveillance. Being careful.

Joseph Guion

CHAPTER TWENTY SEVEN

Nelson sighed and walked into the den at his Chevy Chase mansion. Best had alerted him on an unsecured line. "More trouble?" He insisted on switching to voice on the secure phone. "What do you mean, you lost two men? What the hell is going on down there? Do I have to come down and take over?"

"That won't be necessary." He explained the situation from Murphy's report. "It's under control. They've snatched one man's body and they'll dispose of it. Nobody knows where the other one is or when it might wash up on shore someplace. The guy was a pro, no ID, no weapons with any tracing possibilities. Two men are watching the frogman. I have a bridge on his telephone. If he calls the cops, we can switch it and answer it ourselves. I have two men with police IDs ready to roll."

"That would only delay the inevitable. We've got to find out what he knows and if he's told anyone else. What about her?"

"On the way out. I'm sending them out to deep water. It takes maybe two-three hours. They should be ready in about another hour and a half."

"Let me think. I'll call you back."

Wallace placed the phone back carefully and drained a tumbler of Black Jack. "Damn that frogman." He called back. "What does she know?"

"From the tapes I heard she has suspicions. No actual facts. Knows about special projects but not what is in them."

"Has she told the frogman or anyone else?"

"Hard to tell. She says he doesn't know a damn thing. He's been alerted now after being attacked. The girl pulled off a shrewd bit. Left her ring on the boat. If he didn't talk to himself, we'd be in the blind. How about her as a hostage?"

"Let me think about it. You say we have about an hour and a half?"

"Probably closer to an hour. But you never know with those bastards. The Mechanic is something. He gets anxious sometimes and might move up the schedule. I wouldn't want to be in her shoes, I know that."

Nelson grunted. "A priest called him? What about him?"

"Yeah, before the drunk got here. They're buddies, pals or something. The guy needs a shrink and the priest helped him. I think he's clean. We'll find out more when they start talking."

"Yes. I don't want any foolish moves until we find out everything that is said." The voice turned quiet and deadly. "You know, this is a screw up of royal proportions. I cannot afford another one. Now that the man is alert, he'll be harder to handle. His Navy record is pretty impressive except for the end of it. They don't pick shrinking violets for SEAL teams. I imagine he's deadly in the water even though he's out of shape."

"Yeah. I admit that we might have underestimated him. But that won't happen again. How is he going to stay in the water and stop us? He's alerted, but he doesn't know where we're coming for him or when. We pick our time and place."

"It better not be in the water." Nelson paused for that to sink in. "I don't think that you understood my words before. I am reluctant to say this. I can and will go down to take charge if necessary. The plan must work. I'll make sure of it, if no one else can!"

"I haven't let you down before and I won't do it this time. You're the boss. If you want to come here, okay. I wouldn't suggest it."

Nelson wanted to get closer to the action anyway. Remote control work wasn't quite satisfying. "I'll call you back in half an hour."

He poured four fingers of Black Jack. He downed the bourbon and called for a stand-by aircraft. Packing quickly, he thought. "I'll finish off that bastard of a frogman myself if I have to."

The boat rolled and pitched in a jerky, irregular motion. Beth felt motion sickness again. She lay on her back naked, tied up on a double bunk in the after cabin. The mauve and blue ceiling was so close that it increased her nausea. The cabin was climate controlled and cool, but she was perspiring.

Oh, my God, what is happening? Who are these people? They must have something to do with the network, the computer system, and Tony's death. She felt near death herself. Oh, my baby, my poor baby. She moaned, thinking about that awful day, that terrible decision she had made when she was desperate and aborted her child. The bruises on her face throbbed. They were minor, the nausea worse.

She knew what was going to happen. It would be a relief. Drowning in the cold, deep water would end it. The mocking cruelty and the absence of any human feeling in the snake-eyed monster ripped away all hope. The man they called The Mechanic would torture and rape her, then he would kill her. She prayed. "Oh, Lord Jesus, help me die in your favor. Forgive me all my sins. For my sin of killing my baby."

Up in the milk-white cabin Ace told The Mechanic. "We got over an hour left. Let's tie her up and get a drink."

"No! I got business with her." He worked on the stained knife blade until it sparkled in the cockpit lights.

"What you gonna do, cut 'em off?" Red asked.

"Yeah. But first, I wanna see how good a whore she is. You guys can have sloppy seconds if you want." He left them.

Red shivered. "Ace, where the hell did you dig up that bastard? I've seen some crazies, but this one takes them all. And them eyes. I never saw the son of a bitch blink."

Ace chuckled. "Yeah, The Mechanic ain't to be trifled with. He's like a pit bull after a bone when it comes to a kill. Nothing stops him. He caught one in the side from a .357 Magnum, rolled back up, and planted two between that cop's eyes. He picked off the guy's partner running away. Don't screw with him. Give him orders and stay away."

"You gonna try the woman?"

"Sure, what the hell. She ain't no virgin. Course you might get lost in there with that little piece you got."

"Bullshit. Come on let's flip for seconds."

Beth could feel the man's presence with her eyes closed. The creeping cloud of sweet perfume that he wore made her stomach convulse. She squeezed her eyelids as much as she could, trying to shut out the pain and devastation of the rape.

"Hey, bitch. Open those big blue eyes. I got a present for you."

The voice had the piercing sound of sliding a steel plate along another. A chill ran through her as he laid the cold knife between her breasts. He patted a fleshy mound with the flat of the blade, "It ain't that bad, bitch. I'm gonna give you the last good screw you'll ever have. Open your eyes or I turn the blade."

He was naked, bending over her. The look in his eyes was more repulsive than a rape could be. She pleaded with him. Again. Again. Closed her eyes once more and prayed.

Wallace called another contact in Virginia Beach to explain

what had happened. "Remember, I gave you a Plan B about confusing that frogman bastard?"

"Plan B? Oh yeah, I remember."

"You remember the details?"

After hearing the man recite the steps over the secure phone, Wallace said, "Okay. You do it and I'll tell my other group to work with you on it. They got fake cops already lined up. Make it work. You got that!"

"Yes, sir!"

Wallace shut off the conversation without another word. *Now I've got that frogman by the nuts two ways. Time for more Black Jack.*

Stone cursed at the ringing telephone. "Don't that bastard trust me?" It wasn't a contact. He coughed and disguised his voice. "No, he ain't here right now. I'm one of his buddies from the UDT. He went into the water a little while ago. He'll be back soon. You want him to call you, Father Stew? No? You'll stop by. Okay. I'll tell him."

"That freaking priest friend of his again. Better check in." He dialed the stakeout number and talked to Best. "Hell, I don't know where he went. I think he's in the water, maybe searching for Fred. I don't know. Well, we got a call from the priest guy. I don't know what the hell for. He's coming here. Look we can wait and jump him easy. Well, if that's what you want. Yeah, I'll wait till you call back."

Stone called his men together and explained their orders. "You don't like it, tell the man yourself. Now hit it you two. Me and Nip will wait right here for that fucker."

Two men left Haggerty's boat and went to the parking lot out of sight. They drove back and parked by the pier. After placing the dead body in the car trunk they waited for their victim. Two were on deck, one below, and the other up on the flying bridge where he could see around the marina. Ten long minutes went by. They jumped when the phone rang. Jeff disguised his voice. It was his contact. "Yeah? Oh shit. Yeah. We got the stiff stuffed in the trunk. How about leaving somebody here on board? Okay you're the doctor."

Haggerty had worked his way around so that he had a clear view of his boat. He watched four men shove off. Two drove off in the car near the boat. The others went to another vehicle and drove out of sight. He wondered. Anyone else aboard? Damn! Wish I'd a brought a weapon besides my K-bar knife. It would have to do. If he could get aboard and find them fast enough, he had a chance. He swam back silently, thinking about Beth. He had to find her fast. What kind of danger was she in? What was it all about? Was this real? Damned sight right! Am I in a war? He was dying for a drink. Was that the way to go?

Wait one. If I can grab one of those bastards, I might be able to get him to talk. A knife prick or two at the throat is a convincer sometimes. Better be careful, Cat, you ain't up to speed yet. Stay alive! Beth needs you.

CHAPTER TWENTY EIGHT

Blustery rain had pelted down on the Hampton Roads area, leaving a chill in the air and in Dan's heart. Who had taken Beth? Why? Where was she? He sat on the boat's transom, dazed. He couldn't believe that the killer's body was missing. Traces of blood on the bunk had disappeared and there was no evidence of a fight, except on his person. He had a welt on the side of his head, another on his cheek. The cabin reeked of booze, as if someone had spilled a bottle. Had he?

Father Stew stepped on the boat. "What's going on here? Someone on the phone said that they were on board. A friend from UDT? You look like you had a fight. What happened?"

"Huh? UDT?" Dan wagged his head. "Nobody's here! Stew, sit down. I don't know what's happening." He held his head with his hands. "I'll tell you what's goin' on. Then you can help. See if I'm dreaming or somethin'."

He told the priest about the attack and fight with two men. He mentioned the mixed emotions about being back in the water on a mission. "Stew, I don't know what happened to the dead body, or the one in the water. But dammit, there was one aboard."

He pointed at the spot. "It was right there, against the bulkhead. I slugged him and he fell, hit his head on the cleat there. It killed him. I checked his pulse. He dint have any. I checked it before I went back in the water."

Stew seemed interested, perhaps skeptical. "You were in the water? What for?"

"Thought I better search for the body of the guy who knifed me. Geez, I forgot. Look here." He pulled the adhesive off the wound. Blood oozed out of the cut.

"You'd better get that looked at. Why haven't you called a doctor? The police?"

"Don't think I got internal injuries. Hey, it's a damned good thing I dint call the police. What would they say? No bodies. No sign of a fight. How much have you been drinking? I, I just need to think this thing out."

"What thing? What is going on? Where is Beth?"

"That's something else. I don't know where she is. She was here. Yeah, look. Here's her ring." He slipped it out of his pocket. "It was on my bunk in the covers. There were traces of blood down there too."

"Traces of blood? Show me."

Haggerty shook his head. "It aint there any more."

"What? You can't hide bloodstains. If there was blood, let's find it."

"No use. I looked damned careful. I pulled the sheets off the mattress and turned the mattress over. Nothing. The blood was on the sheet and maybe on the cover. But now? I'm not sure. That's why I had a few scotches. Other reasons too."

"You're sure it was blood, and not something else."

He sighed. "I seen too much damned blood not to know what it looks like; fresh, semi-fresh, old, dried up. The whole bit. I tell you. This thing is like a dream."

"Well the knife wound isn't. Where did you get that? And those other bruises? You were drinking again weren't you? Could it have happened in a bar?"

"You don't believe me, huh?" Haggerty was getting pissed and anxious. Did he really have a fight on the boat?

Didn't he? Maybe he had been at the Anchor Inn.

The attempted rape ended when she vomited into his face.

He coughed, jumped off her, and slapped her with both hands. He screamed, "You fucking pig! Whore! Bitch! I cut off your tits!"

The stench made it worse. Beth kept retching until nothing came out. She turned her head sideways so that she wouldn't choke herself to death. He hit her so hard that she lost consciousness. She slipped into comforting darkness and prayed that she wouldn't come out of it.

The others charged in. Ace frowned but stayed silent.

Red said, "Jesus, you sure screwed the puke out of her. Man what talent." He was shoved against the bulkhead and slapped three times before he knew what had happened.

Ace stepped in. "Cut it out, dammit. I ain't gonna fool around here. We got a job and we do it. The screwin' is over. Clean yourself and her up. I'll get the crewman to clean up this mess. You don't know how damn finicky the owner of this boat is. After she's cleaned up, we tie her up. The weights are on deck. I'm not waitin' till we get out to the Norfolk Canyon like we said. You two are too damned dangerous."

"No you don't!" The Mechanic snatched up his knife. "I cut her before she goes."

Ace looked at death in the man's eyes. He knew better than to cross him. "All right, Mechanic. But do it out on deck where the blood can get washed over the side. Let's go."

Lights of a car coming into the marina toward them stopped the conversation on the boat. The Cat was wary. When he saw that it was a police car, he clenched his fists.

A uniformed officer from the Norfolk Police and a plainclothes man climbed aboard. The latter asked, "Which one of you is Dan Haggerty?"

The Cat stood and weaved. "I am."

The plain clothes flipped open a wallet showing a police id. He closed it quickly. "I'm Sergeant Thomas. This is officer Clemens. And who may you be, sir?"

"I'm Father Steward from the Hampton Retreat Center."

"Glad to meet you, Father. You been here all night?"

"No. I just came aboard about ten minutes ago. Why, what's going on?"

"Not much, Father. Just a little disturbance down the road a piece. Your friend here got in a knife fight with a guy at the Anchor Inn. The other one went to DePaul emergency, but he's been released. This guy was gone when we arrived. I wanted to check his story with the other man and witnesses. The other guy won't press charges. They were together in UDT. Eight witnesses say he started it over some gal, uh wait."

He flipped open a notebook and read. "The gal's name is Elizabeth Olson. You know her Mister Haggerty?"

Dan stood there, mouth open, cow-like; with a vacant expression on his face. He couldn't believe this. Father Stew was looking at him like he was an idiot. "Uh, yeah, I know Miss Olson. Where is she by the way?"

"Well, I'm not at liberty to say. You see, she said that she didn't want to see you again. She's afraid of you. That's why she asked if we'd pick up her ring." He grinned. "That's what the argument was about, Father."

Stew cut in. "Would you please identify the ring?"

"Sure." He consulted a page in the book. "It's a birthstone ring, uh, dark amethyst. Yellow gold with her initials on the inside." He grinned. "It's okay Father. She isn't going to press charges either. But she sure doesn't want to see him again."

The detective held out his hand for the ring and Dan handed it over in silence. He was dazed. What the hell was going on?

"How's the stab wound, Mister Haggerty? Better get it looked at by a doctor. You never know. Will you be here tomorrow? Me and my partner may come back and ask a few more questions in case there are charges filed. Here's my card. If you decide to leave town, maybe you better call me huh?" He waved a salute and they left the boat.

After a long silence Haggerty rose slowly and went to the bar. He poured a large scotch. "You want one Stew?"

"No! Please give me the bottle. Drinking into a stupor won't help to settle this." The priest took the half-filled glass from him. "Now, let's take some time. Sit down and tell me everything that comes into your mind. It doesn't matter if it's incoherent, stark reality or fantasy. Maybe start somewhere else besides tonight. The last few times we were together you were getting close to telling me about Viet Nam. Could you go back that far? Or farther?"

Haggerty felt like hell, beaten up, unable to understand what had happened. The only reality was the knife wound. It gnawed at his side like a rat trying to pierce a wall.

"Father I don't know where to start. I don't know what's real and what ain't. This thing tonight." His voice trailed off. He looked away. "Tell me. Am I going off my rocker? Did I have a blackout or something?"

"I don't know, Dan. I just don't know. Uh. Let's just say you could have had a blackout. But, let's work up to that, okay? Just a minute. Let me make a phone call."

Haggerty waved at the phone and went aft to look at the water. Maybe that was the answer. Down into the depths, into the sea, the sea that called to him. What would it be like drifting off down, waiting for death. It would be easy. No dreams. Nothing.

The priest dialed Beth's apartment. After two rings a woman answered. Father Stew identified himself and asked for Beth.

"Father, I'm sorry but Beth is asleep right now. She had a terrible experience and the doctor prescribed a sedative." The woman laughed. "I guess I'm sort of baby-sitting tonight. I'll make sure that she calls you in the morning."

"Could you tell me what happened?"

After he heard her the same story as the detective's with

small differences of little consequence, he shook his head. When he told Dan that Beth had verified the story, he saw Haggerty's entire body sag.

"You're telling me I'm crazy?"

"No, Dan. I'm just telling you that there's been a big mistake. You had a fight in a bar and you thought that it was on board here. Maybe you—."

"Get the hell of my boat! Get off! Dammit, you're just the like the rest of them. Pat the vet on the head. Tell him he's a nut case. Well, Bullshit. I don't need you, priest!"

Stew backed away from the menacing figure. There was a wild look in Haggerty's eyes. The clergyman retreated from the boat and called back, "Call me as soon as you can."

"Dammit! Get the hell out of here!" He drained the bottle of scotch. "God, Tony. Bobby. Beth? Where am I? What's going on? Jesus." He was overwhelmed. Whispering. "Watch it Doc, two o'clock." In a ready weapons crouch, he looked down. The green bottle was in his right hand. His index finger was searching for the trigger.

Wallace called Ace from the Lear aircraft and switched to the scrambler mode.

Murphy reported. "Your idea is working great. The guy is really screwed up and our cops did it just right."

"Now we're getting somewhere. I must find out what they know. What about playing one of them against the other? Threaten her with death in front of him."

"So you want me bring her back in. We'll use her as a hostage too."

"Fine. Unless we can take the SEAL alone."

After they ended the conversation Wallace told the radio operator to call the boat again. The radioman reported, "I think I've got him, but it isn't quite clear."

Wallace heaved his bulk out of the chair. "I'll do the talking. You said that everybody and his brother are able to hear it."

"Anybody can listen." He called the boat twice, saying, "Urgent message for you." He gave Wallace the handset.

"Good Haven, this is N. Come back right away without dropping off your load. I mean it. Come back right away. Uh. Over."

There was static on the receiver speaker, but no words.

"Shit, I better try again."

"Wait one. If that's all you have to say let me try it. Good Haven. Good Haven. This is N. I repeat N. Urgent message. You must acknowledge. Return to port immediately. Do not, repeat, do not drop off load. Acknowledge!"

On the boat, the Mate had throttled down and that increased the rolling motion. He jockeyed it around to bring the swells off the port bow. Night floodlights illuminated the open stern. The woman's nude body was lying on the open deck of the fantail. She was tied, arms against her body and legs out straight. The fishing port was open, enabling them to shove her directly into the sea. An old anchor, hanging outboard, would take her down into the depths.

"Okay, Mechanic. She's all yours. Just get through with it and push her over."

He turned to his pleasure. "Open your eyes. I'm the last man you're gonna see."

Beth was beyond crying or calling out. She was simply a limp body of flesh, waiting for the torturer to put her beyond the horror. Her throat burned from the vomiting and there was searing pain from the rape. She wondered if the Jews felt this way in the concentration camps. No hope, no chance, only the blessed release of death.

Oh, Dan. She prayed for him and had thoughts of Jesus on the cross, dying for her and her sins, for all sins. For sinners. And she was an awful one. She had killed her baby. Could she be forgiven for the abortion? If she could forgive first. Could she forgive the rapist? Satan personified? She prayed for that strength.

Stolen Votes

    The Mechanic bent over her, his face gleamed in the lights with anticipation and pleasure. The boat rolled and Beth heard shouts from the flying bridge. She blinked and watched two men grab at the monster. One pulled back the man's knife, the other turned him around. He fought them and she saw blood spilled. They subdued him finally. She closed her eyes and silently prayed her thanks to Jesus.

Joseph Guion

CHAPTER TWENTY NINE

The next day Ned Henshaw hurried out of Reverend Creed's office. The techs had called for him at the Computer Center. As time ran down for the plan's full operation, he became more irritable and nervous. He had emptied a half bottle of antacids, but the hot burning in his stomach hadn't been quenched. It was all for GRASS ROOTS, so it had to be correct, righteous.

At the computer center Doug was acting as Ops System boss, because Ned had sent Dawson to Williamsburg for liaison. Sam was the computer operator and Jules worked to check the satellite feed. The latter nodded, "Looks like we've got it. The signal was too visible before, needed a little tweak, but she's perfect now. Take a look."

Ned watched the television monitor. The regular Truth Network program was coming through with a perfect picture. He noticed a slight indication of normal interference and asked, "Is the data going out right now?"

Doug grinned, "You bet. Can't tell huh? See that touch of random blips? That's it."

Ned watched the printer grind out data pages and

cracked a rare smile. He tilted his head. Yes, it was working. The data was piggybacked on the television signal at random times. At the receiving end, a special decoder unscrambled the signal.

Ned remarked, "Incredible. The thing will work. What's to prevent the FCC or someone else from decoding it too?"

"Can't. You need a big number cruncher to recognize that there's anything but random noise. Besides that, we're shifting at odd intervals to squat bursts. You know, sending the signals in microsecond pieces. It would take a long time to monitor all that with an IBM 360 or better. Heck, it'll be over in less than fifteen hours."

He wet dry lips. "Yes it will be. Uh, how's the feedback checkout?"

Sammy punched in codes. The printer stopped momentarily and resumed. Doug waved. "Take a look. That's the input from the receivers. I set up a line to check 'em out."

Unidentified columns of numbers appeared on the paper. Without the column heading templates, it was impossible to tell what the data meant. Doug showed how they matched.

"Nothing to it. This is the last test run. We've got the whole weekend, plus. We're ninety-seven percent accurate. With some built in redundancy, maybe ninety-nine plus."

Ned sighed. The success of the system boosted his morale. He had to get back to his office. He had to call Cherry to see if she and the kids were all right. Were there any threats from "C." He had promised to call his contact back. What was wrong? He shuddered. If his contact was in trouble, where did it leave him? If the thing worked and no one discovered it, he was going to be free. There was no way to stop the system now. He leaned on that as a life-giving crutch.

The killers held Beth in a rented house in Sandbridge, a remote area of Virginia Beach. She drifted in and out of consciousness, sometimes into reality. She had little fight left, feeling a half step from seeking the release of death. She moaned with pain. Her breasts burned. Her right eye was closed. "Lord Jesus. You died for my sins. Help me."

When lights were flipped on and a woman entered, Beth spoke. "Oh, thank God. Please help."

"Thank your ass, sweetie." She turned and called behind her. "The big bitch is awake. Who gets first crack at her."

The sneer on the woman's untidy face made Beth gasp. She looked like a long distance runner, slim and muscular. Long unkempt hair was parted carelessly in the middle over a pockmarked square face. The woman leaned down to pat Beth on the butt. A sour, sweaty smell made Beth nauseous.

Realizing that she was still captive was bad enough. A disgusting dyke handling her body crushed her spirit. Her dry heaves returned. She wept.

Ace walked in. "Shit, she's bawling. Hey Lonnie, what'd you say to her?"

"Nothin.' Just told her I'd have my turn." Her lop-sided grin disclosed a gap between teeth.

He shook his head. "Stuff some coffee in her and some toast. Gotta make a call."

When Lonnie approached, Beth cringed. The suggestive banter made it worse. She could barely down the hot coffee and the toast without feeling ill. She struggled with the food and asked to go to the bathroom. The woman ran her hands up Beth's legs before untying her. She stood over her victim in the bathroom watching as she relieved herself. Lonnie ran her hands over Beth's body on the way back to the bed. The sick feeling the woman created made Beth feel degraded, totally without hope.

Ace returned with The Mechanic close behind. He jerked his thumb at the snake-eyed killer. "You know this guy?"

Fear turned Beth's face to a Halloween paste mask.

Murphy grinned. "Yeah, you know him all right. I'm only gonna tell you once. We're gonna call Father Steward. The frogman's friend? You tell him exactly what we tell you. No more, no less." He pointed at The Mechanic. "You pull any fast ones or say anything we don't tell you, he gets you."

She scrambled to pull the covers up to her chin.

"You gonna do what I tell you?"

She nodded, her rounded eyes were fixed on the knifer.

"Remember, I pulled this guy off you last night. He's pissed, anxious to cut you up. You don't want that. Do you?"

Frantic nods. She clutched the covers, grasping the only reality she had.

"You say hello like a nice little shit and you tell him exactly what I wrote here. Read it back to me. I want a good performance."

She read it with the words blurred from tears. She had to tell Steward that she was all right, that she was going to Williamsburg for the convention. Then she would ask him to tell Dan that she never wanted to see him again. She had to talk about a fight in a bar. She would thank the priest for helping to get her ring back. It was confusing. She had to do it. Beth repeated the story three times before Ace dialed the retreat house.

When Father Steward came on the line he announced, "Father this is a friend of Beth Olson. Yes, she's fine. Wants to talk to you."

The dark eyes held her in a death grip. Her hand shook so much that she could hardly hold the phone. She uttered a silent prayer and engaged in some small talk first. A poke in the ribs was her reward for not answering the question about how she was.

"Oh, yes. I'm fine. The Network was very kind. They let me take off to Nags Head. It was so peaceful down there." Then she went through the entire message without a slip. When she finished, she wanted to hint at her plight.

Apparently Ace had the same idea. He motioned for The Mechanic to lean on the bed. Cold snake eyes watched her. He was sharpening his knife. She couldn't try anything.

The priest asked if she were going to Williamsburg, and she faltered for a second. The knife touched her belly. "Oh, the Network people are staying at the Inn. But I'm going to be at the Magruder. It will be away from things and I can rest."

"Great! I'll be up at the same motel. I'll call and look for you."

Beth thanked him. She was crushed when they snatched the phone from her.

Ace remarked, "Ain't you a nice sweet little thing. For that you get me!"

They watched as Lonnie tied her up and fondled her before pushing her down on the bed. Beth closed her eyes as the men trooped out. Would she be safer with them?

A bleary-eyed, on-the-ropes Cat dragged himself out of the bunk. Hurting all over. His head hurt the most. Head job. That's what he was. Screwed up. What a night? Did I kill two men last night? Where are the bodies? He couldn't seem to concentrate. His head felt like a scrambled mass of tangled wires. He stopped to think how he could turn on the shower.

Cat, are you crazy? Did you dream all that shit? Stew didn't believe him. Like he was giving me a pat on the head and saying, 'you poor war veteran. Go on, tell your story.' Was it a 'Nam flashback? Where was I last night? On the boat? In a bar? Beth's ring. Gone. Beth, Baby. Gotta call Beth. He stepped out of the shower half-soaped and dialed.

A woman answered. "I'm sorry, she isn't here. She said she doesn't want to see you any more Mister Haggerty. I think you should respect her wishes."

He had some fight left. "Bullshit! Let her decide. Where is she?"

"I'm not at liberty to say."

He wanted to blast the woman, but he slammed the phone down and looked at himself. He had forgotten that he had started a shower. Jesus, better watch it. The Cat is crazy huh? Crazy Cat? He laughed. A high-pitched, idiotic laugh.

He eased the bandage off the knife wound. It was still oozing. He dashed peroxide on it. By the time the body's impulse to react arrived, his mouth opened without a sound.

Pain cut through fog. Pain in the head, arms, shin, side and back. Walkin' wounded.

He drove to Beth's apartment. On the way he noticed a car trailing a half block behind. It seemed familiar. Shit. First you black out after a fight in a bar. Then you're on the boat killing guys. Now, being followed. Paranoid? Get hold of it!

At Beth's apartment a woman cracked open the door and kept the chain tight. "I told you. She's not here. She's gone away for a while. You didn't help her with that fight and the knife business. Now, please leave. I'll call the police if you don't."

The Cat could have broken the door chain with a shove from his shoulder. What the hell good would it do? He had to think. Get away. Yeah. Run away. That's what he had done after Nam. He cursed and hit the door jam with his hand.

CHAPTER THIRTY

A cold front moved rapidly into Hampton Roads. Dan didn't notice until he stepped outside and felt a chill northeast wind blow a grey cloud overhead. It was as if someone were sliding a vault cover over a casket, his. Shitty day, all over. He put on an old Navy foul weather jacket before he left the boat.

A sense of hopelessness broke over him like a rouge wave. He checked with the marina office and trudged on his rounds, going through the motions, checking security and the boats. Rage over Tony's death and the physical beatings had sapped his energy and his mind. An idea pinged at him, and then slipped away. A thread connecting him to reality?

The killing on the boat and in the water had become superimposed. Did someone try to garrote him? Did someone stop a bar fight with a cord making the mark on his neck? What happened to the body on the boat? The other one? When did he take Beth's ring? Last night he was back in an ambush with Doc. That wasn't real. The smell was missing. The God-awful stench of 'Nam, death, rot, jungle. Mildewed boots, sapping humidity, all missing.

Who was missing? Bobby? Tony? Steward? Smitty? Oh Jesus, poor Smitty. Impaled for hours on a pungi trap before we found him with wooden points sticking through him. He begged me to kill him. I shot the poor bastard between the eyes to put him out of his misery. We took almost an hour to pry his body loose so that we could carry it back to base.

Was there life left in The Cat? Another life? Something jigged his brain. Something was not right. He grasped at a thread. No. It's something else. Somethin' saying, "Bullshit!" You killed Tony. You killed Bobby. Smitty! He padded slowly toward the boat. Lifting a hand, he tried to touch the wind, or was it to touch the thread?

If the men tailing him realized The Cat's condition, they could have walked up to him and led him to his death without resistance. His will to fight was long gone. He was drawn to the sea, to find the answer, or the end. On automatic, instinct. He methodically unhooked the shore power and took in the lines. He lighted off the diesels as the boat drifted off the pier. He swung out the stern and headed toward the channel.

He passed within twenty feet of the Hatteras that had arrived shortly before. He didn't notice their frantic effort, breaking the phone lines and getting ready to get underway. He had to get to sea. The answer was out there, in the depths. He should have called Stew, given him the computer. Given Beth back the Nag's Head mug. Beth. Oh, God, I love her.

The first welcoming roll outside Cape Henry usually gave him a sense of union with the sea. But he was too far-gone. The stunning slap of a six-foot wave in the ocean and its dousing spray snapped him from his vision of a thread.

Man, that's cold! He grinned. "Damn! Loose gear down below."

He checked sparse traffic outside The Cape and secured the wheel with the sea coming in twenty degrees off his port bow. The loud "swish" and "thud" of waves hitting the boat sounds made him grin. A big sports fisherman pounded along behind him. He slid down the ladder.

"Shit!" Forgot to secure the computer for sea, could have

lost that bugger. He worked rapidly, tying loose gear down. He finished with a fresh pot of coffee secured in the rack on the stove. The jarring motion stirred the Cat's seagoing juices. Was there a glimmer of hope someplace? Back on the flying bridge, he inhaled the fresh breeze.

A gray squall dropped a soft curtain in front of the horizon. When it passed over him, it washed the salt off his lips. He sipped black coffee laced with bourbon, watching waves attack the boat, shoving her around. She wasn't fast, but she was comfortable in a sea. The horizon beckoned ahead, fuzzy, light grey, with a somber backdrop behind. Where was he going? How far? Did he have enough fuel? Didn't matter. Nothing mattered, except to open his mind up to nothing, allowing the sea and wind to sweep out skeletons.

A shaft of dazzling white light pulled his eyes. The sun stabbed a probe into the heaving sea two miles away. Silver and chrome shining like a new bumper on a gray car. It disappeared when the shining jewels in the sea were cut out, like switching off Christmas lights.

He started to doze. The motion lulled him, wrapped him in a cocoon of safety, even with a boat trailing him. He woke later, starting from a jumbled dream. Bobby's face, Tony's. Screaming at him. A gory mess closed his eyes, eyes sticky with blood. He rubbed at them, sticky and gritty from salt. He bumped against the frame of the canopy and shivered. Geez. Wind chill must be down in the thirties. He pulled the jacket collar up around his neck. A thought made him shiver too.

He knew why he was on the boat, steaming zero nine zero. He was giving up. He had come to sea for The Cat's burial. The aimless trip would certainly end at sea. The realization unrolled like a chart. He'd stay on that easterly course till the boat ran out of fuel. Then he'd get into his diving gear and slide down to meet his end. He'd find peace. He'd see Bobby, Tony. He snuggled against the side of the chair. It would be so easy.

He dozed again. The thread was finally there, in front of him. It slowly drifted away and came apart at the same time.

Threads parting without a sound. Strands unraveling. Now down to only two of them. Did it really matter?

He could end all the shit he had lived through since he had killed Bobby. It would be so damned easy just to let everything go to hell, where he'd end up anyway.

On the trailing Hatteras, a few of the less hardy souls were feeling the effects of the sea's motion. As usual, the men who never had motion sickness were riding their ill companions unmercifully. One of them spoke to the unfortunates lying in bunks and groaning. "What's the matter? Guess what we're having for dinner? Fried pork chops cooked in their own grease and fat." Their response included more groans and barfing into buckets.

Another man who had a hitch in the Navy suggested remedies, most of which would make the seasickness worse.

"Don't eat anything or you'll keep throwing up. Don't stay outside, watching the waves will do you in." The worst idea was, "If you got to throw up, get over on the windy side, it makes it easier to barf."

After receiving some of the vomit back on themselves, two men realized that they were listening to the wrong advice.

Up in the enclosed cabin, Ace was more serious. "Red, what the hell you think the asshole came out here for? It's not a smooth ride. Can you get anything from the bugs?"

"Our freaking radio guy is tossing his cookies. I haven't heard a helluva lot except noise once in a while. The guy still talks to himself. Wind and ocean too noisy, can't get much."

"Are you taping it?"

"Yeah. You think I can't do my job? Maybe the frog is losing it. He mumbled a lot, a piece of it sounded like, '... answer out there' and something about 'not enough fuel.' and 'end it... last dive.' You think maybe, he's gone off his rocker?"

"That would be a help. Don't kid yourself. If this bastard

gets back anywhere near he was in the SEALs, he's a freaking hand full. Make sure the guys know that. And get those sick bastards fixed up. We need everybody ready in case we have to go over there and climb on that boat."

"Out here? You're kidding."

"We follow orders, friend. No matter what they are. We get the word to knock him off; he goes, no matter what it takes. Understand?"

Red nodded. "Better see if I can get a clue from the bugs. Then I'll get the 'sickies' up and push them." He checked Haggerty's boat with binoculars. "The stupid shit is out on the open bridge. It's freaking cold out there. Maybe he wants to freeze to death."

"No jokes. He's checked us in his glasses a couple of times. If he wants to join us and fight we've got him by numbers and firepower. Get going."

Ace sipped coffee and thought about Nelson's plans. If we stiff the bastard at Little Creek it's over. Problem is that the boss wanted to interrogate him. Tough choice to whack him permanently or hurt him and keep him alive. Not a good situation. If they didn't get him on the boat or in port, the next shot would be in Williamsburg with his sweetie up there as a hostage. That had more promise, because they could squeeze the hell out of both of them, to find out what they knew.

He thought of contacting Wallace, but he couldn't do it while they were on the boat. He needed a secure line. He knew that suggesting that they wait until they sprang the trap in Williamsburg would not go down well. Shit! It's his money. Or is it? He didn't want to go there. He didn't want to know another scrap of info that wasn't necessary. That search could get you killed in this outfit. He wanted a long peaceful life after he quit and moved out of the country.

Stolen Votes

CHAPTER THIRTY ONE

The sea showered and slapped The Cat awake. An odd wave had hit the Bertram almost on the beam. It rolled the old boat so violently that it snapped back, nearly throwing him out of the chair. Green water hit the bridge drenching the dozing sailor. He came out of it sputtering.

"What the hell? That was a biggie. Two more coming."

He swung the wheel to port to make the old boat chug up the face of the wave and crash down in the trough. She shuddered and plowed halfway through the next one, water coursing down the deck and into the open stern. The struggle exposed a slim piece of self-preservation.

He laughed. "Come on, you old witch, you can still take it." So could he. Hanging on to that thread.

Dan shook his head to clear it. What the hell was bugging him? The blinding flash of afternoon sun reflecting on the silver water off his starboard sought his attention. His eyes feasted on the sparkling water, foaming and cresting in the sunlight. He grinned and relaxed. He couldn't let go of that slight thread. The shaft of sunlight made it disappear. He reached toward the light. His arm revealed blood and a scar.

He struggled out of the dream, ready for coffee and bourbon. His eyes ran along the fuzzy horizon. The white boat was two miles astern. Followed again? At sea?

The effort required to keep his feet and steer awakened more than aching muscles. The memories were good ones. Steaming at sea, the crazy fun and grab-ass with shipmates and SEAL buddies. Running from an insertion after trying to locate a tax collector hooch in the dark, weapons ready.

The dark side of 'Nam was like the overcast, hanging a darkness over the horizon. "Bullshit!" He stood and grabbed the windscreen. What the hell? Something told him that he wasn't crazy, that he hadn't been into a flashback. The attacks, the bodies were real. He checked gauges. Need fuel.

The expert helmsman was back at his craft. He spun the helm to port, timing his turn to prevent rolling on her beam-ends. He gunned the engines. The boat hesitated at the top of a swell, dipped down into the trough. She leaned hard. The momentum kept her swinging to two seven zero. And the quartering sea caught the stern and lifted it up. The boat slewed sideways, released at the after end and dropped back with a crash. Something thumped down below. The noise returned when she slewed sideways. Thought you'd secured everything sailor. Better check later.

This was fun. Concentration had the juices flowing. He faced astern to watch. He caught a big swell just right and the Bertram skipped forward like a surfboard. He laughed. When he caught another one the same way, he shouted, "Gotcha!"

The sports fisherman came abeam, slowly turned north, then west about a mile astern. "Following me? Tough shit. You can catch me but you can't hurt me."

In the rhythm of the following sea, a single thought kept puttering around in his consciousness looking for an opening. Like the odd wave. One caught the boat wrong and staggered her. Wrestling with the helm, he knew that the hidden thought would come back every so often. One of these moments, he'd snatch it. He heard an occasional "Bang!' below.

Dan anchored three miles north northeast of Fisherman's

Island in the Chesapeake Bay. He needed to think. Six miles eastward Cape Charles Light winked at him. He sat in the conning seat, watching gulls wheel around, down at morsels in the water. Intermittent rain curtained off the Bridge Tunnel that stretched across the bay from Virginia Beach to the Eastern Shore.

He worried. "Beth, I love you. Where the hell are you? Who took you? Why?"

He ducked down into the saloon to search for the noisemaker. Holy Jesus, it's that second guy's shotgun. They were aboard, dammit. Weren't they? He reached for the weapon without a thought and his hands grasped at air. Come on, Cat, grab the son of a bitch. His arms and legs seemed to be immersed in molasses. He struggled to move toward the shotgun. Battling himself, he cursed again and again. Fucking shotguns! He kicked it away, defeated again.

In the gathering twilight, the big Hatteras anchored a mile away in the North Channel. Then it hit him. It hit so hard that it was like taking a punch in the solar plexus. Beth was on his mind. Sometimes we fight. We mix like gasoline and fire. If she saw me pour bourbon in my coffee, she'd throw her mug right over the side.

"Oh, my God! That's it. A fight in a bar with Beth? She wouldn't be caught dead in a bar! Son of a Bitch! Hit it!"

He threw the remains of the sandwich over the side. A gull snatched part of it before it hit the water. He punched the starter button and the old diesels growled into life. Heaving in the anchor, he set his jaw tight. Damn, Cat. Somethin' bad's been going down. It sure as shit ain't a 'Nam flashback. Somebody's after your ass. Bar fight, shit! There was a freaking body on here. And that damned weapon proves it.

He ran her back in fast. Alert now, he eyed the Hatteras as it got underway and charged towards Little Creek Channel. Bet the bastard's after me. This time let 'em come. I'm ready.

If I'm right, then Beth's in terrible danger. Got to find her. This time I'll knock down her apartment door.

CHAPTER THIRTY TWO

A red Mercedes raced down Interstate 64 on its way toward Williamsburg, Virginia. Whitney Carlton weaved in and out of traffic as if she were running for the lead at *Le Mans*. She took her anger out at herself and Magee. He had humiliated her for the last time. Acting as hostess for his wife was awful. When she saw the dog of a Reverend Creed and Magee's mocking smile, she wanted to turn the *hors d'oeuvres* over Frank's head.

That son of a bitch! He wants me in that old place for something special. I'll give him something special. She patted the brown purse in the other seat. A lightweight Beretta was hidden in a secret compartment. It was loaded, on safety, and had a .44 Magnum punch.

"Get out of the way, asshole."

She flipped the bird to a pickup cruising well below the speed limit in the left lane. She glanced at the mink draped over the passenger's seat and afforded herself a grim smile. From here on out, she'd milk everything she could get out of the son of a bitch. And then freedom. A shadow passed in her eyes and in her heart. That bastard had so many connections, and so many hard-nosed people owed him, that escaping from his grimy paws would be nearly impossible.

What did she have to lose? Wes had told her to be nice to Nelson Wallace, Magee's enemy. What was that about? She hated that ass hole too. His eyes had revealed contempt and lust when he saw her at odd moments in DC. If he ever had the guts to take her from Frank, he would rape and batter her. Never happen.

The Reverend Creed and his entourage were traveling to the same destination. His wife and son accompanied him in a black stretch limo headed for the ultimate hotel there, the Williamsburg Inn. The majority of the television evangelists were sparing no expense to be seen and to schmooze at that plush establishment where the televangelists' conference was being held.

He didn't pay attention to his wife's questions about the accommodations and the opportunity to shop at Merchant's Square. His thoughts raced between triumph and disaster. On the one hand, giving up a piece of his cherished network to Magee had been unthinkable. But recent sex and corruption publicity concerning other TV evangelists had resulted in a precipitous drop in donations at the Truth Network. The death of a hated homosexual in his own employ had disappeared from the local news media after his efforts at clever pressure.

Creed had to raise his reputation and influence into the higher echelons of TV evangelism. His plan to achieve this was the use of The Fox's reputation as a winner and great influence in power circles in the nation's capital. He would use Frank for his own purposes, even as he was being used. A fleeting thought of Whitney Carlton helped to start enough perspiration to require the use of another fresh handkerchief.

"Something wrong, dear?" his wife asked.

"No, no. A bit flushed. I have an unfortunate duty to perform. No one has attacked the disgraced preachers for their transgressions. Ah must be the one to call them to task."

"Praise the Lord." She patted his arm. "I know you will perform well as you always do."

"Thank you, my dear." His thoughts of Whitney caused him to tighten his jaw.

Ned and part of the staff, including his financial gurus, rode in different autos. The peons would be housed at the Fort Magruder on Route 60, a few miles from the Inn. Ned was unable to offset the sedan's air conditioning and perspired profusely during the one-hour drive from the network. He didn't want to be at the conference because he wanted to recheck the computer and satellite system. For some reason Beth was absent again. The Reverend told him that she was not feeling well. Creed had assured him that it wasn't serious.

It was better that the Satellite Manager was not at the network. She might have tried to nose around again to find out what was going to be transmitted during the election.

How could he have agreed to get involved with the scheme? In the beginning it had almost seemed like a fun game, no interference in the voting process and no one would get hurt. Tony's death had been a shock, one that he could never remove from his mind. Of course, the programmer was a homosexual, a pervert, soundly condemned in Scripture. But the horror of the shooting and the aftermath of turning aside persistent reporters had drained him.

Now, he could relax for a few days. The system had been double-checked more than once. The reliability had reached ninety-nine percent. A remarkable figure. He felt Cherry's hand slide inside his elbow. He smiled and covered her hand with his. The threat from his contact surfaced and gagged him, so that he was unable to comfort her. How could he keep his family safe?

The Fox flew from DC in his Boeing 707, its communication capability second only to Air Force One. When the scrambler

Stolen Votes

light came on, he sent Estelle to the after cabin. "Yes?"

His contact in Lebanon reported in a flat voice. "Five hundred packages were delivered on the twenty-eighth."

"Already knew of it."

He had received word that the TOW missiles had been delivered to Iran by Israel. His smile reflected his amusement at military designations. The anti-tank weapon was a "Tube launched, Optically tracked Wire guided missile."

"Sir, have you heard anything about some college students in country and another group who might publish info on the whole deal. Might cause some trouble in exposing the thing."

"Yes, I have. The principals are in Mainz, Germany now and the Iranian contacts said they almost didn't get out of the country. Seems like there were several million pamphlets out that opposed the connections between us and their reps. Also Hizballah radicals were reporting in Lebanon about it."

"Haven't seen or heard anything else."

The Fox squeezed the radio handset. "Dammit! I'll have to get after Casey. Anyone on my special list. Are you ready to act when I tell you?"

"Yes, sir. My guys are locked, loaded, ready for bear."

"This thing has gotten too visible. You may be their only hope to get out."

"Understood, sir."

"You heard that the DEA connection fizzled out?"

"You mean Mister Ross Perot's effort? Yes, sir. You'd think after eighteen months of work they would have finished something. Another fiasco run by incompetents."

"That's why I hired you. By the way, Ross received a grateful letter from the president for his attempts last year. He deserved more than that. It wasn't his fault that it didn't work. In your case, I know you can do it."

"Thank you, sir. We're ready any time."

"One more thing. Could you disappear quickly if I need to change my mind?"

There was hardly a pause. "No sweat, sir. We'll jump in

either direction on signal."

"I knew you would say that. Thanks for your readiness and pass that on to the troops."

He disconnected and departed from the communications suite with a set jaw and a frown. *By, God, we'll succeed where no one else has. Or? No. I won't let anything to happen to my men there.*

He motioned at Wes to sit next to him. "We could have a problem. Something about leaflets or publicity about the Iran connection in country. See what you can find out. Now!"

"Yes, sir." Wes headed for the communications suite.

The damned cargo kicker in Nicaragua should have been silenced one way or the other. His interviews had permeated national magazines, and DC reporters kept the story on page one. The President had done a remarkable job of zigging and zagging, as if he were on the gridiron reprising his roll as "The Gipper" in the Knute Rockne film. More deliveries to Iran were imminent and the so-called "residuals" would be earmarked for furnishing more ammunition, weapons, and material for the contras.

The situation reminded him of a ticking bomb. Should he let go of it? Protect himself? How could he do that, with the lives of the freedom fighters in Nicaragua at risk? The battle had to be continued. For the first time, he wondered what he might lose in the eyes of the powerful and highly connected in his realm. His smile was thin, grim.

Many people in DC owed him. He had markers ready for collection from many members on The Hill and in the White House. Then there were the media types who owed him too. *Not to worry, Fox. There were many fall guys available, especially a certain NSC cowboy.*

He thought of Whitney for a moment and grinned. What better way to handle her than to hand her over to his enemy Nelson Wallace. He knew the man's reputation with women, worse than his dealings with men who had crossed him. He didn't own the man, but he could have. Certainly, he had enough on him. *Give Whitney to him? Fox, you are a real son* of a bitch!

Wallace had the most crucial reason for traveling to The Colonial Capital, and it was not to admire the restoration. He had to destroy Haggerty and his girl. Magee's invitation to meet him in the area was puzzling, especially since they had cursed each roundly at their latest meeting with Speaker Tip O'Neil. Was The Fox telling the truth about handing over his contract with South Africa? He wondered how truthful and honest the sudden peace offering could be.

He sipped a Black Jack in his private Lear and frowned. That bastard had something he's going to pull. Wallace had alerted his second-in-command Pat Yoder to find out if the African government had financial or other problems. Their representative had asked for an appointment the next day. But Wallace delayed it to learn more.

His people in Norfolk were executing Plan A and able to shift to the B plan if their original attempt at killing the frogman failed. He slammed the empty glass on the table. That bastard is getting under my skin. Best better produce, or he'll be long gone too. It seemed like the SEAL anticipated some of his moves. I'll get that bastard on this round.

This time I have workable alternatives. He grunted. More like plans A, B, and C. The "vic" was on his boat. Fifteen minutes after Wallace notified Ace Murphy that he was in Williamsburg, Murphy would place a call to occupy the frog.

At the same moment, two first class hit men would attack him on the boat. Randy was another expert in the double tap, putting two bullets in the same spot in a second. The first round that he used had pellets to spread when they entered the target's head. The second was an enhanced bullet that would pulverize the brain. Lukash, the second hit man preferred a highly accurate .22 caliber because of his shooting expertise.

Two divers would be suited up, standing by in the event

that the bastard entered the water. They were as professional as any SEAL and possessed the latest re-breathing diving equipment, silent and almost impossible to detect.

Murphy had seven killers in and around the connected room where Beth was constrained. The Mechanic couldn't wait to get Haggerty in his clutches, the first one-on-one battle he had ever lost. Payback time. The men in the motel rooms were fast shooters, accurate and fearless.

Ace had three rings of defense outside. Men at the entrance, several in the parking lot and each door covered by at least two men. They'd grab the frogman, immobilize him, and remove him so quickly that no one would notice. If anyone did see it, five of his men wore police uniforms.

He finished off another bourbon and punched the armrest of his easy chair. That's going to be you, you fucking frog-head! He wondered if Frank had Whitney at the Lodge or in the Magruder. As soon as possible, he'd find out. Then he'd rape that little bitch!

Stolen Votes

CHAPTER THIRTY THREE

The Williamsburg Inn had the faded grace and expensive charm of an "old money" matron. She had entertained kings, princes, presidents, and her share of knaves. Three of the latter were busy toiling to bring together a number of loose ends as a spider might after a windstorm. The Fox had one of the largest suites with a second next-door crammed with communications equipment, including protected lines and a special safe for the KL-43 secure machine.

He invited retired three-star general Newman to have another bourbon.

"General, things seems to be getting out of hand. Those dolts from the White House are making a mess. I believe that the connection between the contras and the Iranians will be public knowledge quite soon. Still we may get one or more hostages out." He didn't mention his readiness to act with the men poised in Lebanon, his 'third channel."

"You think that both ends, the hostages and funds for the contra supply will be exposed?"

"Probably the missile end, but the less anyone knows, the better."

"That helps. Sounds like things coming apart."

"And we still have deliveries to make to Iran and the contras. It's a god-awful mess. Problem is the key person is a rank amateur in complex plans and operations. I think he's over his head in this job. Some smart aleck decided that the guy needed an insurance policy to protect his family if he were wasted. And that, my friend is illegal."

His companion laughed. "You're worried about illegal? You're talking to me."

The Fox played the innocent altar boy. "I always remain on the side of the law."

"Which side is that? You're a trip, Fox."

"It's extremely valuable to have friends and debtors in the correct places. The President signed the revised Contra Aid Bill, so I might be able to slip away from that without being involved further. Of course, it will take the CIA some time to match our system. In fact, we might have to continue for a while until they're actually ready to take control."

"Sounds good to me."

"I was curious about your quick trip down this way. Anything I need to know?"

"No. I figured your invite to stay here was a chance to get away from DC bullshit."

The Fox nodded. "Thank you. I'll see you later."

Wes was admitted to the suite by Magee's valet. "Wes, come in. Have a seat. Anything new on our projects?"

"No, sir."

"I've been thinking. With the use of my access to the media I need to turn to a broader view of the country. Yes, this is the time to move the nation in the right direction." The end would justify the means in such a sinful country.

The possibility of guilt moved him to bring up his mistress. "Wes, new subject. I brought Whitney down here for final pressure on that bumpkin Creed. The winds have shifted in my direction. The videos are more than enough to make him come across."

"Yes, sir. I had a session with her earlier, and she's

really pissed, if I might use the word. She knows why you have her here."

"Not a problem. My friend, we've known each other for a long time and I know you trust my judgment. However, I'd like your opinion here. What would you think if I gave her to Nelson Wallace? He's quite taken with her, even though she's an ungrateful little bitch."

Wes frowned. "Sir, that's quite a switch isn't it? You and Mister Wallace have been fighting for years. Why the sudden change? Is there something I've missed in your plans?"

For Magee, Whitney had outlived her usefulness. Far worse was the fact that she had screwed another man, albeit at his direction. She was damaged goods. He picked a piece of lint from his pin stripe. "He'll enjoy her for a while and then realize that he has a wildcat by the tail. And she deserves rough handling anyway. She's gotten too uppity for me."

After shaking his head, Wes said, "Sir, you're the man who knows more than any of us. I'm sure you've thought it out well. I don't quite get it. What do you want me to do?"

"Nothing at all. I'll take care of it personally. Make sure you know where she is."

Wes nodded and departed to carry out his assignment.

The Inn was overflowing with TV evangelists, supporters, groupies, and the press. Magee had to play the game here very carefully. Rumors of a marginal network takeover had the press and a few high-rolling evangelists salivating. His thin smile was exaggerated, as he entered Creed's suite.

"Reverend Jethro, I'm happy to see you again. I am so grateful for our agreement. A great new network will rise."

The tanned TV personality pumped Magee's hand up and down. "Why, ah thank you, Frank. It was your support and leadership that convinced me that it was the best thing to do. By the way, have you met my Executive Assistant, Mr. Ned Henshaw?"

The handshake was brief, like an encounter between two

fish slipping past each other. Ned's face was as pasty as unbaked dough. Magee spotted fear in the man's eyes and thought that the peasant was in over his head. This was a media event probably worth a few million in contributions for Creed. It appeared that Nervous Ned couldn't stomach it.

The Fox and the preacher went around a small circle. The social talk was inane, almost sickening. Magee was an expert in the field. "Ah, Reverend Smalley. I've seen you on television. You certainly have a strong message, surely others pay as much attention as I did."

"Why thank you, Mister Magee, I sure hope that the Lord pays attention too." His laugh had a booming, jolly quality.

The Fox greeted the covey of top-level TV preachers, thinking, not one of you birds has the substance of Fulton Sheen. Now there was a stirring and holy man. On second thought there were a few he had seen and heard who were dynamic and had a substantive message. They were a mixed bag. Sipping his Perrier, he conversed with an oil-rich Texas preacher who had ascended the rating charts like a NASA rocket because of his alleged healing. The Fox thought, what a monstrous fake. Did this thief know that one of his aides was skimming funds for the JUST CAUSE war chest?

Magee cursed a few for their hypocrisy, milking the poor and living in mansions, while acknowledging that some good came from their efforts. He was going to enjoy their shock when the joint venture with Jethro was announced. Before the official reception, he slipped out to call his suite. "Any word from my secure contact?"

"No sir. Shall I call you sir?"

"Yes. Don't make it obvious. We're going down to the reception now."

"Yes sir."

His brow was furrowed and he rubbed his hands as he strode to catch up to The Reverend's entourage. Damned glitches. They better not screw up my deliveries. I hate to keep my group on hold for so long. We'd better get some hostages out.

Nelson arrived at the Magruder. Ace reported, "We're ready to put Plan A in effect. If she doesn't follow the script, we get into Plan B. We got a choice, hit him at his boat or here."

"Which do you like?"

"I say, knock off the bastard wherever we can take him. They fixed his car so he can't drive it. He gets out to look at it; they're on him. Four with plenty of muscle and they're quick and quiet."

"What if he goes in the water again?"

Ace grinned. "Got two special operations guys, trained in Europe by SAS people and that German group GSG-9. They have the Draeger Rebreather System, no noise, and no bubbles. Damned hard to find them and ex-Special Forces guys, divers like him. He'll be fish bait."

He waited for Wallace to acknowledge the information with a nod and continued.

"She'd spill anything on her mother right now. If he gets away somehow and comes here, we got him. I have an army here with three rings of defense. The outer perimeter will check every vehicle that comes on the grounds. Our people man the surveillance cameras. Three patrols inside the building. The room and those adjoining are fortresses, with The Mechanic, two shotgun experts, two pistol marksmen, and the lezzie keeper. The frogman ain't gonna make it."

"Sounds good. On the outside chance he arrives and there is no shootout, capture him. We can play one against the other. He won't be able to stand any threats against her. If he knows the least bit of information we'll get it out of him. Then they're both finished."

Nelson called another contact on a secure phone. "How did your efforts work out with locating the local computer experts in Virginia Beach and Norfolk?"

"One of them belongs to you. The queer? Weatherby? I've been watching; he's under control. There's a lezzy woman. Don't know if computers turn them that way. Her name's Rita Brennan. She's got blonde hair and gorgeous. You'd never think she was gaga over gals. Got a bull dyke."

"Is she a threat?"

"Probably not. I've got a good line on her. To the outside she's a helluva good bank Operations Manager, sharp cookie and businesslike. She's one of seven people in the vicinity who could possibly get into the system and discover the secret program before it's over. Remember, it took the fag from the network weeks to get into the thing, and he had worked on it before. The lez has a boss who owes me. He has her on special assignment in Richmond this weekend."

"Is she being watched?"

"Got a full-time tail on her. Her apartment is bugged and so are the other five expert hackers. Weatherby too. We're keeping the snoops in business."

CHAPTER THIRTY FOUR

With the trap set and a robotic Beth Olson as the bait, the group of killers moved to Williamsburg at the Fort Magruder on Route 60. They walked Beth through the side exit and set up four L-shaped rooms in a row on the second floor in the North Wing. The beds were partially obscured by the bath wall from the door. They set up fields of fire and blocked the room entrances with chairs. The elevators were several rooms away. If they had to leave quickly, a fire exit was located across the hall. The two end rooms were connected by doors to the inner ones.

Ace and his crew had stripped Beth and tied her, spread-eagled on the double bed near the door. The shame and vulnerability from her nakedness were more discomforting than her aching body. Rape threats from the men alternated with the dyke's fondling. They ripped away her humanity, her dignity, leaving only an animal instinct to survive. She would do anything to sleep, to stay alive.

Ace spoke sharply. "All right, honey. This is the last phone call you'll make, so you better make it right. Do a good job and we feed you and let you sleep. Understand?" He pointed at The Mechanic, fondling the knife.

She croaked, "Yes."

Lonnie untied her. "I won't hurt you, honey. You're my baby, you know?"

Beth watched Ace, perhaps the least threatening. She would do anything to have them leave her alone. When he gave her a note, she realized that she would be talking to Dan. A spark of hope flared up in her heart, until she understood what it meant. Her call would invite Dan here, to his death. She prayed for strength not to betray him. Her stomach muscles contracted when the cold knife touched her. "I'll do it! I'll do it!"

Ace cooed. "Sure you will, honey. Read that over. Don't go nowhere."

He went into the adjoining room. Nelson was waiting for him, puffing on the cigar. Ace said, "She's ready to kiss your ass right now. We'll get that freaking frogman here if he's alone."

"Yes. He might have come back to his boat after telling somebody something on the radio. I have to make sure." A smile showed on his thick lips. "Don't forget to put her under, right after the phone call. In a couple days she'll do anything for some coke."

Murphy spoke. "Yeah. Why the hell did we take her on this trip? We could have ambushed her boyfriend anyplace? Thought we were going to waste him on his boat."

"Don't worry your little head about that. The Pentagon calls it, defense in depth. I've got two rings of guys outside here plus yours. You never know where the guy may show up. I have high-powered people down there with the divers. He won't get away. It's like fighting a sexual disease, have to stop it now before it spreads. But first, I want to find out exactly what he knows and if he tipped anyone."

"Interrogate him? The Mechanic will be in ecstasy." Ace grinned. "Man, you picked a winner with him. The troops are afraid of him. How do we control him after?"

Nelson pointed a finger. "You keep your mind on your

job. Don't worry about anything after this bit is over. That's my job. Don't expect to have a family reunion with these people. I'm going to weed some out permanently. Some know more than they should."

Ace frowned. "I ain't curious, believe me. Jack wanted to know where C was and I told him to keep his freaking mouth shut. I know who owns the biggest balls around here. The Mechanic is dangerous as hell, but he's still just a mechanic."

"Just remember. He works for me, not you."

The telephone rang and Nelson answered. "Yeah? He's back eh. Keep him in sight. When I tell you, jump on him quick. Don't kill him, he has to be able to sing."

Wallace received a call from Virginia Beach on a secure phone that pissed him off. "What the hell are you talking about? Delay the phone call, the whole attempt down there?"

"It's like this. Remember, the frog and his a-hole buddies went fishing and stayed all night when they came back?"

"What, they did it again?"

"No! This time they got some other ape with them on the boat and they're having a freaking party. They got all this gibberish from ops in 'Nam and we can't really tell what they hell they're talking about. Sounds like the new guy is a chopper pilot they knew. He's got more stories than the other three. I say, we better wait till tomorrow. They're some tough dudes. And you don't want to spread this thing out any more than you have to."

"Dammit! You have enough people down there to take on an infantry company."

"They aint gonna go quietly. Thought you wanted no publicity, no extra possibilities of it leaking out."

Wallace shook his head. "You're right. Just keep your people alert, just in case. If they leave him alone, jump fast!"

"Got it. Be back in touch before something breaks."

Wallace grabbed the Black Jack and filled a glass. One day won't matter, especially since we'll have the time to double check our defenses up here.

He wondered where Whitney was hidden in the city. I'd sure like to get in that bitch's pants. I'll have Yoder sniff around, see if he can find out where the Fox has her.

CHAPTER THIRTY FIVE

The next evening, at the pier across from Haggerty's, the first group of killers were primed to attack. One of the divers had donned his scuba gear and was ready to slip into the water. The second one had delayed and asked his buddy for assistance. The man working on the frogman's car had reported that he had completed the bomb installation. They heard the phone ring on Dan's boat. After four rings The Cat answered. His surprise at hearing from Beth seemed genuine.

She said, "I'm in Williamsburg, the Fort Magruder. Do you know where it is?"

He wondered if she tried to alert him with that hint. "Uh. Yeah, think I know it is. What room you in?"

"I'm in room two-twenty. Please come right away. I have to tell you what happened. I'm sorry. I need you, I love you."

"Room two-two-zero. Okay. Beth. Be there soon's I can. Gotta gas up the car. Can I meet you in the bar?"

He had taken a risk. What if Beth panicked and replied with her normal reaction, a sarcastic or nasty remark?

"No, uh. We can go there later."

He squeezed a fist. She had verified that something was wrong. Get off your ass, shove off. Got to get weapons.

Randy and Lukash moved up the pier with silenced pistols ready. They stopped at the boat and Randy peered inside. The saloon was dark, but he heard words from the right side. He pointed to his partner. They slipped aboard and split.

They were unaware that Haggerty had a habit of fiddling with his K-Bar knife when he was talking on a radio or telephone. He felt a slight shift to port as the boat responded to sudden weight. He listened to Beth, and slid sideways into a dark corner, where it would be difficult to find him. He placed the phone on the deck away from him, able to hear it.

His night vision was better than theirs because they had come down the lighted pier. He looked near, but not directly at dark blobs. He saw shapes and the glint of a gun barrel across from him. He launched the knife with an underhand throw, dropped to the deck and crawled sideways.

The K-bar hit the shooter in the chest with a deep wound. "God! I'm knifed,"

Dan heard the gun clatter when it landed and a thud probably from the shooter's body.

Lukash fired his silenced .22 three times into the dark saloon. Haggerty came in low and hard, tackling his assailant below the knees and slamming his fist upward to the groin area. He heard the man gasp and grabbed the gun barrel. They struggled, he reversed the weapon. The Cat forced the trigger backward. The snap of the silenced pistol and the groan of his opponent assured him that the man had been hit.

He located the knifed victim and ground his heel into the man's throat. He felt for the knife, removed it, and plunged it into a carotid artery. He sprang at the second man the same way and dealt a mortal cut. The saloon was silent except for the gurgling sounds from dying killers.

Stolen Votes

They were puzzled on the other boat. "What happened?"

"Hear anything else?"

"Nothin.' Better get over there."

"Wait! They'll tell us if he's still alive. Remember the boss wants to interrogate him. Shit! We can't call them. Gotta wait for them to say something."

They heard movement on the other boat and sound, a loud snap followed by two more that were similar to two silenced shots. Satisfied that the "vic" had been wasted, they couldn't understand why the killers didn't say something. "Dammit, somebody's turned the radio up full bore." He slipped them back on, leaving them just forward of his ears. "That's better," he said. He put the bug back on the speaker for all to hear.

The pull to Williamsburg had been so strong that Dan almost shoved off before he had gathered his thoughts. His SEAL training halted his movements. What the hell you doing, Cat? Are you a professional? You don't attack an enemy till you find out who he is, where he is and what strength he's got. Weaknesses too. If somebody's watching me, I gotta find out.

He felt the small shotgun tucked in a corner. His hands seemed to burn with its touch. No time for that. The snaps that the killers had heard were the sounds of The Cat sliding the magazine into his .45 automatic, bringing the slide back and forth to seat a round in the chamber. He packed a bag silently, thinking as he worked. What if the guys from the nearby boat were waiting to jump him? Beth had tried to warn him that something was wrong when she talked about the Magruder and the bar. What the hell was going on?

Dan checked out his scuba gear and dressed. For the first time in years the familiar routine had a positive psychological effect. Uncertainty and fear faded, replaced by alertness and confidence. He stuffed the weapon inside his wet suit.

Red was the first to notice the silence. "Hey, something's wrong here. I don't hear him. He got off the boat?"

The swarthy big man muttered, "Hell, no. I'm watchin' the pier. He ain't showed."

"Well he's damned quiet, I don't hear a sound."

"Maybe he's takin' a shit." The blond man in the wet suit laughed.

Red called. "Stevie, check his car, he might have slipped off the boat."

The man in the parking lot answered with a negative.

"Jesus H. Christ. We take him now! Gene, you and Mex get over there."

The big man said. "Hey, he's a swimmer. What if he went in the water? Blondie!"

"Yeah. No time for a tank. Zeke, bring scuba gear." He grabbed a facemask and snorkel. Going over the side he made a larger splash than he wanted, but he had to hurry.

Lying in the water near his boat, he heard the diver's splash, then nothing. Shit! Bet the bastard has one of those Draeger rebreathers. Don't look for bubbles or listen for noise. He didn't know who they were. No intel. Time for action.

He parked his tank ten feet away underwater in a cul-de-sac and cracked the valve open slightly to sound like there was a swimmer in that location. He saw the slight ripple and wake of a snorkel coming toward him. The guy was either a sucker, coming alone, or his back up was hidden or late.

Where the hell was the other guy? The Cat felt weak for a second. Sometimes you felt that way. Then the adrenaline charged you up and carried you forward so fast you had to run to keep up. The first diver was close. He'd find out that there was no one attached to the tank. Where was his buddy? The Cat took a chance. He attacked!

Stolen Votes

CHAPTER THIRTY SIX

Creed's speech gripped the hushed crowd in the main banquet room of the Inn. Like vintage wine, his blend of the old and new made it work. He mixed well-chosen biblical quotes and the contemporary sins of society to focus on America, chosen by God to be the guiding light of the world. He threw down thunder-bolts from the right. His corn pone piety and disarming manner disguised the viciousness of his message.

"My friends, the righteous shall inherit the earth. What did the great God mean when he said that? Why, He clearly meant that America the Beautiful, shall inherit this battered earth. Our lovely land, a creation of the Lord, has been become, like Isaiah prophesied, a harlot."

There was an audible gasp from the crowd.

"Yes, my friends, you recoil from those words. Dear people, we are shocked, shocked, I say, at the way our blessed country has turned away from the Lawd. Bleeding heart liberals have turned this land into an idolatrous nation."

He delivered the next words as explosions accompanied by his fist hitting the lectern. "Abortion! Homosexuals!

Drugs! Godless! And yes, my dear friends. I hate to say the word, Sex!" He paused to wipe glistening sweat from his face with a handkerchief as the last word echoed in the room.

"The Blessed Lawd tells us in this great book." He lifted his speech-making bible. The dog-eared book with the red cover was battered and ragged from constant use. "When the people of the land permit the lasciviousness and perverted use of procreation, God will come down!" He slammed the book on the podium. "On those people. His right arm of justice will destroy them. Do I hear AHMEN?"

The crowd roared its answer, "AHMEN!"

"Yes, for God said, 'destroy them.' But, what do we see on television? Abominable perverts, lesbians, homosexuals, publicly, ah said publicly, demanding their rights. Rights? Ah say, they have no rights. No! Except to be burned in Hell!"

A thundering, standing ovation followed his brief pause. A Henshaw shill shouted out from the rear, "AHMEN." "AHMENs" rolled around the room like an army tank.

The Reverend raised a hand to silence the crowd. "Ah know, my friends. Ah know. There is perversion and vice all around us. It is now my sad duty to report that one of our own has fallen to the temptations of the Devil. Like Je-sus, we must throw him out of the temple. Now!" He pointed at a shocked evangelist on the dais, then at the door.

"Out with him! Out with him!" Shouts came from the audience.

Creed nodded, "Yes, I say out with him now!"

Applause and "AHMEN" shouts rebounded from his words. Half of the front rows stood and shook fists at the offender. The man's face was as red as the stripes in the flag behind them.

The chant, "Out! Out!" was accompanied by stamping feet. Jethro stood back, arms folded and glowered at the other preacher. The man seemed to shrivel, as his eyes darted from one to another for aid. With the volume of shouts growing, he crawled away like a dazed rat.

"My friends. With that pervert out of our way I am now

privileged to continue. There are those who would take away our precious right to speak out, to charge those depraved with the sin they have written on their hearts. Ah tell you. It is time to act!"

He paused for effect and shouted. "It is time to take over this blessed country, this blessed land that the Lawd has given to us. It is time to strike at sinners who bring pornography into ah homes. They flaunt their gay. Ah ask, Gay? Rights? Gay means joy and happiness my friends. There is no joy in Heaven with the abominations here among us. We must drive them into the sewers where they belong."

While he basked in their approval, thunderous applause and cheers allowed him a sip of water, The Reverend attacked liberal decisions of the Supreme Court, apparently ignoring a conservative July decision that permitted states to outlaw homosexual sodomy.

He called for the election of the right people. "Think, my friends. The President appoints Supreme Court justices with The Senate's consent. What will happen if the liberals take over that august body? There will be millions of abortions. Eventually a lesbian on the court itself."

Shouts of "No! No!" chorused around the room.

The Reverend wiped his forehead and raised his hand to silence the crowd. "Thank you, I thank you. Please, let me finish. Do you realize that the Supreme Court has more control over our morals than our elected representatives? What can we do? I'll tell you."

"Take control of the courts. There will be vacancies on the Supreme Court. Right-thinking judges must fill them; judges who will reverse those scandalous decisions on abortion. Judges who will refuse to give the homosexuals and the lesbians the right to change our children into perverts? How? By voting in the right men to the Senate."

"Ah started to say, with all humility and prayer to the Lawd. That we must strike at the heart of the perversion and the power of the leaders of the sinners. We must reverse the atrocities against the Lawd that strike at the very roots of our beloved land. And we have many, many opportunities in the marketplace. Yes, we must boycott companies that promote perversion and pornography. Yes my friends. We need help."

He shifted to the election, speaking slowly and more quietly. "We do this my friends, by the precious franchise we have been given by our forefathers. On Tuesday, we have the great chance to attack the perverts and the radicals who have spent millions to buy this election. Ah say, we must vote Tuesday. And we must vote right!" His right arm shot forward with his fist clenched.

Many stood up and imitated the gesture. They shouted, "Vote right! Vote right!" The chant swelled around the room, until all were standing and shouting. Religious leaders on the dais crowded The Reverend to pump his hand. Magee wore a fox-like grin. Creed was good!

CHAPTER THIRTY SEVEN

In the captive's room at the Fort Magruder Inn, Beth drifted to the surface of consciousness. Pain bit into her. She existed in a daze, half in and half out of reality. Giving up was easier, better, because it would end the burning pain. She tried to see, but her left eye was swollen from punches. She was alone, spread-eagled on the bed, naked. She tried to look at her wounds, but the effort drained her. Her head fell back.

The unkempt dyke entered. "She's awake, Ace. Wanna try again?"

Beth shivered. Lord Jesus, if I could only sleep.

"Come on baby. Let me love you up, make you feel better."

Beth felt a cold hand on the inside of her thigh and screamed into her gag. She struggled. The woman's fingers reminded her of a garden slug's slime.

"Hey, Lonnie, cut that out! I told you to hit the other room and stay there. Someone's coming and you ain't gonna see him."

"I don't give a screw about a man. She needs company."

"Bullshit. You aint gonna be here when the guy comes."

Ace followed Lonnie, shut and locked the door.

Beth heard. Another one? What could be worse than what they had already done to her? Raped, beaten, cut. And the slimy woman was the worst. Grimy nails had stabbed into her, and she still burned. She wondered what it would be like to die, to be released from the struggle. What would Jesus look like? Would he forgive her? For her baby's abortion?

She sobbed. Jesus had even forgiven Mary Magdalene. Am I worse? She thought of Dan. Oh God, I've told them everything I know about him. How could I do it? Might as well be dead. She heard voices. "Oh Lord Jesus, whatever comes, help me to be strong."

She felt a large hand on her arm. The voice was deep and seemed to be kind. "Open your eyes, Beth. I want to talk to you."

Bending over her was one of the biggest men she had ever seen. He was dressed in an expensive business suit, a white shirt, and a neatly knotted tie. He seemed friendly.

"My God, what have they done with you? Here, let me take that terrible gag out of your mouth. I was told you were being slightly restrained." His voice rose. He pointed at Ace. "You're responsible for her condition. Get some medication for her. Now!"

Murphy dashed out and Beth was overwhelmed. A wave of surprise broke over her ending in a spread of hope. The man snatched a blanket off the other bed and covered her. Its warmth and the gesture had positive effects. She was grateful.

"Let me untie you. This is terrible. I didn't know they would do this. I'm sorry."

Beth waited as strong hands untied her wrists and then her feet. She curled up into a fetal position, partly to get warmer, partly to protect herself.

"Would you like a drink of water, some tea?"

She nodded. The man opened the door, said something and returned smiling. He was as big as a football lineman, but he was graceful and quick. He touched her brow and moved the hair away from her face. "Beth, please call me N, just N.

Okay?"

"Yes N." She parroted the answer, a little girl reciting to her teacher.

"I'm sure that you don't know why all these things have happened. Again, I must apologize. I can't believe that you were injured. They promised." The voice trailed off.

Was there a tear in his eye? Beth relaxed for the first time since she had been kidnapped. She thought, "Oh thank you, Jesus, thank you."

"Now, listen to me. I'm going to take you out of here to a hospital, to get you taken care of. We're going to find out what this whole thing is about."

"You, you don't know?"

The man took her hand away from the covers and held it. He shook his head. "Not only do I not know what this is all about, but I promised Reverend Jethro to bring you to him as soon as we got you checked by a medical facility. He'd be here right now, but I had to talk him out of leaving the convention in the middle of his speech. I found out that you had been taken to the Magruder. Ace told me Ned ordered you to be held."

"That creep! I knew he was behind all this." She sat, holding the cover to her. Her hair was matted and stiff. She felt a head bruise. "Please. Could I go to the bathroom?"

"Of course, of course. Here. Let me help you."

The man gently lifted her and supported her as they walked toward the bath. Beth wondered if he were coming into the facility with her. He eased her in, stepped back, and smiled. "Why don't you take some time and shower. I'll knock when the tea arrives. Believe me, I'm sorry. These people will pay for this."

She shut the door, locked it, and sank against the wall for a moment. "Oh, my God. Alone! Praise the Lord! I can't believe that I'm out of this."

There was a soft knock. "Beth, here are your clothes."

She opened the door slightly. A pudgy fist held her unwrinkled dress and clean underclothes. She took them silently, closed and locked the door again. She was safe.

When she looked in the mirror, she spoke. "Oh, God, what a mess." Her left eye was closed. There was a fist-sized bruise on her left cheek. She brushed her hand through her stiffened hair to straighten it a bit. Her lip was swollen with dried blood underneath.

She was almost afraid to look at the rest of her body, so she turned on the shower. Hot water gushed and steam rose from the tub. She examined herself. Tears popped into her eyes as she saw the damage. She stepped into the filling tub. "Oh Jesus, thank you."

Outside of the bathroom Wallace lowered his voice. "Quit laughing Ace, she'll hear you."

"Damn, boss, I gotta hand it to you. You're a smooth operator. She's gonna lick your hands when she comes out of there."

Nelson lit a cigar. "Hell, it's no trick. Just the good-cop, bad-cop ploy. The fuzz use it all the time." His expression changed to anger, primarily at himself for holding off on killing the frog on sight. He wouldn't make that mistake again.

"The bastard knocked off the two hitters, and now he's in the water with our two divers after him. It's a helluva lot better to catch him before he arrives. Listen in next door on the bug. As soon as I find out where he might be, get on the horn and call me. I want the three rings of defense rechecked, by you, personally."

"Again? Okay. We've got surveillance cameras around the outside of the buildings. We got guys in the parking lots on the street, in the back and in every building. He ain't gonna make it. As long as you give us the green light to shoot first."

That wouldn't be "the accident" that he wanted, but it had to be accomplished. The SEAL was a tough dude and there was only one thing to do with him. "You got it. Pass the word around. After it's over, I'm gone. You do the talking.

Some Iranian, maybe Middle East terrorists have been after Mister Magee and that TV evangelist Reverend Jethro. Ever since the preacher sent money to help the Iranians and had that hostage released in Lebanon."

"So that's what this is all about."

"Damned right. That's why we got quick support from the police and FBI. You didn't think this was some other caper did you? Anyway, the story is that this guy was a terrorist who was after The Reverend's staff people and he got to the Satellite Manager first. You'll have a PR man at your side in five minutes and he'll take over. By the way, you have to knock her off right after the SEAL gets it. Drag him in here and stuff the gun in his hands. Fire it to make sure there's powder residue on him."

"I got it. Then?"

"We clean up loose ends. I got something on Best. The Mechanic will take care of it. You'll never see or hear from me. Now let me get some dope out of the canary here."

Ace nodded. "I'll be right back, after I get the word out on wasting the bastard."

At night, water looks and almost feels like black oil. It seems sluggish, difficult to move through. The consistency is the same as daylight; it's merely an optical and sensory illusion. The Cat couldn't see the snorkel man's buddy, but he had to be near.

He trembled for a moment, expecting a knife in the back or a blow to the head. He pounced on the killer's back and ripped off the mask. He forced the man's face into mud and pounded him on the head with a billy club. The other diver was extremely strong, but the guy's thrashing legs stopped.

The Cat's hair stood up. Where's his buddy? He had to move fast. He stole the mask and snorkel, then slit the man's wetsuit. He turned to cover his back and felt a hand on his arm. He was in deep shit trouble. He'd never heard the guy.

They surfaced facing each other. In the microsecond it

took the other man to see that he had made a mistake, The Cat plunged his knife into the man's belly. The guy was a warrior. Dan cut the air hose. Both men were on the bottom without air. Haggerty knew it would end soon with the killer's belly cut, but the bastard was tough and even choked him. The Cat was on top of him and worked the knife into the wrists. Winded and shaky, Haggerty dragged him under and held him until the victim's jerky motions ended.

Dan slipped on his tank and was moving before the big man's body stopped twitching. He checked his rear. He zigzagged and doubled back, using other tricks in case he was followed. He surfaced on the west side of the Little Creek Channel and heaved air. He thought of the killings. They're the enemy, Cat. Don't feel sorry for the bastards. If they didn't alert you when they boarded, you'd be crab bait yourself.

He checked his watch. Time was running out on Beth. He had to get to her fast. "Oh, God, Beth. If they got people like this, what the hell are they doing with you?"

He couldn't go back to the boat. They'd have an army there. If he were heading for a trap, he had to know what he was up against. He needed weapons and a damned good plan. How to get in the motel, get Beth and get her out. He needed help. SEALs went into combat in teams with men for fire support, to guard the rear and flanks. When they assaulted VC POW camps, sometimes they had air support. Not this time.

There was only one place for weapons and ammo. Explosives too. One place nearby that had it all. He hated to think about going there. He might have to fight his way in. So much depended on the people on duty. If he were caught, maybe the murders and the mystery could be brought out into the open. But then, he couldn't save Beth.

He squeezed his fists, thinking about returning to his former home, his buddies, his friends, the SEALs. Could he do it? Memories saturated his mind and he felt light-headed. Could he handle explosives again? Was he back to being a warrior? He didn't know. He bit on the mouthpiece and swam toward the east side of the channel. He went behind a tug, on its way to Cape Charles with its barge load of rail cars. He hoped and prayed that he could pull off the most important op of his life.

CHAPTER THIRTY EIGHT

The Fox had insisted that Creed meet him in his suite before they returned to the conference. His valet ushered the TV personality into the anteroom. The Fox seemed pre-occupied but flashed his smile at his guest.

"Bourbon, Reverend?"

His companion shook his head thereby vibrating his jowls. "Can't, Frank. We have to be ready to raise the rafters in our joint presentation."

Wes had bad news to report to his boss, not a happy event. He slid next to his boss and whispered, then stood by the door.

A shadow had flicked over Magee's face during the quick report, and his face matched the red urn standing near him. Wes was supposed to escort Whitney to the suite so that The Fox could shove a blunt reminder that he held a high hole card at his erstwhile partner in the communication game. The fact that she was missing was a glitch, but Wes had brought additional copies of Creed's coupling act with the young woman.

He said, "Let's sit for a moment. It's been an energizing

but tiring experience for me. I'm sure that you're quite used to all this excitement, being so much in the public eye."

A smile lit up the evangelist's face and he responded with a corn pone "Aw, shucks. The people need us, Frank. We need to show them the way. They are lost sheep."

And you've been shearing them unashamedly for years. After that silent thought Fox motioned to Wes, who lifted a large manila envelope from the sideboard. He handed it to Magee and resumed his place by the door.

Holding the envelope in his hand The Fox led Creed through the steps of their financial and control agreements in detail. After each segment he asked if his erstwhile partner remembered and still accepted the statements.

"Remember, Jethro, you agreed that I would eventually take over some of the control for programming and would have veto power there."

"Excuse me? Veto power? I don't recall that being in the papers. Do you have a copy of our agreement there? Let me see it."

The Fox handed it over.

When Creed scanned it he protested. He followed that up with, "No, sir. Ah do not remember that clause at all. In fact, I alone have the power over approving text and video of all programs. I must have—."

The Fox showed the pictures.

"Good Gawd! What are those pitchers? You told me that you gave me all copies. My God. What are you doing to me?"

"I'm doing nothing to you. Just offering you another set that seems to have materialized since we last talked. Here. I'm giving them to you."

"Another set? Oh, my Gawd! I'm ruined. Where? Who?"

Magee's eyes were drill points. "It seems that there are a few more sets of these floating around in the ether. Perhaps you'll have that bourbon now?"

While clutching the pictures, Jethro tried to wipe the perspiration from his face. "Yes, Yes! Bourbon! Never mind ice or water." He gulped at the drink offered by the valet.

The Fox stood and pointed at a chair. "Sit down!" The televangelist obeyed. "I'm telling you this once and one time only. I will have veto power and overriding decision-making on all aspects of this business venture. Understand? You are a figurehead. The face that people see. I am the one who runs the entire enterprise. Period! You got that!"

Creed tried to whine, but Magee shouted, "Shut up!"

The evangelist's hands rose like frightened birds. The Fox continued. "We're going to go out there arm in arm, like old friends who have just finessed the entire television evangelists' market. We will dole out favors to those who accept and promote our cause, the creation of a right-wing, powerful, take-no-prisoners assault on the liberal media."

"You will be the public spokesperson for turning around America. Think of that, Jethro. You, the voice that this country sorely needs to take back our religious freedom, our vote, and our power. The people need a shepherd like you. They will listen and heed your voice. And that's what this is all about. Do you read me?"

The Reverend coughed and wiped bourbon from his lips. "I, uh, read you, sir. I, uh, hadn't thought about being the leading light opening the darkness that we are in. Yes, that's a good phrase, Frank. I'll use that right away."

The Fox patted his victim on the shoulder and grinned. "Spoken like the true believer that you are. Let's take back our Constitution, The Bill of Rights, and our sacred place in the world as its moral leader. Let's go get them! Vote Right!

Although the preacher's hands shook, he echoed his mentor. "Absolutely, Vote Right, Vote Right!"

Wallace walked into the room adjoining Beth's. He shook his head slowly. "She was grateful and damned near licked my hand. But I didn't get shit out of her. I think she knows something, maybe it's mere suspicion. She knows about a secret program and data going out but that's it. Tell me, did they get the frog alive?"

Stolen Votes

When Ace broke the news, Nelson threw the lighted cigar at him. "Damn you! What the hell do you mean he got away? What happened to our frogmen?"

Murphy silently picked up the cigar off the carpet before it singed the material. He was searching for something to say that wouldn't sound idiotic. "They never came back. I got two more ready to come in. They're in DC. Can I use the Lear?"

"No you can't use the Lear. It's parked in Newport News. Get them on a charter. Do I have to do all the work? Damn your ass. You said they were pros."

"They are. The guy must be a pisser. That's—."

"Shut up, dammit! Are you sure they aren't still after him?"

"It's a slim chance. Only one had a tank. He had air for forty-five minutes. It's an hour and a half now. I got two men on the boat waiting for him. Shit, I don't know where the hell he went. He's gotta come back for his car. We know he went in the water, but—."

"But your ass." He slammed a fist on the table and spilled his bourbon. He lighted another Upmann. "Get the whore up. I want to grill her myself."

Murphy's face looked like he had applied white clown make up. Perhaps he realized that he was expendable. He sounded desperate. "Jesus, is that wise? You're still out of it. You want to know what she knows. Right?"

"Bullshit! We know she's only suspicious. I want to know what he knows, NOW!"

"She's a little out of it. We put her to sleep. In case he got away with her, she'd be dead weight. Lemme try. He can't get up here before nine, unless he's got a jet."

His boss jumped up and nearly stabbed him in the eye with a pudgy finger. "Listen you shithead. You get her out of whatever dope you gave her. Right now! Grill her. I mean get on her case. Don't let up. I want to know everything about that bastard."

"I'm gone." He ran out.

Nelson paced. "Damn that frogman!" He blew smoke

and called The Beach on the radio. He shouted his orders to the killers at the marina. "Kill him on sight!"

"Waste him. You bet, boss. Anything else?"

"No. Search the whole marina. I don't give a shit if you need an army. Call when you finish it. And, by God if you don't, your ass is The Mechanic's, got that?"

"Yes sir. Don't worry boss."

He wandered to the window. "Don't worry my ass." This is a three-ring freaking circus. Serves me right for not taking over. He's either the luckiest son of a bitch or he's one helluva tough bastard. I'm tougher. He poured a half glass full of bourbon and sat.

They slapped Beth awake and walked her around the room. They poured coffee in her and kept walking her until there was some response. Ace stationed The Mechanic where she could see the knife. "All right, bitch. Answer and answer fast. Who the hell does that boyfriend of yours go to see when he's got trouble?"

She shook her head. "I. I don't know. No one. He sees Father Steward. Is he—?"

"Shut up. I'm asking the questions. You see that knife, bitch? I'm through screwing around. If you want that bastard Haggerty to live, you answer quick. They're gonna kill him on sight. Where would he go from his boat?"

Beth's eyes became glassy, as if she were thinking about protecting Dan.

Murphy broke in before she could think of a way to prevent him from arriving. She shook her head and staggered when he slapped her again.

"Where does he go when he goes in the water?"

"I don't know. He goes places. Please, don't hit. I can't tell you. I don't know."

Ace punched her in the stomach. "Does he have a swimming buddy?"

She coughed several times from the blow. "No. The only

one he used to swim with, with. Oh God." Tony's death seemed worse than another slap. She recovered, hoping to find something that would save Dan. "It was Tony, that man who was killed. I don't know where they went."

He punched her face and she slumped unconscious.

"Let me at her," the voice was soft, but tough as steel.

Ace nodded at The Mechanic. "Bring her around and find out where he could be. He got away from them assholes."

They tried again. She was weaker now and desperately trying to save herself. Thoughts of saving Dan were gone. If she knew, she would have told them. That thought sickened her. She had nothing left but prayer and hope for getting unconscious. They couldn't get anything coherent out of her.

The Mechanic said. "I'll knock her off, huh?"

Joseph Guion

CHAPTER THIRTY NINE

The Naval Amphibious Base reflected the hind teat position that amphibious warfare had in the U.S. Navy. Unlike the ivy-covered brick and landscaped streets of the Naval Operating Base in Norfolk, Little Creek was a mixture of dogs and cats. It contained a sprawling, disconnected series of frame or concrete buildings and World War II Quonset huts.

The Cat paused outside the headquarters of SEAL TEAM TWO. He was about to enter revered ground, where men he knew had departed on missions and never returned. Too much depended on who had the duty tonight, and if they were alert and ready. The forty-five was heavy in his left hand. He wanted his right available to knock out someone.

He didn't want to shoot anybody. He owed his life to some of these men. Could he attack his own kin? And the consequences? He was pulling off a federal offense. Bullshit! Something heavy and sinister was going down. He was out of shape and beaten up. Six men were already dead, seven counting Tony. Beth needed him. He had to do it.

The sight of the SEAL insignia staggered him. This

Stolen Votes

assault was a gross violation of trust. A betrayal. It was like beating up your family, attacking precious loyalty. Paneled walls inside were covered with pictures of insignia, missions, weapons, and plaques from ships the teams had ridden. Copies of medals and citations, the paraphernalia of a heritage. The Cat had been a professional. A warrior. Was he now? He strangled his emotions and pounced into the room.

"Hey, Cat. Man, what are you doing here?" A six-foot, muscular, black man grinned.

Great! Lousy! His number two buddy, Bennie Jackson, had the duty. His words shot out like bullets. "Bennie, shut up! Down. On your face." He waved the forty-five.

His friend raised his hands and his mustache quivered. Dan knew that Bennie was a hair trigger from jumping him. Could he shoot him? He pointed the automatic at large brown eyes below a crew cut. Jackson stared and jutted out his jaw. He slid to the deck with his hands raised.

The Cat's peripheral vision caught movement. His eyes and the weapon snapped to the danger. Before he could squelch it, he allowed a sigh of relief to escape. It was his A-hole buddy, Doc Warner. He hated the fact that they were here. Doing this to Doc and Bennie was hard, steel hard. They'd do anything for him. He was slapping them in the face. The op came first.

"On the deck, near Bennie. Quiet. Nobody gets hurt."

The Doc's squinty eyes crinkled with a grin. His sparse sandy hair bobbed when he nodded. "Sure, Cat, sure. Hey, I got no weapons." He slumped down near Bennie. "Driver's in the head. Don't know where the Duty Officer is."

"Thanks, Doc. Nobody gets hurt. Don't want to use this or a fist, but I will."

He padded silently to the doorway. Keeping the weapon on them, he waited. A door banged and he heard steps. A stocky black-haired man walked in and seemed surprised.

"Hey, what the hell?" His eyes swung from the two men on the deck to the gunman. "Hey! Wha—."

"Shut up. No noise." The Cat slipped behind him and

twisted his arm up behind his back. "Call the duty officer. Don't warn him or you got a headache."

Doc spoke like he was enjoying the whole deal. "Better do what he says, Curtain. This guy is an ex-SEAL. He knows what he's doin'. He'll bust your ass."

"Ah, Lieutenant, you wanna come out here a second?"

Dan shoved the man away so he couldn't jump him. Silence crowded in like heavy fog. The Navy clock on the bulkhead seemed to tick louder as they waited.

Steps in the hallway were accompanied by grumbling. "Now what?" The officer stood in the doorway, then leaned forward on the balls of his feet. He turned and looked down the barrel of the weapon. "Jesus Christ. What the hell?"

"Knock it off, Lieutenant. Don't get any ideas of jumping me. I won't hesitate." The officer followed instructions and moved away from the man in the wet suit.

"Okay, okay. What the hell is going on, another security alert?" He laughed.

The Cat tossed a heavy cord to the enlisted man. "Here, tie the officer up, then the Doc. Make it quick."

"Hey, wait a minute." The officer stepped forward.

"I warned you. Don't move. I know all the fucking tricks."

Doc helped. "Lieutenant, this guy's a SEAL. He knows what the hell he's doing. He's damned serious. Better do what he says or somebody's going to get hurt bad."

There was still doubt in the officer's eyes when he took a blow to the head and sagged. The Cat snapped at the driver, "Tie him, dammit! I'm in a hurry."

When they were both tied and laid out on the deck, Haggerty pointed at Doc, not wanting to id him as a friend, then Bennie. "Okay, hero. Now you. Get up and tie this guy."

"Roger, I received your message." Bennie was on his feet quickly and tied the Doc. "Okay now what?" Large white teeth flashed in a wide grin. The voice teased, "You gonna tie me up too?"

"No. Put each one in a separate closet. Make it quick.

Stolen Votes

Get the armory keys."

Doc protested. "Oh shit! Cat, come on. Not the armory keys. The freaking Feds will be chasin' your ass forever. Ain't you got some other way? Need help?"

Dan ignored his friend. With Bennie's assistance, they placed each man into a closet and tied the doors shut. They faced each other. "Now what?"

"Let's go. I need weapons, ammo. Some explosives."

"Aw, she-it. You are going to get yourself in a helluva lot of trouble, man. Isn't there something else we can do? Don't you want me to help you?"

"Come on Bennie. You think I'm kidding?"

"Hell no! I've seen that look before. You're going to war. Look, if you need me."

The offer was honest and The Cat knew it. He couldn't involve his friends. He had thought about it. With Bennie and Doc, he could take on anything that was ahead of him. Beth in trouble was more than enough to worry about. He couldn't ask them to join, to be marked for death. He was responsible for the death of too many friends now.

"C'mon, dude, what are you trying to do? I can help get the gear you need, but I want in."

"Can't. Don't want you guys in it."

"Why? We've been in a world of shit before. You got an op, you got two more with you."

He wanted to tell them the truth. He owed them that. But he knew that he'd damned near have to fight them to stay out of it. He couldn't be responsible for two more friends' deaths.

They walked toward the armory, Cat behind with the gun at the ready. "No, Bennie. I have to do this myself. I need fast firing weapons, couple of hand guns."

"You want a Stoner? You always carried one. How close in you gonna be? You used shotguns. You want an Ithaca with a duckbill for short range? An S & W M76, or Uzi?"

"No Stoner. Not enough time to strip it down and make sure it works. I wanna go light with heavy firepower. I'll take the Uzi. You got any squibs and stun grenades?"

"Oh, shit, Cat, yes. I've been saving them. Aw hell, you got 'em. Take my H-vest. You'll be packing too much shit to carry it any other way."

"Okay. Thanks, Ben. You're a helluva man." They were silent until after they loaded the explosives and weapons into a waterproof bag. They worked together like they had before, silently and efficiently. Dan felt he was drifting back to better years. When they closed and locked the armory. He shook out of it to concentrate.

Bennie tied off the bag and hefted it on his shoulder. "Jeez, man. Are you going to blow up Fort Knox? This is a lot of shit."

"Don't sweat it. Know if Doc's got any dynamite sticks? The flares we used?"

Bennie's grin flashed. "No shit. You're going to pull off that one? Geez, you scared the shit out of that CIA guy in Cambodia. Thought he'd shit his pants."

"Don't know what I'll do. Got a job, okay? No questions and you won't know enough to get yourself into trouble."

"No skin off my black ass. Hey, you're my friend. You used to be. Whatever you doing you need somebody to watch your six. Why won't you invite me to your party? I'm getting fat and sloppy here sitting on my ass. I need action."

They dropped the load at the doorway. He motioned for Bennie to go back inside. "No. I couldn't ask for a better man. I don't want you mixed up in this. It's damned dangerous."

"Horseshit! Dangerous? Were we playing grab-ass in 'Nam? Come on, Cat." He touched his friend's arm. "I owe you. Remember?"

Cat saw loyalty, trust, perhaps love in his friend's eyes. The offer was more than tempting. It was SOP. You never went alone. Good mission planning required flank support and backup in case something went wrong. He'd need help grabbing Beth and extracting her safely. Doc and Bennie would leave with him, no questions asked. It was damned tempting, the best thing to do. He thought of the deaths, too many on his head already. He couldn't ask them to risk their lives again for him. He turned away. "Come on, I'm in a hurry."

"Okay, Cat. You're the boss. What happens if you don't come back?"

They stopped at Bennie's locker. "If I don't come back, you leave it alone."

Bennie shook his head. "Yeah, sure Cat. Here's the shit."

They went to Doc's locker. Bennie stood on the other side of the dim hallway as Cat rooted around in the back of the locker and found what he wanted. He stuffed red dynamite sticks into his waist and held explosive squibs in his hand on the way back.

"Are you going to slug me, Cat? You'd better do it. I'm getting mightily pissed at you. You're not my friend if you don't take me along."

The grins and joshing had ended. Cat knew that Bennie would spring at him if he had a chance. He backed off. "Bennie, if I get out of it. I'll call you, okay? I owe you now. You coulda put up a fuss. I'd still be workin'."

"And what if you don't come back? I've got a right to know. I'll be thinking about what I should've done."

The Cat slugged him with the weapon and slipped out with the bag over his shoulder. How the hell do I get to Williamsburg? And what do I do when I get there?

CHAPTER FORTY

At the Magruder Nelson waited again for the report of the frogman's death. Then he'd be on Whitney before she could react. Nothing would stop him. Hell, why not now? He gave orders to the guard at her door and charged inside.

Whitney uncurled from a cat-like position in the sitting chair and stretched a hand for her bag. A vise-grip hurt her wrist. "Let go of me, damn you! Let go of me. I'll tell Frank on you. He'll be so damned angry he'll get rid of you."

"Mister Magee, to you! He doesn't give a shit about you now you little whore. He gave you to me!" He laughed and grabbed her arms. "Come here, bitch. I'm taking you."

She tried to get away. He wrapped his legs over hers, and pinned her arms behind her back. He rolled her over him on the bed and ended on top of her. He pawed at her dress, ripping the front to expose a lacy bra and matching silk teddy.

"Gimme a mouthful, baby. I know you have good tits."

She struggled from side to side and bit his ear until she tasted blood.

"Passionate bitch aren't you! I like combat, honey." He ripped off her underwear. "You want me to hurt those tits? Or will you calm down and let me have it."

She squirmed and fought him until the ringing telephone interrupted their struggle.

"Damn you! You bitch. Stop fighting me!"

The guard banged on the door. "Mister Nelson, you've got to pick up the phone."

"Son of a bitch!" Wallace cursed and pointed. "You stay on that freaking bed. I'm not through with you." He put a heavy hand on her chest and leaned to pick up the phone.

She could barely breathe, so she struggled and fought against his weight.

Nelson slowly released his grip on her and stood. He pulled on his trousers and grabbed a walkie-talkie. "All leaders, report to Room two-twenty right now!" He looked down at the young woman. "You're not going anywhere, little whore. Warm yourself up and wait for me."

He dressed, stomped out and down the corridor. "By God, this army of mine is going to stop that bastard, or I'll kick ass all over."

Before the convention was called back in session, Magee's fists clutched at air in his suite. He had received news about the "enterprise," and none of it was good. When the negotiators offered more TOW missiles and HAWK spare parts, the Iranians stiffed them. And there was no guarantee that any hostages would be released. Should he take separate action?

His armed group in the Middle East was standing down until they received the "go" order from him personally. No one in the other two channels working with the Iranians knew about this covert force. He tapped his fingers on the chair arm, waiting to receive the secure phone call so that he could confer with the leader on the scene.

Dammit, if they don't get to the hostages, it's liable to start a war over there. If we had the location of all of them, we could do something positive. He thought of the abortive rescue attempt by President Carter in 1980. They'd learned a helluva lot from that screw up. At that time, they did not plan well, weather problems had been crucial and they didn't use the special forces properly. In this situation, he knew the on-scene leader well and could judge the man's ability and willingness to carry out the operation properly no matter what happened. He called Wes.

"You had something to report?"

"Yes, sir. Today a US chopper flew North and ex-General Secord from Cyprus to Beirut. They briefed embassy people on intel from the second channel."

"Dammit! No wonder I couldn't get either of those guys. I've tried every means of communication. I have to find out if they know anything about getting hostages out. I can't make a move with my group there with those two present. New subject. Anything new on Whitney's location?"

"Yes, sir. She's being guarded by Mister Wallace's people. I've got an in with his group so I'll keep you posted on where she is. Did you want me to get her out of there?"

The Fox laughed. "She's exactly where I want her now. Mister Wallace will take care of her."

"But I thought—."

"Not to worry, Wes. She's no good to me any more and my former associate deserves her. In fact, they deserve each other. I'll be going with Reverend Creed to the podium shortly. You can accompany me to the conference ballroom and then check on any incoming messages. And get to me immediately if there is a need for me to act."

"Yes, sir. Will do."

CHAPTER FORTY ONE

At SEAL TEAM TWO'S headquarters, Bennie came out of it first. He had a throbbing headache and he was pissed off.

"Son of a bitch! Wait till I get that Cat." He rubbed his aching skull and heard noises. He let out Doc first so that they could confer.

"Untie me, Ben, quick. Don't let the others out yet."

Bennie slit the line with his K-Bar. "Man, I'm pissed. He slugged me."

"You're lucky he did. You and me are prime candidates for suspects. Remember? We're his buddies."

"My black ass. Now what kind of scheme are you thinking?"

"Cat's tryin' to protect us, man." Doc gave his evaluation of the attack. Bennie agreed that he was trying to keep them out of it. They were puzzled.

Doc asked, "You see his face? Somebody beat the shit out of him. Let's find him."

"Or perhaps he's been falling in the gutter again."

Outside Bennie spoke first. "Wait Doc. Where's your four-wheel?"

They stood at the empty parking space. Doc wrinkled his brow. "Cat's got it. It's a helluva lot easier to drive out with my keys. Come on, let's get the other two out." He slapped his hand on Bennie's shoulder. "We're gonna find that Cat, but we gotta get away from here. Let me talk."

"Don't I always, when you trying to put us into some kind of scam."

They released the petty officer first. The lieutenant could be uncomfortable a little while longer. It was his own fault for being a shithead.

"Goddammit, it's about time." The two-striper rubbed his wrists. "What the hell is this about, Doc? You know that bastard, huh? Maybe you know a helluva lot about stealing weapons and explosives." He picked up the telephone.

"Lieutenant, think maybe you better wait before you call somebody. We got a little embarrassing situation here." He lit up a cigar. "Yes sir. Nothin' like four macho-tough SEALs getting their ass kicked by one guy. Makes you wonder if we ain't gettin' soft."

The officer held the handset. "What do you mean?"

"Well, I sure as hell ain't gonna brag about this at the Anchor Inn. An out of shape, over the hill drunk comes in, slaps us around, has us tie each other up, and makes off with weapons and explosives. It don't look good for this duty section."

"Not good fo' securitee." Bennie drawled the words. He liked to play po' black folks at times just for the hell of it.

"What are you sayin' Doc? I have to call the C.O., base security and the gates. The guy could have escaped already."

"He's long gone, Lieutenant. Took my keys, my four-wheeler."

"Yeah, you sure sounded like you was in on it." The petty officer added, "You said he meant biness. How come you knew that?"

"I know that Cat a long time. Too long maybe. He's been washed out for years, a drunk, disgraced in this outfit. But he had a look on him tonight that I ain't seen since 'Nam. He

Stolen Votes

was in a killin' mood. You see them cat's eyes, sir?"

The officer frowned. "So he's a tough bastard. And I got a helluva mess here. You know I have to call the Capn."

"Okay, if you wanna get your ass in a sling. Me and Bennie know where he hangs out. Across the water in the marina off Shore Drive. Give us 'bout twenty minutes to find him. What the hell, it ain't no skin off our ass when it happened." He made a show of looking at his watch. "Maybe just now?"

The officer was a Navy Reg jerk, but a decision maker.

"Go. Get your asses back here in thirty minutes. That's all you've got. Everybody? The break in occurred at 2130."

The two friends dashed out and into Bennie's 280Z.

The surveillance team watched the marina parking lot and the boat. Red, the leader, called them together. He was pissed about the latest orders. "What the hell do they think we are? Search the water? Hey, Mac, when are the frogmen coming down?"

"They're due in an hour. I'll take Mike, walk around the side over there, and see if we can find anything. That's the direction they went."

"Don't waste any time, blast the son of a bitch. That goes for all you guys. You find him you knock him off quick. Marv, come on. You and me are going on that boat, and we're gonna fix that thing so it ain't goin' nowhere."

"Why? You think he's gonna slip aboard without us seein' him? I think the bastard's got you spooked, Red."

"Bullshit. For that, you go for the food later. Come on."

Red watched Marv wire explosives to the drive shaft. The walkie-talkie alerted him. "We got company. Car coming in with two guys. Never saw the car before."

"Watch it," he answered. "Maybe just other boat people. Come on hurry up, Marv. I don't want no more crap coming down."

"Hey, you want this to be covered up, don't you? The

guy was a SEAL. If he's spooked, he'll check over this whole tub."

Red nodded and lifted a snub-nosed revolver. "Okay. I'm going upstairs. Keep at it. Be careful coming back up."

He waited in the shadows of the cabin watching the car park next to Haggerty's. Two men got out and peered at the other car. They headed toward the boat. They were tough looking and wore camouflaged military uniforms. Neither one looked like their quarry.

Red holstered the weapon and walked to the side of the boat to wait. His people started to close in trying not to be seen. He switched on the cabin light.

Doc called out, "Hey, Cat. That you? You bastard, you got some talkin to do."

"That ain't Cat." Bennie tensed his muscles and worked his hands. He glanced over his shoulder. There were two men in the shadows. "We got company, Doc."

The two SEALs waited back to back. The Doc called out. "On the boat. We're lookin' for our buddy, Cat Haggerty. That's his boat. What's the story?"

Red answered. "Come on board. I'm Detective Johnson, Norfolk Police. We've been looking for your friend, maybe you can help us."

Doc went first. He stood over the red-haired man and asked, "You got any id?"

"Why, of course, here." Red showed his wallet with the id of a police detective sergeant. He grinned. "You Navy guys?"

"Yeah. We're old friends. Thought we might come over. He owes me a favor and—." He stopped when a metallic sound came from below. "Somebody doing something down there? And he's not here?" The SEALs separated. With fists clenched, they took aggressive stances.

Red realized they could be trouble. He didn't want any. "That's one of my investigators. It seems that your friend here got himself mixed up with some shady people. You know. Your friend was in a bar, we're waiting for him to return."

"Hey, Doc. If he's gone, how come—." Bennie shut down when he saw the warning look. "How come we have to stand around and wait? That sweet dolly is waiting for me."

"Okay, okay. Bennie. I wanted to see if we could catch the bum before the weekend. You ain't seen him, huh?" Doc moved near the steps heading below.

Red called out, "Hey, Marv, you about finished searchin' down there? We got two of Haggerty's friends here. They don't know where he is either."

The two men in the parking lot moved closer. They were tough looking dudes. Each side measured the other.

Doc moved his head toward the side of the boat. "Let's go, Bennie. Don't wanna have Sheila after my ass for keepin' you away. Hope you find Cat, Detective. He owes me fifty bucks." He wagged his head and muttered to Bennie. "Now he's in trouble with the law. Shit, there goes my fifty."

"So long, guys." Red waved. As he watched the two SEALs walk slowly to the car and drive off, he gave orders on the walkie-talkie. "Follow those tough bastards."

On their drive back to duty, Doc said. "Somethin' stinks. He ain't a cop."

"Yeah, I could smell it. We were up to our ass in shit. You see those hard asses in the parking lot? No wonder The Cat wanted all that shit. He's really into something bad."

"Yeah. Better cover our back with the 'Loot' first. Then we figure out what the hell is going on. The Cat is in a world of shit and he's tryin' to keep us out of it for some reason. What the hell could it be?"

CHAPTER FORTY TWO

Unfortunately, The Cat had an hour to think on the way to Williamsburg. The anticipation and excitement of going on a mission clashed with his SEAL training. The more he thought about it, the crazier it seemed. He had no actual intel, no idea of where the enemy was, the terrain, and no fire support. He was reacting to attacks, spur-of-the-moment actions like some early SEAL Ops in Nam.

He had no backup, no plan, and no help to get away when he grabbed Beth. He thought of three approaches. He could bust right in, call the room first, or create a diversion.

What the hell was this about anyway? What is Beth mixed up in? He'd have to find out where she was located. Was the room number correct? He'd have to surprise and kill an unknown number of enemies. He had maybe a ten-percent chance of success. Think positive! The lobby is on the south side. I can stroll into a motel in a wet suit. Sure.

He tried to check the vehicle's interior while driving through the tunnel to Hampton, but he didn't want to hit the wall. Doc had stuff in his vehicle. You're an ass-hole, no pre-op planning. And what you gonna do when you get there?

If a cop stopped him, that would be all she wrote. No license, no registration, weapons and explosives in the car. He took a chance on being discovered and pulled off near Fort Eustis. He reached behind the seat and found an air tank and material that he tied to pull to him. He checked the rearview mirror and saw a right blinker flashing behind him. Shit!

He slammed the Chevy into gear, flicked the left turn signal on and accelerated. The other car went by with the blinker winking at him. He cursed the other driver and pulled over at exit 57A.

Got to have some cover, or a way to get in without raising suspicion. Shit, all Doc's got is a Navy boiler suit, coveralls that were dark green, with some grease and oil spots. What a choice. That, a wet suit or diving underwear. Do I check in? With what? No ID. No cash. No credit cards. Nothing. Shit!

Wallace grabbed Ace by the arm and dragged him down the hallway to the last room they had. He shoved him inside. He pointed a large finger at the man's face.

"This is getting fucking ridiculous. Every time we have that bastard, he slips away. He's not some fucking magician. He's a washed up drunk. He's either the luckiest shit I ever came across or superman. Get your ass down in the parking lot with a radio. Alert everybody that you're going to try to sneak in here. Try different approaches. Parking lot, lobby, restaurant. Whatever the hell there are for entrances of any kind. Even if it's 'Employees Only.' Understand?"

"Okay, okay. Wouldn't it be better if I picked three of us instead of just me? That way we test the idea a helluva lot quicker. He could be up here in maybe a half hour. I don't mind doin' it, but we could save time and get ready if we find any loopholes."

Nelson slammed Ace on the shoulder. "Son of a bitch, a thinker. Do it! Alert the whole crew, the guys on the cameras, doors, all of them. Tell them to call in to you as soon as they spot you guys. See where you are and get what's his name, Harry, to keep track of the spots. Then you double up the guys to cover those places."

"Got it, boss. I'll report back soon as I finish. We'll get the bastard."

"Yeah, that's what Red and the divers said too."

Soon after Ace had reported and changes were made to insure that no one could sneak in, The Cat struggled to change in the vehicle. Traffic whizzed by heading west. He slipped into the coveralls and stuffed the wet suit behind him. Back on the road and thinking.

Could he handle explosives again? Last time was sixteen years ago. He shut off the question, thinking back to his training and successful ops. How do I get in the place? She tried to warn me. Geez, you're playin' amateur night here. Going into a possible trap without knowing anything about the order of battle. Shit, we did that before.

Beth, I hope you're okay. Dammit, It's couple hours since she called. God, help her. He stopped at the stop sign on Route 60. A frontal assault would be stupid. He drove slowly past The Magruder trying to figure out how to get into the building. Several cars were parked near the entrances with two men in each. Geez. They've got a freaking army.

Several cars jammed with people waited to turn into the parking lot from across the road. They were raising hell, singing and laughing. Many were in costume. What the hell? Wait one. It's Halloween! Got a chance.

Two vehicles turned into the parking lot. He squeezed in behind them in front of three other cars. They parked near each other and party people swarmed around Doc's car. Dan slipped on Doc's sunglasses. Shouldering the air tank and carrying the weapons bag, he walked into the lobby with the Halloween party people. Made it!

A minute later, The Cat knocked on the door to Room

228. No answer. He searched the tools from the vehicle. The pick on Doc's key ring and the knife worked. He slipped into the room, the forty-five in his hand. The room was empty.

Hope this is laid out the like her room. He dropped the bag on the bed, zipped it open and stared at C-4 explosives and detonators. He fisted his hands, inhaled, and dug into them. He worked efficiently, felt good, on top of it.

He thought of his first instructor in SEALs. "Cat, when you go in, expect the worst. You won't be surprised. Surprise the other guy. You got two seconds. That's all."

Two seconds is all I need. He backed against the room's door and rehearsed his entrance. Crap, there's a hidden space on the right from the bathroom. I'll have to jump in farther. He practiced until he was satisfied. If someone were hidden in the corner on the first bed, he was in trouble. He had to move in about three paces and lose two seconds. Shit!

He'd have a stun grenade in his left hand. He hung the S & W machine gun around his neck, put it in the front of the coveralls, keeping it free. He replaced the forty-five with Doc's Beretta in his left side pocket. He had fired it many times a long time ago. He rooted around in the weapons bag and felt cold. He knew what he had touched without looking.

It was an Ithaca Model 37 sawed off shotgun. How the hell did that get in there? He reached to touch it and his hands shook. Jesus. He fumbled with a box of shotgun shells and dropped several. They were identical to the ones he had used when he blew away Bobby's face. Bennie, you bastard. You stuffed that shit in the bag on purpose. Trying to make me a warrior again? He tried to touch the weapon and felt his stomach churn. Dammit to hell! He couldn't pick it up.

"Fuck! I'll use the Uzi." He touched another weapon. His favorite, the Stoner light machine gun. Better not, they need a lot of TLC. Don't have the time to check it out.

He placed dynamite sticks on the dresser top. When he touched the detonator, his hands trembled. He closed his eyes and remembered his platoon leader, Lieutenant DeLong, after Bobby's death. "If you can't cut the mustard, get the hell out.

Now! Before you kill more of us." He fought down the fear of handling explosives again. Could he do it?

The feeling of going on a mission steadied him. He wound four dynamite sticks with a small amount of primer cord, attached a squib, and tied the bomb against his chest. At it again! Cat. Do it! He dialed Room 220 on the phone.

Beth answered. "Hello? Hello?"

The Cat grinned. "Hey, Lady. Is this room two-forty?"

He heard her gulp and, "Who is this? This isn't room two-forty."

"I'm callin' from the lobby, uh. Sorry."

He dropped the phone and headed toward death, success, or something else. He loped down the hallway and ducked into the opening near the ice machine. He watched the hall near room 220, but no one ran out of it. Shit. Thought somebody might show. He shook his head. Come on Cat. Shit or get off the pot.

Grabbing flares from the left front pocket, he bounded down the passage. He heard a noise behind him and glanced backward. People were heading away from him toward the elevator. The Cat lighted off one flare and dropped it at the base of the door at Room 218, then 220, and then 222. He banged on room 220's door and shouted, "Fire! Fire!"

He moved against the far wall at an angle and readied the weapon and a billy club. He heard shouting inside the room. The first door that opened was 218, a thin sharp-eyed man came running out, a knife in his hand. Cat dropped him with the club and a gunman following.

People filled the hallway, shouting and calling as the smoke spread. He watched the rooms across from him. He pocketed the Beretta and lifted out the S & W, waiting for the door to open. The first person out was a woman. Cat kicked her in the stomach, charged in, and lost his two seconds.

A man in tinted glasses raised a gun near the windows. The immediate threat was to the right. Cat caught the glint of a knife out of the corner of his eye. He rolled down, away and fired at the gunman. He felt the sting of the knife in his right arm, and kicked up at the man. Another popped around the corner and took a chest full of his bullets. Screams and noise filled the room. Where was Beth?

He struggled with the knife man face to face and couldn't get his arm free to blast him. The guy was wiry and stronger than he had expected. Fatigue tried to claim him. He was losing it. The knife blade edged closer to his neck. The man's sweet perfume breath was nauseating. The eyes made him think of a snake.

CHAPTER FORTY THREE

The Inn's main ballroom was full of chatter cutting through the rumble of a few hundred conversations. A nervous man in a tux waited at the side of the dais and waved with both arms to get The Reverend's attention. After a moment, Ned caught sight of his assistant and moved through the crowd rapidly. "What is it, Mervin?

"It's trouble, Mister Ned. There was an explosion, fire and gunshots at the Fort Magruder. They think that some people were killed. What shall I do?"

Ned turned the color of the linen tablecloths. "Don't say a word. I'll take care of it." He hurried out.

Magee's valet was at the dais. Otto whispered about the shootings and the fire.

"Dammit, shootings, explosions? What's it about?"

"There are rumors that some people were killed. Some say terrorists were involved."

The Fox frowned. "What the hell is going on? Find out and get back here. No one else hears about this. Understand? No one."

"Yessir."

Magee turned to the gathering around Creed. "I'd better congratulate The Reverend on the speech. Terrorists! Damn, I can use that."

News of the attack at the Magruder buzzed through the room. Reverend Jethro attempted to answer questions thrown at him concerning the alleged terrorist attack. He appealed for calm. He was good at convincing people, and he won over the crowd eventually.

The Fox noted that questions from reporters could end in sound bites on the late news. He could see, "Television evangelist target of terrorists." It could have a positive effect on Creed's fund raising. His mind sorted through alternatives and choices. Were the attacks connected with the hostages? People on the dais looked at him.

The Texas millionaire and faith healer, whispered. "Y'all are on. Your speech?"

His mind raced from ordering his men in the Middle East to strike Lebanon and rescue several of the hostages or to bug out. His people knew where some of the detainees were located unlike the stupes in the CIA. How would that play with the news from Wes that a group of Iranian students were printing leaflets exposing the selling of arms by the US?

Magee squeezed out a thin smile and stood. Picking up his speech, he moved to the podium. Polite applause glided away. Silence greeted him for an embarrassing moment. The speech was familiar, his standard "Right makes Might and Might makes Right." He was an opportunist at heart.

Putting aside his text, The Fox launched into a tirade against terrorism. "There must be, I say, <u>must be</u> a Crusade against terror, foreign and domestic terrorism. Look at the recent bombings in Paris, the murder of Marines in Lebanon, assassinations, mutilations against businessmen of Italy, the Iranian-Cuban connection of terror in Central America, and that of the murderous Sandinistas. It is time to shout, STOP!"

He raised his right hand to emphasize halting terror. For the next fifteen minutes he spoke like a man possessed. The words tumbled rapidly out of his mouth. He kept repeating the phrases, "Crusade!" "Terror!" Killing!" until it became a chant that was soon taken up by the audience.

Articulating and gesturing, he outlined a plan to launch a nationwide assault. "I tell you that violence is spawned by weakness, promoted by the left, and directed against our cherished institutions. Democracy must prevail. We must, I repeat, must sweep out those who would cringe away from direct action against the nests of vipers in Syria, Lebanon, Libya." He connected all terrorism with the "Atheistic Communist Menace."

"I call on all right-thinking people, here present and elsewhere; to join with me now to form a Crusade Against Terror. Yes, my friends and fellow Christians, God is calling us to wipe out the perverts and humanists, just like He called the Crusaders in the 10th century. We must arm ourselves, not just with words and deeds, but with weapons. Yes, weapons. For too long we've been handcuffed by the reluctant ninnies in Congress. It's time to outlaw all gun restriction laws, to get organized with an armed response."

There were puzzled, embarrassed looks at the dais. Reverend Creed's nodding approval helped to convince some. The televangelist's loud "Ah-men!" encouraged favorable responses, repeated by his followers until mob psychology rolled in support.

FX finished his tirade with the phrase, shouted over and over again and taken up by more and more of the crowd. "Crusade Against Terror. Crusade Against Terror." He stood at the podium, awash in applause and cheering.

Creed leaned over and whispered, "Ah never heard you speak with such fire. Magnificent! Magnificent!" He stood up applauding with the audience.

The Fox sat down, emotionally spent. But almost as quickly, he jumped up and lifted the preacher's right hand. Holding them together above their shoulders like a referee announcing the winner, he shouted, "Vote Right! Vote Right!" The chant echoed amid thundering applause.

The Fox was called aside during an impromptu break.

Otto told him that everything was confused concerning the attack at The Magruder. There were several people killed, but he had no names. FX whispered. "Dammit! Get Wes on the radio, he's over there. Find out what's happened."

He turned back to the crowd and received his hot tea. Hands shaking like they did with his first moment before combat, he forced himself to look halfway normal. He tried to update people through the mike. "There are rumors of a terrorist attack over at the Fort Magruder Motel. But rumors only. Some say that a terrorist was killed. As soon as we receive factual information we will give you the truth. You deserve the truth, that's why you're here. Isn't it?"

He was rewarded by a few shouts of "Truth! Truth!" He broke through a ring of people and touched the Reverend Jethro.

The broadcaster shook his head as the reporter shoved a mike in his face. "Ah just don't know if the information is correct about my chauffer being killed. The man was new so ah didn't know much about him. He was a good chauffeur. That's all I know at this time. I'm trying to get all the facts as quickly as possible."

Magee replied. "I hear the police are after them. They ought to set up roadblocks. It's just awful, Reverend. It must have been a mistake. Your network?"

He interpreted the turmoil and announced to all. "I was afraid that The Reverend would be a target. He tried to help achieve peace in Lebanon."

In the room adjoining Beth's, an individual battle raged. The Cat was one slice from death with the knife at his throat. He tried to gain leverage, to reach the knife hand. The Mechanic hissed through a thin mouth "Die, you bastard."

Haggerty rolled, upsetting the man's leverage. He jabbed at the man's eyes and forced his head back. He grabbed and twisted the knife hand. Jumping up, he kicked the bastard in the head. Strong arms pinned him from behind. He tried to break free but the man was like a bear. Cat tried all his tricks and felt his strength failing. The S & W sagged from the sling and he couldn't get to it. He freed his right hand enough to zip down the coveralls.

The big man cracked The Cat's head against the wall. For a second he felt limp, out of it. The guy holding Dan against the wall was big as a grizzly with his arm poised to deliver a blow. He felt sweat as he touched the equipment exposed on his chest.

"Back off, or I blow us all to hell." His opponent seemed paralyzed. Dan had regained two seconds. He stepped closer, exposing the dynamite sticks, the wires, and the detonator. The Cat's hand was on it attached to the dynamite. Could he do it?

Whitney Carlton had to escape. Now! She could take care of the guard while Wallace was out. She made a whimpering call for help through the door.

The guard came in and faced a disheveled woman with a mean-looking Beretta held by both hands and pointed at his eyes. "Step inside, quickly. Get over there and turn around. Put your hands behind your back and don't think I won't shoot."

"Hey look, lady. I don't know what this shit is all about. I got my job and—."

"Move, or the only job you'll have is lying in a casket."

She tied him with his belt and made him lie on the floor where she could see him as she repaired the damage that Nelson had inflicted. She worked the makeup brush with professional care. When she had finished, there was no sign of the assault or the anger. She was a cool, beautiful woman in control of her life. She packed her flight bag, her jewelry and slung the mink over her shoulder.

"All right, fella. You've been a nice boy, but don't get any ideas of following me. If your boss asks where I went, just tell him I hit the bar." She went to the mirror again and touched her hair. Yes, it was fine.

She inhaled and let out a sigh. Well girl, this is what you've been aiming for, being on your own. It was somewhat frightening. Frank had long arms and he could be ruthless. There was one way she could take care of that. As soon as she got away, she'd call him. Maybe.

Another thought. Fox, if you gave me to that damned animal Wallace, I hope you get yours. She felt like slugging the guard. She was angry and alert when she moved toward the door with the Mercedes keys gripped in her hand. Where can I run? That sobering thought remained with her.

CHAPTER FORTY FOUR

Wallace stared at the array of wires and red dynamite sticks in front of the frog's chest. He hesitated, then grinned.

"You're afraid to do anything, you drunken asshole." He pulled out a .45 caliber automatic.

In the room's confined space, the low-level explosion from Haggerty's human bomb ploy sounded as if the four sticks of dynamite had blown. "Blam!" The primer cord and detonator blew flame at the big man's face. He screamed, and dropped the weapon. He covered his face with his hands, fell backwards, and crashed to the floor.

Although Dan had steeled himself for the blast, the explosion shoved him down against the wall. He shook off shock and dizziness. Worked again. Damn, I'm gettin' too old for this shit.

He kicked the big man's weapon under the bed. Hearing noise in the adjoining room, he shoved the door with his shoulder and staggered in holding the Beretta. Beth cowered in the corner.

A burly man with a pistol shouted at him, "Drop it. Or."

Stolen Votes

The Cat's weapon jumped twice and the man slid against the window. He called, "Beth, get up. Come on."

Her eyes rolled. She staggered trying to follow him.

"Stay behind me." He felt her there, sagging against his back. "If I get hit or fall down, run, keep running."

"Oh, thank You, Jesus. Dan are—?"

"Knock it off! Gotta get out fast!"

They came out into smoke and flame of the hallway. It choked Dan for a moment and he hesitated before heading down the hall. He threaded their way through people running and shouting. He felt weak and wondered at his loss of blood for a moment.

"Dan! Beth!"

"Father Stew!" He saw the priest through the smoke. He could take her. Off to his side was the woman he had kicked. She lifted a shiny gun. He threw two shots in her direction. They staggered past her falling body.

"My God, what's happening?"

"Grab Beth, Stew. We've got to get out of here." He felt wobbly, so he leaned against the wall. He felt Stew's hand. "Don't help me, get her out of here."

A young woman with an overnight bag and a mink coat caught his eye. He pointed the weapon at her. "You! Help these two, now!"

She didn't move. "This woman has been kidnapped. She needs help."

Whitney shifted her bag and grabbed Beth's arm.

"Take her, Stew. Come on, we have to get out of here. I'll lead." They dashed to the stairs and down. Haggerty stopped them at the fire exit door. "Stew, take these keys. It's a four-wheel drive, just to your right. I'll go first and I'll cover you."

Hurrying through the door, The Cat led them outside. He expected an explosion of sound and bullets hitting him. There were so many people crowded around that it was impossible to pick anyone out. People ran back and forth, shouting. Dan waved his three captives to the Bronco and stood against it with the machine gun until they got in.

He heard shots, and bullets hit the vehicle. He heard sirens. "Go, take off."

Beth called out, "No. I won't go. Get in or I don't leave."

"Shit. Okay." He pulled himself and the weapons bag into the front seat. "Drive like hell, Stew."

The Bronco jerked into the street from the motel and heeled left, as Father Stew turned right and accelerated. Two cars rushed out of the parking lot behind them. Two police cars dashed into the parking lot, sirens screaming.

Stew asked, "Where's the nearest hospital?"

Haggerty lifted his head. "No hospital. Beth, how bad did they hurt you?"

She groaned and whispered, "No mind. How about you?"

Stew slowed. Dan shoved his automatic into the priest's side. "Keep driving!"

"Hey wait a minute. You're both hurt? You have to get help."

"Take the 199 exit here. I want to see if we're followed." When Stew hesitated, he shouted. "Dammit, Stew! I said pull off. Do what I tell you or I'll dump you."

"All right, all right. What do you mean followed? I don't understand. I mean the shots, the fire? What's going on?"

"Shut up! Kick it up to sixty."

The priest obeyed. "Beth, you talk to him."

"Yeah, Beth. Tell us what happened. What the hell did they do to you?"

"Oh, God. Don't ask me, please. I'm dizzy from the drugs and I, I just don't know what's happening." The anguish in her voice silenced them.

Stew slowed as the entrances to Interstate 64 came up rapidly.

"Pass up the first entrance and slow down to a crawl."

The priest obeyed. Haggerty watched the two cars behind pass the southbound entrance too. They slowed behind them. "Shit! They were dead. "Make a quick u-turn and duck. Those bastards will be shooting." The Bronco bucked forward and swung in an arc. The Cat pulled a grenade from his vest. He saw the flash of gunfire and threw the grenade in front of the second car. Shards of glass flew around the Bronco.

"Blam!" The grenade blew the rear end off the second car. It swerved into the guardrail and started to burn. "Gun it Stew! Gun it! Beth, you okay, Beth? And you?"

"My name is Whitney. Uh, I just happened along, I—."

"I'll let you go as soon as it's safe." The four-wheeler jerked forward and accelerated on 199 toward where they had come from.

"Dan, Stew is hurt."

"Guess I got hit by something, glass I guess. On the arm and cheek. I'll be okay. My God, what's happening?"

"You're in a war, padre. Slow down a bit. See that curve up there? Stop as soon as I tell you. I'll cover you. If you don't see any explosions, get the hell out. Take Beth to a hospital. Don't leave her alone." He saw a car closing behind them.

"God, Dan, don't leave." Beth tried to grab at him.

He shook her off. "Okay, Stop." He slid out and hit the side of the vehicle with his fist. "Go!" He stepped off the road and pulled two grenades. The other vehicle was on him. The grenade bounced partly off the road but it exploded in front of the pursuer making it swerve and slow. He laid the second one on the road and hit the bushes. The grenade blew the tires, sending the car careening into trees where it stopped.

He was behind them as two men struggled out. The first went down with bullets in his back. The other blasted a shotgun at Cat. The S & W silenced him.

Haggerty eased up behind the car. The remaining two in the front seat were badly hurt. He didn't wait to check the ones he had gunned down. He moved in a halting gait down the road. Gotta stop the blood somehow. Don't matter. Beth's safe now. I can train in and secure. Someplace. He lost his balance and fell on the pavement. Jesus. Outta shape Cat. He shook his head and blinked to regain eyesight.

Two cars sped by heading for the Interstate. The lights of a third showed over the hill.

No place to hide. Still got grenades. Go down fighting, Cat. You finished the op. Will I see Bobby? He slumped to a sitting position in the road and reloaded the machine gun.

CHAPTER FORTY FIVE

In Magee's suite, the mood was one of anxiety and wonder. What the hell was going on over at the Magruder? How would it affect his plans? He finished a drink and prepared to rejoin The Reverend and his entourage. Wes strode into the suite face flushed and tense.

"Wes, you seem to be ready to eat nails. What seems to be the problem?"

"Sir, would you please come to the hallway where I can speak in private? It's the terrorist attack at the Magruder."

Magee chose a sitting room nearby with two chairs in one corner. "Go ahead."

"Sir, I'd better jump on the search for the man who attacked those people at the motel. Preacher Creed's chauffer was killed along with four others. Mister Wallace is wounded and in shock. The police have roadblocks, but no one knows where he's taking the hostages. He has two women and a priest. If you approve, I'll take charge, using your comm equipment in your limo."

"Do you think it's wise for us to become involved?"

"Sir, no matter how you feel about Mister Wallace, it's a

breach of security to have a former consultant wounded and five of his people killed. One of the hostages is a woman, the Satellite Manager for Reverend Creed's network. I was sure that you'd want me to get involved for that reason alone."

"You're perfectly correct. Do it. Rumors have it that the man was a terrorist. Should I be concerned about Estelle's safety and mine?"

"I've got two men outside the suite. I'll do the same for Missus Magee. "Thank you, sir. I'll brief you quite often."

The manhunt was intense and extensive. Working out of the Foxmobile in Williamsburg, Wes held constant contact with on-scene commanders. He called in due bills owed by key people in state and local police leaders from the nation's capital to Newport News and Hampton. His federal friends joined in because of the terrorist story.

Magee's contacts brought in expertise and equipment. Air and National Guard aircraft were available. Resources from other government agencies and private sources joined in. Wes had inserted trusted people into key groups with orders to "shoot to kill on sight," regardless of what their superiors said. There would be no live witnesses.

When the former Marine reported back, The Fox sipped Perrier with two television evangelists. "Excuse us for a moment." He led his security chief out of earshot.

Wes pointed at a map. "Sir, I have a couple of choppers from Fort Eustis and from the Coast Guard in Norfolk. The police have the Hampton Tunnel and James River Bridge blocked off. I told them to get after exits to the north, in case they double back. The Coleman Bridge in Yorktown is covered. I'm sending a car to roads that lead away in every direction."

Dan tried to sit up to take on the approaching car. The lights hurt his eyes and he couldn't see what it was. No sirens. No

Stolen Votes

red lights. Must be civvies, FBI, or something like that. Come on, ass-holes. I got something for you. He raised his right hand to throw a grenade. The headlights flicked on "bright," then the driving position. The vehicle slowed. He had the advantage if he pulled the grenade pin and threw it right now. He hesitated. Jesus, the Bronco.

Stew pulled to the side and ran to him. "You okay? You've got to get to a hospital."

"I'm getting too old for this shit. Help me up, huh? How come you didn't keep going?"

"Beth wouldn't let me leave you. I had to come back."

"Make a U-turn and head back towards Williamsburg."

"Williamsburg? Why? Okay, okay."

"They won't follow us now. Got to get you to a hospital, Beth."

On the ramp to Busch Gardens a police car roared up the ramp in the opposite direction. "Well, he'll find something up by the interstate. Let's try to get lost on some side roads. Take Route 60 south whenever we run into it."

They sat in a MacDonald's parking lot so that Haggerty could study a map. Whitney asked, "Please can I go now? I won't tell anybody."

"No! I'll tell you when you can leave."

Stew interrupted. "Hey, look. I'm not going any farther until you tell me what this is all about. Killings, explosions."

"Not yet. Turn left and drive with the traffic. Keep an eye out for roadblocks and police cars. If we're gonna get stopped I'll bail out. You're safer without me. Go!"

"Okay, but I want to hear what is going on."

"Well. I've been tailed and beaten up. Some guys tried to kill me in the water by my boat." He heard Beth gasp. "Beth was kidnapped. She called me and told me to come to get her. But she gave me a warning. There's something damned bad going on. You know that bullshit about her ring and all that? That was all lies. Tell him, Beth."

She told them about being kidnapped and taken to sea to be drowned in halting speech, She left out the gory details of

245

the rapes and cutting.

Near Carter's Grove, Haggerty spotted a roadblock with two police cars.

"Hey, pull off here, into this driveway."

Railroad tracks split their path between the highway and the interstate. Dan directed Stew to back the car, then stop. "Follow me to the tracks. Cut the lights." The Cat stumbled out of the vehicle and fell down, causing the pain in his side to scream. He coaxed Stew along, walking slowly next to the vehicle. He found a spot where they could get over the rails.

Dan cut the fence with Doc's bolt cutters and had Stew haul the fence apart with the Bronco. As they jolted across the tracks, a pulsing light stabbed at them along the rails. A long coal train from the Virginia southwest thundered toward them with its horn blasting as they bounced across the rails. The vehicle sank into a ditch, then leaped up on the shoulder.

Stew speed down the Interstate and grinned, "Well, you brought some excitement into my life, Dan. But I don't know if I can handle this. Where do we go from here?"

"You got me. They're watching my boat. Guess Beth's apartment is out. Whitney, where do you live?"

"DC. Look. My car is at The Magruder. I've got to get back. I don't know you people, so I can't possibly help them do anything against you. Please let me go."

Beth's weak moan answered.

Stew repeated again. "You have to go to a hospital. After that you'd be safe at any of the churches. I'm sure that if—."

"No way, padre. Look, if Beth can take it, we need a place to hide for a while. I mean, we can't show up at a hospital and expect this to blow over. Something sinister is going on. I mean somethin' big, Stew. There's an army after us. Got the best communications and plenty weapons. Those people holding Beth were bad dudes. I almost bought it when that big guy almost bear-hugged me to death."

"Here's an exit, Dan. What should I do?"

"Keep going. If the cops have a roadblock on Sixty, they'll probably have one ahead on the Interstate. The more traffic we're in the better, I think. I've got to get to Southside ASAP! We got two ways, two only. The Hampton Tunnel and the long way around across the James River Bridge. We could run north to Richmond or take the York River Bridge, but I figure they're already blocking those too."

In the corner of a second room away from the TV evangelists, Wes continued to report to his boss. "There's a fence knocked down between Route 60 and the Interstate. Tire tracks from a four-wheeler. They could get away to the north by crossing the median."

Otto signaled at the door. "Mister Magee, I think you'd better come to the suite and see what happened to Mister Nelson."

"Wallace?" He smirked. "I could care less."

"Yes sir. But he's kind of babbling about a terrorist and possibly a threat to you too."

"Hm. After I see the two gentlemen in the next room."

As soon as he could break away from congratulatory offers of financial support and also political backing, he had Wallace brought in. The Fox was shocked at the big man's appearance. His suit was tattered and bore scorch marks. He wiped black powder from his face with the Inn's towels. The most disturbing aspect was the man's face. FX had never seen him frightened. But there was an unmistakable shadow of fear on his face. "My God, what happened, Nelson?"

"Jesus Christ, Frank." He gulped out an explanation, not always clear or coherent. "Terrorist bastard! Killed five guys. That SOB is bad! Got away, two women and a priest."

"A priest? What women?"

Wallace waved to stop questions. "He's wounded. Blew a fucking bomb up in my face. Dynamite strapped to his chest. I don't know how the hell we weren't killed."

Magee was staggered by the explanation and more so by Nelson's manner. He had known the man for years and the rock-like tough was panicked. Magee faced Wallace. A hint of empathy invaded his thoughts for a microsecond. "What can I do?"

"Mister Magee, you have contacts up the ying yang. Help us find the bastard."

"You said he was a terrorist?"

"Yeah. Ex Navy SEAL. Those bastards are killers."

"Should I take cover?"

"Don't think so. He may be with a group in Lebanon or somewhere else there. He was wounded." He shook his head. "Still don't know how the hell the bastard wasn't killed."

The Fox dismissed Wallace's point. His armed people in Lebanon were his first concern. If this was a terrorist attack, could it have a bearing on his people over there?

CHAPTER FORTY SIX

In his suite at the Inn, Magee thought about his armed rescue group in Lebanon. They were more important than the missile deliveries and the contras. He wondered if starting an action in Iran would damn the hostages. How can I bring some of them out without causing more casualties?

Wes interrupted his thoughts. "Sir, it may be that the killer was sent to stir up trouble to get our reaction. I heard from our man in Lebanon. His people are hiding out. Should we have them brought out or should we wait?"

The Fox frowned. Damn! If he brought the crew out of the Middle East now, it would end his special opportunity to save some hostages.

"Send a standby message to our rescue people. Have them ready to attack or bug out. The second channel doesn't seem to be able to guarantee any hostage releases at this time." He inhaled and set his jaw. He could not hide his involvement in GRASS ROOTS any longer. "Nelson, I want this local terrorist ASAP. Got that?"

"Yes, Frank. I'll get on it with Wes. I know where the bastard is going."

"What? What? You know. How?"

"Witnesses say that he had help taking the woman away, a priest and another woman. A woman, by the way, who seemed to look like Whitney."

"Whitney? What the hell? Where was she? How did she get away?"

"I had her, then I had to break off to handle an immediate threat. The terrorist started a fire and in the confusion, she got away. Seems like she's with them."

"That little bitch!"

Wallace shook gray powder out of his hair. "The priest is his friend from the retreat house in Hampton. That's where they're going. To hide out. I know that's where they are."

Magee pointed. "Wes, get on that! Now!"

"Yes sir. I'll get our own cars, our own people, no others. Got a chopper nearby."

"Good." Magee's voice and manner changed again to a modicum of concern. "Well, Nelson, sorry you had to be a victim here. Let me know if I can do anything for you."

"Thanks, Frank. I'll contact Wes soon as I can."

The Fox had dismissed him already. Could he save the missile sales? Bullshit! Those NSC cowboys were on their own. He was out of it! Or was he? He thought of his crew in Lebanon, his opportunity to make a statement to the world about America's power and will. He would never abandon them, but he might have to have them slip away to safety. They were far more important than the pseudo generals of the contras.

The fugitives were heading southward toward the Hampton Tunnel. Father Stew insisted on prying out more information as he drove. "Dan, what's this all about?"

"I wish the hell I knew. Maybe Beth has a clue. All I know is that people have been after me since Tony was killed."

He started to plan the next move. The logical thing

would be to get medical assistance. He didn't know how badly he was hurt and he had to get patched up to protect Beth. She had some bad bruises. She seemed pretty drifty and he wondered about her mind. If they could get to Virginia Beach he could contact Doc. His buddy had enough medical training to determine how badly they were hurt. He hated to involve his friends. But this was war.

"Hey, just in case they have the tunnel to Norfolk blocked, take the James River Bridge. The exit is coming up." The pain in his side kept throbbing. It was a deep wound, but it might not have cut into an organ. He was dizzy again and drifted off.

"What do we do, Dan?"

Haggerty shook himself awake. Stew had stopped on Route 17 in a traffic tie up before getting into the traffic circle east of the bridge. He saw police cars ahead with flashing lights.

"Damn. If they have this closed off, the tunnel will be blocked too. Is there a place we could hide out for a few hours, Stew? A church? Rectory?"

"The retreat house." Stew took a side street, turned three times in different directions, and ended up headed for the Interstate. "It helps to know back streets. We'll be near the tunnel. If that's blocked, we'll get off and go there. I can get a doctor to check you out, but you two still need a hospital."

"We need a place to hide first. Beth has been kidnapped and beaten by some tough dudes. We've been attacked by people who have a helluva big organization with heavy weapons and they aren't afraid of using them. And you want us to go to a hospital?"

Dan's nerves kicked into overdrive as they neared the tunnel. When they came over the crown of the hill by the Veterans Hospital, he saw a long line of red stoplights ahead. "It's no use, Stew. Take us to the retreat house."

"I'll take you there, then it's time for medical help."

"Do it! After we get there we'll talk about next moves."

Whitney sounded irritated. "Wait a minute, Mister Big!

Dan, or whatever the hell your name is. I want out of here. You kidnapped me! You'd better let me go, or the people after you may want me too. And I need to disappear. Right now!"

"Not yet, Beth needs someone to help her, I can't handle it, and neither can Stew As soon as I can, I'll let you go. Believe me, I don't want to be responsible for someone else. I'm sure Father can get you where you need to go. Right, Stew."

"I certainly can, Miss. I do have some connections, not sure if they can help you disappear. Your assistance has been invaluable. You can trust me."

"I've heard that before."

"Not from me. You'll be okay. We can all have a good rest at the retreat house."

No one spoke for a long time on their way to safety. Dan wondered, would it be safe? Would the hunters know about the retreat house? Shit, they knew everything about him. He reloaded the Uzi.

CHAPTER FORTY SEVEN

Friday evening's press conference at the Williamsburg Inn buzzed with anticipation and rumors. The Reverend Creed was the central figure, beaming and nodding his head at acquaintances. Additional news media arrived and crowded into the Inn, drawn by news of a terrorist attack at The Magruder. The preacher warmed up the audience by saying, "Please take a seat and relax. Ah have an announcement to make and then the folks up here on the dais will help answer questions. Thank you."

Reverend Jethro held up his hands to quiet the audience. "It gives me great pleasure to announce to the nation that the Mite Network, formerly owned and operated by the Reverend Lawrence has been purchased by a group of dedicated Christians. The purpose is to offset the distorted views of America spouted by the Satanists and Secular Humanists. This group will form a consortium with my network. We will expand into all areas of our beloved country."

Anticipating a reaction from the crowd, he paused to wait for chatter and noise to subside. 'Yes, my friends, I know that you have many questions and comments about this acquisition. You will receive a press release shortly, and I will be happy to clarify anything you bring up. We do have time for a few questions at this moment."

Several reporters stood and waved to attract his attention. Two shouted their questions about the attack at the Magruder.

"Now folks, I know this is quite a shock, but we live in astonishing times. Please bear with me as we move forward in our program. I assure you, especially members of the press, that I and others will remain as long as you need information. Thank you. Thank you again."

He waited for a moment and continued. "And now I'd like to reintroduce the two folks up here on the dais. On mah left is the distinguished dean of our television evangelists the Reverend Joe Don Bailey."

Bailey was one of the most respected and honored TV evangelists among his peers and the public. He was greeted by thunderous applause. "Now, last but not least, the man who has had a great role in bringing this union into being, the wonderful Catholic layman. An outspoken source of all that is right about America, my personal friend, Mister Francis X. Magee."

The applause was thin until Creed's shills chanted, "Vote Right! Vote Right!"

He allowed the chanting and applause to continue for effect. He thanked everyone, and then invited the dean of religious reporters to ask the first question. It was directed at Bailey. "How do you feel about Catholics being involved in TV ministry?"

The Reverend Joe Don was always sincere in his support of expanding the market for any televangelists. "My friends, we have all come from the same Judeo-Christian roots. The Catholic Church has been in the forefront of issues that are dear to all of us, against abortion, for school prayer and the continuing movement toward Christian Unity. Of course there are times when we might have had a few disagreements, but that is nothing more than honest differences in trying to be true to the Gospel of Jesus Christ."

Creed's loud, "Ah-men!" brought many echoes from the audience. He caught Frank's eye. They both smiled. Yes, they were pulling it off.

Wes was frustrated, even though he had received offers for assistance from every governmental agency involved in law enforcement and intelligence. Reports of the fugitive vehicle were overwhelming, ranging from west of Richmond and to Norfolk. Information from the northern-most area around Matthews, a small community with access to the Chesapeake Bay, stretched to south of the border between Virginia and North Carolina. These inputs of little value tied up phones and radios and contributed to the chaos. He asked Wallace to meet privately.

"Sir, this is a GD fiasco. I can't keep track of all the input. I suggest that we select a leaner, meaner group of people and expand our surveillance out into the water. There are so many places where the frog could get a boat that it isn't funny."

"I agree. Did you get any help from the Coast Guard?"

"Yes, sir, they have three fast boats that they can use for us, but I'd prefer to begin with choppers. They can cover a lot of areas and the boats can do the investigations."

"Sounds good to me. Still nothing at the retreat house. I'm going there. Seems to me that the priest could have taken them somewhere else. Maybe I can find some info." He thought, Damn that frog! He's been freaking lucky. I'll get that bastard, no matter what it takes.

The Cat was thinking faster than Stew drove. Medical help. Yeah. Doc could help. If he called him, it would involve his best friend. Dammit! Gotta keep him out of it. Tactics. Need a diversion. Stew could be kept out of this thing. He could claim that he was a hostage. Yeah, that would get him out of it. I gotta find out what's goin' down. Better to keep friends out of it. What if we borrowed a car from the retreat house? No, we'd still get stopped. If Stew took off in a different direction? First, get Beth looked at and sit for a while so I can figure out what to do.

Half way to the retreat house The Cat made up his mind. His side wound was too chancy. He had to stay awake to help Beth. They needed medical attention. They had to get over to the south side somehow, to get in touch with Doc. How the hell could he make it? The bastards had an army and a half searching for them. With all the clout they seemed to have, they'd probably get choppers after them too.

He caught himself drifting off. They had to get rid of the Bronco. How could they get across to Norfolk? Where was Doc? Could he get hold of him without anyone else knowing about it? Somehow, he had to find out what the hell was going on. Haggerty grabbed Stew's arm a block short of the retreat house entrance. "Stop! Back up. Cut the lights and wait for me."

"What for? We're almost there. We can get Beth taken care of."

"Dammit! Do what I tell you." He stepped out of the vehicle and pointed at Whitney. "Miss, don't get any ideas of takin' off. These bastards may shoot on sight."

The Cat slipped along the brush and shrubs down the long entrance until he had a good view of the parking lot. He ran quietly around the waterside of the house. Coming around on the east side, he saw what he expected. Two dark cars parked with men inside. A police car was standing by, empty. Were they inside searching, or were they out here?

He could have taken the two cars with the grenades in his vest. It would be a mistake. Let them wait where they were. How the hell do we get away now? He slipped into the Bronco.

"Okay, go straight. Keep the lights off. Where does this road go?"

"It heads toward the bay, then dead ends."

"They were waiting for us, Stew. I have an idea. But you'll have to give us a diversion. Course, I'm not sure what good it will do, if we can't get the hell out of here. Slow down. Stop." He pointed at the water. "Is that the bay or is it a lake?"

"It's a lake. Up ahead there's a way to get out to the bay. You thinking of a boat?"

"Don't ask."

"There are some sailboats and power boats at a nearby marina. Can't I take Beth? It's criminal to take her and not get her to a hospital. She's been drugged and exhausted."

"We don't have a choice. Get us as close to the water. Get under a tree. Now!"

The thumping sound of a slick approaching stopped him. He grabbed the S & W and waited, ready to fire. Apparently, the Bronco couldn't be seen where they had stopped.

"Dan, please go and let me take Beth. After all, I'm a priest. I can stay with her in any hospital. You seem to be worried about somebody kidnapping her again."

"Damned sight right! I can't take a chance."

No time for arguments. He'd punch Stew in the face to give him an alibi, then send him north to draw them away. It would be like a fake insertion by a Mike Boat. The argument continued, and Dan began to tremble. Pretty soon he'd be out of it, and where would they be? "Wait one, you wouldn't know a doctor who might keep his mouth shut, would you?"

"I do. But why?"

"I'm fadin' fast here. Beth needs to get rid of the drugs, whatever they were. Is there someone who would be willing to hide us overnight or for a couple hours?"

Stew nodded. "I've got the man who can do both." He drove the Bronco into a neighborhood, turning into different streets, until they were on one with few homes and no traffic.

"Where are we heading?"

"An old friend, a retired doctor who needs company. It would be best if you didn't tell about what has happened. I still have problems understanding what is going on."

"So do I, padre."

When they arrived at the house on a lake, Stew and Whitney struggled getting Beth up the path to the house. Cat struggled too, hefting the weapons bag. He had to keep it with him.

The inside of the house was rumpled and old as was its single occupant. But it felt homey. After short greetings and a quick explanation about Beth's condition, the doctor had them place her on a bed. He grinned behind his white beard and poured drinks for the others. He washed up and talked about the fish he had caught this week.

The Cat flopped into a chair with Whitney opposite, curled on a sagging sofa. He hadn't felt this dragging fatigue since they had three ops in a row in Nam. How could he keep this woman with them so she wouldn't call the cops? He glared at her and remained silent.

She spoke. "You're thinking of how you can keep me here, aren't you?"

"No shit."

"Tell me about the big man who seemed to be in charge."

He described Wallace as best he could and she nodded.

"I know who the bastard is. He tried to rape me earlier tonight. He's a badass from way back and he'll be after your butt forever. I don't know what the hell is going down, but it must be serious. If you think that I'm going to take off and get captured by that son of a bitch, you're stupid."

"I'm going to shackle you to the chair over there."

"Try it and I'll kick you in the balls." She snuggled under her mink and closed her eyes. "Call me for breakfast."

The Cat wanted to get up and use the cuffs on her that were in a side pocket of the bag but he couldn't move. She was asleep. He drifted off and felt a sting from a shot the doctor administered. The doctor cleaned the wound and it burned. He gave him two pills and grinned. "I always wanted to say this. Take two of these and call me in the morning."

CHAPTER FORTY EIGHT

Late that night, Wallace tried to convince the priests at the retreat center that they should disclose Father Steward's friends and contacts. Nothing had worked with the Rector of the retreat center. The latter had sensed that the large man with the damaged face was not the sweet pussycat that he pretended to be. None of the accompanying uniformed police and plainclothesmen had familiar faces. Some could possibly be FBI, but the local Special Agent in Charge was one of the center's staunchest supporters and he was not present.

In addition, any personal relationship with laypersons was the business of the individual priest. The rector knew about the close friends each one of his priests and most of the others. "Pastoral lying" was an avenue of escape that some theologians held.

"I'm sorry, Mister Wallace. I don't know the answers to your questions. I realize that you came here in good faith and have a legitimate reason for asking. But you're intruding on relationships that are often spiritual. Some are so sensitive because they involve confession, which is a privilege that the courts have upheld."

The aged priest with white hair noted the expression that changed on the man's face from softness to an immediate cardinal color and a set jaw.

"You don't know who you're screwing around with here. By God, I'll have the Pope after you."

"That would be a magnificent experience. Now, if you kindly leave our sacred grounds. You have kept us up quite late and we have early rising for prayer and preparations for the lay people in the midst of their retreat."

"Who the hell do you think you are? I'll get a search warrant and we'll turn your place into a shipwreck."

The rector pushed a desk button and two large priests entered. "Father Daniel and Father Zachariah, please escort this gentleman and the others out of my office and off the grounds."

Wallace's last retort was a pointed finger and his threat concerning a search warrant.

A few hours later Wallace returned accompanied by eleven law enforcement officers. Twenty armed men spread out on the grounds. Wallace had the rector awakened and called to his office. The angry visitor pointed to a trim dark suited man who held folded papers in his hand. "Now, by God, you're gonna pay for not answering or allowing me to search."

The gentleman held out the papers. "Rector, you know me well. I am the last person who would disturb these holy premises but I cannot ignore a court order. Here is the search warrant, for the entire premises and grounds, including the rooms of all the people here for a retreat. I'm deeply sorry."

"Tommy, dear Tommy. How is Noreen your dear wife? Has she recovered from her pneumonia? Why, I spoke with her just yesterday—."

Tommy glared at Wallace and stepped back after the rector took the papers. "You ought to read them, Father."

"Signed by the great Judge Monahan, the fallen Catholic. Not a surprise." He turned to his assistant and said, "Father

Joseph, please begin to carry out this order. In the meantime I have a phone call to make." He strode to his desk, paged through his Rolidex, and dialed a long distance number. He had by-passed the Richmond Diocese and called the Papal Nuncio in DC.

"Monsignor Magiori, this is Rector Sullivan from the retreat house in Hampton. I apologize for the inconvenience of calling at this time, but we seem to have a legal problem."

He described the court order and the circumstances. "I am sure that the Nuncio will be interested in this power play by a suspicious lay person. As soon as I hang up I will call our Senators and congressional offices, along with Bishop Navid. I just wanted you to know what is going on."

He stood and faced Wallace. "Please get out of my office. I have more emergency phone calls to make. You can wait in the dining room and my staff will serve you coffee and juice if you wish."

Whitney struggled in her sleep. The mink had slipped to the floor and she was cold. She sat up and checked her watch in the dark. Three A.M. Dammit! She glanced over at Haggerty in the gloom. The son of a bitch was snoring. No wonder she had awakened. She wanted to go to him and punch his nose so that he'd stop. No sense making him more pissed. She checked her purse and in the hidden pocket felt her Beretta. At the proper time, she'd pull it and escape.

Where would she go? With Wallace after my ass and these people, the only hope was to return to Magee. She knew that her days under his protection were waning. Had he already written her off? He was so freaking meticulous, that anything contaminating his food, clothing or his property caused him anguish and immediate cleaning or disposal. And I'm damaged goods with that piss-ant in Hong Kong and the freaking preacher.

She shrugged and pulled the mink over her shoulders. Settling down she promised herself, when I get my chance,

I'm gone. This guy is tough but he's against terrible odds.

The Cat awakened fully alert with his hand on a weapon. Whitney's fumbling and mumbling had brought him out of a deep sleep, one that reminded him of how he had slept after the SEALs Hell Week, and the ensuing groggy and anxious feelings.

Wonder if she'll try to haul ass? I wouldn't blame her. She seems like a tough kid, gorgeous but strong. Better keep a better watch on her. Her story on the guy named Wallace might not be true. Trust your instincts and your training. Yeah, his reactions against the two attempts to kill him on the boat were just that, reactions.

He knew that he was damned lucky to have won the battle against the killers in the room and on the road. Know your enemy. Gather intel. How the hell do I do that and keep Beth safe? But there were too many enemies out there, and they knew what the hell they were doing.

He shook his head. He didn't know squat about what was going on. Dammit! I don't want to do it, but I need help. And I know two buds that will jump in if I ask. But what the hell would I be bringing them into? Sure death? For what? Who are these people? What the hell do they want?

He slipped silently into Beth's room, touched her softly, and said a prayer. Gotta get you back, sweetie. Nobody's gonna hurt you again.

The following day, the white-haired doctor made sure that they had a large breakfast. He told Dan that Beth needed hospital care and soon. "Above all, she needs to get the drugs purged from her system. I'll do what I can. How long do you want to stay?"

Dan sighed. "Could we hang here till dark? We'll take off then and let you alone. I can't thank you enough for helping us. You could get some trouble with the police, or whoever. I'm not sure who these people are. All I know is that they have *mucho* clout."

The doctor grinned. "I love working against powerful people. They always have to come to a doctor and, or, a funeral director in the end."

The Cat spent the day sitting with Beth, or cleaning the weapons and thinking. His intel was zip shit. He had no clue where the enemy forces were, nor how many of them were on the hunt. Snippets of the story cut into TV programs during the day.

Whitney said, "So you're a terrorist. Never met one before. Are you a Muslim, or just a dupe?"

He gave her a hard look and went back to checking the action on the Stoner machine gun.

She pointed. "What is that ugly thing? I've never seen anything like it."

"It's a Stoner light machine gun, a helluva weapon for laying down bullets in a hurry. It's temperamental, like a woman."

"Bullshit!"

"Well, it needs a lot of maintenance to keep it in shape. Have to make sure the action ain't sticky or the barrel don't slip out from the receiver. Happened once or twice at a critical time. I used it a lot in 'Nam." For a moment he was sorry he had mentioned that bastard of a place.

She asked more questions and he refused to answer, his mind focused on the enemy. Much depended on their ability to search and pounce quickly. All the roads, tunnels, and bridges were surely blocked. A boat might make it if he could find one tonight. They had choppers and probably boats, so he'd have to be ready to fight and or run somewhere else. I'll use Stew as a diversion whether he likes it or not. Have to depend on this chippie even more. Shit!

Joseph Guion

CHAPTER FORTY NINE

After sunset, Dan checked boat candidates in a small cove connecting to New Market Creek. A sullen Whitney held Beth to prevent her from falling. A sailboat could be difficult to handle, but he felt it would be a better type to slip by the hunters. Whitney helped to lift Beth on board. They brought the boat around to slacken and disconnect the anchor line.

"Okay, I better keep pushing. Wind's against us and the tide may be too. Can you steer?"

"Can't you tie the helm? You're pretty beat. I'll push."

They worked side-by-side, swinging the boat around and shoving it away from the shallows behind them. He didn't dare start up the engine. He slipped into the cold, dark water. Felt mud under him. Slid under water. Came up coughing and spitting. The mud. The sucking mud that held him captive so many times in 'Nam when the squad was running from an ambush. Geez. He was in a crouch, dizzy.

He felt a hand under his armpit and heard a musical laugh. "Come on, Danny Boy, don't quit now." She boosted him up on the boat. He pulled her aboard and said, "I ought to leave you. I've got enough trouble."

"You have my mink. I don't want it wet."

She had more than the coat on her mind. If Wallace were involved, Frank was not a part of it. No, the fight the men had two years ago had severed their relationship. If she stayed with the fugitives, she might not be able to get back in Frank's graces, to save her ass, and her Mercedes. She'd hang on until she saw a clear path to freedom. Then what?

Father Stew missed the turnoff into the forest alongside the northbound Interstate. "Damn!" He backed up slowly, hoping that no one would come by. Why am I doing this anyway?

This is crazy? I shouldn't have let Dan talk me into this. His cheek burned from the bruise caused by Haggerty's fist. That was meant to add credence to the story that he had escaped from the fugitives. He turned into a dirt road and drove slowly, to stay in the middle. There were deep culverts on each side. "Oh, Lord, help us out of this."

The Bronco dropped into a ditch and ground its way into the mud. "Oh, God!" He reversed and tried to walk it out with the four-wheel drive. It went in deeper. He saw lights from a vehicle around the next curve. He shut off the engine and stumbled out, crawling and scratching his way into the bushes at the side of the road. He started back toward the highway. The other vehicle approached and stopped. Stew realized that he was making too much noise moving through the brush. He halted. Voices drifted toward him.

"Looks like a bad 'un. Say, any tracks around?"

"Somethin' over heah. Engine's still warm. Must a jes happened. Think we oughta take a look around, Jeff?"

"Yep. Take the shotgun. Don't want nobody to know we was huntin' early."

Stew heard them approaching. Running wouldn't be smart. He found a broken branch. Easing himself down in the leaves, he tensed, and then struck himself in the forehead with the wood. It hurt enough to cry out but he stifled the sound. Could he pull off the story? He lay there praying. Twigs snapped nearby. A light crossed over his face.

"Looka here. Some guy, in a black suit."

"Is he out? Check his pulse."

Stew felt the man examining him.

"Gotta pulse. Think he's got any money on him?"

"Why? You gonna roll him 'n make him disappear?"

Stew thought of the '72 movie *Deliverance*. Enough of that, he groaned.

Haggerty and Whitney struggled for an hour to get the boat into the Chesapeake Bay from Newmarket Creek. Dan was so cold that his legs were numb. Damn! Like I'm back in BUDS. Shit, we sat in fifty-degree water till some got hypothermic. You can do it, asshole. A helo thumped nearby. God he was wiped out. Bullshit!

He anchored. They moved Beth into the cabin and Dan fell on the deck. The throbbing of a Huey broke him out of the dizzy sleep. Was he in 'Nam? No. He tried to move quickly, but he felt as if he were under a pile of sand bags. A searchlight stabbed down from the chopper. It hovered for a while. Was Whitney on deck signaling?

"Oh, God, don't let them come down." He had the S&W, other weapons and explosives. He felt his will slipping away with fatigue. "SEALs don't quit!"

The helo dipped, swooped forward, and thumped away. He had to get out of confined waters, get sail up. Dragging up the ladder to the main deck he waited for his strength to return. The familiar sound of a slick approaching made him roll against the cabin's overhang to get out of sight. Was he fast enough?

The chopper went into hover; close enough to feel the wind stirred up by the blades. It dipped so low that he could have hit it with a rock. He was okay, as long as they didn't see him. He heard Beth calling. She sounded like she was coming up the ladder. Damn! Where the hell is Whitney.

He shouted, "Whitney, keep her down there, there's a chopper right on us." He had left the S & W below. Dammit! You're getting' careless.

Their room at the Peninsula Airport was crackling with radio static and animated conversation. During a short break Wes received the report that the priest had been captured. He asked Nelson, "How did he get up there when the main search is down the peninsula?"

"He claims they dumped him out on the highway. The Bronco was there. There's no evidence that they're up that way. I wouldn't give up the south side." He eased into a chair.

"Let's be practical. What do they gain if they head north? What is their goal? Even though we didn't get anything out of the retreat house, roadblocks are the best bets. If they get across Hampton Roads he has friends, SEALs. And they're near the network."

"You think they want to attack it? Could they get in?"

"No. If they find a computer whiz, they might gain access with a local call. I have people who owe me in high places. They'd need a mainframe computer to get into the system. Well, enough about that."

Wes frowned. "A system? What about the terrorist?"

Wallace didn't answer. "Any progress with the priest?"

He wagged his head. "He's sticking to his story. Experts covered that Bronco inch by inch. Others were in it, but it's impossible to verify when or where they left. They have fresh prints of a fourth person."

Wallace nodded. "Yes. Remember, I said that a woman similar to Whitney was with them. She tied up the guard. Her bag and mink have disappeared. It's a wild goose chase. I still believe that they're down south, between here and Hampton Roads. The men at the retreat house haven't seen anything. A chopper is wheeling around there. All of the people are ours. They have their orders."

"Yes, sir. They won't live more than five minutes."

Out in the Chesapeake Bay, the boat was spotlighted three times by choppers. Each time, Dan played the friendly sailor and waved at them. His hair was covered with a dark watch cap and he stayed in the shadows. Whitney steered with her dark auburn hair loose and free. They took a chance that no one knew she was along. Haggerty headed due east, then northeast, away from Virginia Beach. If they were attacked, his weapons were in the cockpit at his feet. The helo thumped away. "Beth, you want to come up?"

She stepped into the cockpit and hugged him. "What if they send a boat after us?"

"That would be tough. If the Navy and Coast Guard get involved, they have some pretty fast boats. That would be all she wrote. I've got a plan, but it's risky."

Whitney asked, "Any riskier than what we've done?"

Nelson was livid. He grabbed the helo pilot and shook him. "Dammit! You said that the boat was heading out into the Chesapeake so you let it go. Identify it. What was it's name? A man in Hampton reported that his thirty-eight footer is missing. You get that freaking helo back up there and find that thing."

A Coast Guard officer approached. "Mister Nelson, I've been authorized to give you all the assistance possible. I have two fast boats ready. Where do you want them?"

Wallace was ready to point at the track the helo pilot had scratched on the chart. If he used them, they would not be under his control or orders. They'd capture the fugitives and the legal wheels would turn. He couldn't afford that. "Thanks for the offer. Let's hold them in place right now. I want to make sure that we're going after the right boat."

"Yes sir. They're all set, any time."

Beth touched his cheek. "Is your side hurting? Your mouth is all pinched up."

"It's better, kid. Hmmm. Guess I could use some coffee. And a kiss."

"You give the lunkhead a kiss, I'll get the coffee."

Beth kissed him and snuggled next to him. Yeah, if they sent a Coast Guard boat out after him, he'd be in a world of shit. "Maybe I can make 'em think we drowned." He told Beth about his idea. She shook her head and passed out when Whitney gave him coffee. He told her about it.

"You, my friend, are out of your frigging mind. Get me to do that? Hell no. I'll stay here and wait for them to come. I won't tell."

"You won't have a choice. These people tortured her, doped her up. They can make anybody talk." He had her take the wheel and searched for his last hope.

Joseph Guion

CHAPTER FIFTY

Haggerty's idea was risky, more likely crazy. The tug with its railroad barge was two miles to the northeast, heading toward Little Creek from Cape Charles on the eastern shore. Dan had seen it hundreds of times but never paid attention. How fast was she going with the barge? He'd set up a collision course to come alongside with only one shot at it. If he didn't time it right, he might fall behind and never catch up. It was going to be dangerous lifting Beth over to the barge. The tug probably had him on radar but it couldn't be helped.

Dan had considerable boat-handling experience, but this would be tough. With three lives in his hands he had to carry it out perfectly. He raised more sail and set a steady bearing for a spot amidships on the railroad barge. If they could jump on board, they'd get a free ride to Little Creek and freedom. Beth wasn't capable of jumping. Without Whitney, it would be impossible. Would the pursuers find them first?

"Whitney, you seem like you can handle a boat?"

"No problem. I've sailed and ran a few powerboats in my time. What do you have in mind? You going to flag down that tug?"

"Hardly. We've got one chance. I'll get in close. You throw on left rudder and smack it alongside. As soon we hit, we'll bounce out. Hold Beth and grab something solid to make sure you don't lose your footing. I'll snatch the barge with a line. When I have us secured alongside, I'll come back and help you with Beth."

He steered close to the barge. As the wake from the vessels converged, the "hiss" and "slosh" of the bow waves hitting each other became louder and the spray spit at him. The wake pushed him away but he worked the boat back in. Whitney took the helm and drove the boat against the barge. He jerked from the collision, jumped on the barge with the line wrapped around his wrist, a safety violation at best. He fell, scrambled upward and threw the bight of the line over a bollard, twisted and secured it.

Whitney shouted, "I'm losing it!"

"It's okay. I got it secured. Now ease in slowly."

He boarded the sailboat and they secured it alongside. Whitney helped him lift an unconscious Beth aboard. He went below for several minutes. When he came topside, Whitney held a knife to the bow line. "What the hell are you doing?"

"You bring my mink or I'll cut it."

"Shit! What the hell. All right. He brought the fur coat and his weapons bag. "Here, stuff it." He threw the coat at the shivering woman. He took the knife from her and cut the sailboat loose. It stayed alongside and then drifted aft. When it was free it turned to the northeast with the helm lashed in place. "Keep sailin' you mother."

Safe for a while. Were they? He eased Beth under a rail car and used a stolen boat cushion for a pillow. "Say. Thanks, Mink Lady. Are you okay?" She didn't answer. "Stay under cover, huh? Just in case." He searched to the west. Flashing lights of an aircraft were coming from Hampton. He heard the thumping of a Huey.

They hid underneath one of the swaying, creaking cars. The chopper's searchlight picked up the sailboat five hundred yards behind them. It was sailing well, still heading northeast. The helo hovered over the boat. He hoped that they wouldn't send divers to search. If they found no one aboard, they'd probably chase after the barge. He checked his watch. "Shit!" Five minutes to blow. He should have set the charge for three.

The helo stood off from the sailboat and swung toward them. "Watch out! Stay hidden." He grabbed Beth and held her close. God, we have to get away from these bastards. The chopper made a pass at the tug and barge, then headed toward Hampton. He couldn't believe it.

"Man, the Lord was with us there."

"Thank God. Now what do we do, Dan?"

He held a moaning Beth. "We enjoy the ride."

Dan checked his watch. Was it time? He watched the fuzzy image of the sailboat on the surface of the water. No sound. Did the detonator work? The C-4? He searched with the sailboat's binoculars. The mast hung at an angle. He grinned as it leaned and slowly dropped into the water. The hull was visible, on its beam now. Gradually, it turned over. Would the other charges work?

Nelson stomped up and down the airport operations room. The helicopter had no one aboard to check the boat. He wouldn't have another available for five minutes. At least they knew that the boat spotted was the one missing from Hampton. Nelson told the Coast Guard Officer to send his boats back to their base. He didn't want any interference or witnesses when he sent his bird with the frogmen. They would eliminate the fugitives immediately.

His helo searched back and forth, and then spiraled outward from the last known position of the sailboat. The pilot cursed the people from the other aircraft and their lousy navigation. He checked with Wes. "I can't find the damned thing. I'm at zero eight eight, two point four miles from Point Charlie. Making an expanding circle and I can't find the

Stolen Votes

damned thing. You sure they knew where it was?"

"You got anything on radar?"

"Nothing but the ships and barges around. Wait one."

He curved off to the northeast. Keeping the searchlight on the water as they skimmed along, the gunner spotted something in the water. The helo went into a hover.

"Got parts of a boat here. She's upside down. Wait one. Got the right name. There's charred pieces in the water and she's barely afloat upside down. I'm sending them down."

Two frogmen dropped into the water and swam through wreckage to the remains of the hull. They searched. One waved his hand and the other joined him in the water. They held up burned and torn clothing. They continued to search.

They were aboard twenty minutes later and the lead diver pulled a piece of a woman's dress out of his wetsuit. He shouted over the engine and transmission noise. "This hers?"

The investigator examined it carefully and consulted his book. "That's what she was wearing when she was seen last."

"Yeah."

The other diver gave him pieces of Haggerty's clothing. The odor of burned cloth cut into the noisy cabin. The investigator sniffed at the clothes. "Something not right here. Burned clothes, no burned people. How did it happen?"

"Looks like an engine room explosion. I smelled fuel, but diesel shouldn't blow that easy. There was a cooking stove that might have done it. Don't think he would have left this." He pulled an Uzi out of a bag. "Been used, but it's got a lot of rounds left."

The chopper returned to its search, expanding outward until it was over Thimble Shoals Channel. Two miles south the tug hauled the barge in close to bring it alongside before mooring at Little Creek.

Nelson wouldn't believe the reports. He sent for his frogmen. "What the hell is this crap about no bodies, no sign of them on that boat? Did the thing sail out there by itself? I thought there was somebody on board earlier."

The older man looked like a worn out boxer, face blunt and spread from punches. His voice sounded like a growl. "You wanted my take, you got it. I say they wasn't killed in the explosion. Wasn't the guy a SEAL? He knew explosives, he could'a blown it."

Nelson thought of Haggerty and his explosives. He was still unnerved by the expectation of being blown to pieces when the frogman had fired off the device in the room. "So where the hell are they? There's no sign? No boat around? Did they get picked up by a helo? A boat? Get out. Stand by. Uh. Thanks, you know your business."

He needed to talk to the first helo pilot. Didn't he say something about a tug and a barge?

With dependents housing nearby, a man and a woman trying to hold another woman stand up outside the fence at the Amphibious Base wasn't too weird. Still, they'd be damned lucky if a police car didn't come by and cut off their escape. Whitney gave him change for a phone call. Haggerty sneaked across Diamond Springs Road to a gas station. He was close to the SEALs. Did he dare call? Doc had the duty on Friday evening; did he have it the whole weekend? What if Doc's phone were bugged? He had to risk it.

After three rings he heard the sleepy voice, "Yeah. Who the hell is calling at this hour?"

"This is Sea Bass One."

The answering voice was sharp, alerted by their squad's voice call. "Roger."

"Need a rendezvous. You may have a tail. Remember the party for Bennie two years ago? Meet me there ASAP. I'm gone." He heard two clicks and hung up.

After a long, worried wait, Haggerty was surprised to see Bennie's 280Z. The Doc's anxious look switched from the Cat to Beth to Whitney and back again. "You look like shit, Cat. Who's this dame? Let's get the hell out of here."

Doc half-turned in the driver's seat. "So you think there's somebody tailing me? Keep an eye out there, Cat. Nobody followed me here, and nobody's around now. Where to first? You two need a doctor, hospital would be best."

"No way. You're the doctor. We need a safe place for a couple days. How about the beach house in Sandbridge?"

"It's vacant far as I know. Can I pick up Bennie? He's worried about the car. I don't blame him. That must have been my Bronk they picked up near West Point, huh?"

"Yeah. I'm real sorry about that, Doc. I still have your Beretta, though." He hated to get Bennie involved too. He had no choice. He was damned exhausted. He needed the Doc for Beth, and Bennie for security. With them involved, they were in danger too. He was too tired to figure out another way.

"Do we swing by Bennie's or do we call?"

"Better call from a booth. He could be bugged too. Make sure you tell him to watch out for being tailed and don't give any hint of where we're going to be."

"Give me a break, Cat. I know what I'm doing. Wait one, here's a booth."

The Doc was back. "He's gonna take the long way. He can shake anybody. Hey, it's a damned good thing I stocked this thing with my tools. Let's get to our hospital."

The fugitives were in the beach house at Sandbridge, at the south end of Virginia Beach. There was one road in or out. Only a beach buggy could make it to North Carolina along the beach and dunes and they didn't have one. Beth was laid out in one room, where the Doc had given her an IV and a sedative. Whitney was asleep in another room.

The Cat was in a third bedroom watching Doc work on his knife cut. It had been cleansed and sprayed with the best the Navy had in infection fighting compounds. The Doc was pretty sure that there weren't any organs touched. Bennie was on watch hiding nearby with an Uzi and a radio. Doc checked his patients, did a two-click radio check with Bennie and hit the rack. He wondered what the Cat had gotten them into.

Before Haggerty dropped off, he sighed. "Safe."

Whitney woke sometime during the night. *I better see how I can call Frank. I don't have anything against these people, but I have to get away before anything happens to me.*

Wallace downed three fingers of bourbon before he made the phone call. He knew what kind of a reaction he'd get.

"Wes, I'm up to my ears in shit. The frogman made it to the southside. Don't ask me how. The other two SEALs got away from the tails, so they're probably together somewhere. Wounded or not, that frogman is damned dangerous. We tell the terrorist story and search like hell. I'm heading there."

"I'm coming down there too, sir. Mister Magee wants me on the scene. He's getting inside help because of the terrorist angle."

Wallace's voice had a tinge of anger. "I don't need any of his GD help! Think about it."

"Sir, Mister Magee's exact words were, 'this fiasco has gone too far. Wallace is on shaky ground. Got that!'"

He knew before Wes had completed the words that he was in deep shit himself. His only out now was to get the frogman and his group. It would be a firefight, but he had the army to win it. "Tell your boss that was a good speech and there's been a good reaction." After Wes hung up Wallace downed the bourbon and lifted a middle finger at the phone. *I want that son of a bitch myself.*

There seemed to be love in this beach cabin. The way the SEALs kidded and fooled around together, even in these stark circumstances they showed care, respect, and a camaraderie that was close to love. She longed for that. Originally she thought her relationship with Frank was love, but she had awakened to the truth in Hong Cong when the bastard pimped her for a business deal to a merchant. The cold hard facts had shaken her that her relationship with him was nothing more than sex.

But he might take her back. Staying with these men was interesting, even fun. But the odds against them were too high to take a chance. She shook off thoughts that could make it worse for her and decided to stay alert and ready to jump in either direction. Frank or these guys? Was there a real choice?

Magee received a secret report that LTCOL North and Ex-General Secord had been flown by Army chopper from Cyprus to Beirut. Late that night and on into early morning, they had briefed the American Embassy on the possible locations where the hostages would be released. He raised his right fist and said. "About time!"

Later in the morning The Fox heard that the White House was so sure that hostages would be released that it had alerted Jim Wright, the House Democratic Leader. Nothing happened that day. He shook his head and grimaced. More stories instead of facts? He knew the source of where that kind of smoke and mirrors came from. Dammit! Was it true or not? He was unable to contact his troop leader in Lebanon.

Joseph Guion

CHAPTER FIFTY ONE

It was Sunday afternoon before the fugitives stirred from exhausted sleep. Doc and Bennie had switched guard duty during the night, and Dan had relieved Bennie. Armed and with the radio, he settled underneath a cottage on pilings where he could observe Sandfiddler Road in both directions and remain hidden. He sipped on coffee.

Whitney stretched and yawned. Shaking her head and wiping sleep out of her eyes, she was somewhat disoriented. Where was she? At a beach cottage, in a place called Sandbridge. She slipped on borrowed sweats and strolled out on the screen porch overlooking the ocean. The tang of the salt air felt delicious. There was no one on the beach. She needed to run, to get the kinks out, and to think. To get away?

She had felt something strange when they moved into the house earlier. There was some kind of latent power, like giant storage batteries, generated in the building that could be unleashed in seconds. She had always been drawn to powerful men, but this was different. She felt an attraction to the SEALs that disturbed her. Bennie brought her a coffee.

"Want brunch, lady? I've got eggs, bacon, toast?"

"You mean I'm going to be served? How delightful?"

In the close quarters of the kitchen, she became charged up, excited. Brushing up against them brought a surge of awareness, erotic in its effect. The SEALs were like two coiled springs. She couldn't help but feel their alertness, their potency. It was like being in a cage with two wild animals. It was exciting and dangerous.

She was good at her trade. Her physical attraction was enhanced by an intuitive sense of male behavior. She went to work, jockeying around the small kitchen, making sure that she touched them. She slipped into a relaxed, joshing mode, so that soon Doc and Bennie were kidding back.

"Watch it, Ben, she's got a knife."

"Yes, and I'll use it if you get too close."

"Why honey, doan do that. We jus' doin' kitchen duty heah. You fixin' chitlin's?"

"What?"

"He likes to play the shuffling, black boy sometimes. Pay no attention. He's got more bucks than most, college degree plus. He's a con artist. Not like me."

"Bull! Watch Doc, honey. He's the con man."

"Who me? Hey, woman, what are you lookin' for?"

"Don't you people have any fresh garlic? Honestly, how can I do up a first class salad and an entree without it? Doc, would you mind going to the store and getting some? I need some olive oil, fresh parsley, oregano, maybe some fennel, would they have it?"

"I thought we were gonna have breakfast. Keep it simple. We don't have time for fancy stuff. You see what I'm sayin'? We do the best we can, a good cook can make do."

"You really want that, uh fennel?"

She touched Bennie's arm before she answered. Her smile was sweet and her eyes were alight with promise. "Of course, I wouldn't ask if I didn't need it. Would you mind going? Maybe they have chitlin's?"

Bennie left for the store with a grin on his face.

After a late heavy brunch Haggerty was back on watch

and Whitney sat on the porch with the two SEALs. They were powerful, dangerous men. Dan seemed to have the tenderness inside that she longed for. He was already taken. Wasn't he? She wanted to learn more about him. "Doc, how come Dan isn't in the Navy like you guys?"

The Doc frowned. He didn't want to tell her a damned thing about The Cat. It wasn't any of her freaking business. She managed to wheedle a few remarks out of him. With Bennie in the conversation, she worked them slowly back to a focus on Haggerty.

"How long have you known each other?"

"Bout fifteen years, right, Doc? Doc knew him before me. You were in UDT and SEAL training together huh?"

"Yeah." He grinned. "Me and The Cat had some fun times, specially when we were instructors."

Doc told about how he and Dan had lost some neophytes in the swamps around Camp Lejeune on a training exercise. When the new SEALs were rescued the next day, one had quit and another wouldn't come down from a tree. "The Cat brought the kid down by lowering him on a line."

More stories eased the tension. It was like two brothers and a sister kidding around at home. Whitney enjoyed it, but she had to know more. Bennie mentioned 'Nam and she asked about it. Doc looked grim. She invited Bennie to speak.

He swallowed, and then blurted out. "I owe my life to Cat." He exhaled. "I had rear guard. We hit an ambush. The retraction Mike boat grounded, so we had to stay and fight longer than we wanted. When the squad was ready to haul ass, the VCs were racing to cut us off on both sides of the canal. Got caught in mangrove roots, flipped upside down, and damned near drowned. Every time I stuck my head up, bullets punched the water next to me."

"By God, my black ass was hanging out. Surrounded by shooters I couldn't see. Thought I bought the big one. I hear a Stoner screaming rounds damned near creasing my scalp. The Cat high stepping up the canal. He pulled out every damned thing he had in his H-harness and spread the ordnance. I mean, grenades, smoke, even a parachute pop flare. Guess he confused the slope heads enough to cut me out of there. We hauled ass."

Bennie was sweating, perhaps embarrassed at displaying his emotions. He glared at Whitney with a look so fierce that she backed away. "I'll go anywhere, do anything for Cat. Including, killing anyone who puts him in danger."

Whitney swallowed to regain her breath. Dan wasn't a subject they wanted to share.

Bennie went inside. She worked the conversation with Doc around to Haggerty again, remarking about the television news of the assault and escape.

Doc's eyes held her. "I don't know what the hell your game is. You stay off Dan!"

"I was just wondering. The TV called him a 'Crazed Vet from 'Nam,' is that true? He looks pretty normal to me and pretty tough, in charge throughout our escape."

"They pull that shit all the time when some vet gets in trouble. You see what I'm sayin'? It don't matter if a guy was rear echelon or in Saigon. If a 'Nam guy gets in some kinda shit, they say he's a 'Crazed Vet'."

"Yes, but they said something about alcohol problems. An estranged wife?"

Doc slipped his K-bar out of the scabbard and held it up in front of her. "You see this? It's seen a helluva lot of shit. Slit Cambodian throats, too many VCs too. I'm only gonna tell you once. Stop pushin' us on Dan. We're in a freaking war here and I ain't gonna let us lose. Anybody gets in our way, anybody; and I'll use this. It don't know male or female when it comes to protectin' The Cat. Get me?"

Whitney held her arms tightly to her body. "I'm, I'm sorry if it appears as if I'm nosy or prying. I was snatched up into this the other night. I don't have any idea of what it's about. Believe me, I want to survive. This isn't my war, and I—."

"You're already in it, sister. Keep your freakin' questions to yourself. Stay quiet. You'll stay healthy."

Whitney watched the waves pushing against the shore. They looked like they'd never stop, just like Doc's eyes, mirrors of his threat.

Wes was on the secure phone with Magee, who chewed on his Upmann and sipped at scotch in the private control center. "Sir, I hate to tell you this but our little bird, Whitney, has flown the coop with the frogman."

"What? That can't be. How could—?"

"She was in the hallway after the fight in the room. The SEAL grabbed her and the priest. They helped to carry the woman outside. The priest finally admitted it."

"What did you do to him?"

"Oh, Wes and the boys convinced him that it would be in his best interest to cooperate. He described the other woman. It was Whitney. So now she's with the frogman, helping him too. I knew she'd abandon you some time, sir."

The lobbyist swore, stomping up and down in the room. "That little bitch. I gave her everything. I trusted her. I. I." He rattled off a litany of gifts that he had given her.

"Well, we still have the Mercedes. Sir, maybe we can use it to lure her back."

"Lure her back? For what? She's no use to me. Well, all right, what about the car?"

"She'll probably see the news sometime. Aren't you going to be interviewed on TV today? Set it up with the little red wagon of hers in the background. You know, sort of lean on the car, as you talk casually to the press?"

"Hmmm. And the message?"

"And the message is, 'I still own you, honey, don't forget that. If you want the car back, come to Daddy. And tip me off where they are.' That Whitney is a sharp cookie, she doesn't miss much. She won't miss that. You could work in a remark of some kind. Maybe something that will jog her memory about how many gifts you gave her. "

"I'll do it! She knows too much about me."

Stolen Votes

Wes nodded. "Once she makes contact, we can trace the call and attack them. Then, I'll take care of her. You won't have to see her again. Ever."

There was enough light to avoid the land end of the waves lapping up the sand, as Dan and Whitney strolled on the beach. "Thanks for letting me come along, Dan"

"I had to get out and think. Thanks for the chow. You didn't have to do that."

"I know. It was my pleasure."

They walked in silence. Should she ask him? How would he respond? "They said on television that you were a Viet Nam Vet. Do some of you have flashbacks, or whatever?"

"Some do."

She touched his arm and felt his muscles tighten. "If you'd rather not talk about it, please don't. Honestly."

She waited as they walked, listening to the ocean's rhythmic thump and roar. She managed to stumble once and grabbed his arm. She didn't let go and he didn't seem to mind. She glanced at him. He was staring straight ahead.

"It's not easy to talk about. Some people had damned bad things happen. They thought they could handle anything. Some did, some didn't. The first tour over there was easier than the second. And, well, let's turn around. I want to see how Beth is."

As they approached the cottage, she touched him once more. "Dan, I'm really sorry that I asked you something that you'd rather not talk about. Please forgive me."

"It's okay, no sweat."

"I was dumped into this, not knowing what's going on."

"Yeah, I know. Better watch yourself. There's some big operation goin' on. I don't know what the hell it is. Seems like a secret government job with instant communications and weapons. Two divers jumped me, they had the latest gear. Somebody's got max money; power, both. They're trying to kill me and get something out of Beth. Right now I don't trust nobody but Doc and Bennie."

"Yes, I understand."

When Haggerty mentioned power and money she began to rethink about who was behind this awesome murderous plot. Nelson was the one Haggerty had fought, so he was involved. Could Frank be a silent partner after they had fought so publicly? Nelson had worked for Magee for years. She had to call her mentor to find out without the SEALs knowing it. Which one would be the easiest to fool? She shook her head, even she could not fool them all the time.

She sat on the sofa and watched the snapping fire. The lights were off so the reflection of the flames on the wood walls was eerie. She was waiting for the opportunity to sneak the call. When the master bedroom phone was off the hook, there was no indicator light in the kitchen to show it. She wondered who would be on watch next. Would it be a betrayal of the SEALs? She was confused about them. They reminded her of Frank, but in a different way. They were tough, but straight shooters, not like that slimy bastard.

That Haggerty. He was strong, yet he had an air of vulnerability. Probably the first man she had met like that. She wanted to learn so much more about him. Maybe he would open up to her. She was good at getting men to unload their hidden feelings. She longed to explain her story to him, how she had little choice about getting into the business. She wanted him to like her. After a long sigh she straightened her shoulders. Dammit! Keep your eye on the target. Frank? Freedom? The SEALs? Which side would be best for her?

CHAPTER FIFTY TWO

That Sunday afternoon Nelson was groggy from the lack of sleep and the constant badgering by Wes. They were on the SEALs trail. Soon, they'd find out where they were hiding. They kept at it without police assistance, so they'd have the fugitives dead before anyone knew what was going on. He called Wes on a secure phone in Virginia Beach. "What about that service record check on those two SEALs?"

"Sir, I had people interviewed at Little Creek. The two SEALs have a beach cottage down in a remote area of Virginia Beach, called Sandbridge. I have a local government guy meeting my man at the court house to search real estate records."

"Who's after them? What are their orders?"

"I'm delaying the info to the police and FBI to make sure that our own group gets them first. The place has limited access, so they're boxed in. The follow-up groups are a mix of locals and ex-feds with our guys in each unit. The orders are, shoot to kill on sight."

"Everybody?"

"Yes, everybody. Guess Mister Magee will get the red

Mercedes back."

Wallace frowned. Too bad about Whitney. She was a beautiful girl, but she knew too much about him. Well, there were many more where she had come from. Whitney had pissed him off when she bit him. He cut her out of his thoughts and concentrated on the plot. Two days to go. There would be no one to stop them. He grabbed another bourbon.

Wes gathered the assault group. The leader was a former special forces guy who had been fed up with the chicken shit aspects of military service. He had years of experience in many different assault ops. They had automatic shotguns, assault weapons with high rates of fire. The men were tough, deadly. They had the numbers, a four to one advantage in personnel. Similar to SEAL operations in 'Nam with their concentrated and awesome firepower, this assault group would also bring that shock to the battle. In addition, they knew where the fugitives were.

Wes was quite positive that Haggerty's people had no clue that they had been located. The SEALs didn't know where the attacks would come from or when. Surprise was a tactical advantage and often carried the day. Nevertheless, Wes and Sal knew that they could not bank on anything except a quick and deadly firefight.

On the beach at Sandbridge a pale sun prodded a dark overcast, creating a feeble shadow of a lone figure striding along the beach. Doc's eyes took in any hint of human activity in the oceanfront cottages that he passed. He'd remember which were occupied and which weren't. He was gathering intel so that they could move quickly in the proper direction. He wondered what they were facing.

The Cat's story seemed so weird that he wondered if the bud was back in 'Nam. Bennie had agreed that Dan seemed to be almost the warrior he used to be. Doc moved back to the oceanfront hideout in a roundabout way, doubling back to check on anyone following. Their bachelor pad was a refuge for them, often with the dollies they had entertained. How long would it stay that way? If they were found, Sandbridge's limited access was a disadvantage. He signaled Bennie to unlock the door.

The exhausted escapees were still asleep. Perhaps the sea's soothing whisper had lulled them into a false sense of security. Doc checked the women. Whitney was covered by her mink coat. Shit, she's worse'n a kid, with a favorite blanket. Her handbag was partially under her pillow.

Doc wasn't curious, just damned careful. He slipped her bag out and padded into the bathroom. He went through the contents swiftly, pulling out an expensive wallet and a deadly, small Beretta. Son of a bitch. She's armed. He checked through the wallet for IDs and his eyebrows raised.

He slipped into Haggerty's room, covered Dan's mouth and whispered, "Cat. Doc. You needa look here quick."

The Cat blinked, holding his weapon ready. "What?"

Doc showed the pistol. "This buddy. Our friend Whitney is a shooter. No shit. She got yellow-tinted shooter glasses, an NRA member, and a marksman; or a marksperson?"

The Cat hefted the weapon. "This is a real light piece."

"Yeah, but it's a nine mil, packs a punch like mine. What the hell you think she is? I mean, she got cards from private shooting clubs up the ying-yang. Got a license for the piece, credit cards, driver's license, no pictures. I mean zip. Strange huh?"

"Yeah, strange. She's damned pretty; slim and strong. She's in great shape."

"No shit, she's got a freaking shape that would make Miss America envious. She's got a couple of health club memberships, maybe works out. I found a model agency card and an ID for some kind of professional models organization. A union huh?"

"Yeah. Listen, before you put the piece back."

The Doc nodded and grinned. The Cat was sharp even

when he was flat tired. He patted his friend on the shoulder. "Okay, pal. Get some sleep."

Haggerty was awakened by a noise and voices. He heard Whitney blasting Bennie for following her while she ran on the beach. "What the hell's going on, Ben?"

"I caught Miss Mink trying to get off the beach. She was heading for a phone booth. I told her to head back for the house or else. She didn't like it, so I said I'd flatten her pretty nose." The wide grin of white teeth against his dark face was far from friendly.

She shouted. "I wasn't trying to make a damned phone call. I was tired and didn't want to sit in the sand in your precious, stinking sweats."

"Don't give me that shit, baby. You weren't even panting. She was trying to—."

"Okay, knock it off. Whitney, you better explain. What were you doing at The Magruder? How did you happen to be right there when I attacked it?"

"I don't have to tell you anything. Listen, I helped you out, dragging that woman along. I was shot at, damned near drowned, and now you're accusing me of pulling something." She pointed. "You're the one who owes me an explanation. Who are you people and what is all this killing? If you don't tell me dammit! I'm leaving. Now!"

"You are not going nowhere, lady. Not till I'm satisfied about who you are and what you are, so start talking. Let's start with, where you live and what you do."

She snapped a nasty look. "I'm not saying a damned word. Go screw yourself."

Bennie made noises. "My, my, such language from such a pretty girl. Cat, you think we got some kind of, of a professional woman here? Like a working girl?"

"You shut up. I'm not talking to you. I want out of here and now, or else."

Cat's answer was, "Or else what? You going to karate us

to death or something?"

She stood, reached quickly into her handbag, and had the Beretta in her hand before they could move. They were too far away to jump her. She pointed the weapon at Cat's head in a two-handed grip.

"I said I'm getting out of here. Now get out of my way."

The Cat's eyelids drooped as he turned to face her. "Give me the gun, please. Be careful. Nobody's going to get hurt."

"Stand back and don't take another step. If you think I can't shoot you, you're badly mistaken. I can hit a bull at a hundred yards and I'm not afraid to shoot you."

"Cat, she can't get both of us."

"Hold it, Ben. Look, shootin' targets is a helluva lot different from firing at people. It's easy squeezing off rounds into a bull or a man-shaped figure. Shooting somebody face to face is tough." He eased toward her in sliding, half steps.

She backed against the wall. The weapon was as steady as a battleship's sixteen-inch gun turret. She was tough. Would he be able to finesse her or should he jump? She was liable to get panicky if they both moved. He waved Bennie back and slid within reach.

"That's it!" She gulped in air and her voice pitch rose. She seemed to get control. The green eyes looked like cold jade. "Move one more inch and I drop you. I mean it."

The Cat took the half step needed to lunge for her. She moved the weapon slightly and squeezed the trigger.

CHAPTER FIFTY THREE

Wes met the killers on the road toward the remote area of Sandbridge on the southeastern part of Virginia Beach. He pulled a map and laid it on the hood of the lead car.

"Soon as I get the address, you move in." He pointed to the map. "Right now, head out this way to Sandbridge Road. Wait here before it splits north and south. You'll have them blocked. Nobody gets away. Got that!"

"No sweat boss. We'll eat them SEALs. Always hated those glory bastards."

Two thirds rode off in the sedans, the remainder traveled in the extended pickup with the direction finder and locator bug. FBI or police manned the units closer to the fugitives. They would be called in when it was over. Wes withdrew and sat in Magee's Foxmobile as his control room. He reported in and asked for at least one helo to give air cover.

Doc didn't receive a response on the radio so he raced to the cottage. Bennie was pumping his arms, pacing and shouting at Haggerty. Whitney was tied up against one of the roof supports. "What the hell happened?"

"Dammit, Doc. The Cat didn't tell me about the frigging weapon, so I'm about to get my ass wasted to save him. I dive at her, come up a pace short and he's got her weapon and a silly grin on his puss. Je-sus, Cat. Don't do that to me."

"Sorry. I didn't have time to tell you. We found the weapon. Doc took all the rounds out of the clip and the chamber." He turned to Whitney. "You goin' to tell me the truth or do I keep you gagged? I'm in a frigging war here. Why were you at the motel?"

She shook her head. "You get nothing!"

Beth called out from the bedroom. "Dan! Dan! Help!"

He ran. She was fighting the twisted sheet and blanket. "Beth, honey, it's okay. It's just the sheet. Easy, now easy." He stayed to calm her down. He told her where they were and what was happening. He told her that they were questioning Whitney.

"She's here? Oh my God. She's one of them. I saw her. I saw her." She struggled away from him and staggered to the doorway. She pointed at Whitney. "That's her. Yes, there was a women with them." She shook her head. "She, uh, looks different but she was with them. I know it."

Dan brought her back to bed and covered her. He stroked her hand and whispered to her. "It's okay, honey. I won't let her or anyone else get to you. You're safe now. Are you sure she was with them? Who are they? What's this all about?"

"Oh, God! It was awful. That snake-eyed man, he, he. Oh God! Dan he cut me. He. Don't touch me. Get away. Help!"

Dan eased away, mighty pissed. If Whitney was one of them, by God, woman or not, he'd interrogate her until she told the truth.

He had her head against the wall with her chin cradled in his left hand. A big fist was poised to punch her in the face. "Now, you talk, dammit, or I'll punch that pretty face into a mess. What were you doing there? Talk! Now!"

"Kiss my ass! Go ahead. Hit me!"

Dan's eyes had granite in them. He raised his fist.

"Wait. All right, all right, don't beat me. You want to know what I was doing there? The truth huh? Well the truth isn't pretty, but if it will save my butt, here it is."

She appeared thoughtful as if she were trying to decide what to disclose and what to hold back.

"My mom had a terminal disease and I had to get a considerable amount of money in a hurry. I ran into a woman who knew a very exclusive madam in DC, someone who ran a group of high-priced call girls." She explained that the johns were wealthy and could afford high prices. She wanted security and freedom, so she bought jewelry and expensive clothes from the proceeds for her future.

"That's how I got the mink. It's quite a lucrative business in Washington. We do favors for lobbyists, government and business people, foreigners too. I bought the gun to protect myself. The jewelry in my bag is expensive, and real."

He prodded a finger into her waist "Okay, so why did you go to Williamsburg?"

"Well, sometimes we have to travel to be with the john. I mean, we're talking high class and expensive people who stay at the best hotels and resorts. I was set up with this, this big guy you were talking about. He hurt me. Honestly, I don't know a thing about this other stuff. I was getting ready to leave when you blew the place apart."

The Cat frowned and took in a deep breath. Was she telling the truth? Was the story about the big man true? Besides the diamonds and other jewelry in her purse, she had keys to a Mercedes. She must have been a real money machine. He looked at her, man to woman. Yes, she sure was a looker. She had that haughty, patrician look that might give the impression that she was hard to get, unattainable. The Grace Kelly mystique.

"All right, I'll buy the story." He caught her eyes with his. "You aren't as tough as you think. Before you squeezed the trigger, you shifted the piece."

"Bullshit! I was aiming at your heart."

He untied her hands. "I had to tie you up 'cause I gotta find out what this war is about. This is the deal. You're free to do anything you want except to run away or to make a phone call. And don't attract attention in any other way. Okay?"

His reward was a punch in the gut that made him cough.

"That's for searching through my things. You and your apes better stay away from all my stuff."

"Yes, Ma'am. Don't you get physical on me." He drew back. "So you're an expert shooter? How about teaching me some tricks." He ducked a wild swing from her right hand and caught her by the wrists. "Take it easy. We'll leave you alone. Just don't pull anything, okay?"

"No. It's not okay. Get out of my face. This place smells like a horse barn."

The Cat realized that this woman was something, sharp, intriguing. No wonder she was good at her trade. SEALs were good at theirs. They'd watch her without her being aware.

"What about her, Beth? She's mistaken about me being with those men. You should take her to a hospital, to a doctor. She's really on something or she's had a terrible trauma."

"Yeah, I know. I can't do anything till I find out what this war is all about. Then I can get her taken care of. Uh, thanks for thinking about her."

The three vehicles stopped where the road split at the beginning of Sandbridge. The pickup pulled off to wait, to back up the assault group in case they had a problem. There would be no avenue of escape past the backup, no road leading out to safety.

Wes radioed. "The address is 2351 Sandfiddler Road."

Sal had been through this before. "You got maybe a bad address? Odd ones don't seem to be on the ocean side. I don't wanna hit the wrong house."

"Wait one. I'm getting an update on the location right

now. I'll call back. Remember, nobody gets out alive. I don't give a shit if it's woman or man. They're all targets. The primary ones are the three SEALs. They're fast and tough. Don't kid yourself. They won't show mercy. You better not."

Sal made each man show his weapons. A few griped but he told them to shut up. "I don't accept any fucking mistakes. Lock and load, no screwing around. Remember, nobody's gonna count the rounds you used, or ask for the weapons back. Use everything you have to finish the job. I'm setting you up to keep the bastards in a cross fire situation. They'll have too many targets to take on. Don't think I have to warn you about killing each other."

He repeated the orders and added, "Drive slow. Fifty clicks from the house, Lou and Don slip out. Lou on the beach. Don goes along, house to house. Red and I will get out by the house itself. Hube, stay in the car. You guys in the first car drive past and anchor to the south about fifteen clicks. Put somebody on the beach, another around the cottages, and move slowly up in our direction. Let's go."

Sal entered the second car and thought about all the elements in their favor. They had three SEALs and two women; one of those was drugged and pretty much helpless. Ordinarily the thing would be a piece of cake. But he knew how badass SEALs were. It would be tough even with the advantages he had. Surprise was their ace-in-the hole.

Stolen Votes

CHAPTER FIFTY FOUR

After dinner Doc was on watch as darkness began to creep over the beach. The others rested. In the master bedroom Beth had told Whitney about the kidnapping and the election plot. Now she was asleep and the door was closed. No one would know. Whitney picked up the phone quietly. Should she call Frank? Was he involved? Could it really be Nelson? He was a rotten bastard, full of devious and cunning tricks. They had become bitter enemies. Yet, she wondered.

She had enjoyed the first class flights to exotic places, exquisite food and wine. And always the surprise gift from Frank. Damn him! He pimped her for that Reverend. Worse, he rubbed her nose in it by making her hostess a dinner in his home, his wife at the table. Having the woman who whored for you hang over the guy she screwed was some kind of shit.

She squeezed the phone. You son of a bitch! I would have done anything for you. You let Nelson try to rape me. He wouldn't have done it without your ok. He hurt me. Even a whore deserves some dignity. Even a whore can say no! Bastard! On TV Frank leaned on her car. Her car! Giving her a chance to come back? She'd call his private number.

Magee's valet burst into the sitting room. "Sir? An urgent call, for you from Miss Whitney. They're tracing it."

The Fox leaped out of his chair. He could nail down their position. He'd call Nelson. I'll play her along. She was too trusting to catch on. "Whitney, my dear. I've been frightened to death about you. What's happened? Where are you?"

"Never mind that." She whispered. "I want to know something. Are you involved in some kind of manhunt? Is there something going on with the election?"

"The election? Why, my dear, you know I've been deeply involved in trying to get a right-minded Senate in office and the same with the House. Of course I'm involved with the election. I'm funding many candidates too. Why do you ask?"

Otto shook his head. They didn't have it traced as yet.

"Why did you have me come to Williamsburg? Was I supposed to be paraded in front of that reverend again like you did at your home? Or have you nailed down that deal?"

"Why, how could you say that? I don't understand, paraded in front of whom? The reverend? What reverend?"

"The one you are now in bed with. I saw the two of you celebrating on television. Is it just taking over that network or is it something sinister to do with the election?"

"Sinister? My dear Whitney."

"What was Nelson doing in Williamsburg with that kidnapped woman? Why was she cut? Raped? Drugged?"

Otto interrupted, "They've got her. It's a different address from the one Wes had. There's a unit on the street near them. Another is close by. They want to know how many people are there, if they have automatic weapons, and explosives."

He waved him away. They had them now. He had a grim grin on his face, imagining them being blasted to pieces. He couldn't resist taunting her. She'd think of him as she died.

"Whitney my dear. Do you know that the birthmark on your right buttock will be seen by thousands of people? I have a video of your remarkable performance with my partner in the network agreement. You provided a stunning effort."

Apparently, she had caught on to his blackmail scheme with the Reverend. The Fox heard fury in her voice.

"You rotten son of a bitch! You twisted piece of dog shit! I'll get you!"

He laughed and hung up. Explain to her? That was rich. Too bad. You were a beautiful woman and a wonderful bed partner, but you've outlived your usefulness. He went to wash his hands as if he were getting rid of her. He smiled and washed his hands again.

She gasped. Frank's tone and manner told her the call was a monstrous mistake. She had heard it before when he had written someone off. His people had traced the call. Oh, God, what have I done? Was he involved with the kidnapping? That plot?

Dan struggled out of a dream. He leaped toward the door, toward voices. He heard Ben.

"You bitch! I'm gonna slit your throat! You tipped them off where we are."

Haggerty swept into the master bedroom, a .45 in his hand. Bennie had Whitney by the throat with his K-bar poised for an artery cut. "Ben, stop! Stop! I'll shoot if I have to."

"Cat, I caught this freaking bitch on the phone, talking to some guy. She'll get us killed. Let me finish her off."

Whitney shouted, "Oh, God! No! No! It was a terrible mistake. Please don't kill me!"

Joseph Guion

CHAPTER FIFTY FIVE

The Cat glanced from Bennie to Whitney's frantic look. Her body trembled and tears overflowed her eyes. He felt the adrenaline rush course through his body. His face seemed to be carved from granite, the whites of his eyes showed.

"No time for that shit. Pack up!" He called Doc. "Doc, we're moving out. The bastards are on their way. Keep under cover. I'll set up an ambush here. Ben will have the car and women ready to roll. Ben, get below with the rest of the weapons. If I say 'Hit!' head south like we planned. If you don't hear from me in five minutes, take off."

He turned to Whitney. "You little freak! Get Beth ready." He pointed the .45 at her face. "You do somethin' wrong and I won't hesitate. Move!"

She obeyed without question. Then she pleaded, "Please, please. It was a terrible mistake. I thought. I wanted." She shook her head. "You wouldn't understand. I'm sorry."

She swept up Beth's clothes and dressed the struggling woman. "Okay, Beth. It's me, Whitney. We have to run. If we hurry we'll be safe."

Bennie called. "Cat, car coming down the road. Block

away. Guy on the beach."

The Cat was so pissed he almost left the grenades and the grenade launcher.

The radio crackled and Bennie spoke. "Doc." He heard a double click. "Second car's comin'. First one kept going by, waiting now south. I can check it."

"Careful. I'm covering the a-hole on the beach. There's another one alongside the third house from C. C?" He heard two clicks.

Cat spoke. "Ben, I'll take the first one. Use my Mark forty-eight."

Ben and the women slipped down the inside stairs. He sent them into the car.

"Whitney. You drive! When I tell you, or if we get the shit kicked out of us, drive like hell out of Sandbridge and stop the first cop you come to. Tell him you got to get her to a hospital quick. Understand?"

"Yes, but—."

"But, shit!"

The southernmost vehicle turned into a driveway and come out heading slowly North toward the house. The second car eased in closer from the opposite direction.

Haggerty was on the roof with a clear field of fire for both vehicles. He avoided looking at any light to build his night vision, for soon it would be difficult to see.

With his Starlight scope Doc saw that the first beach killer had an automatic weapon trained on the house. He clubbed him quietly and took the man's weapons. "One down. I'll get the guy by the houses." He heard two clicks.

The car to Dan's left turned and stopped, blocking most of the street. The second was one house away to his right and stopped. They waited.

The Doc shot the second man with his silenced S & W hush puppy. "Two down."

He heard acknowledging clicks. "Comin' up behind."

"Ben, take the beach side. Work with Doc on the north car. I got the other one."

Doc was nearest to the car. He took the biggest risk with four people in the black sedan. He ran up to the car from the left rear and shined a flashlight into the driver's face. "Hi. Looking for somebody in the neighborhood?"

The driver shouted, "Hey! Turn that off flash. I can't see." He tried to open the door but Doc had his weight against it. "Dammit! Let me out!"

"Oh, sorry. Who were you were looking for?" He spotted Sal on the passenger side with a radio in his hand. He pointed his Combat Masterpiece revolver at the man's head. "Drop it fella, or you're dead. Show me your hands." Sal complied.

Bennie was at the rear quarter panel unseen. The men in the back seat moved and brought him into action. He swung the door open and blinded two men with his light. One had his hand inside his coat; the other reached under a blanket.

"Hey, what's this? We're Virginia Beach police on a drug bust. What the hell are you doing with that piece?"

Doc hauled the driver out of his seat. "Keep your hands where I can see 'em. Bee?"

"I'm watching hands, one hidden. They better come out empty."

"Hey, you got us wrong here. I got nothing to hide."

Before the man could say another word, Bennie stripped off the blanket, uncovering a sawed off shotgun. The other handed over his .357 Magnum.

"Your ID, man, quick."

The other car wheeled around and charged up the street toward them. Shots from that car ricocheted off metal. The driver grunted and fell to the ground. Cat fired the grenade launcher at the southernmost car and the explosion jarred the car and its occupants. He counted on the SEALs to finish.

The explosion ahead seemed to shock the northern car killers. "Jesus. What the hell was that?"

"ID's now! No bullshit."

"Okay, Okay. I'm reachin' for it in my rear pants pocket, here it is."

Doc backed off with the identity card in his hand. It

looked authentic. So did the others.

The man in the front seat asked, "Say, who are you guys? You know it a federal offense to have automatic weapons? Let's see some ID yourself."

"Kiss my ass. Hands behind you." He handcuffed one. Bennie did the same to the other. Doc checked the driver. "He's gone." He disarmed a silent Sal and said, "I'll get the first two."

He walked up the street to immobilize the ones he had knocked off earlier. Bennie searched the car. There was some C-4, weapons in the trunk and several radios. The equipment was top of the line with government IDs.

"Ben, keep an eye on the other car. I'm coming down." Dan heard the engine start up in the garage. He leaped off the porch and charged the door. Whitney swung the garage door open and stood there.

Cat covered the burning car. A man staggered out on the near side. He fell, and then aimed a shotgun at the other vehicle. Dan knocked him down with rounds from the Stoner. A second tried to stand up in back of the car; he fired at The Cat and dropped from a burst. Dan ran to them. Two bodies were still inside the car. He scouted around. No one else. He trotted back to Ben covering the northern crew.

"Keep an eye on 'em, Bee. I'll check 'em out."

"Hey, guys, if headquarters doesn't hear from us in ten minutes, they'll be—."

"Stuff it!"

Doc returned with two prisoners. "Just like comin' back from the TinTin with a couple of gooks. Wanna interrogate them? Or do we just shoot' em?"

"I'd like to strangle the bastards."

Doc said, "Hey, I got some garroting wire."

Sal put up his hands and shouted. "Wait! Wait! We were hired to do a job. That's it. We don't know from shit. I know when it's time to train in and secure."

The Cat shook his head. "Sounds like a Navy guy. Doc, hand me the fucking wire. We'll see who knows the most."

Sal tried to save himself. "Geez, don't you guys believe us? Shit. All I know is I get a phone call an hour ago to saddle up, bring my piece and report in."

"Where? Who did you report to?"

"Some warehouse in Virginia Beach. The guy who gave us orders was a tough looking dude with steel eyes. We got orders and here we are."

"Any others?"

Doc interrupted. "Come on. Let's stop screwing around and kill these bastards." He pulled out his K-bar and shoved it at the first man's face.

"Okay, okay."

Sal shouted, "Shut up. They're bluffing."

Cat knocked him out with his weapon. "Go ahead, bud."

"There's a pickup waitin' at the road before you get here to Sandbridge. He got us covered with a radio and bug finder. They're comin' soon."

Doc slugged him anyway.

Whitney bent over outside of the garage door. She could not control her trembling hands or her racing heart. She had never experienced anything so violent. Although she did not see all of the fight, she heard and saw the explosions and the rattle and thumping of weapons. When she saw the carnage in the street, the burning car, and dead bodies still oozing blood, she had slipped out of the car and vomited. Wiping her face with tissues from her bag, she could hardly believe the speed of the action and its finality.

Thank God, the SEALs had won without any apparent casualties. She grabbed a water bottle from her carry-on to moisten her parched mouth. God, if this was what war was like she didn't want any part of it.

The TV pictures from Viet Nam didn't do the violence justice, for they were only pictures. The screams and moans of the wounded and dying before they drove off pierced her heart. She knew that this baptism of fire would never leave her and she wondered how these men could live with it and themselves afterward. She knew that they were exceptional people, trained, and bloodied. How could they do this? Head for sudden and violent death, and still press forward.

She swallowed more water and slowly wagged her head. Could they hold off even more attacks? She had a lot of thinking to do. Which side could she choose?

The Cat gave orders. "Okay. We're all goin' for a ride. Tie 'em all. Put two in the trunk, the others in the back seat. Follow me." Bennie tied their legs and arms so that they couldn't move. He drove off slowly southward with Doc fiddling with the radios.

Dan drove Bennie's car with the two women and all of their gear. He continued south for a mile and crossed over to Sandpiper Road, which ran parallel to Sandfiddler. He headed north, hoping to evade the pickup on the way to the one road away from the Sandbridge trap.

Joseph Guion

CHAPTER FIFTY SIX

Dan spotted the pickup ahead and pulled into a driveway and Bennie drove into another. He gave The Cat directions to his girlfriend's house. While he was talking a low flying chopper thumped their way and swung low along the beach. Five minutes later the pickup roared toward Sandfiddler. The Cat drove off and Bennie followed.

Haggerty heard a thumping chopper on the road away from Sandbridge, he stopped under cover and waited for the slick to disappear. They took a side road, hit Indian River Road and then separated at Princess Anne Road. They split up with Dan heading for Gloria's house.

Bennie drove westward to The Great Dismal Swamp where they tossed the prisoners into the weeds off a deserted road. He drove the car into the water and hid near the road. A pickup with two men eased to where Doc was finishing off. They started for him with shotguns, but Bennie knocked one out from behind and covered the other. They tied up the killers and hid them in the bushes. The pickup had listening equipment and a direction finder in it. The black car had been bugged and followed. The SEALs knew they were in a world of shit.

On the way to rejoin Haggerty, Doc asked, "You got any ideas? These guys got max equipment. They're gonna be hard to shake. Think they trailed The Cat? Better haul ass to Gloria's house."

Nelson was in Virginia Beach, coordinating the search. He was pissed. The SEALs might have been caught if he hadn't been a hog, trying to have his own people get them without letting the police in on it. From now on, he'd use everything, everybody.

Wes handled the official search through the police forces and the federals. The loss of two units had become apparent when they didn't check in on the half hour. A strike team with a helo made it to Sandbridge after the fugitives had escaped.

Assault teams fanned out from Sandbridge, the Dismal Swamp and into the rest of the city. They received a break. One of the interviewers had picked up the names of Bennie's girlfriends from SEAL Headquarters people. The private army, the FBI and Virginia Beach police flocked toward four addresses. Gloria's was number one.

CHAPTER FIFTY SEVEN

In Williamsburg Nelson was excited. They were closing in. The frogman had two other studs with him, but there was no way this army could fail. They had the word, "Nobody lives."

He had assigned people in strategic places, including the Hampton Roads area, ready to insure that the terrorist attack story would be accepted. Members of the media, police, and influential people could be counted on to enhance the ploy.

He reached for the phone and waited. A shadow dashed across his face like a cloud passing between the sun and the earth. He threw down the cold cigar. Anger bloomed in his face. Better wait till I get the phone call. That dude is damned lucky or smart or too much of both.

At Gloria's home, Whitney was trying to control her racing heart. She had been frightened before, especially when she was in Miss Barbara's stable of high-price prostitutes. Some men needed to demonstrate their power and since they were paying for a woman's time, they demanded the right to get physical. Fortunately, Miss Barbara would cancel out the man's name and would never accept another assignment from the ass-hole. Frank and the SEALs held her in a tug of war rope. Which way could she go? Haggerty was tough like Frank, except that he had a soft side that she had never seen in her benefactor.

Haggerty handed over her pistol. "It's loaded. Have to trust you to help Beth."

She received the weapon with a grim face. "I'll try. You've got to get help for her."

"I know that! Do what you're told and I'll see if and when I can let you go."

She trembled, certain that she was dead meat with Frank or Wallace. If she remained with these men, what were their chances against Frank's power, money and influence? The immediate problem was to live through another gun battle. She wondered if she could face it, She checked her weapon.

Magee was in his suite reading the local newspaper about the freeing of Lebanon hostages. A wry smile acknowledged what he already knew from his NSC contact, that they were coordinating and monitoring the situation. He made a fist when he glanced at the article that the damned government troops in Nicaragua had chased contra fighters three miles into Honduras. Damn, those wimps in Congress! We should have had more than enough missiles and firepower to beat their ass.

When Reverend Jethro burst in unannounced, The Fox jumped out of the chair and the paper slipped from his hand. "Frank! Frank! Have you read the paper? We're going to lose the election! It says right heah that we'd have to win five of the seven closest states, so we could get a Senate tie. You know, like fifty votes for them and fifty for us."

Magee nodded. "That's not critical. And after all, Vice President George Bush could make the vote ours. Try not to worry."

He held a newspaper and pointed. "You've got to see

this article. Those liberal donkey Democrats could win in Florida, Maryland and Nevada. And if they can take Colorado and win two of the other six closest states they could have a majority."

The Fox patted his partner on the shoulder. "Jethro, my friend, that's a lot of 'ifs.' Didn't it say anything about our winning possibilities? I believe that I read that there are a lot of undecided people in Carolina and we put a lot of money in there. Come on, friend. Let's now get panicky here. We still have unfinished business here. Let's talk about that and let our PAC money and people on the scene to carry us through to victory."

The Reverend shook his head. "You sound mighty sure of yourself. I just could not stand it if those baby killers won over the Senate."

"Not to worry. Let's complete our ideas for the departure press conference. Settle down and have a bourbon."

Creed reluctantly took three fingers of the heavy brown liquid and gulped it down.

The Fox knew that the media had predicted more states as too close to call. His scheme had to work. If they didn't keep The Senate, the country would continue to turn for the worst. They needed right thinking judges in the Supreme Court to reverse liberal decisions. The Star Wars program could be sacrificed to budget cutters and arms control wimps.

Reactions from his speech continued to arrive and they grew in intensity. The liberal press called it demagoguery at its worst. He didn't give a damn. Fund pledges were rolling in, to The Reverend and to his own JUST CAUSE. The TV and newspaper pictures of the partners with arms upraised and hands clasped together were an interesting sight. For a moment, he saw the '88 Republican Convention with the same picture. He dismissed it. Or did he?

Creed's face turned sunny from the drink. "Frank, y'all coming with me to the next conference?"

"I'll be there shortly. Go ahead, you don't need me now."

Stolen Votes

A grin split the muffin face like a knife opening up a biscuit for buttering. "Vote Raht!" He raised his right fist and The Fox responded in kind.

The first killer car nosed around the corner two blocks from Gloria's house. Four men wearing FBI jackets and carrying heavy weapons got out and walked toward the address. The driver reported to a second car heading for a cut off point.

The helicopter checked in to the leader. "I'll be overhead in five minutes. Any sign of anything?"

"No. Just get the hell over here fast, no slipups."

"That's a Roge."

The leader directed the other three to spread out and begin walking toward the target's house. He had decided to walk in his men while the other cars were arriving. You never knew if something could spook somebody. He figured that the helo might flush them out, and his orders were, "No warnings, shoot to kill."

He checked out his automatic shotgun and set the choke for medium distance. It would hit with a blob of pellets, knocking anyone down. Then he'd blast the man or woman. Without an investigation afterward, they could use forbidden weapons and ammo. They had the bastards cold.

In Gloria's living room, The Cat had a taste of the past that was like bile. Once again, he was responsible for the lives of friends. And people were trying to kill them. He had to be right, to make the correct decisions. Should they run? Now? They were in a race for survival. If the killers found them at Gloria's place in Kempsville Lakes, it would be all she wrote. Bennie was outside on watch in radio contact. He argued with Doc. "These guys have access to cops, everything. What if they track down Bennie's girlfriends?"

"Shit, that'll take two weeks."

"Sure. How'd they find us in Sandbridge?"

"That was Miss Mink on the phone."

"No way! They knew where we were before she called. We're lucky she did. It alerted us to move out. We'd been in a world of shit with no warning."

"Cat, you're in no condition to take off. You needa rest. You see what I'm saying? Let's take some time off here. If you don't do what I tell you, I'll ship out of here."

"Go ahead, Doc. I don't need you any more. Look, the outfit after us has max stuff. They gotta army for cripes sakes. They'll be sneakin' around the neighborhood ASAP."

"Then what? We can't beat the firepower they got."

"What the hell did we do in 'Nam? Sneak in; overwhelm them with firepower, pull off the mission and run like hell to be extracted. Let's go!"

"Where? You got a Swift boat or a medium some place? A hootch somewhere? Shit, I say we stay till Beth wakes up anyway. She needs sleep."

The Cat frowned. Where could they go? Who would be willing to hide fugitives? Other SEALs? Which ones? These two were the most trustworthy. Who else? His mind raced around like a dog chasing a rabbit. He frowned. Would those people help? He had to try. "Yeah, I know some people. They'll hide us." He checked the phone book and dialed.

"We move now! Tell Bennie to stay where he is. Gloria, take the 280Z and run like hell. We take the Volvo." They packed the car. Bennie called, "Slick comin'. Get out!"

The helo swooped down two blocks away and began a low-level search. Bennie called again. "Better duck, folks. FBI in the next street."

Gloria blasted out of her driveway in Bennie's 280Z. She drew the helo and the running men when she swerved around the corner. The fugitives piled into the Volvo. Doc picked up Bennie and they headed for Norfolk.

The press conference was top level for media interest drawn by the terrorist connection and the startling religious news.

Reporters from news services, three major networks, major newspapers, and the DC press were on hand. Creed's brief announcement of their joint network with its coordinated programming bounced off the walls in the sudden silence.

Questions machine-gunned at the preacher. Reporters jumped up and shouted to be heard. After fifteen minutes of bedlam, detailed press releases were handed out.

A network reporter asked, "What about the relationship between you and Mister Magee? Are you calling for people to 'VOTE RIGHT' for your candidates?"

"Ah'd like to ask Frank to come up here." When The Fox arrived, Creed took his hand and raised it above their heads.

"Yes, folks, on Tuesday, Vote Right! The terrorists are after me and my network. With Frank Magee and all the loyal Christians that we represent, we will scourge them from this land." He chanted, "Vote Right! Vote Right!"

The crowd rewarded Creed with a standing ovation that lasted for twenty minutes. Reporters dashed for telephones and other rapid means of communication to their editors.

Joseph Guion

CHAPTER FIFTY EIGHT

The SEAL faces in the car looked grim, determined and at least somewhat satisfied. They had escaped again. Whitney was shaking and holding a passive, nauseated Beth.

Bennie broke the tension. "Damn, Cat. You just cost me a nice girlfriend. They probably tore up that car too. She's gonna be pissed when they start questioning her. Where's the next hideout? Can they find that too?"

"I doubt it. None of us are tied to this outfit. Think they know how to keep us hidden too. One thing guys. None of your shit. These are gays. No smart freaking remarks."

Bennie grinned. "Why, thay fella, you never told me."

"Dammit to hell! That's what I'm talking about. Turn here. Doc, we've got to do the hidden vehicle thing again. What do you think?"

"Let a queer hide it under his skirt. Aw shit, Cat, I won't make a pass."

"Stop!" The Cat got out and held the door. "Now listen you shitheads. My life and yours are in the hands of people you may hate. Some of them are a helluva lot tougher than you are. Don't give me, or any of them shit. If you're going to

Stolen Votes

keep it up, shove off."

They nodded. Doc said, "Aw, Cat. Lighten up."

"No! I won't lighten up. If you guys don't want their help, take off. I'm taking the women and we're going to be at their mercy. Don't forget, they're damned good at keeping secrets. And I don't want any talk about what this freaking chase is all about. Okay?"

They moved into a contemporary condo in the Ghent section of Norfolk. Pete Dunn grinned and shook Haggerty's hand. "Are you the people in the news?" His manner changed when he saw grim faces. "You can move into another place every night or several times a day through this complex. We can switch houses anytime. I used three drivers to hide your car. Each one knew only his part of it. Is that satisfactory?"

Doc nodded. "Sounds great, Pete. Say you got some coffee?"

"Certainly, decaf or regular? Cream, Sugar?"

"Man, I'd like the regular with a stiff shot."

"Bourbon, brandy, or liqueur?"

Doc grinned. "This man's okay. I'll take all three."

"Dan, would you like to have a doctor come in? I mean a very discreet one."

He sighed. "No. We'll be okay. If we have to spend more than overnight, I'd like to have Beth looked at. No skin off your nose, Doc. I need to find out what they gave her."

Doc went with Pete for the coffee. Bennie turned on the twenty-five inch console. He kept touching the "Up Channel" button to search. There were no news bulletins. "When do you think I can call Gloria? They could put the squeeze on her. I put her in deep shit."

"Probably better not, Ben. I'm sorry as hell you guys got into this."

Bennie headed for the kitchen. "No sweat. You'd do it for us. What's for dinner?"

After an excellent meal, Dan and Doc settled in the paneled den in front of the working fireplace. They needed an intelligence conference. Ben was on watch, hidden outside.

Whitney was in a bedroom with a young man outside the open door. He was in a macho gay uniform, tight jeans molding genitals and cutoff sleeves to show off biceps. The Cat wouldn't let Pete sit in with them, explaining that it was safer for him to stay out of it. He reluctantly agreed. Beth sat next to Cat wrapped in his arm.

The Doc sipped at the neat bourbon silently. "Who the hell is behind this, Cat? I mean, you're telling me they got an army, police in their pocket. They got slicks, communications up the ying yang. Who the hell could it be? Feds?"

"I don't know. It could be. How the hell could they cover up those deaths in Williamsburg? In the water? I mean, they've got one helluva outfit."

"You've been damned lucky. It ain't gonna continue. My guess is, Beth has some info they need or don't want spread. Maybe they were trying to find out how much she knew. See what I'm sayin'. You come along and it's a new ballgame. They tried to take you out. They couldn't, so they tried the trap. That didn't work either because you pulled that freaking mad bomber shit. Honestly, Cat, when are gonna grow up?"

Doc's soft laugh gave his seal of approval. "Seems like we better try to find out what it is they're after, then we figure out some counteraction. How long can we stay here? Are these people secure?"

Dan reassured him and they tried to question Beth. Her information brought in Tony and the computer system at the Network. They tried to dig deeper into the situation.

Beth leaned against Dan on the deep-cushioned sofa. Still groggy, she tried to speak. "I think, uh, think it might have some uh, something to do with a secret program in the network computers. Don't have proof, ummm, I know where to find out."

"Where?"

"The Reverend. Dan, you don't like him. But he's knows everything that goes on."

Doc interrupted. "I thought you said that his assistant might be involved."

"That's what the big man said at the motel. He blamed Ned for everything, even said he was going to straighten things out and take me to Reverend Creed. That was before you broke in. Thank God you did."

"No sweat, babe. Okay, say it's a very secret computer program. For what? Why would people be so damned nasty about it? Corporate secrets? Breaking into bank systems? I mean, I read some of Tony's books about computer fraud and crime. But this seems to be some kind of government job, maybe CIA. What about Russians?"

Doc said, "Yeah, could be I guess. Don't some big corporations have muscle too? 'Specially if they're in foreign countries. Isn't the CIA into the contra crap? That poor ex-jarhead got shot down delivering weapons. Could that be it?"

Dan thought. Tony, computers. "Tony left some stuff on my monitor when he was working heavy. Some people told me it sounded like he was trying to break into a program. He had a Trap Door and a horse. A Trojan Horse. Maybe Pete knows somethin' about computers."

Haggerty came back grinning. "I talked, well Pete talked to an expert. You use a Trap Door to have the computer hide things for you. The machine runs along and when it hits a certain operation or code, it dumps stuff off in your account."

"You mean like a bank account?"

"Maybe, sort of. It's a reference file, or address. Anyway, a Trojan Horse is an instruction hidden in a computer system. When it's triggered, it makes the computer do things the operator don't want it to, and the operator may not know it."

Bennie was relieved outside by a gay Norfolk Policeman. While his friend had a beer, Dan brought him up to date. "Cat, you think Tony was trying to get into a secret program at the network. And that's why he was killed?"

"I don't know. You see, Tony's killer shouted, 'Take that you fucking queer.' He could have been killed because of that. Or they wanted to cover the computer bit. Wait."

Ben shook his head. "I've seen that look before. Doc

we're in a heap of—."

Cat cut him off. "A couple of gay people quizzed me about Tony's death. A computer guy from NOB named Bob Weatherby said the same words the killer shouted. Far as I know he wasn't at the murder and the exact words were never made public."

"You think those people had something to do with it? What did they say?"

Dan shrugged. Beth shivered and he held her close. "He said, 'Take that you fucking queer.' Shit, I don't know. The thing gets confusing as hell."

Bennie grinned. "Why don't we check them out? Invite them to discuss it in a nice way? What do you think, Doc?"

"Yeah, an Uzi between the eyes helps a guy to remember lots of stuff."

Dan turned them down. He didn't want to expose them to anyone else. So far, he felt pretty secure with Pete's people. What about Rita Brennan? She was a computer whiz. She didn't ask about the exact words, or did she? He found her phone number and called. Her answering system came on. He hung up. There was no way that he'd leave a number.

Nelson almost throttled the man who had reported in. The frogman had outflanked him again. He had to see The Fox before the shit left Williamsburg for DC. He could call to bring the Foxmobile from Williamsburg, but that would take at least an hour. The hell with it. I'll drive myself.

The man on Magee's switchboard nodded. "We got 'em." He dialed Nelson's number. Wes answered and said that Wallace was on his way to Williamsburg, that he couldn't get in touch with him for an hour. The switchboard man said that he'd try to set up a trace on the next call. He asked for instructions. He was told to wait.

Stolen Votes

CHAPTER FIFTY NINE

Dan carried Beth into the bedroom and placed her on the bed. Whitney sat in a chaise filing her nails. Sometime after he left Beth stirred and moaned. Whitney leaned over the woman. "What's the matter, Beth? Are you okay?"

"Where's Dan? Who are you?"

Whitney reminded her who she was, that they were still trying to hide out and remain safe. After a while, they opened up. Beth unloaded first, speaking now with more clarity.

"I spent my first year in college working my way up from students to faculty to businessmen. Nothing but a medium-priced whore. Could Dan ever forgive me?"

Whitney sighed and put her arm around Beth. "He seems like a real great guy. I'm sure, uh, sure he will. It's a good idea to get it all out. It will help you to be free."

"Where's Dan? Where are we? What day is this?"

"Guess he's sleeping. We're at Pete Dunn's place. We're trying to hide out from some terrible people, remember? I helped you get away. Do you remember the escape? The boat? It's Sunday, uh, November second."

"November second! Oh, Lord Jesus. The election is days

away. Got to stop them."

"Stop who? What are you talking about?"

Beth rambled on about her suspicions of secrecy and the kidnapping. "They took me to Dan's boat and that awful. Oh, Dear Jesus, that devil. You should see his eyes; he's like a snake. And he, he—. " She covered her face with her hands and sobbed.

Whitney held her, patting her and whispering that it was all right; she was safe. She wondered how safe they actually were with Frank's minions after them. Could she still go back to the bastard who had pimped her twice? She asked about the snake-eyed man.

"Please, he, oh Lord Jesus, he raped me, raped me!" Tears flooded her eyes.

Whitney hugged her. "Beth, I know. I know." She rocked the big woman in her arms.

"It's so God-awful. I know. I was raped too. You feel so disgraced, so filthy. Your most private places have been ripped open raw and everyone in the world can see them. Everyone you meet, you think, 'They know! They know I've been raped.' Most of it will pass after a while. I'm afraid that you'll never be the same. Oh, Beth, I'm so sorry."

The women whispered their feelings for a time. Later Beth brightened up. "You know, the Reverend Creed can get it straightened out. Whitney, he's the most wonderful person in the world. He took me out of the gutter. He helped me to see Jesus. He'll save us." She shivered and talked of the rape.

Whitney said, "I thought I could never let another man touch me, I did and then it wasn't so bad. But I still feel it, fear it more than anything in the world. The first thing that hits my mind when I see a man is, 'Will he rape me?' "

Beth prayed aloud and slept. She woke later, thinking about The Reverend, how he could rescue them. He was on the bedroom television. His face drew her to him. She wanted to call him, but she forgot when he was supposed to return to Norfolk. The news conference made her smile. "Oh, thank you, Jesus." She wondered if Dan could work with her for

Jesus. It might help them to resolve their differences. First they had to get out of this terrible situation. She prayed. Decided. She had to see her mentor

Dan contacted Rita. After her initial surprise, she was quite interested about his questions and of computer secrets. She asked where he was. He frowned. "Don't you know what's been going on here for the past couple of days?"

"Not really. I was in Richmond for five days working on some accounts that they couldn't straighten out. I fixed them and drove here to the beach. Why?"

"You'll hear a wild story about me in the news. They're calling me a terrorist. I rescued Beth from kidnappers in Williamsburg. Had to fight them. Some people were killed. We hid out at Sandbridge and we were attacked again. So, I'm a fugitive."

"What does this have to do with computers? Um, anyway, can I help?"

"Try to get some info for me. Like you said, Tony was such a hacker, maybe he did some things with, uh. You called it an electronic bulletin board? How soon can I call you back?"

"Better give me about an hour. Good bye and good luck."

When Dan called her back Rita sounded excited. "What was Tony's full name?"

"Anthony Louis Garbossa."

"Hmm. Know anything about his birth date, home address or phone number?" She explained that many people used familiar numbers and names for personal codes. "Well, anyway, here's what I've got. He was in the Unnamed BBS in Virginia Beach the day he was murdered and left a couple of messages. One in plain language for you and another one is coded. It will take time to break it. The message is pretty interesting. You were right, there is something."

"Stop! Can you bring that message where it's safe?"

"Safe? I saw the news about you. Let me think about this. Call me back in ten minutes I may have something by that time."

Dan talked to Pete. He agreed that they should take precautions and move to another place. When they packed for another move, they realized that Beth was missing.

The Cat had Whitney by the shoulders and shook her. "What the hell happened to her? Where did she go? Why didn't you stop her?"

"When the hell did you put me in charge of her? Where was the young butch? I thought he was watching her."

Dan shouted at Pete. "Where did that guy go? Wasn't anyone watching her?"

"I'm sorry, you wanted to keep us out of it and I took him off the bedroom. Look, Dan, she couldn't go far in her state. I'll send a bunch after her."

Dan asked Whitney, "Did she talk to you about leaving? Where did she go?"

"I don't know. She did say something about going to see Reverend Creed."

"Oh, Jesus." The Cat felt that he was rolling backwards, into disaster, back to 'Nam. He had lost Beth. Like Bobby. Like Tony. He felt threads coming apart in his head. Hands against his temples, he tried to press his brains together.

Doc called him back to the moment. "Hey, Cat. Me and Bennie will find her. You keep on this shit here. Try to get it figured out so we can find something to attack. You hear?"

"Yeah, yeah. But I ought to go. I lost her."

"You shit, man! This is a freaking team. Stay at the base for more intel. Okay?"

Bennie reminded him that Rita had only talked to him. "She doesn't know us." He slapped Cat's shoulder. "We're gone!"

Dan and Whitney followed Pete through a yard into another complex. Walking briskly together in the dark, they crossed two streets, turned down another and found a phone booth. Dan called Rita and gave her the new address. They hurried to an old frame house, just off Stockley Gardens.

They were greeted by a tall, energetic young man with the unlikely name of Buck. The rooms were well furnished, less opulent than at Pete's place. Dan paced, worrying about Beth. He wondered if Rita would follow instructions. He jumped when the phone rang. Buck answered and nodded to them. "Pete?"

Dunn listened, asked two questions, and hung up.

"You were right. She was tailed. My people couldn't pick her up. But they're trailing them all." He nodded at Haggerty's expression. "It's amazing what gays have to do sometimes to keep out of trouble."

"Pete, I don't know how to thank you. I mean you're sticking your neck out."

"We're doing this for you, your friends, Tony too."

Rita stepped into the room. She looked fresh in a grey fall suit with an electric blue shawl. She was even more beautiful than Dan remembered. She hugged him tightly, stepped back and looked at his eyes. "Are you all right?"

"Yeah." He sent everyone else out of the room. "Now let's get to it."

She explained that Tony had indeed left a message on the electronic bulletin board. In it he warned that if anything happened to him, like a sudden death or anything suspicious, Dan should be wary. Someone had tried to prevent him from getting into a secret program in The Truth Network. Beth didn't know about it. It had something to do with the election.

"The election? What election?" He shook his head and paced. "What the hell?"

Rita watched. "Dan, I couldn't believe it either. Nobody tries fooling around with an election with computers. I don't understand it. I mean a local election, maybe."

"Local, my ass. These birds are far from local. They got connections with police, federal people. Yeah, it makes sense. This had to be something damned important. They got a big gang with all sorts of weapons and communications. The Russians!"

"But Dan, think about it. What can you do playing with an election? And for what reason? They use computers to predict outcomes and to tabulate results. But—."

"And why The Truth Network?"

"That's another good question. I just can't see what could be done."

"Skip that. Why use the network's computer system? Is it the latest or best?"

"Hmmm. Not really. There are larger, faster mainframes that can do a lot of sophisticated research. I don't know why, Dan. Maybe because the persons worked at The Network."

"We need Beth. Why haven't those guys called?"

"Dan, if I could get back into the BBS I could get into the secret message. I'm stuck here. I used my PC at home."

He asked Pete to find another PC and modem for Rita. The Cat had to sit down. An election being played with? But why the network? What did they do differently than a bank or company with computers? Something was kicking around in his mind.

When Rita returned, the high color blush on her face contrasted with an ashen look.

"From Tony's BBS info I learned the mainframe number at the Truth Network to call and the password, so I could get into the system. It worked."

"You got me."

"Well more and more entities that have mainframes have set up a system where each remote terminal could be reached by a special telephone number. You dial that number and the mainframe answers."

She sat down and sighed. "Here it is, Dan. It's incredible. They are going to use the Truth Network's satellite system to transmit data all over the country. I'm not sure how it would work at that end. They have data flowing in some way from outside to the computer for processing. Instructions go back out. I can't find out what they are."

She frowned. "You know, this could be some innocent attempt to beat the other networks in predicting the winners. There's nothing really wrong with that."

"Is it enough to kill for?"

Rita shivered. "No. It will take me some time, probably three or four hours to use Tony's stuff, to penetrate the system and try to find out what is going on."

"Can you crash it?"

"Oh, that's the easiest thing to do. But then what? They must have backups. If you crash it they'd close out outside access. I'm not sure about theirs, but in ours, you can't take data out from inside without special encrypted codes. I'd like to try to get into this thing and see what is really going on."

"What could we do? Uh, to stop what they're doing?"

"I could put in a logic bomb that would trigger and destroy data and parts of the system. That's almost the same as crashing. They'd know it pretty soon. Look, let me try to get into it and see what I can find out."

"You see, when computers are manufactured they are given standard passwords so the persons testing or installing the system always knows how to access it. You type in a sequence, like 'TYPE TEST, USER, SYSTEM,' or even 'PASSWORD.' You have to keep at it, try different words. There are other ways in. Better go, I'll get back to you."

God, another one I'm responsible for. He took her hands and looked into her eyes. "Rita. Please don't do anything that could get you into danger. Let me go with you."

She shook her head. "No. Please, it's sweet of you to be concerned. Remember, this is involves Tony and other good friends. I've got a stake in this thing too. Don't forget that."

Pete had her escorted and guarded by a Norfolk police officer. One of theirs.

Beth almost reached safety. The taxi drove up to the entrance to Jethro Creed's mansion on the water in Elizabeth Shores, Norfolk, when a police car blocked the entrance. The cabbie was frightened until he saw that they were after Beth. He was so cooperative that he babbled. "Yes, I picked her up at Colonial and Brambleton. Alone."

They sat her in the police car for a while interrogating her. She went into shock. The previous captivity jammed her mind and blotted out reality. Safety was just up the driveway. She pleaded to be taken to the reverend's house. They refused. Doc and Bennie arrived just as they drove off with two other cars. The SEALs followed.

CHAPTER SIXTY

Bennie arrived at the new hideout with a worried look on his face. "Cat, I have bad news. The police picked her up at the preacher's doorstep. They never took her to a station. Doc's tailing them. If they roost, you want to assault the place? They got maybe three cars full of guys and heavy weapons."

God! Beth. Captured again! He wanted to find her so badly that he lurched toward the door. Then he stopped. The best way to beat the bastards was to beat their game. He had to take that chance. He had to find out who the hell was behind it. The sooner Rita got into it, the sooner Dan had some bargaining power. He'd bargain Beth for the system. The election was important, but not as important as she was. What could they do anyway?

The Doc showed just before two am on Sunday. The look on his face was enough. "I tried. Man, I tried to hang onto them. They used three cars to stop me. Blew out my tires. Had to slip out from under. Sorry, Cat. Give me an hour rest. Me and Bennie will—."

"No. You did all you could. I gotta leave her in the hands of God, and Rita."

At three on Sunday morning in Williamsburg Francis X. Magee stalked around his former lieutenant and jabbed him with words that were pointed enough to draw blood. "Once again, you had him. A phone call traced, and then? They're gone again. How could you let that happen? You're through Nelson. Through! I'm taking charge, now!"

He called his valet. "Otto, get me into a good downtown hotel in Norfolk. I'll be there for a day or two. I'm riding down. When you have the accommodations, get Wes and have him meet me." He eyed Nelson, "You're coming with me. Leave your car."

Two hours later The Fox had set up his suites including a separate one for his communications and computers at the Omni Hotel suite overlooking the river. He called a local mole on the phone. The man sounded frightened, but eager to help.

"Yes, sir, yes, sir. I was contacted earlier about a couple of computer questions, but I wasn't sure it was them. Yes sir. Believe me, I'll do it. Should I make the approach?"

"I have other means, Mister Weatherby. Wait for a call. Be very cooperative. Do anything they ask, even if it seems destructive, or illegal, or quite out of the ordinary. Then call me at this number. Thank you, Robert."

Magee rubbed his hands and went to wash them again. The program leader reported that the system was running and one hundred percent accurate. He had the election. He had the frogman's girl friend. He'd have the frogman too, as soon as the bastard tried to get into the program or when Weatherby was called in. Then Nelson. First he'd make him sweat.

The phone call came to their third hideout late that afternoon. Haggerty had slept fitfully, dozing, wondering how he could rescue Beth again. The familiar smell of WD 40 permeated the room. Doc and Bennie were cleaning weapons in the den, working quietly, faces set, not speaking. He heard the "snap" and "click" of different weapons being checked. Pete handed him the phone.

Rita's voice was hushed as if she were trying to speak without anyone hearing. "Dan, I'm sorry. I couldn't get here early enough to get it finished. I started into it. I should be able to finish after the first shift is gone. I just don't know how long it will take."

He thanked her and hung up. He walked the den, clenching and unclenching his fists. It was hard to sit and wait, with Beth at their mercy. Doc and Bennie had searched all day long. The SEALs didn't have the resources that the other side had. Several times he had thought about calling the FBI or the CIA, or any federal agency. He went through a list of SEAL names, active duty and retired in the area. He knew that he could call on half a dozen of them for help. But what good would it do? Where were they holding Beth?

He asked his buddies. "Should I contact news people? If the story was made public, then what? An investigation?"

Doc answered. "That's bullshit, Cat. Who the hell can you trust? You need people with ideas, connections. Get Pete involved. He knows a helluva lot of people."

"I hate to bring him into this freaking mess."

The Cat told the story to a very eager listener. Pete asked questions periodically. Once, Dan felt that a question was too good, too precise about what might be going on. Shit. He wondered, now you're suspecting Pete. If it weren't for him, you'd still be on the run or dead.

"Dan, there's an excellent computer man who could help. I believe that you know him, Bob Weatherby. He could give you some ideas on how to tackle this thing." He smiled. "Of course, you realize that this thing is like a totally wild story."

"No shit. I don't believe it myself half the time. Some son of a bitch has an idea or plan that's worth killing people over? I didn't dream these damned attacks. The killers after us at the Magruder motel were heavily armed. And the bastards had first rate communications."

"What about soldiers of fortune? Or Survivalists?" Pete paused. "No... No. They aren't that well organized and they don't have that much clout. What about the motel? Have you thought about what you faced there? Would that help to figure out something?"

"Good idea." He told that part of the story, answering Pete's questions as they came. He asked what the people were wearing, the men inside the room including the big man.

"Well, he's about a half head taller than I am. That would make him a good six four, or six seven. Probably weighs close to three hundred. The guy was a real bear. Kind of like a defensive lineman in the NFL. Well-dressed, black hair. I didn't recognize him."

Whitney had been listening outside the door. She stepped in. "That was Nelson Wallace. I know him. I'm pretty damned sure that I know who's behind all this."

"The hell you say!"

"The hell YOU say! Sit down, Mister SEAL. I'm going to tell you a rotten story." She told them about Magee at length, about his connections to the White House, Congress, both political parties and powerful people who owed him in and around the Beltway. She tried to impress them that the man always got what he wanted. She tried to convince them of how ruthless he could be.

Pete asked, "How could he have so many contacts all over the country? Would they break the law, hide the bodies? Come on, Whitney, it can't be one man."

"I didn't say it was one man. I'm saying that there is one man who is capable of controlling enough people to do it. Let me ask you, Pete. How's your credit? Good huh?"

He nodded. "What does that have to do with it?"

"Who controls a major credit bureau? Francis X. Magee. He has access, and access in DC is gold. Access to credit records is platinum. Did you hear this year about the defector with defense secrets? The Russians recruited him because he was in financial trouble. Many people would compromise themselves to keep financial problems secret."

Pete nodded. "Yes, that's a way to gain leverage."

Dan shook his head. "Okay, so this friend of yours, he's a real power man. But this is lethal, kid. How far would he go to get what he wants?"

"Haven't you seen him on television the past two days? Wake up! He's preaching about installing an ultra right wing government." She pointed at Pete. "How would you like to have a guy like that running the country? What do you think would happen to gays?"

Pete looked like he had been stabbed.

Bennie disagreed. "He's not going to run the country."

"Bullshit! He might as well be doing that if he gets his people in The Senate. Then, The House and the presidency. Remember, The Senate consents to Supreme Court judges."

"Come on. A guy's gotta be a cold-hearted SOB to do this kind of deadly stuff."

"Dammit! You want to hear what the bastard will do? Pete, I need a drink and a cigarette. I haven't smoked for two years." After she had downed half a scotch and puffed half a smoke. She told them about her being his mistress and how he had treated her.

"See this nose? It didn't look like this last year. Francis Xavier Magee broke it in Hong Kong because I wouldn't whore for him with a banker. Then he had the plastic surgeon fix it slightly off line so I couldn't get top modeling jobs." She lit another smoke and told them about the whore job he had set up with The Reverend, to blackmail him into a TV deal.

"And, guys, picture this." She jabbed a red-nailed index finger at them and leaned forward. "He forced the woman who whored with that freaking preacher to be a hostess at a dinner in his home. Why? So he could grind it into the poor bastard that if he didn't come across on their special deal, the videos of us fucking will be publicized. The son of a bitch threatened that if I didn't come home to him, he'd show my ass on TV."

She paced and puffed. "The dirty bastard has my red Mercedes and he's going to burn it in front of my eyes. Is he a rotten bastard? You bet your ass he is! And he'll kill to get what he wants." She fell into an overstuffed chair and cried.

Dan put his hand on her shoulder. "It's okay, kid. Take it easy. You're, uh, you're a helluva woman. So he could do it."

Pete asked, "Well, Dan, what say we get in touch with Bob Weatherby, see if he can help us."

Dan nodded. He thought of Beth. It was hopeless. There was no way she could be found. The only possibility he had was to break into the computer system and hold that hostage like they were holding her. Beth's life was in his hands. If he hadn't been so damned stupid and left her alone. If he hadn't shouted out Tony's location, the killer wouldn't have found him. If he hadn't fired the shotgun without double-checking, Bobby wouldn't have been killed. If. If. If. Dammit it to hell!

This thing was incredible. There was an army after them. Soon he'd make a mistake and get these people, his friends, his SEAL buddies, killed! He was tired of the responsibility. Oh, God, what can I do? Beth? He imagined the torture she was going through and it made him sick. Everything was slipping away. Bobby. Tony. Beth.

The threads were coming apart in his mind again. He set his jaw. There was one way to end these feelings and the bastards behind all this. He had enough explosives to blow himself into tiny, unrecognizable pieces. Those fuckers too!

The periodic sounds snap of weapons being checked and loaded penetrated his thoughts. Doc and Bennie had no hang-ups. They were on an op. They'd go with him to the end, no matter what. He sat, reached into the weapons bag and felt like he had a giant bee sting. He had touched the sawed off shotgun. He dropped it as if its temperature were five hundred degrees. He pulled out his favorite, the A-63 weapons system, the Stoner. He broke the weapon down and grabbed WD 40. He and the rapid firing weapon would be ready. By God, they'd get her somehow.

The Fox stood and held a drink at the window of his suite in downtown Norfolk. Below him was a tug-busy river; across the way two large Navy ships were in dry dock.

Wes barged in with good news. "We've got him! I just got off the phone with your homo mole. He's been called in to help the frogman find out what's going on with a computer system. I told him, go along with it. Keep us informed."

Magee's thin smile never touched the rest of his face. "Where is he?"

"Don't know yet. He's in Norfolk here. It seems that the homos have been hiding them out. I have to hand it to you boss, your foresight having a mole here was twenty-twenty."

"Are the other SEALs there? Can you find out how much they know? What about the, you know the, uh lesbian?"

"Her boss is keeping her extremely busy, sir. I asked him to send her out of town again, but he couldn't do it. He's trying to keep her under close surveillance. I've added more guys for that and they'll stop her if she gets ready to leave."

"You're sure of that?"

"Absolutely!"

The Fox turned away. "We have to find out what they know. So the news is spread around the homosexuals. God, what next? Thank you, Wes."

The thin, disheveled computer systems man slouched in. He reported on the latest test. Magee pressed him on its accuracy. The answers weren't quick enough or reassuring. He swore at the man and stomped around the suite.

"Dammit, look at these newspapers! Predictions that The Senate will be turned over to the liberals. Dammit to hell! I want no interference with the program. This is a test run for Eighty-Eight. If I can control an off year election, in two years I'll be able to control The Presidential. Then The House."

"We could cut off the outside input to the Network. They'd never get into it."

"But then we lose the up-to-date data input."

"Well, okay. But the thing will still work. The telethon

gives us the opportunity to have a voice back up by having all those people on telephones along with our own. I tell you it will work. We're only using key precincts anyway."

"Dammit! The Vice President can cast the winning vote if we have fifty seats. But not all of the fifty are in our pocket. We need at least four or five extra. If the media predictions are halfway correct, we'll never make it."

Magee dismissed the systems man with, "It works, or else! Got That!"

CHAPTER SIXTY ONE

At a secure room in the Truth Network's Main building, Beth was barely hanging on, drugged and exhausted. She babbled on about everything they asked. In halting tones she tried to describe the house they had been in. She couldn't remember names except for Dan and Whitney.

They persisted. "What tipped your boyfriend to leave?"

"I." She lapsed into an unseeing, drifting haze. She was enveloped in a white mist, spinning first slowly, then faster and faster. Dan always out of reach, chained in front of her. calling, 'Beth.' 'Beth.' "I. I don't remember what you asked."

"Why did you leave?"

"I don't know. Dan just made us pack up and go."

"Where were you going?"

"I. I'm not sure, some, uh some other place around." She drifted off again.

The leader remarked, "Shit, she's hopeless. Let her sleep it off. We'll try again."

"The Mechanic could."

"The Mechanic could shit. She's too far gone to threaten us any more."

The man in the white doctor's coat sighed and shrugged. "The woman is barely functioning as a human being. She might have slipped into a mental state that is irreversible. I've done all I can. I doubt if I can save her mind now." He almost looked sorry.

At nine p.m. Bob Weatherby arrived at the fugitives new hideout. Weapons had been cleaned and re-cleaned. Whitney had brushed her hair for the twentieth time. Only Haggerty was at the end of the hanging noose. Beth's noose.

Weatherby seemed very interested. He didn't challenge Dan's story of controlling the election. Haggerty wondered about it, and then chalked it off because of his fatigue.

The Cat said, "So, our only chance is to break into the computer system, find out about it, and threaten to expose it. That way I can get Beth back."

"Well, we need access to a computer, and I need to see the other—. " He looked around.

"You need what!" Dan sought to challenge him.

"I thought you said there was someone else who had uncovered this program. Someone who said that there was a message of some kind."

"I did?"

"Certainly. When you were describing poor Tony's part in this. Oh, God, I miss him. He was a real friend. We've got to do something, for him."

"Yeah. I don't have the whole message. It described a way to penetrate into the program through a Trap Door." Dan pulled out a paper. "Here it is, I don't understand it. If you use these you can get into Tony's access. Guess it saves time."

"You bet. Can I can I take this? Unless you have access to a large computer, I've got to get to the base and use ours." He checked his watch. "We're in luck. At NOB the second shift will soon be on a break. I can get into it before they're all back. Wish me luck."

Dan wondered, frowning. What was wrong? It sounded

Stolen Votes

like the man knew what he was doing. Maybe Rita could help him sort out his questions. Wish she'd call. Not much time left. The polls would open in, what? Ten hours? He queried Pete about Weatherby.

"I've known him for fifteen years. What's wrong? Your antenna working again?"

His smile was reassuring. Or was it? Was Pete really what he claimed to be? The man seemed as masculine as Doc and Bennie. "You got another place to run to, quickly?"

"Sure, not to worry. You want me to set it up?"

"I thought it was."

A headshake. "It'll only take five minutes. What about your three friends?"

"We go as a team."

Rita's phone call ended the discussion. Dan explained the conversation with Weatherby including fears about the man. "What do you think?"

"What did you tell him about getting quick access?"

"I gave him the paper that included Tony's trap door. Why?"

"Nothing. Okay, here's my story." She laid out her plans, apologizing that she couldn't get into the computer space for another hour. She was set up to penetrate again. Once in, she could find out in ten minutes what it was about.

"Thanks, Rita. Say, I've been wondering. Let me send Bennie over there to nose around. Your boss has been on you so much that you haven't been left alone. Could he—?"

"Oh Dan, you're getting too edgy about this. Jerry is fine, a bit over controlling sometimes, but that's his way. No. If I need some help, I have the security people here."

"Thanks."

The systems man returned to Magee, who was studying the printouts. Weatherby's call came in and FX motioned for the computer man to listen in.

"I don't have much time. Here's the message on how to

get into the program. Tell your people to change Section eighteen of the Access Codes. Tell them to crash operating section B-2-F-6. That's Bee Two F, like Fox, Six. That will keep her from getting back in. I'll keep playing with them. When will you take them?"

The Fox sent the systems man off. "Just get on it. See if you can get into it. I'll let you know what to do then." He was relieved and his mind churned out rapid scenarios. He had received good news. David Jacobson, one of the hostages had been released. At last some positive progress.

"Wes, you have the assault team ready for the SEALs?"

"Yes, sir. Got the area closed off. It's a go as soon as you give me the word."

"You have the cover story?"

"Practically have the headlines and the lead paragraphs written. My boys are anxious and ready, same with agents. I could have taken them an hour ago. I'd feel a helluva lot better with the frogman in a body bag. Can I dump his girlfriend? She's nothing but excess baggage now."

"No. She's still my ace in the hole. That Haggerty has impressed me with his resourcefulness. What if? Hmmm. I want her held and ready to be moved. Have your men attack."

The network verified that the last Trap Door had been destroyed.

Weatherby called. "I've tried every way I could think of. There's no way to get into the system from outside. I keep getting 'CODES LOCKED OUT.' Now what?"

"Come back downtown. I'm moving in on them now, but I want you around."

Rita's phone call was switched to the new hideout. They jumped at the first ring. Sitting together they drank coffee in the living room of the old brownstone. The "click" and "snap" of additional weapons verified that they were ready. Bennie brought out another Uzi from the weapons bag and began to field strip it. Pete laid out three more places to go,

Stolen Votes

just in case. His police contact reported that the last hideout had been searched. The cover story was a drug raid.

Doc grinned. "Well, Cat, you sure are stayin' a jump ahead of the sheriff."

Rita reported to Dan. They had closed out Tony's trap door. A new security guard had arrived and a new computer operator too. They seemed to be curious about her work.

"You want someone there?"

"No. I'll be all right. I set the clock. If I don't log out in twenty minutes, the silent alarm will go off. This place will be full of police in five minutes. Here's what I found."

Her story was just unbelievable. Input would be received from many different stations. She couldn't identify them, but the plan had to be larger than any local or even statewide election. She had uncovered another piece when her access was broken off. She was going to play around with what she had. "I'll meet you somewhere."

This was getting to be too much of a thinking man's game and he was a warrior. "I'll let Pete give you directions. Thanks. Are you sure you're safe? Once you're out, we're stuck, right? We have to go with what we have. Is there any other way to get in?"

"I'm building in another trap door. Wish me luck."

He passed the phone to Pete and paced, holding the loaded Stoner on safety in his hand. The election plot was awesome. No wonder they had an army of killers. How could you change votes? There was no way anyone could change your vote, or was there? He wished that he could talk to someone with some voting information. Maybe Pete knew somebody. Dunn had incredible contacts, gay contacts in every business, government. What if?

He glanced at Pete on the phone. Hell, could this be a gay plot? Maybe to get homosexuals and lesbians in office? He trusted Pete. But, how come the bastards found them so often? Was there a mole in Pete's organization? Maybe we're inside the election plot outfit already without knowing it? Why was Pete so eager to help? One way to control an opponent was to let him in and make him think you were helping. Then, you'd ace him when the final step came. He made a decision. They had to get out. Now!

Pete gave instructions to Rita on the phone where they would meet in three different places. The Cat stopped him. "Hold it, Pete. We're pulling out now!"

"What? My God. There's no place to hide. I've got things all lined up. You'll be safe for at least twenty-four hours. I have a way to get you out of the country too."

Pete seemed honest. Was he helping too much? A notion bounced around his mind. This was the enemy. What better way to disguise something than to use the opposition. Dan wagged his head and swung the Stoner toward Pete. "Sorry. Thanks for everything you've done. Time for the SEALs to move. We'll meet Rita. Then I'll decide what to do."

Pete raised his hands. "Fine. Whatever you say. Here are the next three places in case you change your mind. Take my Buick." He tossed the keys and moved closer, probably to shake hands. He stopped. "I hope that you aren't making a mistake. You still don't know who's doing this."

"That's for sure. I don't." He looked the man straight in the eyes for a long time.

At the door, Pete whispered, "Go with God."

Twenty well-armed men converged on the house. There was no escape. The leader checked them out. "No firebombs till I give the word. Shoot to kill everyone."

A small explosive charge blew open the front door. It could have been mistaken for a car backfire. Within two seconds three men in body armor charged inside, tense fingers on triggers. No one was on the ground floor. Teams took each floor. Slowly, methodically, they searched every corner of the place.

Wes screamed into the phone. "Damn you! What do you mean they're gone? It's the right house! Empty? They have to be nearby. I'll get the local cops on a search. Have Jimmy report to them as soon as they arrive, he'll stick with them. Stay in the vicinity." He slammed the phone handset down; it bounced up and fell to the floor.

Magee stood. "So he pulled it off again. Well, Wesley, this man's too lucky or too cautious to be dealt with by a blunt instrument. We'll use finesse the next time."

"If we get another chance."

He knew that his cold, determined security man was on the ragged edge. The Fox grunted. He felt stronger, more alert. Yes, this SEAL was a worthy opponent. The Fox was always at his best dealing with the best. He modified his orders and relaxed.

Joseph Guion

CHAPTER SIXTY TWO

The SEALs and Whitney rode away in a different automobile and turned a corner. At the same moment, the killers broke from their instructions half a block behind them. Neither group knew of the others' location. The fast move saved the fugitives again from a bloody end to their preparations.

The Cat led them into another house. A young woman wearing a "butch" cut greeted them. "Hope you guys are okay. Pete said to make sure you had something to drink and sleeping accommodations. Would you like something to eat?"

Bennie stepped forward. "Certainly, Miss. I'm Ben and always ready for chow."

Doc nodded. "You asked the wrong question. He's the Navy's greatest chow hound. They've been tryin' to discharge him to save some big bucks, but he's found a home."

The woman grinned. "Not a problem." She brought them to a sitting room with a credenza with cut glass decanters on display. Silver chains on their necks identified their contents. "Help yourself. I'll take the big guy into the kitchen and see if we can fill him up."

The Cat broke his solemn manner and grinned. "You'll never do that. Brenda, you got a bed I can lay down on? I'm pretty beat." He followed her into a bedroom and flopped on a queen size bed. He dozed for a short while.

Dan jerked awake and stared at the wall. The strain of worry about Beth and the constant running were suffocating him. He closed his eyes and tried to settle on the bed. Like all military ops, it was hurry up and wait. Checking weapons, rechecking them again, going over the mission. This time, waiting filled his mind with the possibility of failure, of loss. Beth. Oh, God.

Whitney came in quietly. She sat against the headboard, and crossed her legs. She stroked the Cat's hair, his head in her lap.

"Dan, you've got to stop blaming yourself. You couldn't predict that Beth would leave. I talked to her. I tried to talk her out of leaving. But she had to find out for herself if all her trust had been misplaced. Believe me, I had to find that out too. That's why I made that stupid phone call to Frank. Maybe it was a good thing I did call that creep. Otherwise."

"Yeah. You forced me to haul ass. I was pissed at you at the time. I could have belted you all the way to the car." He didn't tell her how close he'd been to give Bennie orders to kill her. "This freaking thing has my head crashing around into things. I just can't get hold of what is going on. Then Beth. God I pray that she's all right."

"So do I. Now you'd better get some sleep. You're the one who keeps this outfit going. Doc and Bennie are tough and smart, but you're the one who keeps us one jump ahead of the bastards. Come on, let me put the light out."

"Yeah, I don't want you to see a grown man cry."

"That's no disgrace. You've been through a lot here. If this is what war is like, I don't want any part of it."

"War is hell, Whit. God. I can't let anything happen to Doc and Bennie. I lost enough buddies to last two lifetimes. It's like going through it again. Ever since Tony's death."

She stroked his hair and waited.

"It was just like 'Nam, I. I had a real good friend. I mean closer than Doc and Ben. We were swim buddies in BUDS, the Basic Underwater Demolition/SEAL training. His name." He had to swallow twice before he could say it. "Bobby Douglass. He. I. Oh Jesus, I can't talk about it even now."

She stretched out next to him, lifted his head and slid one arm underneath his neck to hold him. She caressed his face. "You need to tell somebody. You can trust me. Honestly."

The words came out slowly, then more quickly, until it was a torrent of jumbled emotions and pain. He ended, "Whit, I killed him, killed him. We were in a dark night in bandit territory, VC all around. I heard a noise from a free fire zone, no SEALs there. I swung the Ithaca, uh, that's a shotgun, and blasted him. He wasn't supposed to be there! It was awful. God! Blood, brains, pieces of scalp all over me. I couldn't see much. I came apart. Blamed myself."

"And Tony. I killed him too. I called out his name at the parking lot. I bet the killer didn't know where he was. Next thing you know, Blam! Shot in the face. Another friend blown away. My fault. God, I can't stand it."

He lay in her arms with tears running and his body shaking. She kissed him then, first on his cheeks and then on the mouth. Soft, caressing kisses. He quieted down.

She gave him a hungry, exploring kiss. "Oh, Dan. I want to help you. If you want me, you can have me. Do you understand? Let me love you, now."

He couldn't. He had betrayed too many people and he wasn't going to betray Beth. "You're one helluva woman. But, Beth, I, I love her.

She kissed him and settled against him.

"I told you something I haven't told anyone else. Maybe it's time you told your whole story."

She shook her head and blinked away tears.

Magee watched the busy Elizabeth River from the spacious suite window. Tugs constantly pulled or shoved barges. The shipyard across the way was working all night with cranes and people moving about. This was the eve of his triumph. He sipped at a Rusty Nail, a tribute to tomorrow's beginning of a new era in American politics. He was due at the Truth Network for the morning program before nine. He and Creed would be on the air for a while, speaking about voting and about the new television network. And he could approach it secure in his mind.

Wes reported in person. "It's all set, sir. I got a call from an old friend. Seems like the SEALs have taken off again. They're in a light blue Buick. The license number is being transmitted to the police as a stolen vehicle. They'll be swarming all over the city, working out from Ghent. Maybe the frogman's luck has run out."

"Thank you, Wes. Whether or not his luck has run out is not the question. With the lesbian in custody quite soon, he has no one else to help him to penetrate the system. Let him try. His last resort is a physical assault. I want you to check on our small army around the Network grounds personally. With your expertise, I'm sure that those bastards will never get near the place alive. I'm counting on you."

"Yes, sir. I'll check out their free firing lanes and make sure that everyone knows they have orders to shoot on sight. No delays, no hesitation."

The Bank Operations Center was well lighted for that late in the evening, part of the security system. Access and egress were strict and tightly controlled. Slightly tinted bulletproof glass surrounded the security booth at the only downstairs entrance. Remote television camera pictures were displayed on screens around a large console. Another security booth was located outside the secure computer room on the next floor. Up there, a new security guard watched the five people inside the room, switching from one monitor to another.

Inside the computer center, Magee's man sat at a console and worked at a desk. He kept track of everything that the good-looking blonde was doing on his monitor. He wagged his head. The gal was really tough stuff. She pulled off a maneuver that he hadn't seen before. He watched green tinted letters when suddenly the screen went blank. "What the hell?"

He jabbed the Escape button twice. The picture returned with the screen covered by a mass of numbers, letters, and a running cursor. He jabbed the Escape button several times, F1 and the ENTER button. He typed in emergency break codes. The computer wouldn't accept them. He went into another emergency mode. He was so intent on trying to find out what happened that he didn't see her leave.

Rita stopped at the upstairs booth. "Say, I don't now what your name is," She bent closer ostensibly to look at the man's ID badge. He did what she expected, he leaned over to see the cleavage she had exposed with an opened blouse. She flipped the switch to shut off his connection to the main entrance without disturbing his stare. "There's something wrong with the door over there, I can't get in if it's stuck."

He stood, eyes still focused on her breasts. "Yeah, I'll check." He went to the door and tried to open it. It was stuck; then he remembered. He had to use the cipher lock. He punched in the numbers and heard the buzzing sound. "Hey, Miss, it's okay."

She was gone. He ran to the booth and checked all the monitors. A door to the fire escape was closing. He called the main floor. No answer. "Dammit!" The switch had been thrown. He flipped it and called for help. "Stop her, stop her!"

"Who? Where?"

"The blonde coming down the fire escape."

"Why? What's the matter?"

"She's stealing a tape."

The downstairs man opened the booth, walked rapidly to the fire door, and drew his gun. Nobody could get out of the place with a tape. They hammered that rule at you.

Behind him, the elevator door opened and Rita peeped around the door jam. She had twenty feet to get to the booth and another thirty to the door. The guard opened the fire door and stepped inside. Before she ran for the door, she punched all the elevator buttons. The guard left the fire door and ran to the elevators. He turned back when Rita opened the first door to the outside. He dashed to lock the front door but it was too late. He punched the emergency alarms.

Rita ran to her car, tossed the tape on the seat, and drove rapidly out of the parking lot into a trap. A police car with lights flashing closed off her escape. Two other cars sped by on the way to the Operations Center. She squeezed the wheel. Could she crash into this car and get away? The policemen approached with guns aimed at her head.

"Oh, my God."

They made her bend over, her hands on the hood of her car. The dirty bastard ran his hands over her breasts twice. Then he went up each leg on the outside, then the inside. She thought thank God for panty hose. The beefy cop let his hand linger between her legs.

She was furious. "Get your dirty hands off me, you pig!"

"Not a bad piece here. Too bad we gotta call for backup."

"Here it is. Hey lady, what are you doing taking this tape away from the bank?"

"How do you know what it is? Get this bastard's hands off my ass, you creep."

She felt fingers tighten on her right buttock. The other hand reached around in front and started to work inside her pantyhose. "Stop it! You freaking son of a bitch!"

Wes reported that he had checked his men surrounding the Truth Network with instructions to kill on sight. The Fox nodded. He had a flash vision of the past. He was freezing his ass off with the Marines near The Chosin Reservoir in the Korean War. The Battalion Commander had ordered him to remain behind with a spotter to knock off Chink officers. He sighted the first leader, a Colonel. The bastard never took another breath.

    He clenched his fists and squeezed his drink in the suite. By God, I'd love to pick off that son of a bitch frogman myself with my sniper rifle. He called his butler at home and told him to air express the weapon to him immediately. You never know. His eyes were black marbles.

CHAPTER SIXTY THREE

Outside the Operations Center, Rita was spread-eagled over the car's hood. She was so angry that she tried to stomp on the cop's foot, but it had slipped away. The hand on her buttock slackened. The other hand under her bellybutton had slipped out of the panty hose. What was happening? The man on the other side of the car had disappeared.

A hand grabbed her arm. "Come on Rita, let's beat it!"
"Dan? What?"
"Got the tape, Ben?"
"Yep. Let's blow this place."

They ran to the car and pulled Rita between them. Dan spoke. "Here, the back seat with me." He slammed the door and Doc blasted the car forward. He made a feint toward the expressway, then past it, taking a side street. He spoke, half-turning, "We better ditch this car."

"Not a bad idea. Bennie, see if you can pick a good one. Nothin' new."

They waited. Rita blurted out her story. "I set the guy up on his monitor. Glitched up his remote. That got him off my case enough so I could slip out. The guard was easy. You men are all alike. Show a pair of good breasts and you guys can't take your eyes off them. Guess I was afraid for a time."

Dan patted her on the arm. "Thanks."

"Anyone says, 'Good Girl' and I'll kill him."

Doc laughed. "Not me."

They headed back toward Norfolk in a green sedan that wore battle scars and North Carolina plates. On the way Dan asked Rita about Pete. He told her of his suspicions.

"You've got a helluva nerve thinking that. From what you told me he's saved your butt. What about me? I'm less trustworthy, a lot worse. Remember, I'm a lez."

"Sorry. I keep thinking, tryin' to figure out how to stay safe for eight more hours. Maybe more than that. Let's call a truce."

"Fine. I'm hungry."

They ate hamburgers from an all night restaurant, parked on a side street near the first new hideout that Pete had given them.

Rita outlined what she had found. "They know I'm into the system. They cut off my access twice."

"How did you get back in?"

"Easy. When you told me about the questions concerning Tony's trap door, I built in a couple of my own. They found two and cut them off. Not sure if they found the last one. With this tape, we have to get to a mainframe. I doubt if I can get access to any except through a good PC and a modem. They can't close out all remotes because that's how they'll be getting their input. If they don't cut it out, we're in business."

"Sounds good."

"Have you tried to figure out who this might be?" She grinned. "Outside of being a homosexual and lesbian plot, I mean."

"Whitney says it's her ex-boyfriend. But it would take a helluva lot more than one man. My guesses are three. The Russians because they'd love to control an election. Or some extremists of some kind, maybe even another country. And some big business outfits want to control the government."

Stolen Votes

"Four. The Right-wingers."

"Aw come on."

"You come on. Who's so damned concerned about trying to make all of us moral? Those people want to force us to behave the way they want. The self-righteous bastards."

Dan drifted off with her words. Vote right? The Moral Society? "What about the freaking liberals? They ain't been in power for some time. Have they?"

"Come off it. The liberals are so damned screwed up. They promise you the world but break your heart. Like a guy trying to get into a woman's pants. No! It's the extremists. The far out right-wingers. They don't promise you anything. You do what they say or they break your ass."

"Geez, you're cynical."

"I ought to be. Grow up, Dan. You're a good guy, but you're naive as hell. There are extreme right-wingers in this country that would love nothing better than to remake it into an ultra conservative fortress. They have connections in every powerful group, National Rifle Association, JUST CAUSE, The Moral Majority."

She asked, "Did you hear two of them the night your boy Reagan was elected? One of them reminded me of Hitler. They said on TV that if the president didn't do what they wanted, they'd get rid of him. Who the hell elected them?"

"You sure you're sex choices aren't making you pissed about them?"

"Give me a break. Contrary to many theorists my sexual orientation is not my choice. I was born that way. Listen, underneath every blind power move are extremists of either the right or the left. Now that I'm no longer famished, get me to a mainframe."

Haggerty waited. Where should they go? She was right. Unless he could threaten them by screwing up the election plot, he couldn't force them to give up Beth. He hated to do it. He still had doubts. "Doc, run us to the next hideout. I want to talk to Pete."

Dunn met them at a suburban town house off Virginia

Beach Boulevard. He told Dan that he had switched cars and drivers on the way and was sure that he was not followed in the end. He relieved Rita of the tape. "Are you sure you trust me with this?"

Dan fixed him with a glare. "Do I have a choice?"

Wes arrived and his shoulders were not at attention. "I'm sorry sir. We lost them again." He appeared to be fatigued enough for The Fox to wonder how sharp he was.

"Take a seat and relax for a while. I want you in four-oh form in the morning. It's the day of all days, and I suspect that we will have an armed confrontation with those damned SEALs. Say, take a look at my sniper rifle. I've had it flown here. By God, I'd love to have that bastard in my sights."

His security chief took the weapon as if it were holy, examined it and checked the loading and action. "Mind if I field strip and make sure everything is in working order?"

Magee nodded. "Ask Otto where he placed the oil and maintenance equipment. Everything should be available. If not, have him get what you need from a gun shop. I'm sure that someone will open up at any hour for a price."

"Yes, sir. Have you heard about the publicity on the Iran Contra situation? Seems like—."

The Fox rose and gestured. "Dammit! Get Farnsworth on a secure phone ASAP. He should have called me. Go! Go!"

Otto stepped in and reported. "Sir, Major Farnsworth is on the secure line."

The Fox grabbed the phone. "Dammit, Farnsworth. How come I'm the last one to hear about your inside information?"

"Sorry, sir. This Puzzle Palace has been bouncing with people and questions from the media, Congress, and the White House. Couldn't get away till now. A news flash from *Al Shirraa* stated that the U.S. has been negotiating with Iran to release hostages. What would you like me to do with all our contacts and records? Our friend in the NSC has been shredding documents for days. Quite a story, and the White

House is fumbling the ball again."

Magee delayed his answer for a micro-second. "You'd better destroy everything. And remember that some of our computers will not delete completely on that command."

"Yes, sir. I know. I'll take care of that personally. I'm not going to get out of here tonight anyway. I'll double check everything before I leave."

"Thanks, Major. Remember, I do not know you."

"Aye, aye, sir. *Semper Fi.*"

He poured a straight blue scotch. Those hapless idiots in the White House. The President had some dolts working on very dangerous areas and now the damned screw-up was exposed. I'll have my top lawyer prepare a news release of regret and that I had stepped out of the efforts months ago. The poor assholes. Somebody's going to be the slain lamb. Probably my NSC guy.

He shook off his connection to the Iran Contra effort as if it were rain from an umbrella that would disappear without a trace. They had to get all the opposition players out of the election game permanently. And Whitney was expendable. Nice piece of ass. Too bad. He knew the best way to take them all out. And she would not enjoy Wallace's rapes and brutality. Nelson would kill her and he'd be eliminated too. He knows too much. Magee had a list of others in his private safe. His smile was thin, grim.

I'd better get my people out of Lebanon before they are discovered. He shook his head. Damn! I wanted to pull off that coup to show the world I had more power and punch than anyone would believe. *C'est la Vie.* And like MacArthur said, "I shall return." And like him, with more power than ever. No one will be able to stop me.

Whitney watched the SEALs carry out their routine, cleaning their weapons in silence, except for comments about past ops. The Cat disengaged and flopped on a sofa in an adjoining room. He looked exhausted and worried, probably thinking of how to rescue Beth and how they could stop the election plot. That damned Fox would use Beth as a hostage to squeeze Haggerty. She wanted to tell Dan more. Why again? Was she getting interested in him? What could he do for her? He was in love with Beth anyway.

Maybe some other time.

Stolen Votes

CHAPTER SIXTY FOUR

Magee hadn't slept, a rarity. Wes woke him during the night with a report from his troop leader in Lebanon. The Prime Minister there had been blowing the whole cover in a speech to Parliament. Time to cut his losses? Another source told him that the NSC boys wanted to keep the enterprise going. He shook his head and gave orders to his troop leader.

"Get out, now! It's over. Let me know when all hands are safe. Thank them all for their efforts."

"Yes sir."

He wondered about the security of his GRASS ROOTS organization. It was incredible that the SEAL had anticipated his moves. Was there a homosexual organization that had penetrated his own? What about his moles? Were they loyal or double agents? It was too late to worry now.

At breakfast, the network systems man reported on a secure phone. "Sir, the system has been cleansed of all Trap Doors and possible intrusions. We're clean, up and running."

"Thank you. I'll keep in touch on line. When I'm at the network broadcasting theater, I'll get direct info. Thanks."

He had worked years for this day. He should have been

triumphant, but he had an uncommon worry that something could go wrong.

The early poll reporting was inconclusive. Votes began to take on a direction, one that was the opposite of his winning plot. He followed the data carefully with a PC in the suite connected to the totals. Then his plan began to take hold. The early swing to the left was neutralized. Then, as other states reported, an insignificant but right wing move began. By the time he had showered and dressed, the battle was on.

He dismissed the morning news reports that there would be a liberal Senate. He was due at the Truth Network for the morning program in an hour. He and Creed would be on the air for a while, speaking about voting and the new television network. And he could approach it all secure in his mind.

Let the damned SEAL try. He was closed out, finally. The enemy's last resort was a physical assault, opening up the bastard to a logical and judicious end. Security around the network grounds had been reinforced with his own army. There was no way the SEALs could penetrate the buildings.

Dan was back in the hands of Pete's people. Rita had a new PC and modem access through a large business computer to break into the network. Doc and Bennie were standing by, rechecking weapons, sipping coffee, ready for a fight.

Rita penetrated so easily that Dan wondered if something else was wrong. "Could they have set up a dummy system to let you in and then stop you?"

"I really doubt it. I tried the other trap doors and they're all gone. What they forgot was the designer's usual break-in method. I found one, and it worked. Now that we're in, what do we do? I still think it's a bad idea to crash it. From what the guy on the phone just gave me, there isn't anything that seems like a trend or direction. We can monitor it and try to slip in changes."

"In what direction. Where? Do you know enough about

the national election scene to tell us what to look for, or how the election actually ought to go?"

"All the papers and news media are predicting a loss of The Senate to the liberals. Now that would be important. The Senate does a lot of things. Remember, Tony said that a great coup for a right winger would be to ease new judges into the Supreme Court."

"What about left wingers?"

"You're something, all right. Okay, but the arguments just don't seem to be as strong." She keyed in some codes and the monitor showed totals in various states. She pointed. "See, the totals seem to be quite even. Some states that were predicted to be a toss up are leaning to the right."

"So, you're saying that anything that goes against the trend that everyone expects is suspect, or is it just that you're against the right wingers."

"Let's prove who's correct." She keyed in several codes. When the monitor gave her prompts she kept punching in her codes. She said in a half whisper, "I'm in. You're the boss."

"Well, how about if we stop input?"

"And cut us out? No. How about cutting the output? If there's no transmission to their selected addresses there won't be any finagling."

"Okay." He watched as she keyed in more commands. Then they sat and watched the totals. Nothing happened for a while. Then there was a slow movement back toward the predictions. Rita had set up a table that showed the predicted average of the polls as a guide. Underneath the predictions were the actual reports as they came in through the phone lines and the computer system. The actual votes started to shift back in the predicted direction.

"See?"

"Yeah, but maybe it's just a leveling off."

"Maybe, we'll have to see if they try to cut me off."

Two coffees later, she pointed at the monitor that had changed from their tabulations. "There! See, they've cut into my access." She typed rapidly, talking to herself. "No you don't. Hah! Gotcha! Hmm, there they go again. Now take that!" She leaned back. "I've locked them out. Let's see what the totals are again." The trend was in the predicted direction.

They watched the voting tabulations unfold, somewhat satisfied until—. "Dan, telephone."

"Who knows I'm here?" He took it from Pete. He could barely make out the words, but he knew who it was. "Beth. Oh, God, where are you?"

A heavy male voice came on. "That's to let you know we have her, Haggerty. Now get off that goddamned program. Or she's dead."

His body sagged. How could they know where he was? If they did, why didn't they assault their hideout? He turned and saw that they were all looking as startled as he felt. His voice was weak, uncertain again.

"They, they have Beth. Threatened to kill. They'll kill her if we don't get off."

He heard the man cursing at him on the phone. He said, "If you're so freaking tough, why don't you try to rescue her again. I'll tell you right where she is. She's in the number one reception room at the Truth Network. It's located in the main building on the second deck. Come and I'll see you in hell."

He let the phone slip out of his hand. God, I can't take Beth's death in my hands. "Shut down. Shut down! For God's sake, shut it down."

Rita looked at him sharply. "You sure? I could crash it."
"No, please, no!"

He lurched out of the room and into the bathroom. He felt nauseous and weak. The way he'd felt when Tony was killed. When his bud was killed. What's the use? He had that awful urge to get stoned. His back muscles jammed pain into him and a stomach fire lighted off. He had to run, to get away.

Doc stood over him. "You okay? What's going down?"

"They got her at the network. It'll be like a fortress. They'll kill her. It's hopeless."

The Doc looked at him for a long time. "Yeah. Guess we

better give up, Cat. Like you did when Bobby was killed by his own mistake." He walked away.

Whitney stood next to him and stroked his arm. "What can I do? I want to help."

"There's nothing anyone else can do. Except me." Yeah. He'd assault the place. So what if it was a freaking fortress.

Did the asshole tell him the truth when he gave him Beth's location? The only way he could have a bare-ass chance would be with Doc and Bennie. He couldn't ask them. Could he? It was a suicide mission.

CHAPTER SIXTY FIVE

In the network auditorium, thirty people were off to the side near the stage. They answered telephones and reported on a secure line to the Computer Center. The Reverend Creed had the center position on the stage and he was enjoying himself. He was in his element, the focus of the cameras, and the head of the network's telethon. He left the stage several times in the first two hours of the program so that national news media could interview him. Each time he returned, he seemed more alive and energetic.

The Fox kept a running total of the election results on a PC near his left shoulder. He would whisper to Creed when he could show him the good news of the swings toward a right wing Senate. When Rita had penetrated and locked the network out, his face became crimson. His mouth was tighter than vise. He had sent Wes on a run to call the frogman and give him orders to stop at the risk of his girlfriend's life.

Shortly afterward Wes slipped around the stage and whispered to Magee. "Sir, I told the frog right where we had the woman. Why don't you let me take a group and attack the SOB where he is?"

Stolen Votes

The Fox turned from the camera. "I thought about it. But I want him here! He's been so damned lucky and slippery that he could possibly avoid you. He could have moved out already. Take another inspection tour around the grounds and make sure that your people know what the orders are. Shoot first to wound. If possible, take him alive. Do what you want with the others. I don't want them alive."

"Yes, sir. What if I put a tail or two on them when they take off from where they are? That way, we'll know exactly when they're coming."

Magee nodded. "Good idea. Your men will shred those SEALs like useless paper. I want you here with me. When we have a break, slip out my rifle and recheck the action. I'd love to have the son of a bitch in my sights."

"Understood, sir. I'll be over in the wings out of sight with it. I've got my Combat Masterpiece loaded along with my Glock."

The Fox grinned. "Always ready. Thank you, Wes."

At the latest hideout, The Cat clenched his hands and tried to clear his head. What should he do? He knew how terrible the odds would be if he and his buds were to assault the place to rescue Beth. He also knew that they would join him, if he asked. But he would be asking them to commit suicide. Knowing the size of their enemy, their capabilities, and their willingness to fight were all factors that mitigated against it. I'll go by myself.

He picked up the Stoner light machine gun, checked the safety, and cycled the action. He frowned at the slight noise he heard. He loved using the weapon, but it could be skittish. He started to field strip it in silence. He found that the action was sticking once in a while. That was unsat.

Doc wandered over and sat with him. "Got a problem? Something wrong with it?"

"Got some kind of a burr here. You got a file?"

"No sweat." He dug in the weapons bag and handed his

friend two files. "What you thinking about? Gonna try to rescue her, or what?"

He waved him off. He knew that they would go with him, no matter what the odds. Could he ask them to go on a suicide op? He filed the tiny burr down and tried out the action again. He added some WD 40 and the weapon was slick and ready. Was he?

Bennie was at his side too. "What's goin' down? We got an op here?"

"I'm going. You guys. Well, you have a choice. I can't ask you to go. They're all waiting for me. The bastard told me where they were holding her. I can't ask you to go. A daylight assault? Unknown odds? Guys, it's too damned dangerous."

"What the hell'd we do in 'Nam? Sounds like near a routine op for us SEALs. Right, Doc?"

"She-it yes. And a big Hoo-yah!"

"Come on, guys. We don't have enough firepower."

"The hell we don't. I forgot to tell you. Before we untied the other two that night you busted in on us, Ben and me figured you'd need a helluva lot of stuff. So we requisitioned the things we'd need if we had to take on a VC munitions factory like we did couple of times." Doc grinned and slapped his shoulder. "I'm in!"

Ben nodded. "Me too!"

Whitney pleaded with him. He shoved her away.

She stood in their midst, fists in jammed into her waist. "Damn all of you! By God, I've got a right to be with you. Somebody give me a smoke." She accepted a lighted cigarette from Doc. "Listen to me you shit heads. I earned the right to shoot that bastard Magee."

"I'm going with you. I'm an expert shot. Maybe I can cover for you, and when you get Beth, I can take care of her. At least I could drive, and leave you guys to go charging in."

The Cat stood. "Okay with me but it's up to these two. Having an amateur, even a good shot, is too dangerous. We know where the others will be and their firing lanes."

Bennie nodded. "Wait one. I'll teach her some basics. Come, on honey, let's pick a weapon or two for you. We like max firing power ASAP. Shock value gives us an edge for some seconds. Might want a Stoner, might be a bit heavy for you, but it's got terrific firing rate."

Doc anteed up. "Far's I'm concerned, she's in. Cat, you better pick your weps too. Let's check everything out. And, Cat, we're goin' in blind here. Got any intel?"

"Gotcha." He went to see Pete and they heard him ask for paper and pencils or pens.

When he returned, Whitney spoke, her eyelids battling tears. "Thanks, guys. You, uh, you're like brothers that I never had. I won't let you down."

Joseph Guion

CHAPTER SIXTY SIX

Dan borrowed a pad of legal paper from Pete's people and gathered the three volunteers around a dining room table. He started to sketch block-like buildings, marking the rooms with numbers. The second page looked like the outside of a large building with several satellite dishes on the roof. He marked entrances and drew lines from the doors out to some vague square.

"Okay. What I remember from a couple visits there, the buildings are set up in a u-shape. At the base of the "U" is the main building, and our target. There are several entrances to it, where the asshole said they held Beth. The main double door is here at the front of the building facing the open space, plus two side doors and one in the rear. I set up fields of fire from the sides of the other buildings. Can't be sure how accurate this is. Got no specs; no measurements."

Doc spoke. "Wait one. We come in the front door, they got us in a helluva cross fire."

"Yeah, I know. They'll have the main entrance covered damned well. The back entrance will be covered too. Our best bet is, come in from the left side of the main building heading toward the back. It gives us the most cover."

"Not from any entrance, right?"

"Right. There's a brick wall around the whole compound about chest high. We get over that no sweat. Like I said, we drive on the outside of the "U" toward the back of the main building, drop Ben first near the end of the building nearest the biggie. Drop Doc near the corner of the wall. I'll jump close as I can to the main building. We hit 'em with smoke first."

He pointed. "Give me cover, and I'll run my ass off to get to this side door. Ben can cover you, Doc, so you can hit the main door and join up. I'll be inside the hall waitin' around this corner. I'll be on the deck, anything knee-high and up is free fire. Ben, there's shrubs around the base of these buildings, but I can't tell you where. Get cover fast as you can, where you can see the both of us comin'."

"This looks like a bad-ass job, Cat. See what I'm sayin.' Can't we loosen them up first with some grenades or maybe even a LAW?"

Whitney broke into their circle. "What's a LAW?"

"It's a Light Assault Anti-Tank Weapon. Might not be reliable. If you got one Doc, take it; don't count on it. We don't know where they might be, so they get the first shots. We use max firepower up front, grenades and whatever you want to use. Knock down all you can. The only prisoner pickup is inside the building."

Whitney interrupted. "Dan, I can keep the car close to the wall and fire at anybody who is firing at you."

"This isn't your war, lady. And it's better if we do the shootin'. We know where the other guys will be, even when we move. Thanks for the offer."

"Wait a sec, Cat. You change your mind about lettin' her in? This girl is a shooter. She can do us good. Her driving the car gives you four, five seconds extra to get cover by the wall."

"I don't want her there, Ben."

Doc spoke. "Wait one. This freaking mission is a world

of shit. We all know it. Give us one more shooter. We need all the firepower we can get and then some. You see what I'm sayin'? I'm not complaining about the op. Just factual here."

Haggerty sighed. They were right. He was asking them to join on a one-way mission for some, maybe all of them. He was willing to risk his life for Beth. They were doing it for him, out of loyalty to the SEALs and their friendship. Could he be wrong?

"Okay. You're in Whit. But, you need a flak jacket. You need two fast-firing weapons."

Ben said, "Already started with her, but I'll run through them again. She's a quick learner; she knows how to load, put 'em on safety, some tricks about firing. I told her she'd get a helluva kick from them, more than she was used to."

Doc spoke. "Cat, I don't know if you want your Stoner. I brought a couple other toys, maybe you and Whitney might wanna take a look. How 'bout a cut down model 37 for you, with a duckbill? You're gonna be in close, beats shit out of people." He showed the weapon.

Whitney shook her head. "What is that thing?"

"It's a shotgun. The duckbill on the muzzle shapes the charge so it comes out more horizontal. Deadly. Whit, you won't need it where you be, but Cat might."

Dan stared at the weapon, identical to the one that he had used to kill Bobby. He felt perspiration break on his forehead. Could he use it? He couldn't afford a second of delay or any fumbling with a weapon. He exhaled slowly. "Maybe. You got an M-sixteen combo with a one-forty-eight?"

Bennie handed over the M-16 rifle with the grenade launcher under the barrel. "Probably need the launcher on the way out."

"Yeah. I'm gonna take M-26 frag grenades. You got any 'chute flares?"

"Sure. What the hell you gonna do, call for a medium to extract us?"

"No. Just want to have all the shit I can carry."

Bennie took her to the next room to help her decide on

Stolen Votes

the best weapons for her. When he spoke it was to open up a new avenue of thought.

"Listen, honey, it isn't that Cat hates you, he knows how fast and furious combat is. And, I think he's afraid that you might get hurt or worse. Now before we select your weapons, tell me what was the fastest thing that ever happened to you? I mean, an accident, or something unexpected?"

She frowned. "I don't know, uh, I did have a collision learning to drive. Why?"

"That helps, but." He stood and waved her to do the same. He slipped his k-bar out of its sheath and handed it to her. "We're going to have a demonstration. You attack me with the knife. I mean do your best to get me."

She shook her head. "Ben, I can't do that. Maybe a half-hearted attempt."

"No good. You have to be pissed off. How about this scenario. You have a knife and I'm Magee and I'm laughing at you. Maybe I'll broadcast a picture of your ass—."

She swore and lunged at him. In less than two seconds she was on her back on the floor with the knife dangerously close to her eyes. "Oh, God, don't!"

He grinned. "Never happen. Come on, up." He helped her to stand and noted that she was shaking.

"That's what I meant, fast. I wanted you to experience an inkling of how fast things happen in combat. You have no time to think; you react. That's why Cat is worried. You don't have the training that we've had. My first time in combat, everything was a blur, things went too fast to think. I reacted automatically from SEAL training. You don't have it."

"I, I don't know what to say. I want to help, I want to, to kill that bastard Magee."

"That's fine. But you have to realize that you're going to be seconds behind everything that's going on, seconds that can mean somebody's life. After we pick out your toys, you and I are going to do some quick rehearsals. Okay?"

"Thanks, Bennie. I never thought about what you said.

You know the movies show the person in slow-motion like time slows down and there is time to think."

"That's bullshit! Thinking comes after it's all over. It's react, react, react."

He showed Whitney his weapons. "This here's a CAR fifteen, short-barrel M sixteen. You put it on full auto and it gets out rounds fast. Or maybe you want a Smith and Wesson M 76. Good submachine gun. If you can heft it, you might bring an M-60 too. Lots of firepower there. Take two weapons and you don't have to reload right away."

She selected the S & W and handled the M-60. "It is a bit heavy."

"We cut down about seven pounds to maybe sixteen, shortened the barrel and took off the regular stock. Replaced it with this rubber cup here. It's heavy weapons job. Maybe you ought to take a Stoner. Lighter weight, puts out a thou rounds a minute."

"Guess I'll take it. I'll be near the wall and the car."

They rejoined Cat and Doc.

Dan said, "Remember, this is a hit and run job against a static defense, in depth too. VC wouldn't stay and fight unless they had a max number of shooters or somebody important to keep out of our hands. Long as we use the main building as a block they won't get much cross fire."

"Unless they got shooters outside the wall."

Cat grimaced. "Yeah, they could have shooters all over the place."

The SEALs fieldstripped their weapons again, checked them carefully, and reassembled them. They worked all the mechanisms carefully until they were satisfied. The "snap" and "thock" of weapons being readied were the only sounds.

Whitney worked on her chosen weapons and watched them, fascinated as they quietly readied themselves. Their faces seemed to be transformed, into something different, not mechanical, but professional and deadly.

Bennie had Whitney practice; loading, carrying, shifting weapons and fast loading from the "H" harness he gave her.

"You got four extra Stoner mags with a hundred and ten rounds each plus the full load in the weapon. You're loaded for bear, kid. The first thing you do is start firing as soon as we do. Lay down all the covering fire you can. Reload and keep firing. Try to keep their heads down. Make sure you check your rear, in case somebody sneaks around behind you. Watch for us coming out of the smoke. Fire over our heads or to the side. Use all the ammo you got ready, haul these extra mags and save a couple for when we bug out."

He patted her shoulder. "No sweat. Stand up now loaded, move quick, and see if you can carry all that shit."

She followed his instructions. "Hmmmm. It does take a lot of strength and energy to haul this stuff around. "Okay."

"Now follow me with the Stoner."

He jumped a few paces to the left and pointed a revolver at her. "Come on, I just killed you. Faster."

He used the room furniture to hide and jumped out from different sides with the pistol in his hand. He shut the door and broke in low and rolling to his left. He kept on her for a half hour until she was soaked with perspiration.

He patted her shoulder. "Good going, kid." He fixed his gaze on her eyes. "You still want to go with us?"

"You're damned right I do. Let's try some more."

"Later. You have me perspiring too. Let's say you're behind me. I say, 'Left.' You drop down on the deck to my left. I'll point down too, in case you can't hear over the noise. Just the opposite with the right. Okay?"

She nodded. He grinned, slapped her shoulder and they joined Haggerty and Doc.

Cat nodded. "Okay, troops. Here's what I remember of the layout for the stairs, rooms on the first and second decks. Over here are the TV and satellite control rooms. We skip them. Prisoner rescue is first. Beth should be in one of these two rooms. When we get outside, we'll be running like hell. Doc and I will probably be dragging or carrying her. You two have to raise all sorts of hell to keep them down. That's a good time for grenades and more smoke. Whitney, you better have that car engine running."

"I will. Better show me how to throw a grenade."

"No thanks, Whit. No time. And you gotta have a real arm."

"Want to check my muscles?"

"Sorry. The thing is, we work at top speed, running like hell. So don't get away from that wall. Stay near the car. Make sure you see us before you start blastin' away at anyone comin' out of the smoke. We don't want no friendly fire casualties. Okay. Anything else, guys?"

"You want to cammie up? A little disguise? We come out of this, somebody's gonna be searching for three SEALs."

"It wouldn't hurt. You got any face masks?"

Bennie answered. "Yep. Just happened to have enough. Maybe Whitney won't want one. Don't want to cover up that gorgeous face. Right?"

"Get off my case."

"That it?"

The SEALs agreed. Doc asked, "What about the rest of this shit we requisitioned. I'd like to throw it in the car, in case we change the plan a tad."

"Fine." The Cat tried for a British accent. "Let's select our weaponry, gentlemen and lady. We'll give the peasants a good run for their money."

The three SEALs cammied their faces. Ben had a great time working on Whitney. "Certainly beats that blush makeup you use, honey."

Cat checked everyone's weapons, vest and belt loads. He adjusted the straps on Whitney's H-vest and nodded. No one spoke. He glanced at the Model 37 shotgun, clamped his jaw, and grabbed it. After loading it he placed additional shells in the side pocket of his vest. They walked in silence to the car and packed everything else into it. No one acknowledged that this was possibly a one-way op for some.

On their way to the network, Whitney drove, following Haggerty's directions. Bennie's question shook Dan. "You say they're all set for us. You got a better plan than a frontal assault?"

"Yeah, Cat. You got some tanks and artillery up your sleeve someplace? Any Black Ponies for air support? I mean, I'm not worried or nothing.' We sure could use a surprise gimmick. That's our meat; surprise, max fire power, speed."

The Cat knew that Doc was right. If only they could locate some support, a diversion. Still, he knew that he was ready. All that shit about Bobby's death had been true. For some reason his bud had stepped into the wrong place, a free-firing zone for this SEAL. The poor guy shouldn't have been there and his reaction had been automatic. But this op? They had to get in fast enough today to come out alive. The whole idea was not to commit suicide, but to rescue Beth. Was there a way? A surprise? It always gained time before the jerks reacted. What could we—.

Damn! Hot shit! We could hit them with a surprise.

Joseph Guion

CHAPTER SIXTY SEVEN

Magee called Wes from the Foxmobile en route to the Truth Network. "It seems to me that they'll probably have to assault the place. Go there as soon as you can. Make sure the woman is well hidden and the shooters are ready. Keep in touch."

Wes covered the entire grounds rapidly, beginning from the rear of the network around to the front. The red brick wall surrounded the open u-shape of the five buildings, with the central one housing the television control system and satellite transmission. Four ten-meter dish antennae mounted on the north end of the main building's roof pointed in slightly different directions. They looked like saucers waiting to receive rain from the sky. The wall could hide assault troops from both sides. He moved several groups to have clear fields of fire inside and outside of the wall.

Three groups were hidden with their cross fire positions covering the main entrance of the central building. If the men at the walls didn't get them, the people at the main building would. He stationed two groups at the rear entrance. The five groups at the main building had heavy machine guns and grenades. He sent two snipers to the rooftops of each of the four buildings comprising the sides of the U.

Uniformed police were stationed at roadblocks on all the streets leading to the network. He stood watching the police check all vehicles coming toward the network. The bastards would never make it. He also had a mobile unit standing by to outflank them.

He reminded the group leaders for the tenth time. "Shoot first. Don't wait. Grab the bodies. Bring them to the south side to the ambulances I have. Okay, let' em come."

When Magee arrived at the network, he had checked on his army of killers. He walked with a security guard toward the front of the network auditorium. Wallace sat halfway back on the aisle in the audience with The Mechanic nearby. The Fox relaxed. His ace in the hole had worked. Using the woman as a bargaining chip was perfect. If Haggerty were stupid enough to attempt an assault on the network, he would be dead. All opposition to the plot would be eliminated.

Wes had reminded him about a possible leak.

"Sir, we know where that computer lezzie and the queers are. I have an assault group ready to annihilate them at your command. Can't let anyone get away."

The Fox smiled. "Good job, Wes. I forgot about them with the impending election and the SEALs assault."

He ascended the steps to the stage, shoulders back, and head up. The figures he received showed that the program was on line and working. No one could stop them. He shook hands with Creed and sat next to him. They discussed the apparent direction of the voting and congratulated each other.

"It's a fine Election Day, Jethro. We're going to win!"

"Yes, Frank. Vote Raht!"

The cameras rolled in closer. The Reverend stepped up to the podium. The man with the earphones counted down backwards, showing five fingers, then four, and down for the live broadcast.

Wes had placed Magee's sniper rifle hidden under the

tablecloth on the dais near the owner's feet. As the program commenced, The Fox reached down to touch it. He checked it rapidly and assured himself that it was loaded. He placed it on safety and straightened up.

God, I'd love to squeeze off a round into that frogman's face. He'll never make it in here. But if he does by some fluke, I'll polish off the bastard myself.

He sipped water and leaned back with a satisfied smile. This was his day of triumph.

The inside of the SEALs car was stone quiet. Each person focused on the unthinkable, unwilling to share fear, anxiety, hope, or anything. The Cat's laugh shocked them. "HooYah! I got it, troops! Turn here. Whitney, get on the expressway. Head toward downtown Norfolk."

Doc asked, "Where the hell we going? Thought it was over near the airport? You gonna circle them and come in around a different way?"

Dan grinned. "Nope! We use a Parakeet Op."

Whitney asked, "What is that?"

"It's a chopper insertion. Come in fast over the trees; hit that frigging place from the roof before they know what the hell happened. Of course, we won't have any gun ships for support."

"You got a slick someplace, smartass?"

"No, but I know where there could be one, fueled and ready to go, pilot and all."

"Little Creek's back the other way. Hey, if it was like 'Nam sometimes, we couldn't get a slick for three days, and by that time, the American prisoners would be long gone."

"She-it no. We'd never get near it. You ever hear of the Nightingale?"

Bennie sounded excited. "The medical helicopter? Son of a bitch, he's right!"

"Bet your ass. Like he said on the boat, Charlie's been flying birds for the MedEvac at Norfolk General. Unless

Stolen Votes

they're out on an emergency call, the slick will be fueled and ready on the pad. We rush the office, grab the pilot, convince him that he'd better fly and we're on our way."

Doc grinned. "Is that all? I never liked helo insertions in 'Nam, but I sure like this. Kinda changes the odds a bit."

Whitney argued en route to the hospital. She insisted on going with them. "You'll need your hands for weapons, I can help carry Beth to the helicopter. Besides. I've got to see if that rotten bastard Frank is there. The paper has him on this morning's program."

"I ain't gonna be responsible for another woman's life. No! You don't go! You'd be in the way. You don't know anything about this."

"I'm a damned good shot. Come on, Dan let me help."

The Doc tried. "She's right, hoss. I don't mean about bein' a good shot, but we could use somebody to help get Beth back to the chopper. One of us could buy it."

Haggerty shook his head. "We don't even know if there's a bird there."

"Case there is, let's run through procedures. Here's what we do, kid. Pilot flares out, I mean he lifts his nose and starts to stall to lose air speed. Chopper can shake like hell. He hits the ground, in our case, the roof. Hey Cat, any kind of shit there? Air conditioning trailers?"

"Not sure. They have four satellite antennas on it, but they're off to one end. Don't know which way the wind is."

Doc continued. "So, anyways, we jump out and go to work. Cat and me head down; you and Ben hold the roof and suppress the gunfire with max firepower. Use grenades, all sorts of shit. The idea is to keep 'em low and confused. That okay, Cat?"

"Yeah, but we better have you and me on the landing skids firing as we come in. If we can't land, we'll have to fast rope. You got gloves?"

"She-it yeah. You think I ain't prepared?"

Whitney asked, "What's fast roping?"

"The chopper hovers and we slide down a rope damned

fast, Gotta have gloves or your hands get burned pretty bad. If we have to do that, you may have to stay on board."

"Like hell! I'm with you guys all the way."

Doc winked. "Sounds good to me when some dolly says that."

The Cat turned away from them. The chopper had to be there! If it weren't, the hope for a surprise attack that would gain them a quick, but short advantage would be gone. He heard some kidding in the back seat with his buds and closed his eyes. He wasn't a praying man, but he uttered a silent prayer, for Beth, for his buds and Whitney. He left out himself. God knew how bad he'd been. Was this a possibility for redemption? He shook off thoughts to concentrate on changing their assault plan. If—.

Stolen Votes

CHAPTER SIXTY EIGHT

At the network, Creed was holding forth in one of his better speeches. He kept emphasizing the need for a "right" Senate. He spoke directly to the large audience present.

"You wonderful people, you first class citizens, your presence heah demonstrates your commitment to our blessed country. Ah thank you, for giving up some of your time on such an important day. Election Day! I pray that you will vote, if you haven't already. Remember that is has become right easy with our up-to-date electronic voting machines. We will welcome you back during this telethon, regardless of the time."

His smile lighted up his face. "And, Vote Right!"

During the massive response of applause and scattered shouts of "Vote Right," Magee's valet Otto, slipped behind his boss and whispered. He handed a slip of paper to The Fox, who glanced at it and nodded. His eyes roamed around the auditorium and he spotted Nelson and the crazed killer, The Mechanic. Nelson, too bad your partner is going to knock you off. You know too much. After the election had been won, he had a list of people who were dangerous. Hit men had been assigned to clean the slate. In two years he'd have the presidential election to control, first with his financial and power-laden access and then this system, refined and ready.

Creed's voice reflected excitement. "Folks, ah have good news for you. The predictions that the Senate would fall to the liberals are not to be. The key precincts in the east and our beloved south show that our right-thinking, truthful senatorial candidates are forging ahead."

"Remember, when you vote today, let me hear it please." He cupped his hand behind his ear and the shills in the audience began a chant, "Vote Right! Vote Right!" He raised his hands above his head, clasped them together, and joined in the chanting through the mike.

Half listening to Creed, The Fox took a fleeting look at the paper. A thin smile flickered on his face. The SEALs were already on their way to certain death. Wes had assigned two vehicles to trail them and he would update their progress. He could count on his security chief to give them orders to keep them in sight and at the same time, warn the killers around the network of their progress. This was getting too easy.

He reached down and patted the stock of his sniper rifle. Too bad I won't get a chance to kill the SEAL myself. He's been a terrible pain. But the frog's final pain will be his failed rescue attempt. He smiled and joined The Reverend to hold their hands high in a victory salute.

The Cat turned the rear view mirror to see behind them. He kept checking "Doc, think we're being followed. Maybe two cars. Whitney take a right at the next street and floor this thing."

As they accelerated, he saw that the autos behind were trying to catch up. They were in an industrial park area. Whitney burned rubber in three rapid turns. The same cars raced after them. Yeah, they were being followed.

"Quick, take a fast left and stop. Doc, Ben, bail out and get their tires. We'll circle around and pick you by this building we're passing."

He heard two "Rogers," before the doors opened and were slammed closed.

"Hit it, Whitney!"

Watch me." She slipped around a tractor-trailer that was backing to a loading dock.

The acceleration jerked Cat against the seat. She barely slowed and screeched the vehicle around the corner to race parallel to their previous path.

He pointed. "Easy coming around the next corner and slip into that parking space."

She skidded the car to a full stop and smiled at him. He grinned, "Nice job. If I ever need a gateway car, I'll call you." He turned to watch for the SEALs. "Come, on, guys. Hustle."

Doc and Bennie ran to them at full speed and jumped through the opened doors. "Got 'em, Cat. They weren't too happy. Guess they'll report in."

"Yeah, but they don't know what the surprise is going to be. Whitney, go back the way we came into this park and watch your speed. Can't afford cops."

The Cat ran through the expected change of plans. "We got our surprise. They'll be expecting us from ground level. It will take half a minute maybe for them to realize that it's an air assault. If we can land on the roof, we can jump out, and head down the ladders to the second deck. If we fast rope, we do the same."

Doc said, "Cat, wait a sec. Maybe we oughta not open up right away. What's the chopper look like?"

"It's red and white." He paused. "Yeah. They might be confused. It could look like there's an emergency at the network. Might buy us some time."

He ran through the changes needed in the op and they agreed. He looked at grim faces that seemed to wear the touch of grins. This changes everything. They really had a chance now. God, please help the bird to be there.

The raucous chanting in the auditorium settled down and the audience continued to buzz with excitement. The two leaders congratulated each other when Otto ran to Magee wide-eyed and wearing a crimson face. He handed over another paper. "Sir, here. Problem, sir. I'll keep after more information." He disappeared.

"Somthin' wrong, Frank?"

The Fox swore silently. Son of a bitch. They shot out the trailing cars' tires. Damn!

"Nothing, Jethro. You probably should acknowledge the support."

"Join me, Frank?"

"No, of course not. This is your triumph."

Wes arrived somewhat out of breath. "Sir, you received my note?"

"Dammit, Wes, how come the cars were that close that they knocked out both?"

"Sorry, sir. I told them to have distance between the cars, but the SEALs car accelerated so quickly that they bunched up. I've got the police alerted with an APB. They're on it already."

"Where were they heading?"

Wes seemed puzzled. "Away from here to Norfolk."

"Anything down there we should know about?"

"No, sir. I'll keep in touch. I tightened the security around the network. We're ready."

The Fox nodded. What the hell was the frog doing now?

The Cat's luck held. When he and Doc jumped from the car and ran to the helo, Bennie was already pulling their pilot buddy with him. A screaming woman in a flight suit charged at them. Dan fired a burst over her head and removed her aggressiveness. The chopper's twin engines wound up and

Bennie shouted, "Charlie, Baby, look who wants a ride." He slung the large bag inside and helped Whitney get on board.

"You bastards! I might have known. Good thing you have a pro able to fly without a co-pilot." They were airborne so quickly that Doc hadn't grabbed a seat. There was no chitchat; the pilot knew that they meant business.

Haggerty stood next to Charlie and had to shout the plan over the chopper's noise. "How long will it take to get there? We've got to get in fast."

"Five, ten minutes. Where do you want me to drop you? I've got a winch back there, if you want to go down on a line. I've got a stretcher too."

"How about landing on the roof? They got ten-meter satellite antennas on the west side of the roof. I don't think there's anything on the east side. What say?"

"Geez, another parakeet op? At least it won't be like landing on a hootch roof. We had a couple of disasters doing that in 'Nam. We have a north wind. Any idea of the layout? Where's north there?"

"Hell, I don't know. If you can't land, we'll fast rope to the roof, all of us. Charlie, we won't forget this. If they catch us, you'll be clean. We forced you."

"Yeah, sure. What the hell, I needed some excitement. You want a fast drop, right? Want me to hang around to retract you?"

His buddies looked at him. He knew damned well that they'd do whatever he wanted. They deserved a chance to get away. "Fake some mechanical problem and hover nearby. You got any radios we can borrow?"

The pilot pointed to the racks at the compartment's side. "Three minutes to touchdown. I'll go into a hover close as I can to the roof. They got any overhead wires?"

"Not that I know of."

"You must be getting old, Cat. You forgot to cover the LZ. You want I should drop somebody first to do that."

Dan slapped him on the shoulder. "No. Think if we just slide in like you have an emergency, it could buy us some time. They won't know what the hell is going on. Can you look it over first? Think there's a helo pad somewhere with a windsock. Maybe see what the wind direction is?"

"Okay. I'll pass near the main building toward the open end of the 'U.' That way you can spot the sons of bitches too. If I can land, I'll do it."

They went in fast. The helo beating the air surprised all the ground forces around the network. They were all oriented outward, expecting an assault from the streets or the small forest nearby. Cat saw someone pointing at their chopper and upturned faces. But there was no gunfire. Charlie made his approach toward the open end, turning the helo hard left.

Doc shouted, "Cat, people on each roof with weapons."

"Right, Doc. Wait one. Then you and me on the skids to suppress 'em. Ben and Whit will drop smoke like we talked about."

The chopper flattened out and slowed to land on the roof. As they passed the four buildings, Doc and Cat hosed fire at people on the roofs and knocked them down.

Bennie shouted. "Drop smoke, now! Ready, drop smoke now." He and Whitney dropped eight smoke grenades to provide some semblance of cover for the aircraft when it was most vulnerable. Doc and Cat continued their rapid fire on anyone visible.

"Down. On Deck. Haul ass, guys."

Stolen Votes

CHAPTER SIXTY NINE

Cat and Doc dropped on the roof followed by Bennie and Whitney. Charlie applied power and lifted away. Cat pointed at her to take the east side of the roof, "Keep 'em busy"

He pointed at Ben and motioned toward the satellite antennas. He spotted a group of armed men at the nearest building and fired the grenade launcher. He pointed down at Doc and ran toward the door to the stairs. He slung the M16 on his shoulder and cycled the shotgun as he ran.

Bullets hit the bricks and concrete around the roof and Whitney returned fire. Bennie tossed grenades at the group on his side and searched for sharpshooters on the roofs.

Doc blasted the roof door. They ran down two flights of steps. The Cat motioned toward the reception room where Beth had invited him at the dedication of the building. They stopped at a corner. He sprawled on the deck and Doc fired over him, dropping two men outside the door. The Cat was halfway down the hall when the door opened. Doc dropped the first one out. The second man rolled out on the deck and the Cat hit him with the shotgun. He was at the door and inside, knowing that Doc was coming up fast. Two people shot at him and he leveled them with the Ithaca. A quick glance around. Beth wasn't in the room. Where the hell did they hide her? Keep searching dammit! Force them to tell.

The Fox gripped the armrests of the plush chair and waited for Otto's report. He was astounded that Wes rushed to him.

"Sir, the fucking SEALs used a chopper to land on the roof. They dropped smoke to hide the aircraft. They've penetrated the building and are searching for the woman. Our guys were caught by surprise and they're taking casualties from somebody on the roof of this building. The bastards have machine guns and RPGs."

Magee stood and shouted at Wes, silencing Creed and the audience. "God-dammit! What the hell is the matter with you? Find out where they are get rid of them."

"Yes, sir. I'm on the way."

The Fox realized that his tirade had been heard in the auditorium. He felt his face cooling as he regained control. He grabbed the mike. "Ladies and gentleman, I apologize for my words and anger. I received a report about some terrorists in the area, not here, of course. But, things are under control. Reverend Creed, would you please continue your important message?"

The crowd buzzed with noise and some people stood and departed rapidly. The preacher's jaw dropped and his mouth hung open. He cleared his throat and regained his poise. "Folks, please do not be alarmed. Our security people are in control of the situation. Please do not leave. I will report to you as soon as I receive facts. Thank you."

Creed shifted papers and tried to speak over the audience noise without success. At that moment a dull thud occurred somewhere. The lights dimmed and returned to full brilliance. They dimmed again and went out. Emergency lights flashed on and focused on the dais and front sections of the seating. The balance of the auditorium had darkened like an hour after sunset before moonrise.

Stolen Votes

The Fox pulled his rifle from the floor, checked the action again behind the tablecloth, and verified that it was on safety. He pointed at Wallace to alert him that something was going wrong. He saw Nelson lean toward The Mechanic and another gunman next to him.

The Cat's eyes had expanded and looked like gun barrels. He grabbed one victim and jammed the shotgun muzzle between his eyes. "You got three seconds. Where is she?"

"I don't know. They just took her out."

He slammed the man on the head and hit the door. Doc was against the wall.

"She's not here."

Doc pulled his K-bar and knelt by one of the wounded. "This is in your throat. Tell me where they took the woman."

The knife drew blood and the man tried to turn away.

"Okay, okay. They took her downstairs. Outside, side door. Don't kill me."

Doc called Ben and Whitney on the radio to watch the side doors. The Cat was running before Doc hit the man and followed. They ran down stairs to the first deck. A door was closing ahead of them. They went through it without caution. Surprise saved them. Two men were dragging Beth, her feet slid along the floor and her head was canted at an angle. Two others raised their guns. Cat took the nearest. Doc the other. Both opponents went down.

"Let her go or you're dead."

The last two dropped their weapons and Beth. Her body flopped like a bag of wheat and her head hit the floor hard and bounced.

Haggerty shouted on the radio. "Bennie, come! Bring Whit. Got Beth. First deck left door from stairs."

"Now what, Cat?"

He glanced at Beth. Oh, God, she was unconscious and bleeding from the mouth and nose. "You and Whit take her. Ben gives you cover. Call in Charlie. I gotta finish it."

"Screw it man. Let the thing go. "

"No. I have to stop this thing now."

Bennie and Whitney backed in. "Now what?"

"Doc, you're in charge. Get the chopper and take her to a hospital, then take off. Don't come back here for me."

"Bullshit! SEALs never leave a man, dead or alive."

"Okay, I'm with you." He covered them from the roof. He sprayed grenades and smoke below as Charlie came in fast and hit the roof hard. They put Beth into a stretcher. Cat checked heads to see if they had made it.

"Where the hell is Whitney?"

Bennie shouted, "I told her to come. She was right with me. I'll go get her."

"No! Come back in five minutes. If I'm not outside, head for the nearest hospital. You're on your own." He slapped his buddy. He saw Bennie hesitate. "Do it!"

The two SEALs were on the skids, firing as targets appeared. The helo dipped and lifted rapidly away from the firing down below. Dan emptied the Stoner, slapped in another magazine and emptied it again. Okay Cat. Let's do it. While running down the stairs he reloaded the shotgun. Where was the satellite control center? Near the studios and the control room.

The door was marked as a security area, so he pushed it open. "Shit!" It was the television control room next to the glassed-in columns of computer and electronic equipment. Could he stop transmissions from here? He pulled grenades and shouted, "Everybody out. Grenades gonna explode. Out!"

Occupants scrambled for the door. He followed the last one out and lofted grenades in different directions. "Dammit! The Computer Center is in another building. Should I try it?"

A door opened and two armed men ran in. He dropped one; the other caught him in the hip with a bullet. Cat went down but blasted the guy against the wall with the shotgun. He felt the explosions in the control room. The lights went out in this section and the emergency lighting flickered and flooded the space with light. He limped into the auditorium.

Stolen Votes

The snake-eyed man rose from a seat near the back of the room and pulled a pistol. Dan blasted with the shotgun. He couldn't tell if he hit him. He felt the hip pain. He struggled against the urge to sit but flopped on the deck anyway. Can't make the computer center.

CHAPTER SEVENTY

As The Fox and Wes slipped around the end of the dais, the majority of the telephone people had run off. Magee swore at them for abandoning their responsibilities and the break of the voting input. The woman in charge remained with her earphones in place. He heard several explosions. He asked. "What's happened?"

"Somebody blew up the radio, TV and satellite systems. We're done here." She placed the phones on her desk and walked rapidly up the aisle.

"Son of a bitch! The bastard blew our capability. Kill the frog, Wes."

"Yes sir. From here?"

Magee could have stayed on the dais; he was still the marksman. "No, I want the ass hole to know who killed him. You can wound him, but let me do the *coup de gras*."

"Aye, aye, sir." Wes took the lead, hunched down in an infantryman's crouch.

Cat dragged his way along the deck, his leg hardly usable. He

Stolen Votes

waved the weapon. There were five people on a stage. On the main floor people ran past him and screams cascaded around him. Everyone was watching; eyes bugged open. Up above them was a bright banner, VOTE RIGHT! Where the hell was Whitney? He crabbed around the room, looking for snake eyes. Catching movement to his right, he drew his S & W semi-auto pistol and threw several shots in that direction. Turned back the other way. He sagged and slowed, damned near out of it.

The snake-eyed man was on him with his knife. The Cat was weak and desperate. He slipped a stun grenade out of his vest and worked the pin loose. The guy about had him. He stuffed the grenade inside the back of the man's belt and tried to hold off the knife with both hands.

When the grenade exploded, the knife hit Cat's throat, but he jerked his head away before it penetrated too far. The killer flew against him, thrashed around, screaming until he quivered and stopped moving, still on top of him. Dan only heard a solid ringing. Dazed and almost unconscious, he saw the big bastard approaching brandishing an automatic.

The Cat couldn't get out from under the dead man. He pulled out a grenade and rolled it toward the big guy who dove behind empty seats. After it blew The Cat wriggled free and waited for Wallace to appear. The stupid ass popped up over the seat and took a shotgun blast to the head. Dan swung the weapon to another gunman and the chamber was empty. He reached for his Combat Masterpiece. Behind him, The Fox stepped forward.

"Haggerty, meet your death."

The Cat fell and heard a noise cut through his damaged hearing. He turned to face a neatly dressed man with black hair and a touch of gray standing near him. He had an M-16 rifle with a sniper scope in his hands. Next to him was a tough looking guy with a dark face and eyes, who raised a forty-five automatic. The sniper leveled his weapon at the prone Cat. The Fox grinned, one that only showed on his mouth. Francis X. Magee was back in combat. He had the frogman.

Dan was unable to move and he saw death in the man's eyes. He prayed that Beth was going to be all right. Did they save the election? He didn't care. Where was Whitney? Would he see Bobby? Tony?

With a last gasp of strength The Cat rolled a grenade at the shooter. The pistol-packer's mouth opened as if he were shouting and threw himself over the explosive. It exploded and the victim bounced upward. The sniper's face never twitched or changed to acknowledge his man's sacrifice.

Cat saw the muzzle hole of the sniper rifle slide directly at his eyes. He was helpless. He saw a grim smile on the shooter's face. It was over. He relaxed.

Through the ringing in his ears, he heard Whitney shout. "You son of a bitch! Take what's coming to you."

Magee turned toward her and The Cat saw a puzzled look on the man's face. He swung the rifle toward her and then back at Dan. Before he could fire, Whitney emptied the magazine of the Beretta into him and screamed. "Die, you bastard!"

Haggerty saw death for them and he tried to swing the shotgun around his neck to reload and fire at a figure rushing toward him out of the grenade smoke. Darkness intervened and enveloped his eyes, body, and brain.

Stolen Votes

CHAPTER SEVENTY ONE

Ten days after the election, sound trickled by and a distant syncopated reverberation. The Cat drifted in and out. He tried to move but was constrained somehow. A hissing sound, a distant voice? No, softer, close by. His body was one big ache. He inhaled and heard the hiss again. Sea streaming by a boat? Ship? He felt a presence, someone bending over him. He blinked and saw Doc. He coughed and asked, "Doc... uh. Doc, wha... ?"

Doc glanced at the door behind him. "Easy, Cat. I ain't supposed to be in here. Me and Bennie takin' turns checking. I had to warn you soon as you come out of it. FBI guys pushing to question you. Here's the skinny. Don't say nothing. Understand? Be back soon." He slipped out.

The Cat sagged and shook his head. What the hell? Where am I? He drifted off.

Noise awakened him. A disturbance? He blinked through gritty eyes through a half-opened door. Two men in dark suits gestured at a uniformed police officer.

"No jurisdiction..."

"Kidnapping means FBI."

"Doctors say no visitors."

"Bullshit! We're no visitors. Now step aside officer."

"No!"

There were sounds of a scuffle and Cat thought he saw the cop falling to the deck.

The black suits shoved their way into the room. The lead flipped open a wallet badge and ID.

"Federal Bureau of Investigation. Name's Special Agent Sims. Partner's name is Special Agent Romiano. We need to ask you some questions about the assault you were running. First where did you get your weapons and ammunition?"

"Huh?" The Cat wagged his head, half-awake.

"No bullshit. It's a federal offense to have government weapons."

Romiano spoke. "Who was in charge of the murderous assault of a dozen people at the Truth Network?"

The Cat sagged to the side and breathed deeply. "I—. What? Who?"

A doctor wearing green scrubs rushed in. "Would you gentlemen please leave this room. My patient is not available for questions or visitors." He showed an ID. "I'm Doctor Randall, head of the ICU. You do not have my permission to ask questions or even being present. Now, please leave or I will call security."

The agents exchanged glances. Sims spoke. "Apparently you do not know what is going on here. This man with several others killed twelve people at the Truth Network. We come here with the authority of the highest level in the Justice Department."

"And I'm the highest level to allow or deny access to my ICU and bothering my patients. Once again, do I call security, or do I call the Attorney General?"

"Now wait a minute, doc. You don't have to get so difficult. We're just doing our job."

"And so am I. Please leave. Now!"

The agents looked at each other. Sims said, "You haven't heard the last of this."

Stolen Votes

The physician remained as the agents left. He stepped to the bed and checked the monitors over Cat's head. "Stupid asses! Are you okay?"

"Ummm. Thanks. Uh, doc. What's going on?"

He grinned and shook Haggerty's hand. "I'm a friend of Peter Dunn. I'll keep everyone out until I feel you are able to talk clearly. See you later."

Later Doc Warner returned. "How you doing, Cat?"

"FBI guys were here. Glad the doc threw them out. What the hell's going on? Where am I in ICU? Where's Beth? How did you get away? Thought, uh thought everybody would be in jail. Weren't you guys UA? How the hell did you get out of that?"

His bud grinned and pointed at his chest. "Me and Ben? Unauthorized Absence? Dirty our spotless records? Why we recovered stolen weapons and ammo that some asshole made off from SEAL TEAM TWO. The Lieutenant gave us leave chits for the days we were gone."

The Cat wagged his head slowly.

"Charlie jumped slick too." He laughed. "Convinced the investigators that there was a fourth man on board who forced him to do the assault and retraction. How's that for a smartass idea?"

"A fourth man?"

"Yeah. The bastard forced us to load a car with weapons and ammo, stole the Nightingale and the rest of the story. Nobody knows when or where he jumped off. Must have been when we come back for you on the roof. Soon as we got you back we went direct here."

"No shit."

"You needed a hospital, Cat. I couldn't fix that hip."

"I told you not to come back."

"You know we never leave a man dead or alive. And I outrank you, sand crab."

"Where's Beth?"

Doc stared for a second and placed his hand on Cat's shoulder. "We dumped you and her here at Norfolk General.

Sorry, Cat. Beth bought the big one. She—."

The Cat struggled to get up against the straps holding him down.

"Easy, Cat. Easy. Don't pull out that IV or I'll smack you. When they dropped her on the deck she got a fractured skull and brain injuries. She was in a coma for a while and then faded away. The autopsy showed that after the drugs they fed her and the beatings, she was probably near brain dead anyway. Real sorry, man."

Dan's head and shoulders dropped him down on the pillow. He covered his eyes with his left hand and started to shake.

"One more time, Cat. It ain't your fault. You did all you could and you got the rest of us outta there alive and kickin.' And you're back bein' a helluva warrior. You see what I'm saying? Remember, the fourth guy was some kind of terrorist. He caught us unprepared and threatened to kill Whitney if we didn't do what he said. That's our story and we're sticking to it. I'll fill you in on details later. Got that?"

"Thanks, Doc. I mean—." The Cat felt a pat on the shoulder before he passed out.

The next few days were a blur of hospital procedures, doctors poking and prodding him, nurses and aides waking him up during the night for vitals signs and telling him to go back to sleep. Whenever he was awake he thought of Beth and tears flooded his eyes. Another op, and with a terrible cost. Was it worth it? For what?

Doc and Bennie took turns repeating the story of the fourth man and how they had been ordered to attack or Whitney would have been killed. He asked about her and Doc told him, "Don't worry about her. She's good at takin' care of herself."

In a few days they made him get up and try walking. The hip hurt like hell. A young woman came in and worked his legs till he was ready to kill her. She called it "Therapy."

Stolen Votes

After they moved him from ICU to a regular hospital room, the ICU doctor stopped in and told him that Beth would have never recovered. "I'm sorry Mister Haggerty, she could not overcome the drugs they gave her, much less the injuries she sustained. Just try to remember the good things about her. You'll need counseling. I've made arrangements for that. Hope to see you released in a week or so. Take care."

"Uh, doc, thanks for keeping those FBI buzzards off me."

"Frankly, it was my pleasure. You'll have to get an advocate here since you're out of my jurisdiction. I've made suggestions to Doctor Sloan who is in charge of this floor."

He noticed a Norfolk police officer stationed outside the room in the hall. The man in blue followed wherever they took him. Well, they got me. Guess the next trip is the slammer for a long time. He remembered killing the snake-eyed man, The big hulk and facing the dapper guy with the sniper rifle. Geez, Whitney saved your ass. Where the hell is she?

Joseph Guion

CHAPTER SEVENTY TWO

By the end of the week The Cat was ready to eat nails or punch out the therapist. He hurt more than when he had first come out of it. Still, he could walk part way down the corridor and back with crutches. It reminded him of a bad HALO jump years back. He had two weeks in the damned things. Not this time. He had moments of remorse and even tears about Beth.

Bennie arrived and helped him into a wheel chair. "Where we going, Ben?"

"Gathering of the troops, Cat."

In a small, overcrowded sitting room Pete came over and shook his hand. "I'm pleased that you're doing well. You certainly ended it." He nodded at the police officer. "One of ours. We have a daily watch for you one way or the other. Just precaution." He was pale and bent, unlike Dan's memory of him. Was he sick?

"Thanks. I—."

Rita arrived and kissed him on the cheek. "Hey, sailor. How does it feel to be a hero? You saved an election. Too bad the Demos took The Senate. I brought you a paper to rub it in."

"What happened to everybody?"

She shrugged. I checked with a friend at the network. The Reverend Creed was hiding under the table during the shooting. And, he's thinking of running for the presidency."

He closed his eyes. "No shit!"

"Exactly. Vote right! Only it will have to be in eighty-eight or later. And he'd have a House and Senate against him. Check this out."

She showed him newspaper copy. "A lot of the contests were close. Do you know that a change of around fifty-thousand votes would have ended in a tie? Today it's fifty-five to forty-five favor of the Demos, with a fifty-fifty tie the Repos could have stayed in charge through Vice President Bush's vote. Think of it, Dan. You don't have to control everybody's vote, just a miniscule amount of key precincts."

"That's a lot of votes."

"No sir. That's what you think. This year almost sixty-five million votes were cast in the senatorial election. I checked the math. Fifty thousand is less than one percent. To get technical it's approximately decimal zero eight percent of the total vote. One more thing. There are over one hundred and eighty-eight thousand precincts. And you could identify those key precincts with a main frame in seconds.

The Cat shook his head. "Holy Shit! I mean, that's damned near zippo. I never thought of it that way. You didn't manipulate the voting? By the way, how were they doing it?"

"It was a great scheme. They swapped votes from one side to the other, so the machine totals always matched those of the ballots. And they had key people substituting the locked and sealed carrier boxes with theirs. In other places I understand that they owned some people and convinced them to reprogram the computers. The electronic voting machines are ripe for abuse because many have no paper trail. Even if they do, a programmer could easily have the voting check boxes on the screen show correctly and register the vote in the opposite direction. Believe me, their system would have worked. They could try it again."

"What?"

"Somebody's got the tapes. Who? What are they going to do with them? Kind of frightens you, doesn't it? Nobody seems to know where the network computer people are who ran it."

Pete spoke. "I understand that there was a large shakeup in that department. The systems head and Ned have been missing since Election Day. The police searched Ned's home and it was empty."

"What about the freaking army that was after us? How many bodies were laying there on the grounds? Isn't anyone interested in finding out what they were trying to do?"

Bennie explained. "Do you think that those wonderful people would go to the authorities and turn themselves in? No one knows who they were and they have disappeared. There are many questions left unanswered. The man behind it all is dead, so is his second in command. Apparently, there are too many people in the nation's capital who want to forget the entire incident."

"So, who takes the blame?"

At that moment Whitney made her entrance. As always it was a spectacular one at that. She strolled into the room and removed a dark raincoat to show off a teal dress that plunged lower than the law might allow. She smiled and handed him a large bunch of blooming yellow roses.

"I'm extremely sorry about Beth. She was a fine woman and I know that you loved her. Here's one from the both of us." She bent, kissed him and he had to break off to breathe.

"Thanks for helping me to find the strength to break off from that bastard Magee." She stood next to the bed with her hand on his shoulder.

"Nobody answered my question. Who is going to take the blame?"

They glanced at each other. Whitney explained. "You. You were a 'crazed vet,' so they found their scapegoat." She grinned and kissed him. "Actually, you were the dupe. The 'fourth man' in the helo was the terrorist. You could be an accessory to the killings, not the murderer. He convinced you that someone was trying to take over the government."

She continued. "Remember, I killed Magee. But I have one of the best criminal lawyers available. I might plead guilty due to insanity or intense trauma from being kidnapped by four terrorists. Oh, no, I mean a fourth man who was a terrorist. I'll get it right guys."

"Geez. You're all getting off?"

"Not quite, hoss. Me and Ben owe the Lieutenant a bit, so we got some extra duty. Gonna have an Article Fifteen investigation. No sweat. The main thing is, you're back, Cat. I mean really back!"

He grinned. "Yeah, I know, but I'll be a jailbird."

Whitney grabbed his hand. "I forgot. You have one of the best lawyers too. I didn't need the mink anymore and diamonds go a long way to hire good people."

She wagged a finger at him and smiled. "Don't forget. No one talks to you or asks questions without that lawyer present. Or else."

"I don't know what to say. Uh, thanks! You saved my life, lady."

"It's my pleasure."

Bennie had a sly grin. "It's time for the ceremony."

"Ceremony?"

Doc and Bennie stood in front of him. The Doc spoke in formal tones. "Dan, The Cat, Haggerty, front and center."

Whitney wheeled him closer. Doc lifted a package from a large duffle bag. "For the heroic efforts of a Navy SEAL, who showed his true warrior colors in an incredible assault on an highly fortified and defended compound, who saved the precious votes of our citizens and brought his team back alive, we two representatives of SEAL TEAM TWO hereby present you with a token of our appreciation and thanks. May you always stay a warrior."

The Cat received the package and shook his head. "What the hell is this?" He hefted it for a moment and frowned.

"Damn, feels like a—." He unwrapped a sawed off shotgun. It wasn't a model 37. "Je-sus. What the hell is this for? You said the weapons went back to the armory."

"It ain't USN issue. We salvaged that piece from your boat. Remember, you told us that one of the attackers had one. Thought you'd like to have this one hung up on your boat. They call it a *Lupara*, Sicilian for Wolf. It's a beauty, man. Silver work on the stock, probably worth some bucks. Kind of a reminder of us and all the SEALs we served with."

Haggerty opened the weapon and checked to make sure that it wasn't loaded.

Bennie spoke. "You think we're crazy enough to bring ammo along? We figure you can try it out when we go hunting some time. Birds and game. No people."

The Cat grinned. "Thanks guys."

Doc asked her to back the wheelchair out of the way and sounded off. "Miss Whitney Carlton, front and center."

She inhaled, thrust out her chest, and stood at attention. Bennie strolled up and presented her with his K-bar knife.

"For the most gorgeous, almost a SEAL I ever had the pleasure of meeting. Even though she doesn't like to get cammied up." He handed her a camouflage container.

She grinned and thanked him with a hug and a kiss.

The Doc reached into his pocket and pulled out a six-inch square box. He took off the cover and removed a metal object wrapped in green tissue paper.

"Miss Whitney Carlton, for great bravery under fire with SEALs, for making a helo insertion, for dropping smoke and fragmentation grenades on the enemy, and for saving a SEAL from being killed, it is my great pleasure to award you with 'The Budweiser,' the insignia of the SEALs. You are a true warrior and we welcome you to our ranks. And we give you a big 'HooYah!" Bennie echoed it.

"What the hell?" The Cat couldn't believe that Doc was doing this. It wasn't right. You didn't get the coveted official SEAL insignia unless you went through Hell Week, and all the rest of the shit they threw at you, and you qualified in parachuting, underwater, the entire training. He was pissed. "Dammit! Doc, how could you. Only SEALs—."

Doc fumbled with the award, trying to pin it on her chest. "Here, Cat. Maybe you better do it." He handed over the object. It was a Budweiser emblem cut from a beer can, a close resemblance to the official Navy SEAL insignia, often called "The Budweiser."

He laughed and began to pin the red object on her chest. "By damn, you're right. She is a warrior."

She put up her hand and grinned. "Hey, Haggerty, watch how you pin that thing on me. I don't want you to damage my up-front goodies. You might want to check them out some time."

The Cat shook his head as he finished his task. He stepped back and looked over the most gorgeous and intriguing woman he had ever met. She was beaming, full of herself, and happy.

"I gotta say it again. You saved my life, lady. Thanks."

She smiled and caught him with a glance that went deep into him. "In some cultures, that means I own you."

He bent slightly forward and swallowed. Where would that lead? He couldn't stop staring at her, as if he had seen her for the first time. He sighed.

What the hell could I do with a woman like her?

Joseph Guion

Select Bibliography

Books

Alterman, Eric *When Presidents Lie, A History Of Official Deception And Its Consequences.* New York: Viking Penguin. 2004.

Bosilijevac, T.L. *SEALs UDT/SEAL Operations in Viet Nam.* New York: Ivy Books. 1990.

Bradlee, Ben Jr, *Guts And Glory, The Rise and Fall of Oliver North.* New York: Donald I. Fine, Inc. 1988.

Branford, James, *The Puzzle Palace.* Boston: Houghton Mifflin, 1982.

Dockery, Kevin, and Fawcett, Bill, eds. *The Teams, An Oral History of the U.S. Navy SEALs.* New York: William Morrow, 1998.

Dockery, Kevin, from interviews by Bud Brutsman, *Navy SEALs A History, Part III.* New York: Berkley Books. 2003.

Fawcett, Bill, (ed) *Hunters And Shooters.* New York: Avon Books. 1995.

Kornbluth, Peter, Byrne, Malcolm (Eds) *The Iran-Contra Scandal The Declassified History.* New York: The New Press, 1993.

Mahle, Melissa Boyle, *Denial And Deception, An Insider's View of the CIA from Iran-Contra to 9/11.* New York: Nation Books. 2004.

Marcinko, Richard, with Weisman, John, *Rouge Warrior.* New York: Pocket Books. 1992.

Parker, Donn, *Fighting Computer Crime.* New York: Scribners. 1983.

Rubin, Aviel D. *Brave New Ballot.* New York: Morgan Road Books. 2006. **A MUST READ**

Timberg, Robert, *The Nightingale's Song.* New York: A Touchstone Book, Published by Simon and Schuster. 1995.

Walsh, Lawrence E. , *Firewall, The Iran-Contra Conspiracy And Cover-Up.* New York: W. W. Norton and Company. 1997.

Young, Darrell, *The Element of Surprise, Navy SEALS in Vietnam.* New York: Ivy Books, 1990.

Articles

Allen, Brandt, "Embezzler's guide to the computer." *Harvard Business Review*, July-August 1975.

Broder, David, "GOP hold on Senate endangered." *The Virginian Pilot*, Sunday November 2, 1986. Washington News Service.

Burnham, David, New York Times, News Service, "Computer voting called vulnerable to tampering." A 3. *The Virginian Pilot* July 29, 1985.

Dugger, Ronnie, "Annals of Democracy, Counting Votes." 40-108 *The New Yorker*, November, 1988

Ellerin, Milton and Keaten, Alisa N., The New Right: An Emerging Force in the Political Scene. *USA Today.* National Affairs. March 1981

Hartig, Dennis, "The new election machinery." The Beacon 6. *The Virginian Pilot.* October 31, 1982.

Hofeller, Thomas B, "The Powerful New Machine on the Political Scene." *Business Week.* Information Processing, November 5, 1984

Horyn, Cathy, "I am Who I Am, Ken Warrington speaks out for Virginia gays." B-1 *The Virginian Pilot*, July 9, 1984.

Kleinman, Larry, "Protecting Your Computer and Its Information." *Specifying Engineer*, April 1984.

Lamar, Jacob V. Jr, Reported by Barrett, Lawrence L. "Can the Democrats Recapture the Senate?" 26 – 32. *Time*, October 6, 1986.

Larsen, Erik, "For Fun or Foul, Computer Hackers Can Crack Any Code." *THE WALL STREET JOURNAL.* Wednesday April 15, 1983.

Murphy, Cullen, "Voting Big Business in Ballots.", *Atlantic Magazine*. November 1984.

Ostling, Richard N., Reported by Kane, Joseph J, Leavitt, B. Russell, Wierzysnski, Gregory H. Jerry Falwell's Crusade, 48 – 57, and Ajemian, Robert, "Jerry Falwell Spreads the Word." 58 – 61. *TIME* September 2, 1985

Ostling, Richard N. Reported by Kane, Joseph J. Leavitt, B. Russell, Riley, Michael, "Power, Glory – And Politics." 62 – 69. *TIME* February 17, 1986, *Cover Story GOSPEL TV, Religion, Politics and Money.*

Parker, Donn, Nycum, Susan, Oüra, S. Stephen, "Computer Abuse." *Stanford Research Institute*, Prepared for the National Science Foundation, November 1973.

Perry, Tekla S. and Wallich, "Can Computer Crime be stopped?" *IEEE Spectrum*, May 1984.

Post, Deborah Cromer, Security And Governmental Regulation, Senior Editor *Security World*. June 1980.

Peters, Mason and Reid, Ford, "Undecided voters may decide N.C. race." Staff Writer, *The Virginian Pilot*, Sunday November 2, 1986.

Schweitzer, James A. "Personal Computing and Data Security." *Security World*. June 1980.

Staikos, Nicholas, "Designs for Computer Security." *Security World*. March 1984.

Tengel, Richard, Reported by Chua-Eoan, Howard G., Constable Anne, Taylor Elizabeth, "Sex Busters," 12 – 22. *Time* July 21, 1986

Thomas, Evan, Reported by Beckwith, David, "Peddling Influence." 26 – 36. *Time* March 3, 1986

Thomas, Evan, Reported by Beckwith, David, Constable, Anne, "Reagan's Mister Right, Rehnquist is picked for the court's top job." 24 – 33. *Time* June 30, 1986 Cover

Thornton, Mary, Three part series on Computer Crime, from the Washington Post News service. *Virginian Pilot*, May 28- May 30, 1984.

Verity, John W. "MACHINE POLITICS." *Datamation*, Nov 1, 1986.

Weintraub, Bernard, "Reagan Vows to Finish His 'Revolution' " *The New York Times*. Thursday, November 6, 1986.

Witt, April, "Outcast Gay Christians fight for acceptance," A 1. *The Virginian Pilot*, May 19, 1985.

_____ "Hardware And Training To Prevent Break-Ins." *Security World.* Sept, 1980.

_____ From Wire Reports, "U.S. silent about mission to free Lebanon hostages...." T*he Virginian Pilot*, Sunday November 2, 1986.

Internet

_____ "Nov 3 Lebanese Newspaper Al-Shiraa reports US sold arms to Iran" *The Iran-Contra Time Line, 1979-1987 +*" http://www.schule.de/englisch/state_of_the_union/group7/project/timeline.htm

Acknowledgements

Whatever I have or will accomplish in life has been with the love, support and dedication of my late wife of fifty years, Magdalene (Madge) Oslovich Guion. My parents Marie and John Guion started me on the road and Madge brought me into a loving, stellar relationship. Our four daughters, Kathy, Mary Jane, Paulette and Teresa continue to "mother" me with love and affection. Their ideas, suggestions and patience have made the writing road smoother.

My niece Geri Barbato and her husband Nick have been long time supporters of my writing. My good friend Nancy Guarnieri has made many suggestions for the book and has provided continued support.

I am indebted to my wonderful editor Sofi Starnes. Any errors are mine. Graphics were created by the Wolko Design Group.

The Chesapeake Bay Writers Club has been a source of support and inspiration to an aspiring writer. I owe special thanks and gratitude to Jean Keating, the fine writer of her beloved dog books. Richard and Emeline Bailey, have been more than host and hostess for our bi-monthly critique meetings, a support group of friends that I sorely needed.

I find it difficult to limit a list of so many friends and relatives who have supplied great encouragement and interest for this book. Fellow members of The Emerson Society of Williamsburg have listened patiently to my essays without filling the room with hisses and boos.

I owe the book's title to Sam Horn, a great teacher, keynote speaker and writer.

Reading will never be a lost art unless writers give up. That is the key, "Never Give up!"

Stolen Votes

LOVE SONGS ON THE JOURNEY

Poems and reflections on the journey to and with God

Joseph Guion invites readers to reflect on their love relationships in:
> Book 1 Wandering Songs- God's Love, Personal Love, Nature, Life Changes.
> Book 2 Weeping Songs- September 11, 2001 and Church Illness.
> Book 3 Journeying on Songs- The Journey Continues.

$12.95   Copyright © Joseph E. Guion 2002

Formerly a captain of Navy ships and Associate professor of Business: Joseph Guion served for many years as Chairperson of the Diocesan Pastoral Council in the Catholic Diocese of Richmond, Virginia. His journey includes fifty years of married love before his wife's passing. Mr. Guion has led retreats for parish leadership groups for over twenty years. He is a recipient of the Papal *Bene Merenti* Medal.

READER RESPONSES

A PERSON WHO LOST A DEAR PARENT WROTE:
"It is so uplifting to spend a few minutes reading from your wonderful book of poems."
A PERSON ABUSED AS A CHILD WROTE:
"...after reading the poem, 'Blessed The Abused,' a great weight was lifted from me."
A RETIRED DIOCESAN STAFF PERSON WROTE:
"You have courage writing what you did about the Church."
A WORLD WAR TWO VETERAN WROTE:
"I'm all choked up reading, 'Do I Want Her Back."
BEST-SELLING AUTHOR AND INTERNATIONAL SPEAKER BARBARA GERAGHTY WROTE:
"Barbara feels that 'Companions' captures the very essence of the type of love that uplifts and endures."

Printed in the United States
130915LV00002B/202-249/P